MISTLETOE and MAYHEM

YULETIDE AT CASTLEWOOD MANOR

**VERONICA
CLINE BARTON**

© 2019 Veronica Cline Barton

All rights reserved.

This is a work of fiction. Names, characters, businesses, places, events, locales, and incidents are either imaginary or used in a fictitious manner. Any resemblance to actual persons, living or dead, or actual events is purely coincidental.

Print ISBN: 978-1-54398-930-4

eBook ISBN: 978-1-54398-931-1

As always, I want to thank my husband, Bruce—a thoughtful man who lets my heart soar. This book is dedicated to the wonderful caregivers in this world
who give so much to others in need, God Bless!

'I know a boy
I know a girl
I know my family
They love me…'

Lyrics by Ashlynn and Makara Bean

TABLE OF CONTENTS

A Year of Headlines… 1
Six Weeks Ago… 7
1 Winter Chills 9
2 Let the Plans Begin 25
3 Pass, or Fail 39
4 Homecoming Prep 55
5 Celebrations 69
6 On the Hunt 85
7 A Royal Wrap 99
8 Season's Change 115
9 Chaos and Confusion 129
10 Royal Jingles 143
11 Fit for a Queen 157
12 Regal Intentions 171
13 Tinsel Trauma 185
14 Carols and Crisis 199
15 Christmas Eve I Dos and Don'ts 215
16 Yuletide Showtime 229
17 Mistletoe Miracle 243
18 Untangling the Tinsel 257
19 Midnight Madness 271
20 American Marchioness 285
The Next Four Months… 299
A word from the author… 301

A Year of Headlines…

American Heiress Gemma Lancaster Phillips, PhD - Shot at Dinner Gala Event

The final glamorous event for the 'Castlewood Manor' set location contest ended in near tragedy for the team at Cherrywood Hall. Lord Evan Lancaster's cousin, American heiress Gemma Lancaster Phillips, PhD, was grazed by a bullet fired by a jealous competitor. The competition has been plagued with accidents and deaths of its contestants, leading some to wonder if the contest will continue. Dr. Phillips is expected to recover…

Cherrywood Hall Wins Set Location Contest for New Series *Castlewood Manor*

The New Year arrived with a bang as news hit that Rosehill Productions selected Cherrywood Hall as the set location site for their new period drama series, 'Castlewood Manor'. Lord Evan Lancaster, 8th Marquess of Kentshire, his cousin, American heiress Gemma Lancaster Phillips, PhD, and estate manager, Kyle Williams will be managing the liaison between the estate operations, events, and the studio, as well as coordinating activities with the local village of Maidenford…

Season One Filming of *Castlewood Manor* Begins

The cast and crew have descended upon Cherrywood Hall for the site location filming of season one of the highly anticipated series, 'Castlewood Manor'. American actress Jillian Phillips (mother to American heiress Gemma Lancaster Phillips, PhD) and Dame Agnes Knight have the lead roles as the domineering American mother who is best friends with the Queen...

Fashions of *Castlewood Manor* Promo Feature in the Works

American heiress Gemma Lancaster Phillips, PhD, the marketing liaison at the Cherrywood Hall estate, is working with wardrobe director Penny Atkins and film director Timothy Jones to highlight the costumes being designed for the series and showcase the extensive bespoke wardrobe collection of the Lancaster family now housed in the newly re-designed mega closet at Cherrywood Hall...

Royal It-girl, Lady Evangeline Tilford Lands Marketing Assistant Role

Lady Evangeline, daughter of the Queen's favorite niece, Lady Adela Tilford, global socialite and adventurer extraordinaire, has landed the role as marketing assistant to American heiress Gemma Lancaster Phillips, PhD, for the highly anticipated period drama series, 'Castlewood Manor'. The young royal is expected to be on-site at the Cherrywood Hall estate for the season one filming of the series...

Cherrywood Hall Expands Business Ventures

Sparkling wines and sherry production at the vineyards of the famed estate are about to get a new boost. Estate manager Kyle Williams and his project manager, architect Stephanie 'Steph' Rutherford, have launched construction projects to include a new wedding pavilion and honeymoon chateau available for public and private events. American heiress Gemma Lancaster Phillips, PhD, will oversee business operations for the newest ventures. Publicity firm

Magnum PR, led by owner Elliot Pierce, will be in charge of public relations efforts for the estate...

Tragedy Strikes at Cherrywood Hall Hot Air Balloon Event

Queen Annelyce and Prince Thaddeus were amongst the horrified witnesses to the bizarre death of 'Castlewood Manor' lead writer, Jason Redstone, as he plummeted to his death at the series' promotional hot air balloon event hosted by Rosehill Productions. Passengers in Mr. Redstone's ill-fated balloon included American heiress Gemma Lancaster Phillips, PhD, and 'Castlewood Manor' wardrobe designer Penny Atkins. The ladies were saved in a dramatic rescue by Kyle Williams, estate manager at Cherrywood Hall, and his project manager, Steph Rutherford...

Royal Fashion Show at the Palace for the *Castlewood Manor* Series

Buckingham Palace has announced a major charity event featuring the costumes and garments worn in the highly acclaimed 'Fashions of Castlewood Manor' feature documentary to be held in the regal halls. American heiress Gemma Lancaster Phillips, PhD, locals from the village of Maidenford, and cast members of the series will lend star-powered glamour to the event. Queen Annelyce is expected to attend...

Scandal Hits *Castlewood Manor* after Tragic Death of Lady Evangeline Tilford

In a staggering twist to the murder of Lady Evangeline Tilford last month at Cherrywood Hall, Scotland Yard representative, Chief Inspector Marquot, has announced that 'Castlewood Manor' lead actor, Sir James Dennison has been arrested for the murder of Lady Evangeline and sabotage of the hot air balloon that caused the death of the show's lead writer, Jason Redstone. Sir Dennison was rumored to be involved in a torrid love triangle with Lady Evangeline, her mother, Lady Adela, and Cherrywood Hall dowager marchioness, Lady Margaret Lancaster—mother of Sir Evan Lancaster and aunt of American heiress Gemma Lancaster Phillips, PhD. No statements have been issued at this time...

Kyle Williams, Estate Manager at Cherrywood Hall to be Knighted

The palace has announced that Mr. Kyle Williams is to be knighted at Buckingham Palace for his architectural and technology innovations that have led to modernization features installed at many of Britain's finest estates. American heiress Gemma Lancaster Phillips, PhD, who is dating Mr. Williams, and Lady Adela Tilford, favorite niece of the queen and former best friend of his late mother, are expected to be in attendance...

Cherrywood Hall Scene of Royal Wedding That Was Not

A #RoyalWeddingFail as royal grandson, Sir Timothy Oxmoor, MBE jilts his bride to be, Lady Kimberly Birchfield at the altar of the newly opened Cherrywood Hall wedding pavilion. Shocking his guests, which included his grandmother, Queen Annelyce, and an estimated televised audience of one billion viewers, the wayward groom ran off with former girlfriend, Shelly Townsend, a guest invited by the groom. The quick thinking of American heiress Gemma Lancaster Phillips, PhD, saved the monarch's modesty as she covered the television cameras with her outreached hands to hinder the live coverage of the queen, who had fainted dead away in a very unroyal manner across the lap of her husband, Prince Thaddeus. The clever American with the hands seen 'round the world' earned the cheeky moniker of 'Royal Avenger'...

Castlewood Manor Series Declared Runaway Hit After Wins at the *Telly Tiara's*

After the successful première of the show in London and promotional events in New York City, the cast and crew of 'Castlewood Manor' have even more reason to celebrate! Lead actresses Jillian Phillips and Dame Agnes Knight have received the coveted award show's Best Actress and Best Supporting Actress awards, respectively. Penny Atkins, the series wardrobe director, received a Telly Tiara for costume design. As a final cherry to the cake, Rosehill Productions Executive Vice President, Lucy Etheridge, accepted the Telly Tiara for Best Show...

Castlewood Manor American Tour Tinged with Tragedy

The arrest of the crazed, jilted royal bride, Lady Kimberly Birchfield, for the attempted murder of American heiress Gemma Lancaster Phillips, PhD, who she blamed for jinxing her wedding with a tainted family veil, was not the end of bad news for the cast and crew of the hit series as they wrapped up their American tour. It was announced that Lord Evan Lancaster, 8th Marquess of Kentshire, owner of the Cherrywood Hall estate used as the set location for 'Castlewood Manor', has been kidnapped by a poacher gang he has been at odds with at his ranch in South Africa. Sir Kyle Williams, estate manager and recent fiancé of Lord Evan's cousin, Gemma, will be leading the rescue operation...

Is the Queen About to Right a Royal Wrong?

As the search for kidnap victim, Lord Evan Lancaster continues in South Africa, royal rumors are swirling that Queen Annelyce is about to mend a royal injustice from centuries ago involving the Lancaster family peerage and title. Could American heiress Gemma Lancaster Phillips, PhD, fiancé of Sir Kyle Williams, be the first American woman to assume a British title and peerage in her own right? This story is developing…

Six Weeks Ago…

"Asset spotted…"

My heart skipped a beat as I listened in remotely via Spyke.digital, a secured communications service Kyle had engaged as part of the search to find my Cousin Evan. My fingers squeezed the receiver in a steely grip to try and control the panic-driven chills racing throughout my body. I pressed the unit closer to my ear until it burned, straining to hear anything over the crackle filled transmission.

"Come on, come on," I whispered, desperate to know my cousin's fate.

I heard the horrific war cry of men charging into the room, gunfire blazing. I sat frozen in time, my mouth open in disbelief, tears streaming down my cheeks. I was terrified—not only for what I feared had happened to Evan, but worried sick about my fiancé, Kyle, who led the charge. Tick tock… tick tock, the roar of deafening silence…

"I've got him, darling, oh God…" Kyle's words tore at my heart, one part of me relieved to hear my beloved's voice, the other saddened by his grief-stricken tone.

"Kyle, Kyle—is he, all right? Is he…?" I collapsed on the floor in a flood of emotions; my body and spirit wracked with dismay.

"He's alive, Gemma---but barely. I don't know, darling… I just don't know."

The connection signal went dead. Our lives at Cherrywood Hall changed in an instant.

CHAPTER 1
Winter Chills

The last flickers of light from the early December sky were fading rapidly as I gazed out the French doors of my office at Cherrywood Hall. Darkness fell early these days. The rain-laced winds whipped at the North Sea, creating whitecaps on the waves careening toward the cliffs. I could hear their roar as they crashed against the rocks below, back and forth, a never-ending rhythm that mesmerized me as I stared at the deep blue water. Winter was coming, chilling everything in its path.

"Hey darling." Kyle walked across the office and wrapped his arms around me, holding me close. "You look as if you're a million miles away."

I smiled as I looked into his emerald-green eyes, running my fingers through his jet-black mane, still damp from the drizzle outside. My fiancé, Kyle runs the estate operations here at Cherrywood Hall. He proposed to me during a surprise stopover in Iceland on our return trip from America a few months back. We had snorkeled in the icy waters of the Silfra Fissure where he popped the big question in the same spot where his parents became betrothed years before. As he slipped his mother's engagement ring on my finger, our teeth chattering, we vowed our promises of eternal love to one another. I thought it was one of the most romantic moments I had ever experienced, despite the frosty temperature.

"I was, Kyle. The waves had me hypnotized. Just look at them, I think the winds will have them crashing all the way up to the sea path before long," I said, chuckling.

He gently cupped my chin in his hand and kissed me, his soft lips caressing my lips and cheeks. I tightened my grip around his waist, pressing him into me as our passion grew.

"Gemma, Kyle, come on darlings, it's time for cocktails... oh," Mama said, barging into my office, swinging her red, velvet wrap around her shoulders. She stopped abruptly when she saw our embrace. "Sorry darlings, I didn't mean to interrupt. Brrr, it's absolutely freezing in here. Come on now, Margaret is waiting for us downstairs."

I gave Kyle a furtive glance, my brow tensing. This was the first evening we would be together in Cherrywood Hall since my Cousin Evan's rescue. Aunt Margaret had been terribly upset the past few months. Evan's kidnapping and torture had taken a huge emotional toll on her, not knowing if her son was alive or dead. Her charming, witty personality had all but disappeared, overtaken by her grief. We hadn't had a chance to discuss his situation as a family here at Cherrywood since Evan was airlifted from South Africa to the private care facility in London. She had stayed by his side morning 'til night, holding his hand as he lay in a coma---his brutalized body slowly healing from the weeks of torture he endured at the hands of his kidnappers. The doctors did not know when, or if, Evan would ever regain consciousness.

I broke from our embrace and walked over to Mama to kiss her cheeks. "How is she? Is there any news?"

Mama shook her head, tears brimming in her eyes. Kyle and I linked arms with her on either side as we walked slowly down the stairs to the study on the first floor, a favorite gathering spot for evening cocktails before dinner. Mama was staying at Cherrywood Hall with me through the holidays before season two filming of *Castlewood Manor* began. I was glad to have her company. She always managed to keep everyone's spirits up with her showbiz banter. We needed it, especially now. Everyone was tense and uncertain these days. Without Evan, would our family ever be the same?

We crossed the grand hallway and made our way into the study. Aunt Margaret was sitting on the sofa, gazing down at the flames blazing in the fireplace. She rose when she saw us and gave a guarded smile. I broke away and went to her, hugging her close. I could feel the tension in her body and for a moment heard her whimper as we embraced. She pulled back as she gently patted my cheeks. She walked over to Mama and Kyle, greeting them with hugs.

"Let's sit down," she said, fluffing the sofa cushions. "Kyle, would you please act as bartender for us this evening? I would like a sherry please."

Mama and I sat down on either side of her.

"Of course, Lady Margaret. Jillian, Gemma, what would you like ladies?"

"Champagne please for me," Mama said, her eyes twinkling.

"Gin and St. Germain for me, please, with a splash of lemon juice."

Kyle smiled at me and winked. The gin and St. Germain cocktail had become a favorite of mine the past few months. Kyle's project manager at the estate, architect Stephanie 'Steph' Rutherford, was overseeing a new business venture for us here at Cherrywood Hall, the building of a gin distillery. We were expanding our liquor ventures from sparkling wines and sherry to now include gin. The building design had been completed and permits were in hand. Construction would start in the next few months once the worst of the winter weather was over.

Kyle brought us our libations on a silver tray, bowing with a flourish as he handed us our drinks, sitting down next to me when everyone was served.

"I think we need a toast," I said, holding my martini glass in front of me. Mama, Aunt Margaret and Kyle scooted closer, raising their glasses. "To Evan, may his recovery be thorough and swift. Please let him know his family loves and misses him."

"Hear, hear," we said somberly, clinking our glasses and settling back in our seats. Mama gently stroked Aunt Margaret's arm.

"Yummy, the gin and St. Germain martini tastes divine, Sir Kyle. I think you've mastered just the right combination." I kissed the tip of my forefinger and touched his nose, giving him an impish grin.

Kyle was knighted by the queen last spring for the technology and renovation innovations he developed for use in many of Britain's finest manor house estates. His architectural degree and modernization projects at Cherrywood Hall, as the estate manager, had received global recognition from preservation and historical groups. He loved the older estates and was constantly looking for new ways to preserve their beauty and modernize them with minimal impact on their classical designs.

So much had changed in the year and a half since I had moved from my cozy beach cottage in Malibu. I ventured to England to assist my cousin, Evan Lancaster, the 8th Marquess of Kentshire and owner of our ancestral home, Cherrywood Hall, in a set-location competition for the new, hit period drama television series, *Castlewood Manor*. Our estate was selected from three manor houses, much to our delight after a brutal competition. Season one filming was completed this past spring despite the efforts of some who wanted to stop the show before its first airing.

The global premiere of *Castlewood Manor* this past summer and its subsequent wins at the acclaimed *Telly Tiara* award show a few months back had cemented the series' future, or at least for the time being. The television business could change in the blink of an eye and Rosehill Productions was always looking for new ways to promote and expand the series. Season two filming would begin after New Year's. My mama, Jillian Phillips, was one of the leading actresses in the period drama, playing the role of the American best friend of the queen, showcasing their dilemmas as they raised their daughters and searched for suitable husbands in the halls and grounds of elegant palaces. Mama had received a best actress *Telly Tiara* for her performance, her joy and celebrations cut short when we learned of Evan's kidnapping.

I should take some time to introduce my family, since it's a bit different from everyday American and British lineage, and somewhat relevant to the *Castlewood Manor* series. My name is Gemma Alexandra Lancaster Phillips, and I'm a twenty-eight-year-old California girl, born and bred. I had been awarded my PhD degree a few months before I arrived at Cherrywood Hall last year, my dissertation largely based upon my family's heritage.

My American Lancaster family had been one of the first industrial giants to make huge fortunes as the railways pushed west across the United States. My great-great-grandfather was Patrick Lancaster, an entrepreneur who'd had the brilliant idea that the railways were going to need iron and labor—and lots of it.

I emphasize *American Lancaster family* because Patrick's great-great-grandfather, John Lancaster, had left his ancestral home in England to come over to the American colonies, as they were then known, just before the Revolutionary War. John was the second son of the Marquess of Kentshire, James Lancaster, who lived on the family estate, Cherrywood Hall. Being the second son, the rules of primogeniture prevailed, John would inherit nothing. He thus split with the British family and made the trip to America to begin a new life.

Patrick had two daughters: Phillipa, affectionately known as Pippa, my great-great-aunt; and Lillian, my great-grandmother. Pippa went to England in 1912 loaded with a generous multi-million-dollar dowry Patrick had bestowed upon her. She married her distant Lancaster family cousin Charles Edward Lancaster, who was the 4th Marquess of Kentshire. Pippa was something of a renegade for her time. She didn't want to be just an American socialite living in the hills of San Francisco or New York. She had bigger aspirations, and they included becoming a British *almost royal* living half a world away.

Her marriage to Charles reunited the American and British Lancaster families—a huge event given that we had been separated by years of war, waves of family ill feeling, and miles and miles of sea and land. Pippa had brought a badly needed fortune to the family peerage and the Cherrywood estate. Thanks to Pippa and her American money, Cherrywood Hall had been saved, and my Cousin Evan had become the 8th Marquess of Kentshire, when his father died.

My great-grandmama Lillian became one of the first, female medical doctors of her time, and her daughter, Meredith, followed her career path. Lillian was endowed with a multi-million-dollar trust just as Pippa had been and generously supported her descendants in a very comfortable style of life, which is how I happen to have a rather large trust fund.

My mama, Jillian, scandalously went out on her own to become a successful film and television actress. She married my father, David Phillips, who was then pursuing his doctoral degree in history at the University of California while surfing in Malibu. They divorced when I was two, history and acting not mixing in their case.

I followed my father's academic route, pursuing my PhD at the University of California as well. I wanted to make my own mark, and not just be another Malibu trust-fund baby. I had an enormous appreciation for my family's feats, especially Pippa's. Her reunification of the Lancaster family and her inheritance became the subject of my dissertation: *Twentieth-Century Reunification of British and American Aristocratic Families with the Influx of American Heiress Inheritances*. Pippa and Lillian both believed that a family united was invincible. Evan and I continued in this belief, a family united, British and American, in our new family venture with the *Castlewood Manor* series.

Our family ancestry jaws had dropped a few months ago in Vail, where we were attending the *Telly Tiara* award show. My daddy, David Philips, PhD, had disclosed certain crown-shattering details he had learned about our British and American Lancaster family heritage. His research, done at the secret request of Queen Annelyce, the ruling monarch, confirmed that my American patriarch, John Lancaster, the second son who had moved away to America, was in fact the rightful heir to the Lancaster marquess peerage, title, and property. It was found that his older brother was illegitimate, and thus ineligible to inherit the title and peerage he had assumed. This discovery was quite shocking to us all, for it meant that the American lineage of Lancaster's was eligible to inherit. Mama declined, wanting no part of it. This meant I was now the eligible heir to Cherrywood Hall and the title and peerage as Marchioness of Kentshire, displacing my Cousin Evan.

Evan was often referred to as the 'reluctant marquess', for despite his love for Cherrywood Hall and the surrounding community, including the nearby village of Maidenford, his heart belonged on his ranch in South Africa and being with his long-term love, billionaire heiress Simone Alexander, who ran her father's extensive business empire in Johannesburg.

He was torn between fulfilling his inherited duty versus living out his desires and dreams in South Africa.

We had not had the chance to disclose any of the newly unearthed title and peerage information to Evan. He had been kidnapped and tortured by a ruthless poacher gang he was at war with on his ranch. Kyle had led the extensive search and rescue operation that returned Evan to us.

I was now struggling too, as I weighed out my options. I didn't want to cause any family friction, particularly at this time, with Evan being in a coma. Aunt Margaret bristled every time the subject came up and seemed determined to delay any effort to displace her son as the titled heir. We had a tentative family truce on the discussion of the subject, but the topic was frequently played out in the gossip tabloids, triggering whispers galore in the celebrity scene. Queen Annelyce was also pressing for a decision, causing more than a few icy tensions in her long running friendship with Aunt Margaret.

A log shifted in the fireplace; its crackling thud caused us to jump as we finished our cocktails. Bridges, the head butler at Cherrywood, came to the side entry and announced that dinner was served. We walked into the candlelit dining room, glowing in hues of blue, taking a seat at the end of the table next to a large fireplace that radiated welcome heat. Kyle and I sat across from Mama and Aunt Margaret—Evan's empty chair at the end a sad reminder of my dear cousin's absence.

"Oh, look—Karl has done it again," Mama said, skewering a large, sausage and bacon wrapped date from a tray, tucking into one of her favorite appetizers. Karl, *Chef Karl,* was the creator of our scrumptious cuisine at Cherrywood Hall, and Mama's current love interest. They had taken their affair public a few months ago when Karl walked the red carpet with Mama at the *Telly Tiaras* in Vail. He loved to spoil her with his tantalizing creations, much to the distress of her waistline.

"Better not eat too many of those, Mama, or Penny will have a fit," I said, wagging my finger at her. Penny Atkins was the director of the wardrobe department for the *Castlewood Manor* show. She had also just been awarded a *Telly Tiara* for her fashion designs, which had delighted both her and her girlfriend, Steph Rutherford.

"Believe me darling, I know. Shooting begins again after New Year's and the costumes are already in production for the cast. We all have been warned about indulging too much in the upcoming holiday season. Penny and her team wield a stiff tape measure!" Mama's dramatic grimace made us all laugh.

"She's not the only one ruling with an iron fist. Lucy Etheridge and her assistants will be here this weekend. The staff will begin the Christmas decorating next week. They want to make sure the decorations fit in with the color scheme planned for their major broadcast on New Year's Eve. I can't believe a whole year has passed since the last announcement here at Cherrywood."

Lucy Etheridge was the executive vice president at Rosehill Productions, the studio in charge of the *Castlewood Manor* production. The previous New Year's Eve broadcast was when we found out Cherrywood Hall had been selected as the series' set location choice. Our win had secured substantial financial resources for the estate and surrounding community.

"Any hints, Jillian, of what this announcement is about?" Kyle asked, his eyebrows raised.

"They won't tell us anything. I've been pestering Elliot non-stop, but he's been sworn to silence," Mama said, making a twist-lock motion with her fingers on her lips.

Elliot Pierce was the owner of Magnum PR, the public relations firm Rosehill Productions used for the *Castlewood Manor* series. Elliot's firm also helped with the Cherrywood Hall business ventures that we had started this past year—including the wines, wedding pavilion and honeymoon chateau promotions. He and his partner Max had become close friends of ours, and especially Mama's and Aunt Margaret's.

"Max has been calling me non-stop. He wants me to meet a wedding planner friend of his." I looked over at Kyle and smiled. "I haven't committed to anything, not with Evan…" I stopped and glanced over at Aunt Margaret, who was struggling to maintain her composure.

"You must call him, Gemma dear. Your wedding would be so important to him, you know," Aunt Margaret whimpered, attempting to smile. "We have no idea of how long his recovery will be. It's time to get on with the living."

We sat in silence for a moment, the sadness hanging thick in the air.

"You should go ahead and call him, darling. He's told me all about the fabulous Mr. Gerard. His last event was a royal wedding in Denmark. The guests were treated to an ice castle wedding in the middle of an Indian summer. They had tons of ice flown in and master artisans carved for weeks and weeks. It was quite a spectacle, everyone was there," Mama said, in full gossip mode.

"Reginald Gerard is highly regarded, Gemma dear. He's planned society weddings here too. Many of the dinner events and parties hosted by the queen have been Reginald's creations. He does have that royal touch," Aunt Margaret chimed in, sounding almost like her former self.

"Kyle and I haven't even really discussed our wedding. I thought we might do something here at the wedding pavilion. We both love it."

Kyle placed his hand over mine. We knew we were about to be overruled.

"Let's keep an open mind, darling. Why, you know I'll have to have the *Castlewood Manor* cast and crew invited, and the Rosehill Production executives of course. Your father will likely want some of his academic friends invited as well."

I could tell Mama was mentally clicking away at her guest list.

"You mustn't forget the royals, Gemma. Queen Annelyce has grown quite fond of you as you know, as have other members of her family. Having them in attendance takes your wedding planning to a whole different level."

I could see Aunt Margaret was still trying to keep her emotions in check. I reached across the table and gave her hand a squeeze. "All right, all right, I will call Max first thing in the morning and have him set up a meeting with the fabulous Mr. Gerard. Right now, we're really just at the idea stage. I don't want to make any firm commitments, not yet…" I hedged. With Evan's current status unknown, I wasn't keen to make any final arrangements, no matter how much Mama or anyone else wanted me to.

"Keep a close eye on Max, he'll be pushing you to do the ice castle wedding theme. He has a fabulous, red velvet suit trimmed in white faux fur that looks divine," Mama said, rolling her eyes.

We laughed, thinking about Max prancing around, fluffing his furs.

"He can wear that to the Yuletide festivities in a few weeks. I proposed to Gemma in an icy fissure that nearly turned us blue, I think our wedding ceremony should be in a warmer environment." Kyle grinned, putting his arm around me. "Lady Adela is coming here next week to have lunch with Gemma and me. If you're staying here for a while, we'd love for you to join us," Kyle said, nodding over to Aunt Margaret and Mama.

Lady Adela Tilford was the queen's late sister's daughter, and her favorite niece. She was a global socialite who traveled extensively around the world with a royal aura. Her daughter, Lady Evangeline, had interned with me last spring, meeting a tragic end by the hand of a mad lover who had also courted her mother and Aunt Margaret in a deceptive lover's triangle. The two ladies remained friends, although the strain of the shared paramour was quite overwhelming for them at times. Lady Adela had also been a friend of Kyle's mother, Honey. When her daughter was killed, she became close to Kyle again as an aunt-like figure. She was with him at the palace when he was knighted last spring. I had grown to like her very much myself—her charm and grace always made for a pleasant visit.

"Oh yes, please say you'll be here. I want you to help with the Christmas decorating too—you know how you love it." I looked at Aunt Margaret with pleading eyes, willing her to say yes.

"Let's go into the study for an after-dinner drink. There's something I need to discuss with you," Aunt Margaret said, pulling out her chair to stand.

Kyle poured us snifters of brandy as we took our seats back on the sofa by the fireplace. The wind was howling even more strongly now, its ferocious roar whistling down the chimney. Aunt Margaret gazed at her brandy, swirling it around and around in the crystal glass before she finally took a sip.

"I want to bring Evan back to Cherrywood Hall." Aunt Margaret looked up and stared at us, watching for our reactions. "It is still his home and I've arranged for caregivers to be here with him to provide the same level of care he gets at the London facility. His condition hasn't changed, but if it turns for the worse, I want him to be at home if he passes."

I reached over and put my arm around her waist. "Of course, Aunt Margaret. Cherrywood Hall will always be Evan's home, no matter what happens." I looked up at her, tears stinging my eyes. I never wanted her and Evan to not think of Cherrywood as their home, even if I assumed the title of Marchioness of Kentshire.

"I can have my crew take down the walls between your suite and Evan's, Lady Margaret, if that would make things easier."

"No, Kyle dear, that won't be necessary for the upstairs suites. There are a few bedrooms and sitting rooms here on the ground floor that I thought could be made into a care center of sorts for Evan. There are adjoining bedrooms for the caregivers to stay in and it will mean a lot less running around for food trays and other necessities that he might need. I have a list of medical equipment to be brought in. I thought your staff could take care of that for me. There are electrical and networking requirements that are quite out of my league."

"Of course, Lady Margaret. I'll see to it personally. Don't worry about anything."

Aunt Margaret gave Kyle a grateful smile and sipped her brandy. I could tell she was relieved knowing Evan would be coming home. To tell the truth, I would be glad to have him here too. I couldn't get up to London to see him as much as I wanted the past few weeks. With the upcoming holidays and the New Year's Eve event with the Rosehill Productions, my time would be even more limited.

"How's Simone doing, Aunt Margaret? I haven't spoken to her in a while."

"She's holding up. The poor dear has been flying back and forth between London and Johannesburg. I worry that she'll wear herself out. She's been such a great comfort. I've grown to love her even more as a daughter," Aunt Margaret whispered.

"She loves Evan very much, Lady Margaret—and you too. She was right by our sides during Evan's rescue. Her martial arts training came in quite handy, as the unfortunate kidnappers found out. She has a deadly kick," Kyle said, his chin pointed down in affirmation.

We grinned at Kyle's compliment, but shuddered thinking about the horrible rescue.

"I forgot to tell you, Gemma, your father and Elizabeth want to come to England over the holidays. He asked me if I thought they could stay at Cherrywood Hall… to visit with you." Mama peered at me, watching for my reaction. My father and his then girlfriend, had left Vail suddenly after the *Telly Tiara* awards before we had a chance to meet her. We later found out they had eloped. I had only spoken to Daddy twice since I returned home, our relations were strained to say the least.

I closed my eyes and took a deep breath before I responded. "Mama, I really don't think this is the time, especially with all the holiday preparations and now Evan coming home. We're going to have so much going on…" I looked at Kyle and shrugged. He could see I was growing anxious.

"I will manage them, darling. Give your father and Elizabeth a chance. There's plenty of room here at Cherrywood. It's not like you'll be enclosed in a small space with them. You can have Amy take them on local tours—I'm sure the historical buildings will be of interest to them. Vicar Hawthorne I know would love to be a tour guide as well. He's quite the expert on our area buildings you know."

Amy Princeton was my assistant, helping me manage the *Castlewood Manor* promotional events as well as the private weddings and functions held at the wedding pavilion and honeymoon chateau. She was the niece of Sally Prim, editor of the Maidenford Banner, and our go-to press liaison for local events. Both had become good friends of mine.

"That's an awesome idea, Kyle," Mama said, her interests perking up. "Vicar Hawthorne would be a marvelous tour guide for them. You know how he loves to be in on events here at the Hall." Vicar Hawthorne, the local rector at St. Mary's church in Maidenford, was Mama's most enthusiastic local fan. He had played a few walk-on roles for the *Castlewood Manor* show too, loving any opportunity to hobnob with the cast.

Once again, I knew I was being overruled, but since it was getting close to the holidays, I decided to shelve my concerns. We needed a joyful Christmas and time to celebrate after experiencing so much tragedy the past few months. I raised my arms in a surrender pose. "I'll agree if you promise to help manage everything and not disappear on me. It will be fun to have a crowd here, especially at Christmas."

"I'm glad you said that daughter, Elliot and Max have been begging for an invitation to be here for the holidays too." Mama looked at me, trying not to grin. Her efforts to suppress her mirth didn't work, as we all burst out laughing, knowing that Elliot and Max would make sure our Christmas was very merry—they always had something up their sleeve to keep us entertained.

"I think it will be very good to have everyone here, close to Evan. Let's hope the holiday cheer helps him recover. It will be good for him to have laughter and music around him." Aunt Margaret smiled, raising her snifter.

We clinked our glasses and took a sip of our brandy, hoping her words would come true. A Christmas miracle was needed, no doubt. We spent the rest of the evening giggling and telling more Elliot and Max tales. For the first time, I started to feel some of the weight of sadness lift from my shoulders. The holidays, my wedding planning, and Evan coming home cheered me tremendously. The fire roared away, keeping our room nice and toasty as the gale-force winds increased their freezing blasts. I felt the love of our family in the room, and I knew Aunt Pippa was right by our side.

CHAPTER 2

Let the Plans Begin

I woke up the next morning in my comfy bed, feeling more refreshed than I had been for some time. I adored my bedroom at Cherrywood Hall. It had been my Aunt Pippa's and was decorated lavishly in hues of blues and turquoise, her favorite colors, that reminded her of the sea she loved. I smiled as I rubbed my hand on the side of my bed, still feeling the warmth from Kyle's body. He had left earlier to attend to some business for the new gin distillery with Steph.

I climbed out of bed and quickly showered and changed, anxious to go eat breakfast. I slipped on an emerald-green cashmere sweater and black leggings, tucking them into my over-the-knee, leather boots. The wind was howling up a storm again, the crashing of the waves against the cliffs going non-stop.

I made my way down the staircase and across the grand hallway to the dining room. Mama and Aunt Margaret were seated, eating their breakfast.

"Morning, ladies," I said, as I went to each of them to kiss their cheeks. I grabbed a plate and started spooning on helpings of my favorites---coddled eggs, bacon, tomatoes, mushrooms, and baked beans. I was in love with a traditional English breakfast. I took my loaded plate and sat at the end of the table between Mama and Aunt Margaret. They looked at me in silence for just a moment—it was the seat Evan usually sat in.

Aunt Margaret gave me a heartening look. "I saw Kyle before he left. He has the medical equipment requirements for his staff to get the downstairs rooms ready for Evan's return. I'm so grateful he's taking this on for me. It will be good for Evan to be back at Cherrywood, I just know it. He needs his family close by, now more than ever."

Mama glanced over at me, her concern for Aunt Margaret evident. We both wanted Aunt Margaret to hold onto any shred of hope that made her feel better. "Of course, darling. It will be best for him to return home, especially for the holidays. Kyle and Gemma will get everything readied for him. Will you be staying here until he's transferred?"

"No, I'm leaving for London after breakfast. I'm sorry I'll miss your time with Lady Adela here this week, Gemma. I'll catch her on the next visit I'm sure."

"Don't worry about it, Aunt Margaret. Spend your time with Evan and get ready to have some holiday fun when you return."

"I found the mercury glass ornaments that Pippa had at the Belgravia house. These are blue ones that Charles gave her for her first Christmas here at Cherrywood Hall. I thought I'd bring them here when Evan and I return. We can have a Christmas tree set up in his room to hang the ornaments. Perhaps some of Pippa's magic can help him." Once again, her emotions threatened to get the best of her. Evan's condition was having an enormous impact on her wellbeing.

"I think that's a super idea, Aunt Margaret. We'll decorate his room with lots of sparkles. I know it will bring him some Christmas magic."

"Now, Gemma, don't forget to call Max, darling, to set up a meeting with Reginald Gerard. His schedule gets very booked—we want to make sure he has time for you."

"I will call him, Mama, I promise. I'm making no commitments though—not yet. Kyle and I will listen to what he has to say and decide. Um, you will call Daddy won't you, to arrange things for his travel here with Elizabeth? I think if they arrive the week of Christmas, we can keep them busy with Amy and Vicar Hawthorne's help. Do you want them to be here for the *Castlewood Manor* broadcast on New Year's Eve? I'm sure Rosehill Productions will have many VIPs here for you to mingle with. Will Daddy or Elizabeth's presence be a problem for you?"

"David will be fine, but like you, I don't even know Elizabeth. I'm sure they'll be okay, although if she was overwhelmed at the *Tellys* she'll have the same issue here. Television cameras and photographers will be everywhere."

"It does seem very odd how she left without meeting us in Vail, rude in fact. I was quite surprised David would let her get away with that behavior," Aunt Margaret said, taking a bite of toast.

"I'm not sure that Daddy has any control of her. I'm still upset that they eloped and didn't even bother to tell us until later. Daddy seems to have lost his head with Elizabeth. It's not like him at all."

"It happens all the time, darlings—older men taking off with women young enough to be their daughters. They have to do anything they're asked—they're afraid of being traded in." Mama giggled, shaking her head.

"I hope he signed a prenup. Even after the lottery money he transferred into my trust fund account last fall, he still had a considerable fortune. I don't want him caught in any nasty battles. You know… just in case." I squirmed.

"That's your father's issue dear. Don't worry yourself about it. I'm more concerned that she'll start pressing him to start a family. At his age, it can be quite difficult."

"Oh, I don't think…Well, I don't know really if he would even consider it. He was pretty much hands off when I was growing up, except for holidays and summer visits. I can't imagine him wanting to start a new family now."

"He's a young pup compared to some of the actors and band members that are rolling out their fifth or sixth decade of offspring," Mama said, laughing. "Mickey Bennet is eighty-eight and expecting his ninth child. His oldest son just turned seventy!"

Mickey was a Hollywood heartthrob who had been entertaining generations of people with his movies. Unfortunately, his movie career lasted much longer than his marriages.

"David never mentioned wanting another family during the tour. I'd be quite surprised if he and Elizabeth had children. I thought they were committed to an academic life."

"A hundred million dollars is a lot of incentive to quit academia and start a new life, just saying…" Mama applied a spoonful of clotted cream to her scone and shrugged.

"Please call him, Mama and set up his visit. We'll just need the dates so that Bridges and Mrs. Smythe can coordinate their arrival and needs with the staff." Mrs. Smythe was the head housekeeper at Cherrywood, working side by side with Bridges in the management of the household.

I kissed Aunt Margaret goodbye and pecked Mama on the cheek so that I could get upstairs to my office and start the day's activities. Amy was coming in later this morning. She was meeting with a couple to go over wedding plans for their big day at the pavilion. I raced up the stairs to the third floor and made a pot of tea to drink before sitting down and starting my phone calls. I took the steaming cup over to my antique desk, its gild and gemstones shimmering in the morning light. Kyle had found the heirloom desk in storage and had it restored for me to use. I loved its glimmering elegance. I noticed that Lucy Etheridge had called several times already this morning. I decided to start with her before tackling Max and the wedding planner topic.

"Ms. Etheridge's office."

"Betty, hello, it's Gemma Lancaster Phillips. I'm returning Lucy's calls."

"Oh yes, Dr. Gemma. She's quite anxious to speak with you. I'll put her right on."

"Gemma, darling, thank you for getting back to me."

"No problem, Lucy. How can I help you?"

"Is anyone in the room with you? Amy? Jillian?"

"No, just me this morning."

"Gemma, it's a go. I just received approval. *Castlewood Manor* is being made into a feature film. Timothy Jones, who directed *The Fashions of Castlewood Manor*, will be the feature film director. I'm calling because we'd like to change the broadcast announcement schedule to now include both Christmas Day and New Year's Eve. Now, I know you'll have family and friends at Cherrywood, but I'll bring in first class everything for the announcements, decorators, designers, caterers and extra chefs if Chef Karl approves. Everything will be at your disposal. Prudence Nell will be leading the efforts on our end."

Prudence Nell and Timothy Jones had become an item last spring when we filmed several fashion shoots and a promo film here at Cherrywood.

"Lucy, wow, I don't know what to say. I know Prudence quite well. If you remember, she designed my beautiful office space. Do any of the actors know about the feature film? Mama is going to go through the roof!"

"No, and I must swear you to absolute secrecy, well, except for Kyle, I know he can be trusted. You see, not all the actors in the series will be included in the feature film. We're expecting some ruffled feathers, no doubt. Final decisions on the cast will be made in the next few days. We'd like to have the film cast announcements occur on New Year's Eve, to give us even greater exposure after the Christmas Day feature film announcement. It's all so exciting, and of course we'll have to have new contracts drawn up for you, Evan, and Kyle to go over, for the use of the estate. Oh my, how is Evan? I'm sorry, I'm such a goose."

"He's still comatose unfortunately, no change. Aunt Margaret came here yesterday, she wants to bring Evan to Cherrywood Hall to be cared for by the staff. She thinks being at home for the holidays may bring him some get well magic."

"The poor darling, of course. Is she okay with having us at Cherrywood Hall during this time?"

I could tell Lucy was panicking a bit. "She's fine. We all spoke last evening and agreed the more the merrier. It's been dreadful the past few months. We all need some Christmas cheer."

"Oh, I agree, Gemma. What about your wedding? Any details you can share?"

"Nothing yet, Lucy. Mama is having me call Max this morning. He has a wedding planner friend, Reginald Gerard, who he is insisting I use for our planning efforts."

"Reggie? Oh Gemma, he's the best there is. As a matter of fact, I've secured him to work with Prudence for the Christmas Day and New Year's Eve events at Cherrywood. I jumped the gun and assumed you'd be all right with this. He does the queen's parties you know."

"Yes, Aunt Margaret shared that tidbit with us last evening."

"Reggie, Prudence and I would like to arrive a little earlier this weekend to start going over details, if that's okay. Prudence knows the house, of course, but Reggie's only seen parts of it that have been featured in the show. They want to take a tour of the first floor to scout out the best broadcast locations. Of course, you could talk to him about your wedding while he's there too."

"Earlier this weekend will be fine. I'll make sure Amy can attend. She'll have to be told the news too, Lucy. You know she can be trusted."

"I'll count on your judgement, Gemma. Just please, say nothing to Jillian, not yet. There are going to be some hurt feelings with the cast. Bye, darling!"

We rang off and I refilled my tea before settling down once again to call Max. I wondered how he'd react knowing his wedding planner was now to be the decorator of our Christmas and New Year's soirees.

I was a little worried too, about Mama. Surely, they wouldn't consider doing a feature film and not include their leading actress. Both she and her co-star, Dame Agnes Knight had both just received *Telly Tiaras* for their work, Mama receiving the best actress award and Dame Agnes the best supporting actress trophy. I shook my shoulders to get those thoughts out of my mind before I dialed Max. One issue at a time, Gemma.

"Max Wellington."

"Max, it's Gemma. How are you?"

"Why you little darling, it's about time you called me. We have a wedding to plan!"

I laughed at Max's dramatic tone. I knew there was no way he was not going to be involved in choreographing my wedding, he was on a mission. "It's been a bit busy here, Max. Mama said you have someone in mind that you'd like to introduce me to, a Mr. Reginald Gerard?"

"Oh darling, Reggie is absolutely the best there is. He just got back from Denmark you know. He and I go way back to our university days. We both majored in interior design. Reggie branched out years ago to get in the wedding and party planning event business. Queen Annelyce and Lady Adela adore him. He did the queen's last dinner party, you know."

"Yes, yes, I've heard that. I must tell you Max, that Kyle and I have really not had a chance to discuss any plans yet, not with everything that has gone on with Evan."

"Oh, I know, darling. It's been so awful. That's why I thought you could just let me and Reggie, get started planning all the details for you. We'll take care of everything. You won't have to lift a finger."

I chuckled at his enthusiasm. "I do want to be involved, Max. It is my wedding you know. This month is going to be a madhouse with the holidays and…" I cut myself short before mentioning any of the *Castlewood Manor* events. I was pretty sure Elliot knew about them, but not sure of the extent of Max's knowledge. He loved being in the know and breaking new gossip.

"Darling, let's discuss it this weekend. Jillian has invited Elliot and me to Cherrywood Hall. It will be perfect timing. I understand Reggie will be there with Lucy and Prudence."

Once again, Max was light-years ahead of me in the know, I should have guessed. "I-uh, yes, they will be here. I have some things…"

"Oh darling, it will be perfect. I can hang with you and Reggie and we'll squeeze in wedding talk when we can. This will give him a chance to get to know you, and ahem, see if you fit his services."

I shook my head, was I hearing this correctly—Reggie would be determining my suitability as a customer? "Well, Max, if he has any doubts as to my suitability for his services, I don't want to take up his time. I'm sure he has a list of clients who might be better suited than me."

"Now, retract those bridezilla talons, Gemma. There will be plenty of time for the cat fighting. It just makes sense, darling, to do a meet and greet beforehand. Your wedding planner will be your new best friend for months. It's good business for you both to see if you're compatible, that's all."

I rang off with Max, wondering what in the world I had gotten myself into. I hadn't even thought about the possibility of the wedding planner not accepting me as a client. I had to admit my ego was a bit dented.

"Gemma, so glad you're here. I think I have us another client for the wedding pavilion lined up." Amy Princeton, my assistant walked in, setting her tote on her desk. She came over to air kiss my cheeks and sat down in the chair in front of my desk. "Brrr, it's really getting cold outside."

"Let's sit by the fire to get you warm. We can catch up there."

We took our notebooks and sat in the colorful, wingback chairs I had flanking either side of the fireplace. They were covered in neon-tinted, plaid fabrics; a tad unorthodox, but with the frequent gloomy weather outside I liked the bright décor, it made things cheery. We settled in the comfy chairs and enjoyed the warmth from the fire. I decided to start first, breaking it to Amy that we would be working this weekend. I only disclosed that we would be having events on Christmas Day and New Year's. I did not tell her the reason yet, thinking the fewer people that knew about the feature film the better, at least for now. Besides, Mama would be on her like a tick, wanting any information if she thought Amy knew something.

"Are you telling me *the* Reginald Gerard will be here, Gemma? Oh-my-gosh, he's only the who's who of the royal party set. I can't believe I get to work with him, and Prudence of course. Aunt Sally is going to have a cow."

"Now Amy, we are sworn to secrecy on this. The Rosehill Production executives want to make a huge splash on Christmas Day and New Year's

Eve. Sally will be given details as part of the press release efforts. You can't disclose anything to her."

"I get it, Gemma, my lips are sealed. Ooh, I'll have to get some new dresses for the events—how exciting."

"Amy, I will take you shopping personally to get the works. I'm confident Penny and her talented team will lend a helping hand too. She'll guarantee we'll look beautiful, no doubt about it."

We giggled and gave each other a fist bump. This was going to be a lot of work, but I had a feeling we'd have fun. We poured ourselves cups of tea and went over the event schedules Amy had worked on earlier. The wedding pavilion was going to be quite busy the next few months. I was beginning to wonder if Kyle and I could even squeeze in a date there ourselves.

On Thursday, just before noon, Kyle and I waited in the grand hallway at the entry for Lady Adela to arrive. We had planned on a lunch set up in the conservatory, one of my favorite rooms at Cherrywood. We smiled when we heard the crunch of gravel as her car pulled up. Kyle went outside to greet her and walk her inside.

"Lady Adela, so nice to see you," I said, kissing her cheeks as she entered.

She looked classically elegant, dressed in tan wool slacks and blazer, a navy and red silk scarf tied at her neckline. Bridges took her coat and we started the walk to the conservatory.

"Hello, darling girl. I can't believe how cold it's getting. And the winds—they were pummeling the car. I was afraid of being blown off the road." She squeezed my hand as we entered the conservatory. The plants were twinkling with fairy lights, giving off a magical glow. We sat in the wicker chairs, enjoying the view of the waterfall as Kyle brought us over a sherry to sip on before lunch.

"Ladies, here's to the start of winter. I think this is going to be a cold one," Kyle said raising his glass.

As we clinked our glasses—the winds growled their concurrence, bombarding the glass pane windows of the conservatory.

"We're safe in here aren't we?" I asked, nervously watching the glass shaking against the metal frames.

"No problem, darling. I had the conservatory frames and glass retrofitted years ago, both for energy efficiency and strength. We're safe, even in hurricane-force winds---unless of course the winds decide to bring down a helicopter or plane in our midst. I don't think the warranty covered that." Kyle winced.

"The queen just had a tire of all things crash through the greenhouse at the palace. She and Uncle Thaddeus were in checking on her new orchid blooms when the glass shattered and flew everywhere. The Royal Protections Service members threw them to the ground, thinking a possible terrorist act had been committed. They were chagrined and relieved when they saw the blown tire. A lorry had a burst tire just outside the palace walls, sending it careening over like a missile. It was amazing that no one was hurt."

"I'm glad of that, how frightening for them. I'll be watching the skies more closely."

We jumped as a large branch hit the outer wall of the conservatory. The winds were listening to our chatter.

"I think I'll have another sherry please, Kyle," Lady Adela said, giggling.

Kyle refilled our glasses. I could see his face tense up as he looked out at the howling winds.

Lady Adela stared down at the swirling sherry in her glass for a moment, finally stopping to glance up and look at me. "Gemma, darling,

I need to speak to you regarding the title and peerage dilemma. The queen is wondering what your decision is to be, especially now with Evan's situation."

I sat silent, contemplating the best way to address her question. I knew the queen was growing anxious for me to decide. "It's so difficult, Lady Adela. If I could talk with Evan and discuss it, I'm sure we could have it resolved quickly. In his condition, he doesn't even know about the news. I don't want to make the decision unilaterally—this is a family issue that needs everyone's input."

Kyle looked over at me and gave me a reassuring nod.

"I know it's a difficult time, dear. You all may have to deal with the fact that Evan may never recover. I'm sure this time is especially trying for Margaret. It must be hard for her watching her son in a coma and dealing with the thought of his title and peerage being stripped away. She is a strong woman though; she needs to put the needs of the family legacy first."

"She does put the family first, Lady Adela. She also cherishes her relationship with the queen. She's a very loyal subject and friend."

"No one's questioning her loyalty or friendship to the queen, Gemma. There are times when tough decisions must be made."

We sat in silence for a few minutes, thinking about the issues at hand. Our delicate stand-off was broken when Bridges announced that lunch was served, showing us over to a table that had been set up in a tree-topped niche next to the outer wall. We could see the whitecaps on the sea, the cold water looking almost black. I stared at their inky fury, wondering what I should do.

Lunch was brought in, starting with a creamy seafood chowder and crusty baguettes. The warm chowder tasted especially good on such a cold, windy day. Halibut, fingerling potatoes, and arugula salad were served next. We finished our meal with tea and blueberry scones, fresh from the oven. I decided to change the topic to the upcoming holiday events.

"We're about to start the holiday decorating here at the hall, Lady Adela. We have Reginald Gerard and Prudence Nell coming this weekend to start scoping out the décor. We'll be having two live broadcasts here, one on Christmas Day and one on New Year's Eve for the major announcements from Rosehill Productions."

"I've heard rumors about Rosehill having something up their *Castlewood Manor* sleeve. You'll love Reggie by the way. He has a great eye for fashion, decorating—he's really the best in the business. You should have him plan your wedding."

Kyle and I both smiled.

"So, we've been told, many times. He's a close friend of Max's and I'm pretty sure they've already started discussions without us, knowing him. Max and Elliot will be here too this weekend. I've learned Kyle and I will be hustled away by Max and Reggie for evaluation. Apparently, Reggie has to get to know us before committing to plan our wedding. We're going to have to be on our best behavior." I sighed, giving Kyle a playful wag of my finger.

"What's he going to do, give us an exam, check our bank accounts? I thought planning a wedding was supposed to be a fun experience." Kyle rolled his eyes, not buying into the idea of being evaluated by a wedding planner.

"Oh, I don't think you will have any problem dears. Reggie knows how close the queen is to the Lancaster family. You know, it might not be bad to have him plan your peerage ceremony. I'm sure he would be extra attentive, if he had an exclusive with you for both ceremonies."

"Wait--what peerage ceremony, Lady Adela?"

"As we were discussing earlier, Gemma dear, the queen would like to have the title and peerage transfer completed soon. She wants to have your ceremony at Hampton Court Palace on January 15th. Apparently, that is the day your American forefather, John Lancaster left England to go to the colonies because of the primogeniture issue. She felt it would be a fitting tribute to have the title and peerage bestowed upon you as a remembrance to the legacy he should have had. Of course, this requires your agreement, Gemma."

Kyle and I looked at each other, not knowing what to say. I was slowly realizing that these matters weren't really in my hands—if the queen wanted the ceremony to occur then, there was little I could do, other than back out and risk our family peerage and title be taken away.

The wind's howl grew louder and louder, rattling the panes of glass that separated us from the fury outside. The fairy lights twinkled on and off as the power surged with the storm. Pippa was sending me a message. Would our family's light still shine here at Cherrywood, or be gone with the wind?

CHAPTER 3
Pass, or Fail

Saturday morning started with a flourish of activity as we prepared for our Rosehill Productions guests to arrive. Bridges, Amy and I had the Cherrywood Christmas decorations for the house unboxed and ready to be shown to Prudence and the famous Mr. Reginald Gerard. We didn't know if they wanted to use our extensive collection or bring in all new wares for the holiday broadcasts. Max and Elliot arrived last evening, partying into the wee hours with Mama and Chef Karl. This morning, Kyle and I were first in the dining room, loading our plates with the savory breakfast offerings. The gales outside were once again blowing in frenzied gusts. This holiday season was coming in with a blast, and a cold one at that.

We spent the past two evenings having discussion after discussion about the title and peerage decision I had to make soon. We both knew it was time, and Lady Adela's visit here drove that point home. Truth be told I was excited about the prospect of becoming the Marchioness of Kentshire and righting the wrong done to my American patriarch, John—but not at the expense of any hurt feelings with Evan and Aunt Margaret. The queen's sense of urgency to finalize this decision and have the title ceremony in mid-January was putting a great deal of pressure on me, to say the least.

Mama glided into the dining room looking cheery, dressed in a hot pink, velvet top with paisley, palazzo pants. She kissed our cheeks and went to the buffet. Despite the late night of partying, she looked fresh and ready for the day to begin. "Good morning, darlings. Listen to that wind, I hope the walls of Cherrywood won't come tumbling down anytime soon."

"I don't know how you do it, Mama. When Kyle and I left you last night there were at least three empty champagne bottles laying on their side on the bar top." I grinned at her and shook my head.

"Darling, it's all in the timing. How much champagne did you actually see me drink? I am an award-winning actress you know…" Mama pursed her lips and coyly put her chin to her shoulder. She had made a point, Mama could be quite entertaining without alcohol, and I hadn't really seen her have more than a couple of glasses the entire evening.

Kyle laughed. "I think Elliot and Max did the lion's share of champagne imbibement. I doubt we'll see them before afternoon."

"Don't count Max out yet. Reginald Gerard will be here in an hour with Prudence and Lucy. I'm pretty sure he won't miss his visit," I said, skewering a mushroom.

"Yes, tell me about this visit. I'm intrigued that Rosehill Productions has brought in Reggie. They must be planning something very high brow and very big." She looked at me, her eyes opened wide in speculation.

"Mama, as I told you last night, they're here to scope out the grand hallway and first floor rooms for broadcast locations, and to look at our Christmas decorations to be used for the shows on Christmas Day and New Year's Eve. They're planning the décor for the broadcasts. I'm anxious to hear what they're thinking too. I hope we can use as many of the

Cherrywood decorations as possible. They've been in our family for centuries and it would be so upsetting if they were pushed aside. I'd feel guilty if we left them in the boxes this year." I pouted my lips dramatically and batted my eyes.

"I don't see how they wouldn't use what's in storage. Many of those glass globes are one of a kind creation. You can't get that kind of beauty from plastic and rayon."

"I totally agree, Kyle, but who knows what design plans are in the mind of the fabulous Mr. Gerard?" I shrugged.

"So, why are they suddenly doing two broadcasts, Gemma? The original plan was to just have an announcement on New Year's Eve." Mama was moving in for one more try. She was relentless when it came to scoops in entertainment related news, especially when it might involve her. It suddenly occurred to me she probably pushed last night's champagne free-for-all on Elliot and Max to try and pry details from them.

"I don't know, Mama. What have you heard? Lucy Etheridge will be here too. I'm sure she'll have all the answers to your questions." I decided two could play at this game.

Mama's brow wrinkled in thought. "Yes, well Lucy has been very tight-lipped with the cast. There are rumors that a feature film on Castlewood Manor is to be made next summer, fueled by a couple of tabloid articles. Not that I believe what's written in those."

"Mama, who are you kidding? You have subscriptions to just about every tabloid and entertainment magazine in existence." Kyle and I laughed at her feigned innocence and shook our heads. Mama combed these salacious reads as part of her early morning routine, looking for any articles on her and new tidbits of gossip and speculation that could be used to her benefit. She hasn't missed a morning read-a-thon yet, that I knew of.

"It's important to keep up on the latest details of what's going on in your industry, darling. I'm just doing my research, just like you and your daddy in the academia world. Speaking of which, I spoke to David yesterday afternoon. He and Elizabeth will be arriving here the week of Christmas. They want to stay at least until the New Year, maybe longer."

"Let's hope they don't decide to be a no-show again. I know Amy and Vicar Hawthorne will make time in their schedules to take them around. I don't want them left hanging at the last minute."

"I don't think you'll have to worry about that, Gemma. It seems your father has resigned his position at Columbia. Elizabeth has decided she wants to live in England. They will be looking for a place to live."

"Wow, that didn't last long," I said, surprised by this bit of news. "Daddy just accepted the position there. I can't believe he just upped and quit. Doesn't that seem strange to you?" Mama and Kyle seemed as perplexed as I was at the news. I hoped that I'd be able to talk with him privately when he arrived here for their stay. Something definitely didn't feel right.

At eleven o'clock, Kyle and I waited by the entry for Lucy, Prudence and Reginald to arrive. I was feeling anxious and yet super curious about meeting Mr. Gerard. I had changed after breakfast into a festive outfit of red tartan slacks, black turtleneck, and black patent boots to get into a holiday frame of mind. I wore my hair down, styled with a few golden tendrils framing my face.

We heard the hum of an engine as their limousine pulled up in front of the entry. The winds were gale-force today. We stood at the open door, watching our guests as they struggled to exit the car and come inside. Prudence and Lucy ran to the door, fighting the pull of the wind. Reginald Gerard stood outside the car and walked slowly up the stairs to the entry. He didn't seem to be bothered by the wind at all, his gate strong and regal, a long, black cape billowing around him. He held his head high as he walked and was clutching a bundle close to his chest that I couldn't quite make out. He stood in the grand hallway as Bridges removed his elegant cape from his shoulders. I smiled when I saw his concealed package. It was the cutest little white and brown, long-haired dog I had ever seen.

"Gemma, Kyle—thank you for meeting with us," Lucy said, as she and Prudence came over to shake our hands and greet us. I counted Lucy as a good friend these days, having worked with her since day one of the estate set-location competition. "I'd like to introduce you to Reginald Gerard, our decorator and event planner extraordinaire."

Reginald looked at Kyle and me, sizing us up through his wire frame glasses. He stood at around six feet tall with sandy-brown hair, tastefully attired in a bespoke tan and gray, tweed suit, complete with an embossed gold watch in the vest pocket. His miniature dog started to squirm in his hands as he stepped over to us.

"Patch, please mind your manners now, sir. Let's greet Gemma and Kyle."

To our astonishment, Patch reached out his right paw to shake as Kyle and I looked at one another with glee. We took turns shaking the delightful little pooch's paw.

"He's so cute," I said, tickled as he tried to lick Kyle's hand when he shook it.

"Patch, no licking, not on the first date," Reginald deadpanned. Patch looked up to his master with adoring eyes. Reginald gave him a small treat from his pocket and then turned his gaze to us.

"Welcome to Cherrywood Hall, Mr. Gerard." I held out my hand to shake.

"Enchante, Dr. Phillips. I hope you don't mind that I used your first name with Patch. He has a harder time with surnames and titles you know." Mr. Gerard took my hand and kissed it.

"No problem at all, Mr. Gerard. Please call me Gemma."

"Then you must call me Reggie," he said, a glimmer of a grin on his lips. He turned to Kyle. "Sir Kyle, very nice to meet you too."

"Thank you, Reggie, welcome. You have a most attractive companion there."

"Ruff!" Patch barked, staring lovingly at Kyle. It appeared that Kyle had a new-found friend.

"Would you like a drink and warm up over by the fire? Or would you like to start the tour of the first floor?" I asked.

"Let's start the tour, Gemma. I've heard about the rooms in great detail from Lucy and Prudence on the drive up. And of course, I watch the *Castlewood Manor* show faithfully. Patch and I never miss it on Sunday evenings. We feel like we know the house."

"Ruff!" Patch agreed.

"Let's start here in the grand hallway. We'll have the Christmas tree at the end," I said pointing. "It's over twenty-feet tall and is quite the dramatic piece. We have the traditional family ornaments that we've used through the years, as well as a gilded chair tufted in red velvet for Father Christmas to sit in for our Christmas Eve events with the Maidenford villagers. The tree is quite something to see when it's decorated, and the lights turned on."

"The trees all come from the estate too. We have a designated area of forest that we harvest them from. This year's tree was actually planted by my mother many years ago." Kyle said, his eyes sparkling at the mention of his mother.

I hadn't known this tidbit until now—my heart swelled with love at hearing this. Kyle's parents, Honey and Christian had been the previous estate managers here at Cherrywood Hall. They both had aristocratic backgrounds but decided to pursue the career passions they loved. Honey was also a jewelry maker in her own right. They had both been tragically killed in an automobile accident when Kyle was in university.

"Oh, Sir Kyle, that's so sweet. That's just the sort of detail we need for our broadcast segments when we discuss the decorations. The fans will eat that up," Prudence said, writing furiously in her notebook.

"Christmas has always been a special time here at Cherrywood Hall, especially after Gemma's great, great Aunt Pippa joined the family in the early nineteen-hundreds. As mistress, Lady Pippa made it a point to have every corner of the house decorated."

I saw Reggie nodding his head, taking in every word. You could almost see the little gears in his brain turning, developing his plan.

We made our way into the library, study and dining room next. "Lucy, will you want the dining room cleared as we did for the New Year's announcement last year?" I asked. We had installed stand up tables and small buffets in each corner, featuring different varieties of food for the guests to sample.

"Oh yes, definitely, don't you think? It will give guests a chance to mingle more freely." Lucy looked over at Prudence and Reggie.

"Do you use the dining room on Christmas Day, Gemma? I don't want to disrupt your family plans too much," Reggie said, one eye closed, lips pursed, scoping out the room.

"We have dinner in here on Christmas Eve. On Christmas Day we usually opt to have meals in the conservatory," I said, pointing over to the glass doors on the far side of the dining room. "Would you like to see it? It's one of my favorite parts of the manor."

I led the group through the doors into the marble-tiled room. Fairy lights flickering, it charmed our visitors who oohed and aahed as we toured around the curving pathways, examining the different varieties of plants. Reggie was particularly taken with the waterfall. Patch too—he was struggling to get down and explore.

"Mr. Patch, manners please." Patch quieted down when his master spoke. "I must say, this room is enchanting. We could have one broadcast announcement in the grand hallway, and the other one here. I think this should be the New Year's Eve spot. With the black and white marble tiles we can dazzle the room with silver and gold highlights. It's going to be a stunner." Reggie's eyes glazed over as he went into design mode, making suggestion after suggestion.

Prudence took detailed notes, not wanting to miss anything. We heard footsteps of people walking in behind us, heels clicking on the marble tiles.

"Reggie, darling," Max oozed, gliding over to greet his friend. Mama followed close behind, with a confident, determined look on her face. "I must introduce you to our favorite actress, the lovely Jillian Phillips."

Reggie's face broke into a huge grin. He was obviously a fan of Mama's.

"Jillian, darling, it's so wonderful to meet you at last. Max, you bad boy, keeping this delightful creature from me and Patch all this time."

"Ruff!" Patch licked Mama's hand when she reached out to pet him.

"I'm so honored to meet you, Patch—and you too, Reggie dear," Mama cooed, in her best Hollywood actress tone. She walked over to Prudence and kissed her cheeks, turning next to Lucy. "Hell-o, Lucy. How charming to see you here, darling." Mama clutched her arm. There was no way Lucy was getting out of her grip anytime soon.

"Let's go into the study, darlings. Jillian and I have set out cocktails and Chef Karl has prepared some lovely bites for us to indulge in." Max led us into the study where Elliot stood at the bar, looking dapper in a silk, smoking jacket, cravat wrapped elegantly around his neck, poised to act as bartender for the group. He gave a quick buss to Reggie, Lucy and Prudence.

"All right my darlings, get yourself a plate of the goodies, Cherrywood bubbly is coming right up." Elliot popped open a bottle of the sparkling wine and began to pour our drinks.

We took a plate as instructed and loaded up on BBQ shrimps, canapés with salmon, crème fraiche and dill, slices of Brie drizzled with honey, and of course, Mama's favorite, dates wrapped in sausage and bacon.

"Ruff!" Patch took a seat on the sofa between Reggie and Kyle, who promptly snuck him a piece of shrimp.

"Now Patch, manners boy." Reggie pointed his chin down, eyes looking over the wireframe spectacles perched on his nose. Patch promptly obeyed his adoring master.

Elliot handed us our glasses of the house wine. "A toast please. Here's to the upcoming holidays, may they be joyful, fun, and filled with excitement. And please give the wind a rest!" Elliot enthused, rolling his eyes dramatically.

"Hear, hear," we said in unison, as the winds groaned in the chimney.

"Ruff!" Patch chimed in.

"Lucy dear, tell us all about the big plans here on Christmas Day and New Year's Eve. We're dying to hear all about it, darling." Max gave Mama a wink. It was obvious these two had something up their sleeve.

"Oh now, Max, you know everything's hush hush. I could tell you, but then I'd have to kill you," Lucy deadpanned, rapidly batting her lashes in a teasing gesture.

"Lucy, we won't tell a soul. Can't you give us one hint?" Mama asked, teasing Lucy by fluttering her lashes rapidly.

I felt like we were at a tennis match, our heads turning side to side, from player to player as they volleyed the balls.

"Jillian, darling, you know I can't tell you. Don't you want to be surprised by the announcements on Christmas Day and New Year's Eve? I wouldn't want to spoil the surprise…" Lucy arched her eyebrows, eyes opened wide.

Mama exhaled loudly, clearly frustrated. She popped a sausage-wrapped date in her mouth and chewed, trying to think of a clever comeback to get her the answers she was dying to know. I decided to change the subject while her mouth was full.

"Reggie, what do you think you'd like to do for decorations? Are you interested in seeing the family ornaments for the tree in the grand hallway, or will you want to start with a clean slate? My assistant, Amy Princeton will be here any moment. We've pulled out the family heirlooms for you to inspect. We can go down to the storerooms after we finish here."

"Gemma there's no debate, dear. I want the Cherrywood family decorations used for the Christmas tree in the grand hallway. The centuries of history and family give us the image of opulent years gone by. I feel the love your Aunt Pippa must have had when she arrived here at Cherrywood. In every room you can feel her presence."

"Reggie is a psychic too, Gemma. He's given Elliot and me several readings. I'm completely convinced of his powers to see." Max, nodded his head, panning the room.

Elliot, who was standing back at the bar retrieving another bottle of sparkling wine, rolled his eyes, causing Kyle and me to quickly put a napkin to our mouths to hide our mirth.

"Ah-ha, a psychic. What do you see in store for me, Reggie? Will I be happy with the announcements Rosehill Productions make?" Mama asked, going in for one more try.

Reggie laughed. "I see good things in store for you Jillian, darling… I…" Reggie stopped mid-sentence, his eyes going into a trance-like gaze.

We watched him, not knowing whether to disturb his deep thoughts or let him be. Luckily, Amy came into the entry. The howling wind blowing through the open door caught our attention and snapped Reggie out of his momentary reverie.

"Ruff!" Patch was startled by the loud commotion. His owner shook himself and managed a weak smile.

"Hiya, sorry I'm late. Kyle, I hate to tell you, but there are several trees down near the main gate. I've never seen anything like this." Amy went around the room to greet everyone. She stopped in front of Reggie, speechless with admiration. "Hello, Mr. Gerard. It's an honor to meet you." Amy's star-struck eyes were shining as she gave him a little curtsy. Reggie seemed delighted with her attention.

"Ruff!" Patch extended his paw for a handshake.

"Oh, what a little charmer you are," Amy purred.

We finished eating our canapes and helped ourselves to a lovely assortment of orange tea and lemon curd tarts for our dessert. We were in high spirits, chatting about the upcoming holiday events. I noticed Reggie glancing over at Mama a few times, his face veiled with sadness for just a moment. I wasn't a huge believer in psychic foretellers, but I had a strange feeling about Reggie's haunting gaze. I was growing a bit concerned. Was she in danger or about to receive heartbreaking news?

Kyle excused himself to go check with his crew on the falling trees. Reggie, Prudence, Amy, Max, and I headed down to the storage rooms next to the kitchen to scope out the Christmas decorations. Mama, Elliot, and Lucy remained in the study to talk business. I was certain Mama was going to give it one more heave-ho to find out the details of the studio's holiday announcements.

We went into the kitchen for a quick tour. Patch was left there to nibble on a few goodies while we took inventory of the ornaments and trimmings to be used. Bridges met us at the storage room, where we went around the various shelving units, pulling out ornaments that we thought were unique. Reggie was very impressed and knew the provenance of many of the decorations. I was impressed by his knowledge and began to see why his expertise was in such high demand.

"Look at this—the angel is so detailed. You can see the feather tufts on her wings. I can't imagine the skill needed to carve the molds for some of these. Gemma, your family has a fortune in decorations here. Why, I don't think the queen herself has items of this quality. I understand Lady Adela has been here too of late, you better watch her like a hawk if she attends these celebrations. She and a few other royals I'm acquainted with are known for their sticky fingers, if you catch my drift."

Max and Reggie smirked at hearing this, and I assumed there might be a ring of truth to it. Prudence and Amy stood in shocked silence, not used to thinking of their royals as 'sticky fingered'. Bridges, in his typical fashion, showed no emotion.

"Over here, Reggie, come sit in Father Christmas' chair." Max was already seated, rubbing his hands across the tufted velvet.

"Oh, that is stunning," Reggie gasped, his hands lightly touching the gilded, wood, carved arms. "I've just had the most marvelous idea. We can have Father Christmas make the Christmas Day announcement sitting in this chair. *And now, a message from Father Christmas, from the halls of Castlewood Manor...*" Reggie said, in a dramatic, baritone voice.

"I love it," Max squealed. "Why you can't get a better spokesperson than Father Christmas! Reggie, you are brilliant, darling." Max stood and air kissed his cheeks.

"That is a fantastic idea, Reggie, I agree. Last year, Kyle played the role of Father Christmas, but I'm sure Rosehill Productions will have one of their actors or execs do the honors. How exciting, Father Christmas at *Castlewood Manor*. We'll have to make sure Sally runs that headline," I said, looking over at Amy.

"Timothy would make a great Father Christmas," Prudence said softly. "And he is the new director…" She froze, worried that she had slipped something she shouldn't have. Max's ears perked up immediately, but Prudence said no more on the topic.

"What do you think of photographing a few of the ornaments professionally and have the pictures framed as giveaways for the guests attending the broadcasts? Rosehill might even want to have them made up for the fans of the show," I said, trying to change the subject.

"Brilliant, Gemma, I love that idea. The more we can bring *Castlewood Manor* to the masses the better. It will be a great promo offering."

I basked in Reggie's praise. Was he signaling my passing as a bridal client by chance?

We finished our tour loaded with ideas, picking up a full and drowsy Patch from his new nest in the kitchen. I noticed the staff had placed a comfy pillow next to the fireplace for him during his stay. It seemed everyone was under the spell of the pint-sized dog.

As we walked up the stairs to the grand hallway, we heard a frantic scream. It was Mama. My heart quickened as I raced past the others, worried that Reggie's frozen vision from earlier had come true with some sort of doom. When I reached the study, Mama, Lucy, and Elliot were hugging each other, laughing and crying loudly. The others made their way behind me as we stood and watched their joyous celebration.

"Mama, you scared me half to death."

She turned and pranced over to me, hugging me tightly. "Oh darling, Lucy just told me the most wonderful news. There is going to be a feature film, and, I'm going to be the lead star!" Mama skipped around the room hugging everyone. Max was beside himself with joy, rapidly clapping his hands.

"I smell a *Gilded Globie* next, Jillian!" he said, joining her, laughing and prancing around the room.

"Now everyone, please, this news is not to go outside the walls of Cherrywood Hall. I was given permission to break the news to Jillian, since she will be one of our leads. The other actors are being told today as well by envoys from Rosehill. I must insist you keep this under wraps, because there are a few actors who will not be included in the feature film, which will most likely bring some hurt feelings and short tempers around." Lucy looked at each of us, willing us to stay silent.

"Not a problem, Lucy, you can count on our discretion." I said, making a motion of a zipper being closed against my lips. Everyone else nodded as well, thrilled to be included in this feature film scoop.

Our tour completed, we walked Lucy, Prudence and Reggie to the door to say goodbye, Patch held tightly in Reggie's arms. The winds were still howling as we waved, watching them struggle to get into the limo. Reggie and Prudence would be coming back to Cherrywood Hall next week with their staff to commence the decorating.

Elliot, Max, Mama, Amy, and I went back into the study for a celebratory cocktail. We were in high spirits when Kyle returned from assessing the tree damage, his hair slicked back from the blowing wind and drizzle.

"So, what did I miss?" Kyle asked, sipping his freshly poured bourbon.

A cacophony of voices erupted as everyone tried to talk at once to tell him Mama's fabulous news. Kyle went over and kissed Mama's cheeks. He was very proud of her acting accomplishments. Their relationship had grown very strong this past year. He thought of her as a mother, and she of him as her son.

I sat still, thinking about the happy news as I watched the fire.

As the others chatted, Max came over to me and sat down, snuggling close. "Pssst, Jillian isn't the only one who needs to celebrate. You passed darling, with flying colors. *The* Reginald Gerard is going to do your wedding!"

CHAPTER 4

Homecoming Prep

The next week had Cherrywood Hall filled with artisans, decorators, electricians, and builders as the Christmas decorating began and the rooms downstairs were transformed into recovery and housing quarters for Evan and his caregivers. We were on a tight schedule, Aunt Margaret wanted Evan to be transferred here on Saturday. Kyle's team were working 24/7 to make sure the rooms were retrofitted with the necessary electrical and networking requirements for the medical equipment.

Evan's recovery room was a combination of two existing bedrooms and sitting room used by previous generations of elderly Lancaster's. Three other bedrooms on the floor had been reserved for his permanent caregivers who would work in shifts to give Evan the medical and therapy treatments he needed to keep his body functioning while he was in his comatose state.

Reggie, Prudence and their teams were here executing the decorating of the grand hallway and conservatory for the holiday announcements. It was a godsend really to have them here taking care of things. It freed us up to focus on Evan's return, and for that I was grateful. Aunt Margaret was arriving tonight, so that she could oversee the final details to Evan's new rooms. She wanted everything perfect for him, and I knew she was placing a great deal of hope on Christmas magic reviving her son.

I was glad that she was coming back, for she and I needed to discuss the title and peerage matter once and for all. Lady Adela was now calling and texting me every day, claiming the queen needed to know my answer now, the galley room at Hampton Court Palace was being held for my ceremony. Lady Adela also informed me that the queen had spoken to Aunt Margaret, which made me feel a little better knowing that I was not alone in convincing her.

I had spent the morning and early afternoon reading a few of my Aunt Pippa's diaries. They brought me comfort. Getting to know the friends and family who she interacted with gave me a bird's eye view of her life here in the last century. There was no doubt in my mind that Pippa belonged at Cherrywood Hall. I thought about what her life would have been like being the rightful Marchioness heir herself, and not just through marriage. How would she have reacted? Would it have changed her views on marrying Charles? My speculation was stopped by the ringing of the in-house phone that connected the one-hundred-fifty rooms plus here at the hall.

"This is Gemma."

"Hello darling. I was wondering if you could come downstairs and take a look at Evan's new space. We need a female perspective for the paint color."

I laughed as I made my way downstairs. At least choosing a paint color should be easy. I went through the grand hallway, admiring the garland that was being hung along the walls. It was definitely starting to look like the holidays, and it cheered me to no end.

Reaching Evan's recovery quarters, I was impressed at how much progress Kyle's crew had made. The three rooms had been combined into one great room. The windows on the outer wall had a spectacular view of the sea and the garden vignettes along the sea path. Aunt Margaret wanted Evan's bed near the window so he could see out, if or when he ever woke up. The electricians were installing a breaker box in the room for emergency power supplied by generators that had been placed outside. Kyle was afraid with the winds being so dramatic this season we were likely to have power interruptions. He didn't want Evan's medical equipment to be in any danger of failure. The two fireplaces from the combined rooms were on either side of the space, ensuring that Evan's new room would stay nice and warm even in the event of a power outage.

"Kyle, this looks fabulous. The room is so big. I love the open feel. Maybe we should do this in some of the other areas of the hall." I went over and hugged him, kissing his cheek to congratulate him.

"I am quite pleased. The electrical work is a bit more complex than expected, but I think we have all the kinks worked out. Evan's caregivers won't have to worry about a power failure with the backup system we've installed. I'm thinking it would be a good idea to retrofit the rooms that see major use like the kitchen and study with the generators too. It would be nice to have backup power just in case. I wouldn't want my poor darling to go without her food." Kyle laughed and swept me up in a bear hug, swinging me around the room.

"Stop, stop—I'm getting dizzy." I squealed, trying to escape his swinging embrace.

Kyle set my feet on the ground, holding me close to kiss me. "Amazing how a little construction can arouse one's feelings," he whispered.

Our passion was igniting quickly. I loved getting lost in his kisses.

"Gemma, there you are darling," Mama said, as she walked across the room over to us.

We broke our embrace and straightened our clothing. At one time, I would have been embarrassed at the interruption, but Mama's uncanny ability to catch Kyle and me in a romantic moment made me less and less self-conscious these days.

"This is gorgeous, Kyle," Mama said, walking around the room, inspecting every detail. "Margaret will be so pleased. I know she's frantic, worrying about everything being perfect for Evan."

"You're just in time, Jillian. I had Gemma come down to help decide on the paint color. You can help us choose too."

We walked over to a worktable in the corner of the room made from sawhorses and a plywood sheet. Kyle laid the paint chip tags on the table, giving us a spectrum of violet, gray, teal, and tan to choose from.

"Ooh, I love the violet," Mama gushed. "It may be too girly though for Evan, although I love the cool tone it would give the room."

"That's why I like the tan, Jillian. I think it will bring warmth to the room, a good thing given these never ceasing winter winds. I think Lady Margaret would approve."

"They're both pretty, but I like the gray. It's masculine and provides such a great background to bring in pops of color. The white molding will look super with it too."

After much deliberation, we decided that Aunt Margaret should make the final decision of the two favorites. Kyle had his team paint a large section of wall with the tan and the gray paint so that we could see how it would look both at night and during the day. That decision settled, we went to the conservatory to have tea. Reggie, Prudence and Amy were going to join us. I was looking forward to getting a decorating update.

I was taken aback when we entered the conservatory. Miniature double-sided, mirrored discs had been hung from the taller plants and trees with clear fishing line, their reflective surfaces shooting sprays of light across the room. The effect was spectacular, and I knew at night with the fairy lights it would be even more dramatic. It would be perfect for the New Year's Eve cast announcement.

"Oh-my-gosh, this is beautiful guys. We are never taking this down."

Amy, Prudence and Reggie smiled, pleased at my reaction. Patch wagged his tiny tail.

"Well done folks, I can't believe the difference the mirrors make. They bring a whole new level of Hollywood glam to the room." Kyle put his arm around my waist.

"Ooh, I just had some great gown inspiration, I'm going with red. It will look dazzling with the black and white tiles and the mirrors will reflect it so well. I need to talk with Penny, her team must get a dress designed for me." Mama's eyes were lit. I could tell she was in seventh heaven, thinking of her glamorous New Year's Eve look.

"That would be spectacular, Jillian. With your coloring it will be perfect for the broadcast. Let me know if you want any help with the design, darling. I'd love to assist." Reggie smiled and scrunched his nose playfully at Mama. I think he was becoming smitten.

"Ruff!" Patch seemed quite the fan of Mama's too.

"Tea is served, everyone," Bridges announced.

We took our seats at a large, round table set up next to the waterfall. We helped ourselves to beef consommé served with crusty, Parmesan sprinkled croutons. Open-face sandwiches with chicken salad, Benedictine cheese, and prosciutto were served next, followed by a beef and mushroom tart. Dessert consisted of chocolate truffles, mini cheesecakes, and colorful macaroons. The room was strangely quiet except for the splash of the waterfall and the howling wind outside. Decorating and construction projects had given everyone an appetite.

"I'm amazed you've made so much progress," I said, picking out a cherry macaroon from the tray to nibble on next. "The grand hallway is already looking like Christmas with the garland that has gone up. When do you think you'll do the tree trimming?"

"My crew can have the tree set up at the end of the week. The construction will be completed by then for Evan's rooms. It's in the barn now, drying. You should be able to start decorating as soon as we get it secured." Kyle reached over for another helping of sandwiches.

"It's going to be so festive. We should host a tree trimming party this weekend, as kind of homecoming for Evan celebrating his return. I know Max and Elliot would love to come, and Penny and Steph. Sally and Vicar Hawthorne would probably like an invite too. What do you think?"

"I'd love to come and I'm sure Timothy would too. We'll be staying at my flat in Maidenford this weekend. He's been in non-stop meetings at Rosehill this week for the feature film planning. I'm sure a little tree trimming, and spiked eggnog would be just the thing for him," Prudence said, smiling.

"I know Aunt Sally would love to be here too. She can take photos of the decorations going up. It would be a great promo piece leading up to the big announcements."

"Sounds perfect, Amy. Let's invite Lady Adela, Kyle, to bring in a little royal flavoring to our soiree. It would be fun to have her here. Reggie, you're welcome to stay the weekend at Cherrywood if you'd like. We have plenty of rooms."

"Ruff!" Patch's eyes sparkled. He liked the idea of being a guest at Cherrywood. His pillow down in the kitchen was becoming his favorite spot to get nibbles and naps by the fire.

"That would be a nice treat, Gemma. When Max gets here, we could start discussions on your wedding plans." Reggie gave me a wink.

"We need to pick out themes, venues, dates, and the all-important dress, of course."

"Ooh, count me in for that discussion, Reggie. I want nothing but the best for my daughter and future son-in-law." Mama grinned ear to ear.

She was going to be a ferocious mother of the bride, I was sure. I wondered if Reggie would be a fan of hers after the wedding. Kyle and I looked at one another, our eyes wide in somewhat feigned shock. Could we survive the planning phase of the wedding? Only time would tell.

Pleased with our weekend and wedding planning decisions, we broke up our group and went back to work. Kyle was going to invite Steph and tell her to bring Penny. I made calls to Sally and Vicar Hawthorne to invite them to the tree trimming on Saturday and explained that Evan would be coming home too. As expected, Sally jumped at the chance to get the first look pictures of the decorating and also write a somber piece on Lord Evan's return to Cherrywood. The Vicar was beside himself getting to be with Mama for the decorating, and he wanted to be of comfort to Aunt Margaret too. My final call was to Lady Adela.

"Tilford residence."

"Yes, hello. This is Gemma Lancaster Phillips calling for Lady Adela."

"One moment miss. I will check to see if she's receiving calls."

I waited for just a minute.

"Gemma, darling, how are you? Is the weather still ghastly there at Cherrywood Hall?"

"Yes, I'm afraid so, Lady Adela. Aunt Margaret is coming here tonight, and we have Evan being transferred to Cherrywood on Saturday morning. We wanted to have a gathering this weekend to start the tree trimming here at the hall. It should be fun and having friends and family here will do Aunt Margaret a world of good. Would you be available to come up Saturday and stay the night with us?"

"I'd love to, darling. It's so sweet of you to ask me. I can be there around two. Is that okay?"

"Two will be just fine, Lady Adela; the other guests are coming at four. We should have Evan well situated by then. I'll have a room made up for you."

"Gemma, have you made your decision yet? We must have things finalized, darling."

"I'm going to discuss this with Aunt Margaret when she arrives. I realize the urgency, but we're dealing with a lot as a family right now."

"Gemma, dear, you're going to be Marchioness of Kentshire. I admire your dedication to your family, particularly with Evan's condition. However, you must rise to your position, dear. It's expected."

We finished our discussion and rang off. I sat at my desk, perplexed. As an American, the idea of peerage and title was a foreign concept. I had certainly grown to appreciate it after having lived here, but to me, my family's happiness came first. I went over to the fireplace and stared at a painting of Aunt Pippa. It was one of her in middle age, a profile of her looking out to the sea-swept landscape.

"Okay old girl, what would you advise? I've come to love Evan and Aunt Margaret so much. I would do anything for them and wouldn't hurt them for the world. I need my cousin, Pippa." Tears trickled down my cheeks, the stress of worrying over this issue was taking its toll on me too.

"I think she would advise you to follow your heart and head, dear."

I started. Aunt Margaret stood in my office doorway. She smiled and walked over to me, giving me a hug to buoy up my spirits. We stood in our quiet embrace for several minutes.

"Here, you sit down, and I'll make some tea," I said, pulling from our embrace and wiping my eyes.

"The fire feels wonderful." Aunt Margaret sat in a winged back chair, putting her hands out to warm them. She gratefully accepted her cup of tea from me.

"This is just what I needed. I've never seen such weather. The highways are inundated with blowing signs and trash. Bates had to swerve several times to avoid being hit with an errant piece of debris."

Bates was the chauffeur here at Cherrywood Hall, who often drove us back and forth to London.

"I'm glad you made it here safely. We have a surprise for you downstairs. Kyle's crew has made significant progress on Evan's room. It's beautiful now that the walls of the adjoining rooms have been removed. It's spacious and has a lovely view of the garden vignettes and sea. We have a final decision for you to make. We narrowed the paint color options down to two. You get the deciding vote."

"I'm sure it looks beautiful. The grand hallway is stunning, by the way. I love the garland."

"You should see the conservatory. Its splendid with swarms of little dangling mirrors hanging from the trees and plants. I've never seen anything like it."

"Reggie's work no doubt. He does have a flair for the dramatic."

"We decided to have a small gathering here Saturday evening, Aunt Margaret. Reggie, Elliot and Max, Prudence and Timothy, Amy, Sally, and Vicar Hawthorne are coming over to begin the tree trimming in the grand hallway. We thought it would be fun to have some gaiety in the air for Evan's return. I know the laughter will do us good. I hope it helps him too." Aunt Margaret smiled and nodded her head.

"I think it's a grand idea, dear. Cherrywood Hall was built for entertaining. It's been silent for too long."

"Lady Adela will be here. Kyle and I thought it would be good to include her. This will be her first Christmas since Evangeline's death; things may get a little emotional for her."

Aunt Margaret sat quietly, looking at the fire. "I suppose she is pressing you for a decision."

"Yes, she is, Aunt Margaret. Queen Annelyce wants to have my title and peerage ceremony on January fifteenth. Apparently, that is the date John Lancaster left England for America. She thinks it will be a fitting tribute."

"I understand. What venue has she picked."

"Hampton Court Palace. It's stunning there. I love the grounds."

"Gemma, you know my feelings on this subject. My main concern is for Evan. If he ever recovers it may put him back in decline if he learns he's been stripped of his peerage and title. I cannot have that." A look of sorrow veiled her face.

"Aunt Margaret, I completely understand, really I do. Can't you see how much pressure is on me? I want the chance to discuss it with Evan so badly. You must know too, whatever happens, Cherrywood Hall will always remain your home."

"I appreciate that, dear. This entire situation has hit us all like a ton of bricks. I know you must give the queen an answer. I would just ask that you wait until Evan returns home. Let's see how he responds to treatments here at Cherrywood. I'll speak to the queen again. I'm a bit perturbed that Lady Adela has inserted herself into this situation. I know she cares for Kyle and you—I'm sure it's a blessing having you in her life with Evangeline gone. It's irritating that she is putting so much pressure on you. We'll deal with it, don't worry."

Our teacups empty, we stood and gave one another one last hug and made our way downstairs to see Evan's new quarters. Kyle and Mama were already there, staring at the large color swaths that had been painted on the walls from different angles. They smiled when they saw us walk in. Kyle beckoned us over to see the wall.

"Okay ladies, moment of truth, what color is it to be?" Kyle shined a bright light on the swaths to give us a better perspective.

"I'm torn, I thought tan, but now I like the gray. Is it still your favorite, Gemma?"

"I think so, Mama. It seems so soothing to me. I'm thinking we can punch the color up with accessories. Red or teal, or even tan pillows. Maybe a tapestry pattern?"

"There's a lovely pair of paisley patterned tan chairs in one of the sitting rooms upstairs. They would look splendid down here by the fireplace. There are some matching rugs too, if I'm not mistaken. Bridges would know. We could scatter them around the room to make a few seating vignettes for visitors."

Kyle continued the tour of the room with Aunt Margaret by his side to explain the new wiring and backup power features being installed. Mama came over and stood by me as they made their rounds.

"I take it you and Margaret spoke?" Mama put her arm around my shoulder, giving me a supportive hug.

"Yes, we did. She's empathetic but she doesn't want anything done without Evan's input. I think it's the last thread of hope she's holding onto. She wants me to wait before I tell the queen my decision, hoping to see if there's any change in Evan's condition when he gets back to Cherrywood Hall."

"The poor darling. I know she's heartbroken. I can't imagine her pain. Why if anything happened to you, Gemma…" Mama sniffed and wiped a tear from her eye.

I leaned into her and held her close. "We'll get through this, Mama. I don't know how yet, but we will."

Kyle and Aunt Margaret walked over to us after they completed their tour. Aunt Margaret had a grin on her face that warmed our hearts. She was clearly pleased with the progress.

"I am so impressed. The power backup is a brilliant idea, I hadn't even considered it. Kyle darling, Evan and I are forever indebted to you, I hope you know that." She stepped up on her tippy toes and planted a kiss on his cheek. For just a moment I saw Kyle blushing, but he was pleased, I could tell.

"I think a cocktail is just what we need to celebrate. Shall we go to the study?"

"Lead the way, Jillian. You ladies go ahead. I'll shut down the room. Gemma darling, I'd love a whiskey if you're pouring."

"You've got it—hurry up now."

Aunt Margaret, Mama and I made our way to the study, stopping briefly in the grand hallway to admire the garland. The twinkle lights were on, glittering against the carefully placed ornament clusters, giving a look of Yuletide opulence to the hallway.

"*It's beginning to look a lot like Christmas...,*" Mama sang.

Aunt Margaret and I laughed, watching Mama glide across the hallway. We went into the study. Aunt Margaret and Mama took a seat together on the couch. I poured out a sherry for Aunt Margaret, champagne for Mama, a whiskey for Kyle, and whisked together a gin and St. Germain martini for me. Kyle came in just as I had finished preparing our cocktails. He helped me get the drinks served as we sat down in the chairs across from Mama and Aunt Margaret.

"Here's to Evan and his health. I can't tell you how much your support means to us," Aunt Margaret toasted, raising her glass to us.

"Hear, hear," we said in unison, clinking our glasses.

"Gemma, have you given any thought as to the style of wedding dress you'd like?" Mama asked. "We can have a bespoke dress made for you. I bet Penny and her team would love to design something. They know your style quite well."

"I really haven't, Mama. I've worn so many beautiful gowns this past year for the *Castlewood Manor* events. Most of them have hugged my figure. Do you think I ought to go for a huge ball-gown silhouette to be different? I've seen some dresses so wide you have to step through a door sideways. Then there's the matter of the train, should I have one as long as the hallway?"

Kyle looked over at me as if I had gone daft, his expression causing us all to break out in laughter.

"I've always said, go big or go home," Mama chimed in, scrunching her nose.

"I'm sure Max and Reggie have some ideas too," Aunt Margaret said, trying to stifle her mirth at Mama's and my teasing.

"I am not wearing red velvet, trimmed in white faux fur. A Mother Christmas look is not in the cards," I said, waving my hands back and forth.

"Are there any wedding gowns in the mega closet, Gemma? I know there are, ahem, veils…" Mama coughed.

A family veil drama had caused quite a scandal a few months ago at a royal wedding fiasco down at the pavilion. It made headlines around the world when the queen's grandson jilted his bride to be, a royal wedding first that the queen did not want to see repeated.

"I haven't looked at the wedding gowns there. We could do that on Sunday. I'm sure Max and Reggie would enjoy seeing what's in the inventory, me too for that matter. I'd love to find Pippa's wedding dress."

"I've seen it, many years ago. It was a stunning creation with hand stitched lace and glimmering pearl beads. She was quite the lady. You know, there's another dress of hers that she used to talk about all the time. It was a brocade and lace, mermaid-style dress with a billowing, blue, tulle skirt that was cinched and attached at the waist. I think it was made for an anniversary I believe. I've never seen it—I don't know if it's in the closets or not."

"Sounds gorgeous, Aunt Margaret. I'd love to find it. I'm getting excited now. It will be like we're on a treasure hunt." I clapped my hands in anticipation. This was going to be fun.

We spent the rest of the evening chatting excitedly about Evan's return and the holiday events. I was glad to see the smiles on our faces again. I hoped against hope that Evan would be given the strength to return to us. I knew that I was not alone in this heartfelt wish.

CHAPTER 5
Celebrations

Saturday morning arrived before we knew it. Kyle and I woke up early, anxious to get downstairs in anticipation of Evan's arrival. I stopped for a minute in the grand hallway to stare at the magnificent Christmas tree Kyle's crew had erected yesterday, complete with lights. It stood just over twenty feet tall, its branches spreading out in a glorious, nature-inspired spiral. The smell of pine from the tree was intoxicating and revved up my decorating spirit. My heart was pounding too with excitement at seeing my cousin back at Cherrywood. In the dining room, Mama, Elliot, Max, Reggie, and Aunt Margaret were seated eating their breakfast. We were not the only ones anxious to see Evan.

"Good morning, everyone. I guess we're all early birds today." I went over to give Aunt Margaret and Mama a quick cheek buss before heading over to the buffet.

"I couldn't sleep a wink. I've been waiting for this day for so long. I just hope that everything goes well. Do you think we should call the traffic officers to make sure there's not been an accident?"

"Margaret, darling. Everything is fine. Evan's not expected here for another hour at least. They will call us if anything goes amiss. Now come on, eat your breakfast. You're going to need your strength." Mama gently caressed Aunt Margaret's hand.

"The winds aren't nearly as strong as they have been, Lady Margaret. I'm sure the drive will be much smoother than earlier in the week. My staff is here. They're down in the kitchen being served some breakfast as they wait. They'll get everything carried inside and placed as soon as the lorries arrive." Kyle's reassuring voice was comforting to us all.

"So, who's ready to decorate today?" I asked, trying to change the subject. I took a seat next to Reggie. Patch was in his lap, snoozing away like a baby.

"I am, but I'm sticking to the lower branches. My vertigo kicks in just looking up to the top of the tree," Max said, helping himself to the citrus fruit salad at the buffet.

"I must say, Sir Kyle, the tree is a magnificent specimen. I think the tradition of harvesting the trees you've grown, and planting new ones, is a fine one. I wish more people followed your example." Reggie stroked the sleeping Patch as he took a sip of tea.

"Lady Pippa started it, Reggie. She thought it would be a family tradition that could be passed down through the ages. She was right. It makes Christmas very special here at Cherrywood Hall."

"Has Gemma told you what she has planned for us tomorrow?" Mama asked, giving me a wink.

"Do tell, darling. Just remember, there may be a bit of merrymaking tonight after the tree trimming. Please, tell me we won't be getting up at the crack of dawn," Elliot said, shaking his head. He was not an early morning person.

"We're going on a bridal dress treasure hunt in the mega closet. Aunt Margaret said there were several dresses there that might give some inspiration to my own dress design. I'm on the hunt for a dress Aunt

Pippa had designed for an anniversary celebration. I can't wait to see what we find."

"Oh, please tell me the dresses aren't tainted like that ghastly bridal veil. I don't know if my heart can take another bridal curse," Elliot said, groaning.

"Now Elliot, we all know Gemma had nothing to do with that veil other than picking it to avoid a crisis with the royal wedding. I suppose this go around we should double check the provenance of any gown or accessory we do find. I want Gemma's big day to be without any hitches, curses, or revenge."

"You won't have to worry about anything, Jillian," Max said, taking his seat. He had loaded his plate with Danish pastries to supplement his fruit salad. "Reggie and I will make sure everything goes without a hitch. Or a curse… or… well… whatever. There won't be a repeat of the Lady Kimberly and Sir Timothy royal wedding disaster."

"I just read that Lady Kimberly was transferred to a new, ahem… rest home north of here. The article seemed to insinuate that her treatment was not as successful as hoped," Reggie said.

We all stopped and looked at one another, shuddering, hoping against hope that Lady Kimberly would not be in our lives again. She had tried to kill me during our trip to Malibu in the fall. I did not want to have any contact with her again.

"I'll give a ring to my contacts at the Royal Protection Services just to see what's going on. I'm sure there's no danger." Kyle gave me a loving nudge on my arm.

We finished breakfast and waited together in the library for Evan's arrival. Bridges served us coffee and kept a watchful eye on the entry camera display. We would know when Evan's van and medical lorries arrived.

Aunt Margaret paced anxiously, looking at her watch every few minutes. Finally, our vigil came to an end.

"Lord Evan's van and lorries are coming up the drive now, my lady."

"Thank you, Bridges. Let's go outside and wait for him, shall we?"

Kyle called his crew on his cell to tell them to wait at the back entry to unload the medical equipment. Mama, Aunt Margaret and I donned our wraps and walked down the entry stairs with Max, Elliot and Reggie right behind us. We saw the van as it made its way up the last incline, pulling up in front of the entry. Kyle directed the other lorries to go around to the back entrance.

I held my breath as the back doors of the ambulance were opened. The medical attendants who had accompanied him lowered Evan on his stretcher from the van to the ground. Aunt Margaret made her way over to him and gently kissed his forehead. Evan looked very pale, but his face was fuller than the last time I saw him. The cuts and scrapes had healed for the most part too. He looked as if he were taking a nap.

The attendants lifted him up the front entry stairs as we followed close behind. Bridges directed them to the recovery room where his nurses were waiting. They asked us to remain outside while they made him comfortable and Kyle's crew finished unloading the medical equipment and supplies.

We went into the study to wait. Despite the early hour, Elliot poured us all a sherry, thinking it would calm our nerves. We gratefully accepted the offering, breathing a sigh of relief that Evan was finally back home at Cherrywood.

"I thought he physically looks healthier than the last time I saw him," I said, trying to keep things upbeat.

"I think so too, Gemma darling. The scrapes on his face are healing. Luckily, there doesn't seem to be any sign of scarring." Mama encouraged.

"He looked as if he were just sound asleep. Every time I see him, I tiptoe around him, afraid that I'll wake him up. I do think his face has more color than before," Aunt Margaret said wistfully, taking a sip of her sherry.

I could feel her angst. We waited in the study for what seemed like an eternity.

Kyle joined us, giving us some good news. "The crew has all the equipment and supplies unloaded and the caregivers are getting Evan situated in his new bed. I'm amazed at their efficiency, although I suppose they've done this hundreds of times. It shouldn't be much longer before we can go in and see him." He placed his hand on Aunt Margaret's shoulder to reassure her.

"His team is very well trained. They're the best in the business—very qualified and they have a great way of interacting with patients and their families. I feel sorry for them—at times I'm sure the family and friends are much more difficult to deal with than the patients," Aunt Margaret tittered.

"I think being a caregiver is one of the most noble of trades. One never knows when you're going to need help. I'm very grateful to those who enter the field. I hope if my time ever comes, we can find a team like Lord Evan's," Elliot said.

Max gave his partner a hug and affectionately laid his head on his shoulder.

We heard the soft squeaks of someone walking across the grand hallway. A tall, middle-aged woman came to the study entry, giving us a big smile.

"Hello everyone, Lady Margaret. I'm Nurse Ellie, Lord Evan's primary caregiver. We have him all situated in his lovely new quarters. I know you all are anxious to see him. I have just a few rules, please, before you go in to see him. As you know, as a comatose patient, he is being fed intravenously. He is in a weakened condition. We've begun therapy to try and exercise his muscles to keep him limber—he does have muscle spasms at times. This is normal, please don't be alarmed should it occur when you're visiting him. I would ask that you not touch him or kiss him, with the exception of you, Lady Margaret. Lord Evan's immune system has been severely impacted, we wouldn't want any germ transferred to him, especially now that winter is upon us. Now, if you'd like to follow me, we can go in groups of four to see him."

We followed Nurse Ellie obediently across the grand hallway and over to the recovery rooms. She stopped and looked back at us, specifically at Reggie. "Such a cute little doggie, but I'm afraid he won't be able to come in."

Reggie nodded his understanding.

Kyle, Aunt Margaret, Mama and I went in first. I was glad to see the fires lit in the room. The chairs and rugs that were brought in made the large space seem cozier. We walked over to Evan's bedside and looked down at him. His ash blonde hair had grown longer, soft curls covering his forehead. He looked so peaceful. I closed my eyes and said a little prayer for his recovery.

Kyle, Mama and I left to let others come in and visit him. I was surprised to see a line had formed outside Evan's room. The staff at Cherrywood had formed a queue. Everyone wanted to see their beloved lord. It was a touching scene, beyond words really. I knew that Evan was loved very much. Reggie handed Patch over to Kyle as we passed. He didn't want to break Nurse Ellie's rules. Patch licked Kyle's face and squirmed playfully.

"I think someone has a new friend. Patch is quite taken with you," I said, patting the dog's head.

"Ruff!" Patch's tail wagged in agreement.

"Better watch out, Kyle. It looks like Patch is smitten." Mama teased. "Darlings, I think I'm going to go lie down. It's been an early morning and a somewhat stressful one at that. What time are our guests arriving?"

"Lady Adela will be here around two o'clock, and Sally, Amy, Vicar Hawthorne, Prudence and Timothy will arrive at four."

"Steph and Penny will be here then too," Kyle chimed in.

"Oh good, I have plenty of time to get myself refreshed. What are you going to do?"

"I was thinking of a swim, actually," I said, looking at Kyle. "Jumping in some nice warm water sounds heavenly."

"Sounds good to me. Do you suppose Patch swims?"

"Ruff!" Patch squirmed in delight.

"You darlings have fun. I'll see you in a bit." Mama smiled and gave a little wave at us as she made her way up the staircase.

Kyle, Patch and I proceeded to walk through the dining room and conservatory to go to the indoor pool room. The entrance to the pool was a faux rock door, opened by a hidden switch. I sent Reggie a text message to let him know where we were in case he wanted to fetch his prized pooch back right away. Kyle sat Patch down on the tile floor. He immediately went off to sniff and smell around the glassed-in pool.

Kyle and I put on our swimsuits in the changing rooms off to the side of the main door. I pinned up my long tresses and pulled on a swim cap to keep them dry. I wasn't going to have time to wash and blow dry my hair before our afternoon festivities began. We jumped into the pool, relishing the warm water. Patch ran back and forth around the pool watching us swim laps. He was clearly enjoying seeing us have fun in the water, but he wouldn't jump in when coaxed. Kyle and I swam to the end to catch our breath and to pet Patch.

"What did you think when you saw Evan. It was a shock to me, truth be told," Kyle whispered. "I thought he'd have more color in his cheeks. He seems so frail now."

I smoothed his locks back from his forehead. I knew Evan's condition was upsetting to him. They had been best friends since childhood. The rescue operation to find and save Evan had been particularly brutal. Kyle's nightmares had woken us both up on more than one occasion.

"I know, darling. It's a shock to see him like this. I know his presence is bringing back the awful memories of his rescue too. All we can do is wait and hope being back home will do him good. I know what I'm wishing for from Father Christmas—I think we're all making the same wish."

Kyle pulled me close to him, hugging me tightly. It was so hard seeing someone you loved deteriorate in this manner. We held each other for some time, breaking our hug when Patch started running and barking frantically. Reggie, Max, and Elliot had come into the pool room in high spirits.

Reggie bent down as Patch leapt into his arms, licking his face. "Manners, sir."

Patch calmed down immediately. Reggie gave him a well-deserved treat.

"Come on in guys, the water's wonderful." I splashed some up at them.

"We're going to change now," Elliot said, as he and Max picked a pair of suits off a shelf and went into the changing rooms.

"I think I'll take Patch up and rest a bit before our guests arrive. I've spoken with Bridges; we have all the trimmings for the festivities ready. I have some special gifts for the guests that I think you'll like. You have fun, we'll see you in a bit."

"Ruff!" Patch bid us farewell, as his master carried him back to their guest room.

We spent the next hour swimming and laughing with Elliot and Max. They had brought down a bottle of champagne and opened it. The partying spirit was officially in the air.

Kyle and I left to go up to my room for a quick nap before changing into our evening clothes. We lit a fire and decided to curl up on the sofa to rest. The sky grew darker and the winds once again picked up, howling their chilling snarl. I drifted off, feeling secure with Kyle's arms around me. I looked up at Pippa's portrait above my fireplace before I fell asleep and sent her a plea to please bring peace to Evan. A log crackled in the fire, sending sparks up the chimney. Pippa was watching and waiting.

Kyle woke me up with a kiss to my forehead. "Hey sleepyhead, time to wake up and get beautiful. Lady Adela will be here in a half hour. You go ahead and use your facilities. I'll shower and change in my room."

Kyle stood and pulled me up. He had a room down the hall that held several changes of clothes when he wasn't staying in his house down by the barn. Since we became engaged, he was here at Cherrywood with me most of the time.

I went into my bathroom and turned on the water in the glassed-in shower. I loved the room's decor, complete with a clawfoot tub and fireplace. It had been one of the first en suite baths installed at Cherrywood Hall and was designed by my Aunt Pippa. Bronze sconces in the shape of mermaids framed the vanity mirror. My aunt had named them Pippa and Lillian after her sister.

My shower complete, I dressed in my holiday attire to get ready to greet my guests. I was wearing blue and green tartan pants tonight with a navy, cashmere turtleneck. I decided to wear a pair of comfy flats since we would be decorating the tree. I wanted to be able to move around and climb the step ladder comfortably to hang the Christmas ornaments. I had missed the first part of last year's decorating festivities. I had been grazed by a bullet from some very ill-spirited competitors who were involved in the set-location competition the previous Christmas. I vowed that this year I was not missing a decorating moment.

I met Kyle down in the study. Mama, Max, Elliot, and Reggie were there, enjoying a glass of sherry. Patch was sleeping contently by the fireplace, keeping warm by the blazing flames. Mama looked bright and cheerful in a red, wool turtleneck and matching slacks. Kyle had opted for a navy sweater and plaid pants, much like the ones I was wearing. Max and Elliot were dapper in black slacks and red vests. Reggie had chosen a black turtleneck paired with red, tartan slacks. Patch was wearing a matching tartan bow tie around his collar. All in all, we were a very festive looking group.

Lady Adela arrived promptly at two. Bridges brought her into the study. She made the rounds, greeting everyone with two precise kisses on their cheeks. She dressed for the Yuletide season as well, wearing a gold, lame blouse with ivory slacks. Her brown hair was pulled up into a chic chignon. Patch had awakened from his fireside slumber and went to Lady Adela's side to be regally petted.

"Well hello there, Patch. It's been a while since I've seen you. You look as dapper as ever."

"Ruff!" Patch's tail wagged enthusiastically as he enjoyed his petting session.

"Reggie, the dinner party you planned for the queen and Prince Thaddeus last month was a royal hit. The princesses are all whining that they need your services now. No one wants to risk hosting an event that will be compared to that one. You've set the bar high my friend. You're not going to have any time to jaunt around with me."

"Thank you, Lady Adela. I'm glad the queen and her guests enjoyed it. I'd be happy to help the princesses after the new year. We're going to be quite busy here at Cherrywood with the Rosehill Productions broadcasts. You know though, I will always make time for you, darling." Reggie winked.

Lady Adela gave Reggie a coquettish smile. "I've heard. There are some exciting rumors floating around. I'm sure you're happy, Jillian, if what I've heard is true."

Mama blushed. To her credit she didn't confirm or deny. She knew better than to get on Lucy's bad side.

Our banter continued, talking about the upcoming holidays and of course the topic of Kyle's and my wedding came up. Aunt Margaret came to the study entry to greet Lady Adela. We watched as they kissed cheeks, looking the part of good friends, at least for the moment. She escorted Lady Adela to Evan's room to see him.

We gravitated into the grand hallway. Bridges and his staff had moved several sofas and chairs around the Christmas tree and set up tables to hold the ornaments we would be trimming the tree with tonight. A buffet stand was being set up to serve the holiday yummies for our guests. Chef Karl's menu included prime rib sandwiches, cheesy broccoli soup, stuffed mushrooms and Swedish meatballs, appetizer sized, as the savory bites we would be indulging in this evening. Trays of shrimps, veggies and sweets filled the other tables. No one would be hungry tonight. I couldn't resist taking a few samples to taste test, of course.

At four o'clock our Maidenford guests arrived, windblown as they entered the hallway. Vicar Hawthorne wore a festive red scarf around his neck. Amy looked stylish in a velvet jumpsuit cinched at the waist with a sequin belt. Prudence and Timothy were adorable in matching holiday sweaters.

Christmas tunes played in the background, lending a *tis the season* vibe to our festivities. Introductions were made and the laughter began as we sipped on glasses of wassail and munched on starters being served by Bridge's waiters. Steph and Penny turned out to be last minute no-shows. Steph had sent a brief text message to Kyle that he showed to me. I hoped nothing was wrong with our two friends.

Karl joined Mama this evening—handsomely dressed in black slacks and a red, plaid sweater to complement Mama's red outfit. I had to admit they were a very handsome couple as they snuggled by the tree.

Sally snapped pictures of the hallway and guests for use in an article on the broadcast preparation. Her pictures would be sent out globally for use in other publications. Sally's village credentials, and ties to Cherrywood Hall and Rosehill Productions, had made her services highly sought after by news and entertainment outlets around the world.

Aunt Margaret finally joined our group, having changed and looking very cheerful in an emerald-green jumper and matching slacks. A navy, silk scarf adorned her neckline, giving her an elegant, chic look. She seemed happy and relaxed this evening, greeting her village friends with warm laughs. It was good to see her so joyful.

"Ladies and gentlemen, if I may have your attention." Reggie tapped a spoon on a crystal glass, its clinking getting our attention.

"Ruff!" Patch's master sweetly petted him into silence.

"I know everyone is having a good time, but we do have some work to do. This evening we'll only be decorating the lower branches. I don't think cocktails and ladders would do any of us good."

We laughed at his statement, one shouldn't drink and climb ladders.

As our giggles died down, Reggie continued. "Sir Kyle's crew has graciously secured the tree for us so that decorating can begin. I thought we could do a countdown to show the tree lights that have been installed. Bridges, if you'll please dim the hallway lights, we can begin."

The lights were lowered. We began the countdown in unison. "Ten-nine-eight-seven-six-five-four-three-two-one…" The Christmas tree lights came on, glowing in red, green, and white brilliance. We took a collective gasp of breath, taking in the holiday beauty. Bridges raised the hallway chandelier light level a bit, giving us plenty of light to begin the tree trimming.

Mama and Karl decorated one side with Vicar Hawthorne, Timothy and Prudence. I was sure she was warming up to her new director, and truth be told the Vicar probably was too. There was always a need for extras in a film.

Sally, Amy, Kyle, Elliot, and Max were laughing and giggling on the opposite side, the waiters making numerous runs to keep their glasses filled. I could tell that the hunt for bridal dresses tomorrow morning would need to be scheduled later in the day. I didn't think anyone would be up for an early morning start after the festivities tonight.

Reggie, Aunt Margaret and Lady Adela were in the front of the tree hanging some very special ornaments Reggie had made---two miniature framed pictures, one with a drawing of Lady Adela's daughter, Lady Evangeline, and one with Evan's picture for Aunt Margaret. The two mothers gave Reggie a sweet hug as they wiped tears away from their eyes. Everyone clapped as Aunt Margaret hung Evan's keepsake ornament front and center. Lady Adela stood back and watched. I thought she was looking a little upset, so I walked over to her side.

"Are you all right, Lady Adela? I know this must be a tough holiday season for you. It's your first without Evangeline."

Lady Adela nodded at me and patted my back. "I'm fine, dear. The loss of Evangeline was tragic, there is no doubt. I have you and Kyle now. I want you to have all the experiences she'll never be able to enjoy. I know I may seem pushy at times, but I really do care for you, Gemma. I just want the best for you both."

"You're very special to me and to Kyle too, Lady Adela. It means so much to have you in our lives as well. I know he cherishes you and the friendship you had with his mother, Honey. We appreciate all the guidance you've given us with the peerage situation. I hope with Evan's return to Cherrywood we can get the situation resolved quickly."

Lady Adela smiled and clinked her wassail glass to mine. We were going to join the others when we heard Evan's caregivers running into his room, shouting orders. Aunt Margaret dropped her drink and ran into Evan's room in a panic. Kyle and I were close behind her, afraid of what we would see.

Evan looked as if he was in considerable distress, his body convulsing on his bed. The nurses were on either side of him, trying to determine what was causing his condition. We held on to Aunt Margaret and watched as they rolled Evan on his side, as they examined his tubes and made sure his airways were clear. The minutes ticked by as the caregivers finally were able to stabilize Evan. His face once again looked peaceful and his convulsions stopped, helped by a dose of sedative that was given in his IV. Nurse Ellie walked over to us and led us to the fireplace across the room. She held a section of the IV tube in her hand.

"I think you should know the IV tube had a crimp in it and several holes that may have caused air bubbles and contaminants to enter his system."

"How in the world did his tube get holes in it, Nurse Ellie?" Aunt Margaret demanded, her face ashen.

"I don't know, Lady Margaret, not yet. The crimp and holes look as if they were made by an animal chewing on the line. An animal with very small teeth."

"An animal? We don't have any animals here at Cherrywood Hall, Nurse Ellie." Aunt Margaret said, shaking her head.

At that moment, we heard a bark coming from the grand hallway. It was Patch. A very tiny dog with very small teeth.

CHAPTER 6
On the Hunt

Kyle and I went back into the grand hallway to update our guests on Evan's condition. The group was seated on the sofas by the tree, drinking tea and coffee, the laughter from just moments before now silent. They turned, looking at us with worried faces as Kyle and I walked toward them.

"Evan is resting now, he's stabilized. There was a problem with one of his tubes that caused him to convulse," I explained, trying to be calm.

"How's Lady Margaret?" Prudence asked.

"She's with Evan now. She's sorry for the disruption to the festivities," Kyle answered.

"Oh, she shouldn't worry about us. The poor dear, I hope she hasn't made a mistake bringing Evan back here. The care at the London facility was top notch. I told her…" Lady Adela said, shaking her head.

"Evan's caregivers are very qualified, Lady Adela. This was just an unfortunate incident; we'll get to the bottom of it. I'm sure things will run smoothly from here out." Kyle and I had agreed to keep the crimped and chewed line to ourselves for now, to not cause any alarm or undue blame as our eyes darted over to Patch, who was now slumbering in Reggie's arms.

The festive mood quelled, our Maidenford guests decided to depart once they knew Evan was okay. We waved goodbye first to Prudence and

Timothy, and then Sally, Amy and Vicar Hawthorne as their cars were pulled up to the entry.

Sally pulled me aside before she left. "Please tell Lady Margaret we're praying for her and Lord Evan. I know this is such a bittersweet time for your family trying to celebrate Christmas and having to watch and wait with Lord Evan. Just know that we're with you, Gemma, if you need anything."

"Thank you, Sally, we do appreciate it. You don't know how much…" I reached over and hugged her tight, grateful to have friends that cared. I waved at her and blew a kiss as they pulled out.

The evening was still young, so we decided to salvage as much of the joy of the season as we could. Bridges lowered the hallway lights again as we took seats by the Christmas tree to admire the lower branches of the stately tree that now held the first of the shiny, heirloom ornaments. The lights and the baubles glowed with glittering cheer, as the Christmas tunes played softly in the background, slowly lifting our spirits. Kyle and Elliot served us glasses of champagne from the ice bucket on the buffet table.

"I'm glad Evan is okay, Gemma," Reggie said. "That was quite a scare. These kinds of things will happen though when you have a critically ill person being cared for at home. You mustn't let it upset you too much. I went through this myself with my dear mother."

"Thank you, Reggie. This is new for us. I'm sure we'll experience many ups and downs." Kyle clinked his champagne glass to mine.

"I received some interesting information from Timothy this evening…" Mama's eyes opened wide as she looked at us, smiling.

Elliot and Max were all ears.

"Come on now, Jillian dear, don't leave us hanging." Max leaned in closer to Mama.

"It seems Rosehill is having discussions on not just one, but two feature films. *Castlewood Manor* is hitting the big time, franchise opportunities, spin-offs. It's so exciting!" Mama clapped her hands in celebration, clearly pleased.

"That's amazing, Jillian. But tell me, how can they be planning multiple movies when you've just finished season one? Is there enough material?" Kyle asked.

"Oh darling, of course. There are prequel storylines, future projections of the characters, holiday themed events, weddings. Once you establish a beloved set of characters and storyline, you can take it any which way in time. That's the beauty."

"Let's toast then, to the *Castlewood Manor* dynasty." Elliot raised his glass, his adoring eyes focused on Mama.

"Hear, hear," we chimed in, excited for the new opportunities.

I was glad Mama had interjected some showbiz news into our discussions to take our minds off Evan's distress earlier. As the chit-chat continued, my mind drifted off as I looked at the beautiful tree. I couldn't understand how Evan's line had come to be crimped, nor how to explain what looked like bite marks. I looked over at Patch, who was now awake, being fed snacks from multiple people who thought they were being discreet, slipping him a bite here and there. He was so tiny, there was no way he could have reached Evan's IV line. I was sure that Reggie wouldn't have allowed him in Evan's room, not after Nurse Ellie's instructions to us earlier.

We turned as we heard Aunt Margaret walking over to us. She looked tired, but had a smile on her face. Kyle got up and brought her a glass of champagne, which she gratefully accepted. She sat down next to Lady Adela and Reggie.

"Evan's sleeping comfortably now. I'm so relieved. The tree looks beautiful with just the bottom branches decorated. I can only imagine what it will look like when all the decorations are up."

"The staff will be back Monday morning. I think we'll have everything finished by the end of the week." Reggie smiled.

"Sally wants to take pictures once the rooms have been completed. There are many requests for the shots. Everyone is excited to see *Castlewood Manor* at Christmas. She's planning a special feature magazine pullout to the paper, how about that?" I asked, raising my glass in a mock toast.

"Ruff!" Patch seemed excited at the prospect.

Aunt Margaret glanced at him and tilted her head, as if she suddenly realized he was a small animal with tiny teeth. She shuddered, then smiled, looking at me and shaking her head. I could tell she didn't see how Patch could be guilty either.

"Who's going on the wedding dress hunt with me tomorrow in the mega closet?" I asked. Mama, Lady Adela, Max and Reggie raised their hands. "Kyle, aren't you going to look with me?"

"I would darling, but isn't it bad luck for the groom to see the bride's dress before the wedding? Suppose you decide on wearing one of the family dresses. Would you really want me to see it beforehand?"

"Kyle's right, Gemma. A groom's first look at his bride walking down the aisle is a forever moment you wouldn't be able to repeat," Reggie said, nodding, with Lady Adela and Max in agreement.

"I can't wait to look through the dresses. I'm sure we'll find some that will inspire your final look, Gemma. I'm going to look for some mother of the bride dresses too if we have time. The early twentieth century bespoke creations would be smashing, especially the ones with feather boas. I love that look." Mama waved her hands in front of her dramatically, splashing a little of her champagne on Karl's lap.

"We may find a dress for your peerage ceremony too," Lady Adela said, giving a quick glance to Aunt Margaret. "It would be very poignant for you to wear an heirloom dress from the Lancaster collection, don't you think, Margaret?"

"I think that whatever dress Gemma chooses for the ceremony, should it occur, will be perfect."

Max, Elliot and Mama leaned in closer in anticipation of a regal war of words. Sensing trouble, I decided to break up our soiree.

"I think it's time we turned in. It's been a long day. We'll see you in the morning at breakfast. Get your rest tonight, there's hundreds of dresses to sort through." We made our rounds to our guests, kissing cheeks. I pulled Mama off to the side before we went upstairs.

"Please don't let Aunt Margaret and Lady Adela stay down here by themselves. I don't want them to get into a squabble over the peerage ceremony."

"Go on up to bed daughter, I'll keep watch." Mama planted a kiss on my cheek and swatted my behind playfully.

Kyle and I made our way up the staircase to go to my room, turning once to wave good night to our friends.

As we crawled into bed, Kyle pulled me next to him, stroking my hair as we watched the flames in the fireplace. "It's been quite a day. I don't think any of us were prepared for the emotional toll Evan's homecoming would have on us. Do you think Lady Adela is right, should Evan have stayed in the care facility in London?"

"I don't know, Kyle. Part of me wanted him home so much, but I was so scared this evening when his caregivers went running into his room. I didn't know what to expect. This crimped, chewed line has me worried too. How did that happen? The only animal in here is Patch. He couldn't have done the damage, could he?'

"It's very suspicious to me. There are tons of animals around here, including rodents. But I haven't had any indication they're inside the hall, especially not in Evan's new room. It's practically been reconstructed. Someone either sabotaged that line, wanting to cause Evan harm, or it was a damaged piece, not noticed by the staff, which seems highly unlikely. We may need to face the fact that someone here is up to no-good."

"Oh, surely not. Have all the caregivers had background checks? We better ask Aunt Margaret." I sighed heavily, the worry of a possible friend doing this kind of harm to Evan was overwhelming.

Kyle pulled me on top of him and started kissing me. "Look," he said, as he nuzzled my neck, "I don't want you worrying about this. I'll take care of things. One thing our perpetrator doesn't know is that there are surveillance cameras installed in the area. I'll review the footage tomorrow to see if anything looks suspicious. If necessary, I can have bodyguards hired as well, which may be a good idea with all the public festivities planned in the next few weeks."

I pressed up from Kyle's kisses and looked at him with an adoring gaze. "You really are a knight in shining armor, Kyle. I love you so much." I lowered myself down against my loving knight in a close embrace, feeling safe and protected in his arms. Our passion burned as bright as the flames in the fireplace that night, the troubles of the day forgotten for the moment.

At breakfast, the next morning, everyone seemed to be in a cheery mood. Aunt Margaret had sent a message that she would be spending the morning at Evan's side. Max and Reggie were anxious to get started going through our fashion archives. Mama and Elliot were whispering together no doubt plotting their moves for the *Castlewood Manor* movie franchises. Kyle sat next to Lady Adela, giving her details on our latest expansion into the world of gin, something I was very much looking forward to.

Steph and Penny joined us as surprise guests for breakfast, walking in the room holding hands. Penny was beaming.

"Hi everyone, our apologies for not making it to the tree trimming last night—but, well, we're engaged!" Penny held out her hand, revealing a beautiful, yellow diamond ring, squealing in delight.

We all stood up to give them hugs and congratulate them. Steph was beaming at her petite fiancée who was proudly showing her ringed finger to everyone.

"Penny, your ring is gorgeous." I held her hand, so I could see it closer. It was a round-cut, yellow diamond surrounded by smaller, white round diamonds. It looked like a sparkling daisy, perfect for our friend's positive, can-do attitude.

Penny grinned and winked at Steph. "Thanks, Gemma, Steph designed it just for me. Daisies always make her smile, as I hope to do for her, for the rest of our lives." Steph beamed in Penny's praise, a perfect couple in love.

True to form, Elliot produced a bottle of champagne so we could give them a congratulatory toast.

"To Penny and Steph, may their love be blessed." Kyle raised his glass and kissed the cheek of his university friend.

"Hear, hear," we toasted, clinking our glasses and clapping. We sat back down to finish our breakfast.

"So, when is your big day?" I asked, taking a bite of toast.

"We'd like to get married soon, before the season two filming begins with all its craziness," Penny said giggling. She looked at Steph and winked. "Gemma, is there any possibility we could have a small ceremony here at Cherrywood? It looks so beautiful with the Christmas decorations going up. We aren't having anything lavish, just a small ceremony and ring exchange."

"Of course, Penny, we'll work you in some way, somehow! How about a Christmas Eve ceremony? We could have it in the early evening, after the Maidenford villagers leave. We can have as many or as few people in attendance, whatever you'd like."

"That would be lovely, Gemma, thank you. You've made me and my lady very happy," Steph said, looking at her fiancé adoringly.

"You know ladies, the conservatory with the hanging lights and mirrors would be a spectacular backdrop for wedding nuptials. Now Penny, I know you have a penchant for color---a red, wedding dress would be smashing darling, with that backdrop," Reggie said, nodding his head.

"Yes, yes," Mama chimed in. "I'm wearing red for the New Year's Eve broadcast in there. It would be perfect, Penny."

I laughed as everyone jumped in at once, giving their two pence worth.

Kyle looked over at me and smiled. He leaned over and whispered, "Maybe we should just elope."

I looked up at him and gave a quick bob of approval. It wasn't a bad idea really.

Reggie took out his notepad and started writing. I took in a deep breath when I thought of all we had going on in the next few weeks, which now included a wedding for our friends. I decided to leave for a few minutes to go check in on Evan and Aunt Margaret before we headed up to the mega closet for the dress quest.

Aunt Margaret was seated by the fireplace next to Evan's bed, reading the morning papers. I gave her a wave and went to check on my cousin.

"He looks good, Aunt Margaret—his face is fuller, with color in his cheeks."

Aunt Margaret stood and came over next to me. "I was hoping you'd say that, Gemma. I thought so myself, but I'm always so afraid I'm imagining that he's getting better when he's not. He does have more color, and his breathing seems stronger now too. Maybe that horrible incident from yesterday triggered something."

I gave Aunt Margaret a hopeful smile. Everyone was trying to make the best of this situation, and I wished for Evan's sake our dreams for his recovery would come true. We took a seat next to the fireplace.

"I have some amazing news. Penny and Steph joined us for breakfast. They're engaged and they want to have a small wedding ceremony here at Cherrywood, with all the Christmas decorations. I told them yes, perhaps having the ceremony on Christmas Eve. I hope that's okay with you."

"That's wonderful news. I'm very happy for them. Both are terrific young women and so very talented. With everything that's going on, why not?" Aunt Margaret laughed. It was good to see some sparkle in her eyes too.

I stayed with her for a few more minutes, then raced back to the dining room to gather my wedding dress hunters together. Penny was going to join us, which made Mama very happy. Steph and Kyle left to go to the winery. Elliot was going back to his room to sleep a bit more. I had a feeling he had imbibed a little more champagne yesterday than we knew about.

Lady Adela, Penny, Mama, Max, Reggie, and I made our way up to the third floor. The mega closet adjoined my office. It had originally been four separate rooms that were used to store the garments and accessories belonging to my Lancaster ancestors. We had it converted into one large room earlier this year, complete with climate control, inventory storage, and security features to access and preserve the garments. There were several items that were priceless, adorned with custom gem and beadwork that were one-of-a-kind creations. The inventory system included an automated rack system that allowed you to sort the lot of dresses and gowns that had been categorized by function/occasion, season, color, and date.

We had a few gowns showcased in glassed-in, climate-controlled displays in the center of the room, allowing a 360-degree view. There were runway paths around the perimeter of the room to hold small fashion shows, and a work area for any customizations. Penny's wardrobe team members were here frequently, examining the dresses and gowns for inspiration for their *Castlewood Manor* designs.

Reggie was taking everything in, his smile showing he was in seventh heaven. Penny took us over to the control unit screen, where she punched in search words: bridal, wedding, lace, satin. Within seconds the rack was moving and soon we had all the dresses in the inventory matching that search criteria hanging on the rack against the wall. I estimated at least sixty dresses, maybe more. Each dress was in a sealed garment bag, with a transparent pane to allow us to view the dress before unzipping it.

Lady Adela and Mama took one end of the rack, Reggie and Max the other end, and Penny and I took the middle. I was amazed at the selection of dresses, in all varieties of ivory, white, lace, satin—there was so much to choose from.

"Ooh, here's Lady Pippa's wedding dress," Penny squealed, taking the garment bag from the rack. We gathered around as she unzipped the bag, placing the elegant gown on a form in the center of the room. As Aunt Margaret had described, it was a beautiful, handcrafted, lace creation adorned with miniature, pearl beads. Penny fluffed out the train to showcase its beauty. We walked around and around gazing at the details and admiring the beautiful handwork.

"This dress is stunning. I can't get over the beading. It must have taken ages to create," Reggie exclaimed.

Max was speechless, his hand over his mouth, as he circled the dress.

We left Pippa's dress in the center of the room and went back to our sections on the rack to continue our search. We found ball gowns, trains that were fifteen-feet long, tea length creations---if you could imagine it, it was there. I went from garment bag to garment bag, searching for the lace dress with the blue, tulle skirt that Pippa had worn for her anniversary. It was not to be found.

"You know, Gemma, let me try something." Penny went back to the control unit screen and typed in blue tulle.

To my amazement the rack started moving and deposited more than ten gowns when it stopped. We looked at the bags one by one, all looking lovely, but not the one I was looking for.

The final bag didn't have the see-through pane. Penny took it off the rack and hung it separately on a display rack next to Pippa's wedding dress. The zipper was hard to open, but Penny's perseverance soon paid off. We made a collective gasp when we saw the gown. It was the anniversary dress—an ivory and gold brocade, mermaid-style dress with the magical, blue, tulle skirt that could be attached at the waistline. The tulle had tiny, blue crystals that adorned every fold, causing it to shimmer and sparkle from any angle. I was speechless as I moseyed around the dress taking in all its splendor.

"Gemma, this is your dress," Mama cried, wiping tears off her cheeks.

Max handed her a hanky; he had brought spares for just such an occasion.

"You must try it on, Gemma, it's perfect," Lady Adela said, standing back to observe the dress from a few feet away.

Penny and I went into the changing room where I stripped down to my silk camisole and matching panty shorts. Penny slipped the gown over my head. Pippa and I had very similar figures with the exception that I was a good three to four inches taller than she had been. With a prior dress I wore of hers, things worked out fine—she had worn the dress with heels, and I wore the dress with flats.

Penny pulled and tugged and finally had the dress fitted on me to her satisfaction. I ran my fingers over the ivory and gold brocade that clung to my figure perfectly. It was a thick fabric, but very soft and luxurious, almost satin-like. To my amazement, the length was perfect on me. I might even be able to wear kitten-heeled shoes with it. Penny fluffed out the tulle skirt, filling most of the room with its blue sparkle. We looked at each other in the mirror. The excitement and glow on our faces said it all.

As Penny opened the door, I walked out in the dress, to the oohs and aahs of my dress hunting squad. I swirled and twirled for them, causing tears to flow from everyone. I walked the length of the runways in the room to get the feel of the dress and its flow.

"That's it, Gemma darling. I can't see any other dress holding a candle to this one," Mama gushed.

Max handed her another hanky; his supply was growing low.

"I agree, Jillian. It is absolutely perfect. The queen will love seeing Gemma wear this for the peerage ceremony. She looks like a Marchioness of Kentshire." Lady Adela clasped her hands in front of her, a royal grin of approval spread across her face.

"Peerage ceremony, why no, Lady Adela," Mama said, giving her an astonished look. "This is Gemma's wedding dress. A one of a kind creation only worn by Gemma and her beloved Aunt Pippa. I can see the news and wedding announcement headlines now. It will be sublime." Mama beamed, clapping her hands in an exaggerated fashion.

"It's a dress of the Lancaster legacy, worn by the woman who should have been marchioness, and her descendant that will rectify the title infringement. This is the story that the headlines will cover, approved by the queen." Lady Adela's tone rang with royal overrule; her head held in regal aloofness.

Max and Reggie stepped back to observe the emerging toff tiff. Max could hardly contain himself. Penny and I stole a quick glance at each other knowing we'd better stop this discussion now.

"I need to think about it, Mama, Lady Adela," I said, using my best PhD authoritative voice. "It's a beautiful, stunning dress for sure—I have so much to think about. I think our treasure hunt is complete. Why don't we go down by the Christmas tree and celebrate our find?"

Mama and Lady Adela took the hint, shaking their shoulders to get rid of the building tensions. Penny and I went into the changing room, sighing heavily when the door was closed.

"I thought for a minute they might come to blows," Penny whispered, her mouth in an exaggerated grimace. "Good job diffusing that situation, Gemma. See, your PhD comes in very handy at times," she said, giving me a quick thumbs up before she started to undo the fasteners of my dress.

I looked at myself in the mirror one last time, envisioning walking down the aisle to Kyle, and also to the queen. I had to admit, both Mama and Lady Adela were right, the dress would be stunning for either occasion. I felt like a bride, and a marchioness. I stepped out of the dress and reflected on my options, as Lucy took it out of the room so that I could change back into my clothes.

When I emerged from the dressing room, I gasped. Lucy had staged the gown and tulle skirt on a dress form next to the one highlighting Pippa's wedding dress. The form fitting brocade and sparkling blue tulle once again took my breath away. Mama and Lady Adela had called a truce. The gown had enchanted them to a point where they let their conflict go, for now.

I smiled as I strolled around the gown a final time. I knew this was my dress, I just didn't know what the occasion would be to wear it, yet. I took pictures with my phone to enjoy later. I didn't know if I should show Kyle the dress or not, my first bridal dilemma!

We walked downstairs, laughing and ready to celebrate. To my delight, Kyle, Steph, Elliot, and Aunt Margaret were seated next to the Christmas tree, enjoying the lights and an afternoon cocktail. We joined them and told them of our find, without disclosing too many details of the dress. I wanted an air of mystery to surround it. The final details would be revealed at either my wedding or peerage ceremony, a decision to pontificate on, at least for the time being.

I took Aunt Margaret aside and showed her pictures of the gown. Tears came to her eyes as I flipped through the photos. I could tell the dress had enchanted her too.

"This is your and Pippa's dress, Gemma. It's fit for a bride and a marchioness, a legacy you both will have shared someday. It will look stunning with Pippa's jewels, too. I feel certain she would have wanted you to wear it to continue the Lancaster legacy."

Aunt Margaret smiled and kissed my forehead, making her way back to our guests. I didn't know if she was finally coming to terms with the transfer of peerage, but I did sense a change in her attitude. I looked at Pippa's portrait above the large fireplace in the center of the hallway. The portrait showed Pippa when she was just about my age. I looked at her face, loving its warmth and determination. I hoped that I would have the same courage for my new life path, which was coming soon.

CHAPTER 7
A Royal Wrap

The week before Christmas was moving at lightning speed aided by the non-stop wind gusts that were relentlessly pounding the walls of Cherrywood Hall. Elliot, Max and Lady Adela had left to go back to London for a few days. Elliot and Max would be returning this weekend, staying with us through New Year's Eve. Lady Adela made tentative plans to join us on Christmas Eve and staying with us through New Year's as well, although her decision was somewhat in flux since she usually stayed with the queen at Sandringham for the holidays. No one wanted to miss the Rosehill Productions broadcasts—it was becoming the social event of the season.

Downstairs, Reggie and Prudence's staff were busy as Christmas elves filling the first-floor rooms with holiday decorations and lights galore. It was magical, although the winds had knocked out the power twice. Kyle and his crew were installing the back-up generators for the first-floor rooms and kitchen. He didn't want to take any chances, especially now—we had too much planned for the holidays to let a power outage spoil the festivities.

I rolled over and snuggled close to Kyle, who was still snoozing away this cold morning. I looked over at the French doors that were shimmying in their frames, buffeted by the howling winds. My eyes zoomed in on a dark object, hurling and swirling in the wind, heading right for the French doors.

"Kyle," I screamed, pulling the covers over our head as the object crashed into the French doors, sending shards of glass flying through the room.

Kyle woke and instinctively threw his body over mine to protect me. We stayed under the covers for a few minutes as our bedroom became a mini wind tunnel, knocking over our bedside lamps and flower vases.

"Good grief," Kyle muttered, raising his head from out of the covers to peek at the damage.

The water-soaked, plywood panel that had shattered the glass was pressed against the doors, vibrating against the frames. He started to get out of bed to assess the damage.

"Kyle, slippers!" I yelled, shielding my eyes from the blowing winds.

Debris and rain were flying everywhere in the room now. He heeded my warning, pulling on his slippers, and made his way over to the door, his pajama bottoms billowing in the wind.

"Miss Gemma, are you all right?" Bridges and Mrs. Smythe came running into my room, the noise of the smashing glass alarming them.

Bridges went over to help Kyle move the flying plywood piece in front of the French door frames to block out most of the blowing wind and rain. I climbed out of bed and put on my slippers and robe, glad I at least had on the pajama top that matched Kyle's bottoms now that we had a crowd in my bedroom.

"My goodness, I've never seen such a thing!" Mrs. Smythe exclaimed, surveying the room and the damage.

Kyle and Bridges stepped back from the door. Their fix would be temporary at best. Kyle grabbed his cell phone and called his crew manager, giving him instructions for the needed repairs.

I grabbed a blouse, pink sweater, and jeans from my wardrobe. "We'll go to Kyle's room and change so that the crew can get things fixed."

"Yes, go ahead Miss. I'll have your room cleaned of this mess." Mrs. Smythe said, shaking her head and going over to the house phone to summon help.

Kyle and I left, walking down the hallway to the room he kept here at Cherrywood. It was on the inner corridor and did not have a view of the sea, but it was tastefully decorated with vibrant pictures of horses, hunts and architectural drawings. A large, red Persian rug covered the floors, leather chairs framing the fireplace. He lit a fire to ward off the morning chill. He came over and kissed me, holding me close.

"Well, what a way to start the day, hey?" Kyle teased, grabbing me in his arms and swinging me around. The clothes I held flew around the room.

"Stop," I cried, laughing. "Haven't you had enough hurricane action this morning?"

"Hurricane, yes---but I think I need another kind of action..." Kyle swept me up in his arms and carried me over to the bed. He pulled the covers back and laid me down, joining me in a loving embrace. We would be late for breakfast.

After we had showered and dressed, we made our way down the hallway to check on my room before heading to the dining room for breakfast. The crew had arrived, repairing the damaged French door frame and installing new glass panes. Mrs. Smythe's maids were picking up the larger pieces of glass and debris from the floor, wearing work gloves to protect their fingers from the razor-sharp shards.

"I couldn't believe my eyes when I saw the plywood flying right for us." I said, shaking my head as we walked down the staircase.

"Good thing you did, darling, and very smart of you to pull the covers over us. I don't fancy pulling glass bits out of my head."

We walked into the dining room where Aunt Margaret and Mama were seated, having breakfast.

"Good morning you two. We heard you had a rather wicked, wake-up call," Mama said, her eyes opened wide with concern.

"It was a disaster. We're lucky the plywood was stopped at the French doors. The crews are doing a smashing job with the cleanup and repair though, pardon the pun."

Kyle rolled his eyes at me as he helped himself to eggs, bacon, tomatoes and hash browns. I followed close behind, taking helpings of my usual favorites.

"I'm worried about this wind, and now the flying debris from the sea. I wonder if we should put shutters up in the room to help prevent any shattered glass flying, particularly in Evan's quarters. I wouldn't want one of his windows crashing."

"That's an excellent idea, Lady Margaret. We have shutters in the storage units that we could use. I could have them installed in all the rooms with ocean views. They can be closed at night or secured during a heavy storm. I'll make sure Evan's room gets them today."

"Thank you dear, I'll rest easier."

"Karl is loving the backup generator your crew is installing. He's even brought in racks and a rotisserie unit for the fireplace in the kitchen to use just in case. His chefs will be able to cook and keep things warm in a worst-case scenario. He has chickens roasting now to test out the rotisserie unit. It smells divine down there." Mama's eyes glistened as she licked her lips.

"Yum, I love chickens cooked over a fire. I can't wait for lunch," I said, skewering a bite that included pieces of tomato, mushroom and egg.

Kyle looked at me and shook his head, smiling at my never-ending appetite.

Bridges came into the dining room. "Miss Gemma, the queen is on the line. I have the phone in the library waiting for you."

Mama, Aunt Margaret and Kyle looked at me with curiosity as I stood and left to take the call. I sat in a leather wingback chair in the library and picked up the receiver.

"This is Gemma Lancaster Phillips."

"Good morning, please hold for the queen, Dr. Phillips."

"Gemma, dear, good morning. Thank you for taking my call."

"Good morning, Your Majesty. What may I do for you?'

"I'm asking you and Sir Kyle to join Prince Thaddeus and me at Hampton Court Palace tomorrow. I apologize for the short notice, but an opening came up in my diary. We would be pleased to welcome you for lunch at one o'clock. Are you available, dear?"

"Yes Ma'am of course. Where should we meet you?"

"Just go to the entrance. Hampton Court Palace is open to the public, but we will be in a room that is reserved for private functions. How is Evan, Gemma?"

"He's the same, Ma'am, but we do see more color in his cheeks. We're very hopeful."

"I'm glad to hear it. Evan is a fine man. We're all praying for his recovery. Please tell Margaret I will be phoning her soon. I'd like to visit him."

"I will, Ma'am, that will be of great comfort to her I'm sure. I'll see you tomorrow."

I walked back to the dining room slowly. I knew why I was being summoned by the queen. There would be no more delaying. She wanted a decision. I took my seat at the table, pouring a hot cup of tea, and readied myself for questions.

"Come on, daughter, don't leave us hanging."

I knew I could always count on Mama's curiosity.

"The queen wants Kyle and me to have lunch tomorrow with her and Prince Thaddeus at Hampton Court Palace. We're to be there at one o'clock."

Kyle's eyes widened as he nodded his head in affirmation.

"Are you going?"

"Mama, of course I am, we are." I was flustered. "She's having lunch served in the private quarters at the palace."

"One doesn't turn down an invitation from the queen, Jillian." Aunt Margaret said, slicing her custard tart.

Mama shrugged and plucked a grape into her mouth.

"She said she will be calling you, Aunt Margaret. She asked about Evan too. She'd like to visit him."

"That would be lovely. I'm sure she'll enjoy seeing the Christmas decorations Reggie, Amy, and Prudence have had installed. Perhaps they can give Her Majesty a tour."

"Oh, I must call Max, he'll definitely want to be here if that gets arranged." Mama smiled. "He adores any function with the queen almost as much as I do."

"I suppose she wants your decision, Gemma. I've thought about this a great deal, as I know you have. I just want you to know… you have my blessing dear, whatever you decide." Aunt Margaret looked up at me and smiled, tears welling in her eyes.

I jumped up and went to her, hugging her close. "I'm so sorry it has to be under these circumstances, Aunt Margaret. You don't know…" Our bittersweet hug lasted several minutes as the future of myself and Evan was now decided. It was a moment I will remember for the rest of my life.

Mama and Kyle came over to us and joined in, saying nothing, just expanding our hugging circle.

We decided to go to Evan's room to tell him. I didn't know if he could hear me or not as I whispered what my decision was to be.

"I just want you to know how much I love you dear Cousin. Cherrywood Hall will always be your home. I wish for the day when you'll be at your beautiful ranch with Simone, doing the things you love. No more worries, Evan. Ever. No more worries…"

We sobbed quietly, gathered by his side. Kyle had his arm around me as we looked down on our dear friend, cousin, nephew, son. Logs shifted in the fireplace, sending over a warm wave of air. I believe it was Pippa, giving her family her warmth and love too.

The next morning Kyle and I woke early to get on the road to Hampton Court Palace for our royal luncheon rendezvous. I had spent last evening with Mama and Aunt Margaret in my room after the repairs and cleaning were completed, going through outfits, deciding what I should wear to luncheon with the queen. We went through dresses, pantsuits, skirts, blazers—any and every combination you could imagine.

Ultimately, I selected a navy skirt and matching cashmere turtleneck, with a faux fur stole wrapped around my shoulders. It looked very chic and elegant and would keep me warm. With the winter thrashing we were getting I had no doubt the palace would be on the cool side. I decided on dark, navy tights and blue and green, tartan, ankle boots to finish my outfit. Kyle was amazed at how long it took three women to decide on an outfit, but when I put it on in the morning, he was quite impressed.

"You look beautiful, darling. This is a big day. Are you ready?" He smiled and pulled me close.

"I am. It's a big day for you too, Sir Kyle. Are you sure you want to be the husband of a marchioness?"

"I can think of nothing I'd like more, Gemma. I will follow and support you in whatever you decide to do in this life. You're my queen, Gemma." Kyle took me in his arms, kissing me passionately.

This was another moment I knew that would stay etched in my memories.

We decided to take Kyle's black sports coupe to Hampton Court. We originally were going to take the Land Rover, but with the gusting winds Kyle thought a lower profiled vehicle with a lot of speed might be a better bet. We packed an overnight bag—we were staying in London at Aunt Margaret's home after our luncheon with the queen and Prince Thaddeus. I loved the Belgravia house. It was in one of my favorite areas of London too. I had stayed there a year ago, when I was recovering from my gunshot wound, exploring the picturesque, upscale neighborhoods.

We left Cherrywood at eight o'clock to give us plenty of time for the drive. Hampton Court Palace was less than twenty miles southwest of London, but with the winds and traffic we built in plenty of time for travel, just in case. We could feel the wind hitting our car, the skies growing grayer with each mile.

"Geesh, this is getting pretty spooky. Just look at those clouds over there." I pointed to the ominous skies.

"I'm glad we took the sports coupe. I wouldn't want to be driving any vehicles with a high profile today. Just look at these lorries ahead of us—it's all they can do to stay upright."

"Kyle, what do you want to do for our wedding ceremony? I know Mama wants a big wedding to invite all her acting friends, but is that what you want?"

"I don't know, darling. I was really rather excited about just having a small wedding at the pavilion. I love the setting there and the chapel is so quaint. I know your mama wants something bigger and Lady Adela wants something more regal, for the 'Marchioness of Kentshire'." Kyle raised his voice in a high-brow tone.

I looked at him and punched his shoulder playfully. "Stop it, you're teasing me. I want something unique too, not just another big wedding production. It will devastate Reggie and Max, but I want us to be happy on our big day. We can have the formal parties and receptions afterward to satisfy the others' expectations."

"When do you want to get married, Gemma? My preference is to have a ceremony sooner rather than wait. I want to get you pregnant as soon as possible. The more practice the better. As marchioness you need an heir and a spare, you know." Kyle gave me a wicked grin.

"Wait just a minute—how did we go from what type wedding service did we want to making babies?" I laughed.

"I'm always up for making babies, or at least practicing. I consider it to be in service to the crown."

"Ha, ha, very funny. How many babies do you want? We've never really talked about this." I looked at him with a hint of shyness, loving him very much.

"I don't know darling. Since we're both only children I think it would be nice to have at least two or three, don't you think? That seems like a nice manageable number."

I sat for a few minutes, thinking of having babies with the love of my life, my heart pounding with joy. "I think that sounds marvelous, Sir Kyle. I hereby grant you permission to get me with child."

This time, he startled and swerved on the road in a momentary panic. "Why don't we get married first, darling, and then I will gladly perform my duty to beget you with child."

We laughed as we talked about wedding plans, having babies and the reactions of our family and friends, making the drive time pass quickly. There were a few times when we were slowed down due to accidents— there were several lorries that had been flipped on their side by the wind. Slowly but surely, we navigated our way around London and then on to the palace, which was located in the borough of Richmond upon Thames.

At twelve thirty, we approached the palace gates where we gave our names. Our car was searched before we were allowed to pull into the palace grounds. Since our meeting was with the queen and her husband, we were given an escort to follow as we went down a private lane. We were shown our parking spot and guided into the palace by a member of the queen's staff. We walked down a long corridor of the castle, surrounded by centuries of paintings and artworks.

Hampton Court Palace is best known as the palace of Henry the VIII, the king notorious for having six wives in his quest to conceive a male heir. It was my favorite palace. I loved the grounds with their gravel walkways, manicured trees, and luscious fountains. You could spend days walking and admiring the details of the gardens. I thought the landscaping was just as magnificent as at the Palace of Versailles in France.

We reached the end of the corridor and our escort opened a hidden panel door, taking us into the study where Queen Annelyce and Prince Thaddeus waited for us. For the first time, I curtseyed to the queen and Prince Thaddeus as I greeted them, followed by Kyle, who bowed to both.

As an American, I had usually bowed my head out of respect. By becoming Marchioness of Kentshire, I would also become a British citizen. I decided it was time to start accepting the traditions of my new country.

"Sir Kyle, Gemma, please take a seat here. I thought we could enjoy a view of the gardens before lunch. I'm afraid they're not as beautiful today with the winds and gray sky."

We were served glasses of sherry by a waiter.

The queen stood, as did we, for a toast. "To Gemma and Sir Kyle, Prince Thaddeus and I want to congratulate you on your engagement," Queen Annelyce smiled.

We clinked our glasses, accepting their good wishes and sat back down in our chairs.

"Now Gemma, dear, am I wrong to think you don't know the purpose of our meeting today?"

"I understand, Your Majesty. Our family situation with Evan has been a very difficult time as you know."

"I do, dear. Lady Adela has kept us informed, as well as my conversations with Margaret. I can only imagine the grief she is experiencing—you all are under a great deal of distress and worry. I do need your decision, dear, as to whether you are going to accept the title and peerage of Marchioness of Kentshire. You will be mistress of Cherrywood Hall and known henceforth as Lady Gemma. I would like to host a formal ceremony for you on January fifteenth, the day your American ancestor left Britain for the American colonies. I want to pay tribute to him and for the wrong that was done. Will you tell me your answer, dear?"

I looked over at Kyle briefly for a confidence boost. I was very nervous, but knew this was my destiny, both for myself and my family. I put my glass of sherry on the side table. In my best form, I stood in front of the queen and curtseyed. This time my knee touched the ground.

"I accept the title and peerage of Marchioness of Kentshire, your majesty. I will be of service to you and the people, all the days of my life."

I stood, a little wobbly—I wasn't yet used to the curtsey world. Kyle stood to help steady me. The queen and Prince Thaddeus came to their feet, more to alleviate any embarrassment I felt with my wobble. The queen and Prince Thaddeus shook my hand and kissed my cheeks.

"Well done, young lady, well done." Prince Thaddeus patted my hand.

The queen led us into the dining room where a small round table had been set up near a bay window overlooking the grand fountain in the back of the palace, one of my favorite views. We took our seats, looking forward to a cocktail to celebrate.

"Gemma, I understand you are quite fond of gin and St. Germain martinis. They happen to be one of my favorites too. Will we all be having one?"

I nodded yes, as did Prince Thaddeus and Kyle.

"Kyle, I understand that you are having a gin distillery built at Cherrywood. You're becoming quite the liquor provider in the area with your winery too."

"Yes Sir, the plans and designs have been approved and the permits granted. My project manager, Steph Rutherford, is overseeing the effort for us. We hope to break ground once the worst of the winter weather has passed."

"I'm beginning to wonder if it ever will," Queen Annelyce said, with a royal roll of her eyes. "We're supposed to travel to Sandringham this weekend to begin our holidays. I'm not sure the weather is going to cooperate. Margaret told me you actually had a sheet of plywood crash into your bedroom doors. That must have been frightful!"

"Yes, Ma'am, it was. Kyle's crew is placing shutters on the windows facing the sea. We can close them in the evening or when the storms get bad. He's installed back-up generator systems too. We're afraid power outages may become more frequent."

The waiters served our cocktails and a selection of savory canapés to get started. We took our gin martinis and toasted the season. "To the holidays!"

"Yum, your staff knows how to make a delicious martini, Ma'am." I said, taking another sip.

"Plenty of practice," Prince Thaddeus deadpanned, causing us to giggle.

Queen Annelyce gave him one of her 'the queen is not amused' looks with a quick wink to her husband.

Prince Thaddeus was on a roll. "Kyle, are you ready to be the husband of a marchioness?"

"Well, Sir. I am in fact. I'm looking forward to it very much."

"Best thing is to get her pregnant. Cherrywood Hall needs some children running around the corridors. Gives a place life."

"Thaddeus, really. She's not a brood mare. Why they're not even married yet." Queen Annelyce was shocked at her husband's bluntness, but then burst out laughing.

We followed her lead. I couldn't believe I was having this conversation with the Queen and her husband.

"Gemma, you must learn to put these men in their place. All they want to do is think about impregnating us." The Queen giggled.

I was becoming so tickled by the conversation I struggled to contain my amusement. At one point I even snorted in a fit of giggles. Kyle had to pass me his hanky to dab my eyes. I hoped it was not the first snort they had been subjected to. I could just hear the stories, '*the American snorted in front of the queen...*'

Lunch was served. Lobster bisque to start, followed by baked halibut with wilted spinach, steamed vegetables with sauce beurre, and finally a selection of scones and tarts with tea. The food was delicious and the conversation delightful. We spoke of the upcoming holidays. The queen was very excited to see her young grandchildren, nieces and nephews.

"I spoke with Margaret earlier about coming to Cherrywood to see Evan and the Christmas decorations that have been put up for the big announcements on Christmas Day and New Year's Eve. Weather permitting, I thought Prince Thaddeus and I could stop there on our way to Sandringham. Adela has told us that Reggie Gerard is one of your lead decorators. He's quite talented."

"We would be more than honored if you and Prince Thaddeus would visit us at Cherrywood Hall, Your Majesty. The house decorating should be complete by this weekend. I know the staff and Reggie would love to show you around. It would be good for Aunt Margaret if you looked in on Evan too."

Plans completed, the Queen and Prince Thaddeus walked us to the panel door, where her escort was waiting to take us to our car. We kissed their cheeks, curtseyed and bowed. As I started to walk away, Queen Annelyce, tugged at my arm to pull me down closer to her and whispered in my ear. When she finished, I stood up straight with a blush on my cheeks and nodded "Yes Ma'am." I scurried down the corridor to catch up to Kyle, stopping to wave one last time as our regal afternoon came to a close.

Back in the car, Kyle reached over and kissed me, our passion mounting until we heard a discreet knock on the window. It was the palace guard who had arrived to escort us out. I was flustered being caught but was so pleased with our afternoon I let it pass.

"Come on now, you can't keep me in the dark. What secret did the queen share with you?" Kyle asked, as he shifted gears.

I hemmed and hawed, milking his curiosity for as long as I could. It was fun teasing him, saying that some topics needed to be kept *between us girls*. I finally relented.

"She invited us to Balmoral to stay at the enchanted cottage in the spring. She said it had been a very lucky place for her and the prince when making babies."

CHAPTER 8

Season's Change

I phoned Max on our way to Belgravia to see if he and Elliot wanted to join us for dinner at Chubbies. The popular restaurant club in Mayfair was one we had visited last summer just before the *Castlewood Manor* premiere tour began. He was delighted, and of course wanted to hear all the details of the royal lunch. We planned on meeting at eight o'clock.

Kyle parked in the Belgravia house drive, our exuberance fading after the early morning start and the excitement of our royal luncheon. James, Aunt Margaret's butler, greeted us at the doorway, sending his staff to collect our bags. He took us to our room, a charming suite on the third floor complete with sitting area and en suite bath. We quickly undressed and climbed into bed, nestling into each other's arms.

I yawned. "I'm so sleepy. I think my adrenaline rush has finally crashed."

"Me too, although, sleeping next to a soon-to-be marchioness is rather exciting." Kyle nuzzled my ear, his subtle touch gaining my full attention.

"This soon-to-be marchioness finds sleeping next to a knight quite exciting too."

We slipped into a loving embrace—relishing our feelings for one another. We did get a nap, but it was delayed for just a bit.

We decided to take a cab to the restaurant for convenience. A storm hovered over the city. The thought of driving and parking in a downpour was not high on our list. The cabbie took us right to the doorway of the eating club as we raced in to avoid being drenched. Elliot and Max had just arrived as well. We air kissed our greetings and were led to the private room Elliot had reserved.

I enjoyed the atmosphere at Chubbies—its décor was sleek and modern, filled with holographic lights, glass walls, and tile patterns that might set off warning signals for anyone who suffered from vertigo. Our room was set in a plant-filled niche with steel table and chairs. We ordered our cocktails and got down to the evening's exchange of the latest whispers and buzzes of the *almost royal* set.

"Tempers are starting to fly in the Castlewood Manor cast rooms," Elliot said, stirring his Manhattan. "It seems that someone has leaked who will be in the feature film, and who will not. The 'not' cast is threatening to take legal action. Lucy is livid."

"Can they do that? I didn't think there were any guarantees in the acting business," Kyle said, grabbing a handful of cashews from the snack bowls that had been set on our table.

"It depends. There is no doubt everyone is expendable. Their claim is based on the series being a collective effort. Yes, there are lead actors and actresses, but what makes Castlewood Manor so endearing to its fans are the supporting cast members and the back stories. They've become the living societal organism that allows the main characters to survive. If you strip away the supporting characters and their back drama it takes away from the show's authenticity."

"But won't they fill in new supporting characters and storylines?"

"Yes, of course, darling. But will the 'new' be the 'real' *Castlewood Manor*? That's the million-dollar question, or in the case of movies, the one-hundred-million-dollar question."

"Enough about the movie. I'm sure Lucy will work her magic, she usually does. Now, Gemma, tell us all about your luncheon with the queen." Max gushed.

I glanced at Kyle and scrunched up my nose playfully as I went over the details of the palace and our conversations, omitting the baby making references. I didn't want that tidbit leaked to the press.

"I believe she will be coming to Cherrywood Hall with Prince Thaddeus this weekend. She wants to pay her respects to Evan and get a tour of the Christmas decorations that have been put up by Reggie, Amy and Prudence. I assume you'll want to be there?" Max clapped his hands excitedly and stared at Elliot, pleading for him to answer yes.

"Yes, dear, we'll be there as soon as I finish some last-minute, agency business here." Elliot smiled at his partner, knowing attending the queen's visit would delight Max to no end. He turned back to me, his business face on.

"So, it's official, you are going to be the Marchioness of Kentshire? Gemma, darling, we need to get your press kit prepared and update your dossier. This is going to be a huge story---an American infiltrates the ranks of our nobility! A female American at that. What a way to start the new year. Get ready darling, the storylines from *the royal wedding that was not* from a few months ago will be nothing compared to what you're going to experience." Elliot pulled out his phone and began typing furiously, sending reminders to his assistant on what would be needed in the morning.

"Whoa, I know the locals might have interest, but do you really think anyone else cares?"

Elliot stared at me as if I had gone daft. "Gemma, hell-o. The royals and nobility are a huge business, darling. Every time someone screams '*Bring in a republic…*', the first thing you'll see are tons of press releases on how much tourist revenue the royals bring into the country. Why the little granddaughter princesses are said to be worth billions in revenues to the economy—everyone wants the latest jumper or pinafore that was worn. These things fly off the shelf as soon as the pictures hit the newswires."

"I'm not a little princess, Elliot. Who would be interested in me?"

Elliot's and Max's jaw dropped as they gasped at my naivety. Even Kyle seemed surprised at it.

"Darling, you are an American, coming into one of the oldest institutions on the planet. Never mind that your Mama is a famous actress or that you're a ga-jillionaire. Or the fact that you're engaged to a gorgeous knight. Your forefather lost his title due to an illegitimate lie that was covered up for centuries. You're righting an almost-royal wrong, darling. This is huge. In fact," Elliot typed in some new notes on his phone, "you're going to need a new contract with Rosehill Productions. The net-value of the contract with Cherrywood Hall just increased ten-fold, if not more."

I sat in stunned silence. I hadn't considered the economic impact my accepting the title and peerage would mean, much less the global interest of an American entering the nobility.

"Elliot, my utmost concern is for Gemma's security. When news of this hits, I would expect we will need to up the security services on the estate certainly, but also look into getting a bodyguard, at least initially. I don't want to take any chances. There are too many unsavory elements on the streets these days. We must remember too, that many traditionalists will bristle at the thought of an American coming into the nobility." Kyle reached over and covered my hand with his.

"Most definitely, Kyle. You should get the security ball rolling sooner than later. A bodyguard may be useful too. Gemma, I think I ought to be your publicist for this new role as well. The onslaught of media requests and coverage is about to go global. Amy alone will not be able to handle it."

"You all have overlooked an obvious event that will topple the media ballyhoo, Kyle and Gemma's wedding. You said it yourself dearest, Gemma's marrying a gorgeous knight. This could be the wedding of the year. And," Max bent down and whispered, "you may want to shop the movie rights to their love story and marriage." Elliot bent over and kissed his partner.

"Gah! See, why I love him, he always has my back. That's brilliant darling. I don't know, Gemma, perhaps your contract value with Rosehill is now twenty times more valuable…" Max nodded in enthusiastic agreement.

We spent the rest of the evening at Chubbies ordering dinner (finally) and going over more odds and ends of this new world I had entered. I was a little shell shocked and still had a hard time believing all the fuss. I did trust Elliot though. He was a publicity expert extraordinaire and knew his way around this world much better than I did.

As we left Chubbies, Max and I agreed to do a little shopping in the morning. Elliot and Kyle were going to start working on the security measures and publicity needs. I wanted to look for Christmas presents while I was here in the city and take advantage of my lower profile, enjoying my last few days of semi-anonymity. I had no idea of what I was walking into.

Max picked me up at ten o'clock the next morning to start our shopping trek. He had hired a car to drive us so that we wouldn't have to worry about parking, hailing cabs, or dodging the rain. Storms once again were blowing through the city. We decided to start close to home, hitting the boutiques in Knightsbridge and Kensington. Our first stop made me laugh. It was an antique jewelry store by the name of *Jem-Ahs,* a name twist that caused both Max and me to giggle to no end. We walked into the quaint store, filled with antique showcases. The lights made the jewelry dazzle, taking our breath away.

I wanted to buy Mama and Aunt Margaret jewelry pieces. I was drawn to a tray of antique brooches. Two in particular caught my eye. They were Art Deco pieces; blue sapphires and diamonds in platinum settings from the nineteen thirties. The cut of the stones made them dazzle with sparkling allure.

"Just look at these, Max," I said, as I held the pins up to my shoulder to look in a mirror. "The colors of the stones are amazing. They'd be beautiful pinned on a lapel or with one of Mama's signature, white, silk scarves."

"Gorgeous, darling. Look at these earrings over here. I love them, wouldn't they be perfect for Amy?" Max pointed at a pair of emerald, lever-back earrings. The round-cut emeralds were surrounded by sapphire and ruby gems. They looked very festive for the holidays.

I wanted to give her something special this Christmas. She was working non-stop with Prudence and Reggie to prepare for the Christmas Day and New Year's Eve broadcasts. These would look gorgeous with her holiday outfits.

"Gemma, what do you think of these cufflinks? They're crowns," Max raved, holding them up to his sleeve. There were two pair, in white and yellow gold with pave-set diamonds. "I think we need these for the queen's visit this weekend. Elliot will love them."

I laughed at Max's shopping dramatics as I made a last round of the store. I was quite pleased with the pieces I found. I passed a case that held men's signet rings. I was drawn to a yellow-gold ring with a blue sapphire. A gold crest was placed on top of the stone for a dramatic look.

"It's a beautiful piece, don't you think, miss? It's several hundred years old."

"This crest looks familiar. Do you know its provenance?"

"Yes, ma'am. It is the crest of the Lancaster family."

I gasped when he said this and asked to see the ring. I held it closely and examined it with the jeweler's loupe. It had been engraved near the inner stone setting with the initials '*J. L.*'. Could this possibly be the ring of my American forefather, John Lancaster? Had he pawned it for funds before he left for America? I wasn't going to risk losing this ring. I had a plan for it.

"I'll take it, please. I think I've found several nice presents." I smiled at Max, delighted with my latest find. I was going to have to do some research, but I was convinced this was my ancestor's ring.

The store clerks took care of wrapping our gifts and invited us to sit in their parlor by the fire and sip a glass of champagne while we waited. We giggled like school children, pleased with our finds. We heard the chimes of the entry door ring as another customer came in. We couldn't see who it was from our vantage, but we could hear.

"Hello, your ladyship, let me get Mr. Kincaid for you," the store clerk said.

We heard the creak of footsteps walk over to her.

"Mr. Kincaid. I must have your answer. I expect ten-thousand pounds for the brooch."

Max and I slinked back in our chairs hearing this. We didn't think this customer would want to know she had an audience who could hear everything being said about her financial dealings.

"Your ladyship, we've researched the piece ma'am. This brooch belongs to the queen."

"It most certainly does not. That piece was given to me years ago. I simply find it is not my style. This is my last time here, if you are not interested. Your ancestors have been dealing in royal jewels for hundreds of years. There are other regal, family pieces that I am sure other jewelers would give their eyeteeth to have if you're no longer interested."

"I'll give you the ten-thousand, ma'am." Mr. Kincaid sighed.

"And put in those gold earrings over there for good measure. Your hesitation has disappointed me, Mr. Kincaid."

I heard him as he took the earrings and went in the back of the store. His hesitation had cost him another thousand pounds in merchandise I imagined, but he would still see a good profit. After a few minutes, Mr. Kincaid walked back to the counter and handed his royal customer her payment and package.

"Good day, your ladyship."

"Good day, Mr. Kincaid."

The door chime rang, signaling her departure. Max and I let out a collective exhale. Was one of the royals in financial straits? It seemed unlikely and I was sure the queen would not let her relatives suffer any monetary distress if she knew about it. Whoever this royal was, I was surprised by the tone of her voice in dealing with Mr. Kincaid. The conversation that we overheard today was very cold and calculating bordering on the cruel side. I hoped things would be okay for her, financial difficulties are not pleasant for anyone.

"Dr. Phillips, Mr. Wellington, we have your packages ready."

We paid our bills and carried our lovely, wrapped presents to the waiting car, conveniently parked in front of the jewelers. I decided to call

Kyle and check in. I didn't know if he wanted to leave for Cherrywood this evening or go back tomorrow morning.

"Kyle Williams."

"Hello, darling. Miss me?"

"You know I do. Are you and Max spending lots of money?"

"You know we are. But I have some fabulous Christmas presents. We're deciding where to go next. I wanted to check in with you. Are we driving back to Cherrywood this evening, or waiting until morning?"

"I'd rather go back tonight if that's okay. I've made some calls to some of my systems suppliers. They want to meet me at the estate tomorrow. I also have some chaps I want you to interview with me of the bodyguard variety."

"You have been busy. When will you be ready to leave?"

"I think around five. Will you and Max be done shopping by then?" Kyle laughed.

"I think so, I'll see you soon. Love you." I rang off with a grin on my face, amazed at how diligent Kyle was when it came to my safety.

"You know what would be decadent?" Max asked, his eyes wide. "How about a lovely facial. There's a private spa just around the corner whose owner I know very well. I bet we could get in if we went now. They have a lovely cocktail bar to imbibe from while your mask sets."

I chuckled, thinking of us sitting with bright green clay on our faces, sipping cocktails.

"That sounds delightful. I need to get back to the Belgravia house and pack fairly soon though. Kyle wants to return to Cherrywood tonight. Apparently, we have bodyguards to interview tomorrow." I smiled.

True to his word, Max's friend took us right in, much to the annoyance of others who were waiting for their appointments.

We were escorted into the VIP area and undressed, pulling on soft terry robes. We put our feet up on comfy recliners as the technicians applied the specialized facial clay. It felt wonderful as our face and temples were massaged, the clay causing our faces to tingle. We had thirty minutes to kick back and sip the spa's latest cocktail creation, the *Rosemary Fizz*—a combination of gin, cranberry juice, a splash of sparkling *rose* water, topped with a sprig of rosemary. It was light and refreshing and put us in a holiday state of mind.

After our session concluded, our fresh faces gleaming and our treasured purchases packed away safely in the trunk, we were driven back to Belgravia. It had been a lovely day. I kissed Max's cheeks as I gathered my gifts.

"Gemma, darling, would you mind terribly if Elliot and I came to Cherrywood earlier? I wouldn't want to miss anything, and I promise I'll help Reggie, Amy, and Prudence get ready with any last-minute details before the queen arrives. Would that be okay?"

"Yes… of course. I'll see you when I see you." I gave him a wave and a wink and headed into the house.

Kyle was in the study, concluding his final call. I went over to him and sat in his lap, making it a bit difficult for him to ring off as I kissed his cheeks, distracting him.

"You little minx," he said, putting his phone down, wrapping his arms around me. Our kisses grew passionate, leading to some very heavy breathing. "Your skin smells heavenly, darling." He rubbed his cheeks against mine.

I stood up, grabbing Kyle's hand and leading him upstairs. We stood next to the bed in a close embrace. I moved my suitcase off and sat down, patting the spot next to me. Our departure back to Cherrywood was delayed until six o'clock, a bit later than expected, but well worth it.

I smiled as we left London, thinking about the changes that were coming into our lives. The next few weeks were going to be a whirlwind with family, friends, the Rosehill Production broadcasts and the preparation for my peerage ceremony with the queen after the new year. I felt rejuvenated now that the decision had been made. My only remaining wish was for Evan to recover and begin his life with everything he desired.

"You look deep in thought, are you happy, darling?"

"I am. I'm so glad we met with the queen and made the decision to move forward. I won't have to carry the burden of that decision any longer. What about you, Kyle, are you okay? I have to tell you I was pretty blown away with all the new issues we're going to have to deal with from a publicity and security perspective. The conversation with Elliot last night at Chubbies had me gobsmacked; truth be told."

Kyle smiled at my use of this British term of surprise. "It's a lot to consider most definitely. I have to admit I hadn't really thought about the American entering the nobility angle. I suppose everyone will be intrigued, especially with your family's story. You're going to have to be prepared for the interest, darling. And the fallout."

"I was surprised by that aspect. I don't want anyone to think I'm a brazen American stealing a title. I hope people give me a chance."

"They will darling. It may take some time. You've endeared them already with your work on the Castlewood Manor series and all the events you have organized. No one will ever forget your *royal avenger* hands covering the television cameras to protect the modesty of the queen a few months ago." Kyle lifted his hand off the wheel for a moment to reach out in my now infamous pose. The press had given my hands the moniker of the *royal avenger*, a title I wished would go away.

"Put those hands back on the steering wheel or I'll give you a *royal avenger* slap, Sir Kyle." I shook my finger at him. I did not want a car crash heading back to Cherrywood.

"Kyle, Max and I heard something strange today when we were out shopping. We were waiting for our packages to be wrapped and the bills to be cleared. The shop had a lovely parlor room with comfy chairs by the fire. We were served champagne while we waited."

"Sounds like an expensive shopping spree." Kyle chuckled.

"It was, but that's off topic. While we were waiting another customer came in. It seemed to be a relative of the queen. We couldn't see her, but we did hear everything. She was selling a brooch and the store manager sounded a little intimidated at first. He told her that from their background check it belonged to the queen."

"You're kidding. Why would a royal relative be selling a brooch of the queen's? That doesn't make sense."

"I know. This royal lady sounded very upset by the comment. She told the poor store manager in no uncertain terms that the brooch was hers and she no longer liked the style."

"That sounds credible. Although I find it hard to believe she would sell gifts from the queen. That isn't done in their circles."

"I was shocked too, but in the end her ladyship told the store manager there were many more pieces and if he wanted them, he had better give her ten-thousand pounds, or she'd take her business elsewhere."

"Surely she doesn't need the money. If for some reason someone in the royal family was on the outs, I'm certain the queen would give financial support. Selling off jewels just doesn't make sense."

"The store manager ended up not only giving her ladyship the ten-thousand pounds, she brazenly asked for some gold earrings in addition, to help her get over his initial hesitation. What surprised me the most was the change in tone of her voice. She sounded cruel, Kyle. It was chilling listening to her. There was no sensitivity in her statements at all. If she did have any qualms at selling her gift from the queen, I didn't hear it."

"Did this royal lady see you?"

"No. When Max and I heard her voice and the transaction at hand, we thought it better if we just slink back in our chairs unnoticed. We stayed seated, holding our breath as best we could until she left."

"It does seem strange, but it's really none of our business, darling. I'm sure whoever this royal lady turns out to be she will handle her business transactions as she sees fit. Now, let me tell you about the interviews we have tomorrow…"

For the next fifty miles, Kyle brought me up to speed on the bodyguard candidates we would be seeing tomorrow afternoon. To my surprise and delight, four of the five candidates were women. I was glad to hear that, for I knew a bodyguard would be accompanying me in many places, including those that might be a bit awkward for a man. Their credentials were impressive—martial arts training, marksmanship awards, behavioral science analysis, crowd control, social media monitoring… Today's bodyguards were not mere muscle men, or women.

For the last few miles of our journey, I played around with the radio to get the evening news before we pulled into Cherrywood Hall. I found a station we liked. There was breaking news: *Ladies and gentlemen, the palace has just informed us that the queen's jewelry vault has been robbed of several items. Intruders are suspected. The royal gems are estimated to be worth millions of pounds. More updates as this story develops…*

Kyle and I looked at one another in disbelief. Could the regal family member who I had inadvertently heard selling a piece of the queen's jewelry today be connected to the royal robbery? Should we tell the queen what

I had heard this afternoon? I was faced with my first 'marchioness-to-be' dilemma, and I had no idea what to do.

CHAPTER 9
Chaos and Confusion

I woke early the next morning, still reeling from the news of the robbery at the palace and my suspicions about the royal ladyship's dealings I had overheard. To make my stress levels even worse, the Christmas decorating in the grand hallway had taken an almost deadly crash. The tree tethers had broken away from the wall, causing the stately tree to collapse in the grand hallway, breaking hundreds of the heirloom ornaments and lights.

When Kyle and I walked into the entry the night before, we were greeted by the scene of Reggie, Prudence and their staff picking up the pieces of the fallen tree that now blocked access to the dining room and study. Yellow hazard tape was stretched across the perimeter of the fallen tree, making it look like a giant, green corpse in a crime scene. I did not see how we would get things fixed in time for the queen's visit the coming weekend.

As I stirred, Kyle slipped his arm around when he heard me move. He knew I was worried. "We'll get everything readied, darling. I know it looks bleak now, but it will be fixed. I promise."

"I don't know, Kyle. Your crew will get the tree righted and secured again, I have no doubts. But the ornaments, it broke my heart to see so many of them shattered. They were family heirlooms."

"It is heartbreaking. I don't see how those tethers gave way. They were steel cables, screwed into the wall. My crew will get the ladders up today to see what caused the failure. The good news is there are plenty more ornaments in the storage room, the tree will look good as new before you know it. I'm sure Reggie, Amy, and Prudence will work 24/7 to make sure the decorating gets completed. There is no way Rosehill Productions will lose the chance to have pictures taken with the queen. This is a publicity coup for them."

We rolled out of bed to get ready to go down to breakfast. I was wearing a cranberry, turtleneck sweater over black leggings. I slipped on my leather riding boots to finish my outfit. I had bodyguards to interview this afternoon with Kyle, a task I wasn't looking forward to with everything going on. We were doing the interviews down at the winery so that we wouldn't be disturbed by the holiday hustle of decorating at the hall.

Since the dining room was blocked off, breakfast was being served in the kitchen on a large, round table set in a cozy niche overlooking the gardens. The chintz-covered chairs and whitewashed table made the area very cheery and homey. Chef Karl had the fire in the fireplace roaring, keeping us nice and warm from the chilling winds outside. Mama and Aunt Margaret were seated, tucking into a yummy looking omelet.

"What can I make you this morning, Gemma… Kyle…? Omelets with any filling you'd like and fresh scones, hot from the oven this morning." Karl smiled at us, happy in his beloved kitchen space.

"Yum. I'll have a mushroom omelet with spinach and Parmesan, please, Karl. And definitely a scone or two with clotted cream."

"Make it two please, chef.' Kyle nodded, pulling my chair out for me as we sat at the table.

"What a lovely spot, we should eat down here more often," I said, admiring the view of the garden. I poured Kyle and me a cup of tea, handing his over to him.

"I love it down here. Karl serves me up the most delicious delicacies right here on this table." Mama smiled wickedly.

Aunt Margaret gave her a shocked glance. Kyle and I burst into giggles.

"Mustn't give out the chef's secrets, dear." Karl served Kyle and me our omelets.

"We used to have meals here when Evan was a young boy. It seemed homier than eating in the dining room. It was quite nice." Aunt Margaret smiled, her mind thinking of times gone by.

I noticed that her hand and arm were bandaged. "What happened, Aunt Margaret? Are you all right?" She looked down at her bandages and grimaced.

Mama shook her head in dismay.

"I was sitting by the tree when it collapsed. I had just come from sitting with Evan when I decided to have a sherry and enjoy the tree decorations, just for a minute, alone. I took a seat on the sofa, staring at the glimmering lights. The next thing I knew I heard a metallic scraping sound coming from behind the tree. I stood up to go look when it started to fall. I tried to turn and run away, but I wasn't quite fast enough. I was thrown to the floor, face down. My right arm and hand were covered by the tree, and unfortunately the broken ornaments. The glass was quite sharp."

Kyle and I looked at each other in shock. No one had told us about this last night.

"We had Dr. Moore from the village come over to dress her arm and hand. Luckily, nothing was broken," Mama tsked. "In typical fashion, Margaret didn't want a fuss made."

"The metallic sound you heard was likely the sound of the hooks coming out of the wall. I don't understand it at all. That tree was secure. I don't even think the hurricane winds we've had outside lately would have dislodged it. We'll get to the bottom of this soon." Kyle looked dismayed.

"Did you enjoy your luncheon at Hampton Court Palace, Gemma?" Aunt Margaret smiled, glancing over at Mama. I figured that Mama had either briefed her right after my call to her, or she received the inside scoop from the queen.

"It was very pleasant. Prince Thaddeus is quite the kidder. I was laughing so hard I snorted in front of the queen." I winced in mock dismay, a giggling fit threatening to hit again at the memory.

Aunt Margaret's eyebrows raised at first, but then she chuckled. "I did hear that, actually. No harm done, there has been worse offenses committed in the presence of the queen, I can assure you."

"She's really a very lovely person. I just hope we can get everything put to right before she gets here. She and Prince Thaddeus really wanted to come here to see Evan and the decorations before they headed to Sandringham. Have you heard anything from her about the robbery yesterday? That must have been awful for her."

Kyle gave me a side-eye and nudged my knee with his. He didn't want me to say anything about the conversation I heard in the jewelry store, at least not yet.

"I haven't heard from her, but yes, I'm sure she feels awful. Many of those pieces are priceless. There are very few people who have access to her vault. I'm sure they are being questioned very thoroughly."

I wondered who all the trusted persons with access were. I didn't want to think any member of the royal family was a thief, but after yesterday the nagging doubts in my mind wouldn't let up.

"Kyle, who are these bodyguards you and Gemma will be interviewing today? Elliot is working up quite the PR plans for Gemma, and you, after your meeting with the queen. I have to say I hadn't even thought about the issues you might face, darlings. Elliot was rattling on and on, I couldn't believe it."

"It's going to be a whole new game once the queen makes the announcement of Gemma's peerage and title ceremony. I'm upping the security here at Cherrywood Hall. Steph is investigating an upgrade to the electronic fencing and infrared detection. I've lined up five bodyguards to interview today, in fact, four are female."

"I'm quite excited about that---it's terrific women have entered the profession. I have a bit of a problem thinking about a male bodyguard accompanying me to the lavatory. Some things should just be girls only." I gave an affirmative nod to my point.

After breakfast Kyle and I went upstairs to the grand hallway to watch the resurrecting of the fallen tree. Reggie was holding Patch close, the noise from the winch frightened the little pooch. Reggie seemed as tense as his darling little pup this morning. I was certain he was under a great deal of pressure to get things cleaned up before the queen's arrival. Prudence and Amy were sitting on the staircase. We waved and walked over to them.

"Sir Kyle, your crew has been amazing and so good to work with. We were scared to death when it crashed down yesterday. Poor Lady Margaret, she could have been killed." Prudence shook her head. She was obviously still distressed thinking about it.

"How is she, Gemma? I haven't seen her this morning. Aunt Sally has been buzzing me non-stop to see if there's a story here. She wants to take pictures." Amy held her phone up, showing the list of calls from Sally.

"She's doing well. Aunt Margaret's a trooper. We just left her and Mama down in the kitchen. I'm sure she'll be up in a bit. I'll call Sally later today. I don't think there's a story here, not one we want public, yet anyway." I looked at Kyle, who nodded his agreement.

The winch hummed and buzzed and slowly lifted the giant tree off the floor. There were rattles from the remaining ornaments and lights on the tree, with just a few casualties as loose ornaments crashed down on the floor. I winced every time a branch shook, heartbroken at the thought of the lost family treasures. Kyle walked over and spoke to his foreman to get an update on what had caused the crash. It took a few tries, but the tree was once again positioned in its stand, this time being tethered with double the number of cables.

Prudence and Reggie motioned for their staff to begin sweeping up the debris and salvaging any final ornaments they could. I walked over and looked down at the broken bits on the floor, picking them up carefully in my hand. I was surprised when I examined the pieces closely, for the glass remnants were very thin. Our heirloom ornaments were thicker and heavier, many were hand blown creations. The pieces I held were very light and appeared to be new and mass produced. I picked up a few more samples from the floor and went over to a table to get a piece of tissue to wrap them in, placing them in my concealed sweater pocket. I was going to show Kyle my discovery later when we were alone.

Mama and Aunt Margaret came up from the kitchen and stood by me, just as the tree was straightened for the last time. In a moment of truth, the light switch was turned on, and voila! The lights worked, shining their red, green and white brilliance. Everyone clapped, at least one thing had gone right. Kyle finished his conversation with his foreman. He came over to us, a look of concern on his face.

"What is it darling? Is everything okay?'

"Yes and no. As you can see, the tree has been righted. I have no doubt Prudence, Amy, and Reggie will get things looking perfect in a very short time."

"What's the bad news? You look upset."

"The bad news is that someone unscrewed the tie hooks that held the cables to the wall. This was no accident. It was deliberate."

Mama, Aunt Margaret and I gasped in surprise. I couldn't imagine who would do such a thing, or why.

"I could have been killed." Aunt Margaret's face went ashen.

Mama led her over to a chair to sit down. I motioned for Amy to run and get her a glass of water.

"Take deep breaths, darling." Mama gently rubbed her back, trying to calm her.

Amy brought the glass of water to her, which was gratefully accepted by Aunt Margaret. She drank several long swallows.

"Is everything all right?" Reggie and Prudence walked over, seeing our concerned faces.

Kyle explained to them what his foreman had discovered. Prudence gasped, putting her hand over her mouth. Reggie surprisingly showed little emotion.

"We're going to have to tighten up access to the hall starting now," Kyle said, an edge to his voice. "Prudence, Reggie, you will need to limit access to the hall to only those who have passed background checks. From here on, I'm limiting the times workers will be allowed in as well. I'm sorry, but our situation has changed with the latest breach. Security has been rather lax the past few weeks. That ends today." Reggie gulped.

I could see his forehead tense up.

"Sir Kyle, I must object. We have a ton of decorating to get done here before the queen's visit. I don't know if we can work with limits on staff credentials and time…"

"Reggie, I'm sorry. Your objection is overruled." Kyle stared at him, unwavering.

"I'll get the staff credentials straight away, Sir Kyle. We'll draw up a schedule for you to look at and approve. We'll find a way to work within your constraints," Prudence said, taking notes and giving Kyle a nod. She knew this was not a request to be taken lightly.

"Harrumph," Reggie puffed, rolling his eyes and stomping away.

Patch looked back at us with pleading eyes. I didn't quite like the change in Reggie's attitude, and it appeared Patch wasn't pleased either.

"I'm going into Evan's room for a while. Kyle, dear, please make sure the security is upped as much as possible. I don't like this… not at all."

"I will, Lady Margaret. This stops now."

A new tone of seriousness was in Kyle's voice. I heard it distinctly and so did everyone else. Amy went to help Prudence get the staff credentials checked and verified. Mama went down to the kitchen to tell Karl what had been found out. Everyone's senses were suddenly on high alert, watching and looking for anything appearing out of the norm.

Kyle and I put on our jackets and caps and headed down to the winery to interview the bodyguards. He had a large office above the reception and tasting rooms, resplendent in carved, cherry paneling, rough-hewn tables and a magnificent stone fireplace. His architect drawing table was next to the wall of windows overlooking the grapevines. They shivered in the cold wind, looking forward to the warmth and light the spring would bring.

I started a pot of tea for us to enjoy during the interviews. Chef Karl had sent down boxes packed with tea sandwiches, cookies, sweet and savory tarts, and thermoses filled with hot, tomato and basil soup. I fixed plates filled with the selections for Kyle and me, as well as a tray of sandwiches and sweets to offer our bodyguard candidates if they so desired. I carried our lunch plates and soup cups over to the table next to the fireplace. Kyle finished lighting the fire. He had poured us each a glass of wine to have with our nibbles. We sat down in the leather chairs, clinked our wine glasses and tucked in, enjoying the fire's warming flames.

I took a sip from my cup. "This soup is delicious. Just the thing on a cold day. The wine helps quite a bit too." I laughed.

Kyle smiled, but I knew the tree incident was weighing heavily on his mind. I decided to show him the ornament fragments I picked up this morning. I took the tissue holding them from my sweater pocket and laid them on the table.

"What is this, darling?"

"Look at these up close, Kyle," I said, holding a shard up for him to examine. "These fragments are not from our ornaments. The glass is nowhere near as thick as the heirlooms, and it's so light, I'm not even sure it is glass. These look like new ornaments, mass produced."

We both looked at the other fragments closely, making sure my suspicions were correct.

"How did these ornaments get on the tree and when? The tree was close to fully decorated when we left for London. Who on earth made the switch? More importantly, where are the family ornaments? It doesn't make sense."

"Unless whoever loosened the tether screws didn't want the heirloom ornaments destroyed. Someone swapped these new ornaments for the heirlooms before the tree fell."

We sat and pondered this new revelation, wondering who would do this. Reggie popped briefly into my head—he loved the heirloom ornaments and cherished their provenance. If he loosened the screws from the wall, he could have orchestrated the ornament switch. He was staying with us at Cherrywood since last weekend, so he had unlimited access to the tree at all hours. Kyle looked at me, guessing what I was thinking.

"I just can't believe he would do something like this, Gemma. He's been so nice and engaging. The queen hires him all the time. Max is one of his close friends."

"I don't know, Kyle. Max knew him from university, maybe he's changed. This whole thing with the queen's robbery and now our heirloom ornaments. It's giving me chills."

"Gemma, darling, you can't put the same level of value on the heist from the palace versus the heirloom ornaments. I know you love them, but they're not quite in the same league."

I reached over and playfully punched his arm. He was right, of course, but to me the heirloom ornaments of our family were just as precious as the queen's priceless gems.

We cleared up our luncheon plates and warmed up the tea. Our bodyguard candidate had arrived and was waiting for us in the lobby area outside Kyle's office. Our first candidate was the lone male, Don Quinn. He stood over six foot, five inches, and had a heavy, muscular build. His qualifications were impeccable, and he certainly could physically ward off any intruders into my space.

"So, Don, why do you think I should hire you as my bodyguard?"

He leaned back in his chair, eyeing me up and down from across the table. I felt uncomfortable with his once-over

"I think that I could provide you with all kinds of protection, Gemma," he said, giving me a wink.

Kyle immediately stood and escorted him from the office. The idiot had not realized my fiancé was sitting right next to me.

"Yuck, well that was quick. Didn't he bother to read my dossier?" I asked, chuckling.

"His agency will be getting a call." Kyle said, furiously writing notes.

I had a feeling my fiancé was quite upset.

The next two candidates were much more professional and courteous. They too had excellent qualifications. The first we eliminated due to her schedule. She was only available for the next three months—she was getting married and would be leaving the country. The second candidate was very promising, but she lived in London and refused to relocate. She went over her commute plans, but we knew the route to London very well ourselves and didn't feel it would work out.

Our next candidate was a no show—no call, no message, we never heard from her again. The last candidate was a young woman by the name of Olivia Fisher. She was a Cambridge grad and had worked with several security agencies, both as a full time and seasonal hire. Her skills were impressive, martial arts, archery, and a mastery of several types of firearms. I heard the knock on the office door and went to answer it. Kyle had gone to the WC. I started when I saw our final candidate of the day.

Olivia Fisher was a little younger than me, but physically she was my doppelganger. We both looked at one another, our eyes incredulous and mouths open. Kyle came out of the WC and into the office, stopping dead in his tracks when he saw Olivia. She was wearing a black pantsuit and striped blouse. Had she been wearing a cranberry sweater and black leggings like me, we could have passed for twins, even close up. My manners finally kicked in.

"I'm so sorry, I'm Gemma Lancaster Phillips, and this is Kyle Williams, my fiancé and the estate manager here at Cherrywood Hall. You must be Olivia?" I asked, shaking her hand.

"Hello, Dr. Phillips, I'm just as surprised as you are. I've seen your pictures of course, but up close, our resemblance is rather amazing. That's a good thing though—perps need to be confused sometimes." She walked over to Kyle to shake his hand. "Sir Kyle, very nice to meet you, sir. I've read many of your preservation articles for the manor houses and estates. You have some amazing ideas."

We took our seats at the table to begin the interview.

Kyle started the questions. "Olivia, I presume you've read Gemma's dossier that was provided. Gemma will soon receive the title and peerage as the Marchioness of Kentshire. The queen will be making an announcement in the next few days. We expect a great deal of publicity—some will be kind, and some not so kind. There are many people, including some traditionalists, that may feel a bit of resentment toward an American entering the British nobility as a peer. We have had issues in the past with several ne'er-do-wells that have been associated with the *Castlewood Manor* production. In fact, it was about this time last year Gemma was shot and attacked by an intruder."

"I've read about the prior incidents, Sir Kyle. I understand there were attacks just a few months ago while you were on tour in America. I'm very sorry to hear about Lord Evan's condition as well. You were very brave leading the rescue effort for your friend."

I was impressed that she knew about our latest incidents and was very touched by her mention of Evan. Kyle was captivated too. I glanced over at several comments that he wrote in his notes.

"We have several events coming up in the next few weeks with the holidays. Rosehill Productions will be making two live broadcasts here at the estate on Christmas Day and New Year's Eve. There will also be a village Christmas Eve event and a small wedding with our friends. My peerage and title ceremony will be held at Hampton Court Palace on January fifteenth. We need you to start immediately. Is that going to be a problem for you and your holiday plans?"

Olivia took notes on her tablet, capturing every detail. She looked up at us when she finished her typing and smiled. "I can shuffle my diary engagements around for this position. I have a young cousin, I promised to spend time with. She'll be disappointed, but her father is in law enforcement. She understands that duty sometimes calls, even during the holidays. Annie's a cute little tyke. She says she wants to grow up and be just like me."

"I'm glad you can start soon. Your role, Olivia, is to make sure no harm comes to Gemma. Other security measures are in place and are being fortified as we speak."

"I saw the surveillance drones as I drove in, Sir Kyle. Very impressive, although they were struggling a bit in this wind."

"Thank you, I'm trying to deploy as many types of coverage as possible. There are cameras all around the estate and inside the hall. I'm having the infrared system and electronic fencing upgraded. If you're hired, you will be shown the technologies and will be synched into them for your use. Again, Gemma is your main duty here."

"I understand. Will I be staying on the estate?"

"There are quarters available here if you'd like. I have apartments just down the drive. I can have one of them readied for you. Your travel and expenses will be covered, and you will be provided with any equipment you feel is needed."

"We're a pretty casual group here, Olivia. Most of the time there is no issue. But during holidays, or galas with the series, and my upcoming ceremony, things can get very dicey at times to say the least. Kyle and I are also planning our wedding, which may result in yet another wave of PR, both good and bad."

"I should tell you we're dealing with some situations right now at Cherrywood that are very concerning and dangerous. The queen and Prince Thaddeus will also be visiting this weekend. We're expecting many guests as well. I will be calling in a Scotland Yard contact of ours that we have worked with quite a bit the past year. Unfortunately, I think his presence may be required."

"May I ask who your Scotland Yard contact is, Sir Kyle? I've worked with several employees there myself, in a supporting role of course."

"It's Chief Inspector Marquot. He is usually involved whenever we have situations that involve the queen."

"Uncle Marky? That's fantastic! I'm his niece—his youngest brother's daughter. My cousin Annie is his toddler daughter."

Kyle and I looked at each other in astonishment. Olivia beamed at us, showing us a picture of her with the Chief Inspector and little Annie on her phone. We knew right then that we had just found my new bodyguard.

CHAPTER 10
Royal Jingles

Queen Annelyce and Prince Thaddeus were arriving tomorrow morning. The moods at Cherrywood Hall were on edge as the staff made a last-minute rally in all the first-floor rooms to make sure everything was perfectly in place. Our chief royal enforcer was, of course, Aunt Margaret. Her arm may have been bandaged, her son in a coma---but when it came to the queen visiting Cherrywood Hall, nothing was left to chance. Bridges and Mrs. Smythe followed her as she made round after round, inspecting each room. They took copious notes to ensure there would be no disappointments.

Kyle was completing the hiring package for Olivia. She was moving into her apartment today and would be at dinner tonight to meet my friends and family. We had spoken to Chief Inspector Marquot after she left the interview to bring him up to speed on our situation and the events that had unfolded. He, of course, was very complimentary about his niece, but we knew we could count on him to be honest with us if he didn't think she could handle the position. We told him of the queen's visit and our concerns. He agreed to be here early Saturday morning. The tree incident raised red flags for him.

Elliot and Max had arrived the night before, a little later than expected. Max was in rare form, staying close by Reggie, Amy, and Prudence as the last-minute arrangements were made. Reggie seemed in a much better mood, smiling and kidding around. I didn't know if it was because of Max's presence or the fact that he could see the light at the end of the royal decorating tunnel. We still had our suspicions about him, but when he was smiling, it was hard to think he could be involved in something so dastardly as causing the Christmas tree to crash.

Elliot, Mama and I were meeting in my room to discuss the PR plans he put together for me after our discussion at Chubbies. We sat on the sofa and chairs in front of my fireplace to discuss his proposals.

"I'm glad to see you've hired a bodyguard, Gemma. The more I thought about our conversation from the other night the better idea I think it is. Amazing that it's Marquot's niece, but if she's anything like her uncle you're in good hands."

"We're very pleased she accepted the position, Elliot. She's moving into an apartment on the estate today. You'll get a chance to meet her tonight. I've invited her to dinner as a guest before she starts as my bodyguard. I'm anxious to see what you think of her."

Very anxious, truth be told. Olivia and I were going to be wearing identical outfits and doing our hair up in the same style. I wanted to see the surprise on our guests faces when they saw my new 'twin'. I hadn't even told Kyle about our little charade.

"Elliot, do you really think the public opinion on Gemma will turn once she assumes the title of marchioness? The more I think about it, the more concerns I have." Mama was troubled, worry lines were crossing her normally smooth forehead.

"It will be good and bad, Jillian. Right now, the public opinion of Gemma is very high. The masses love her work with the *Castlewood*

Manor series. All of her events and projects have received high marks. They were, and are, still extremely impressed with her *royal avenger* hands that protected the queen's modesty at that disastrous *royal wedding that wasn't*."

"Oh please, do we have to bring up my hands?" I said, falling into a sofa pillow to hide my face. I was so over all the publicity and the pics seen round the word with my outstretched hands reaching over the television camera lens. The public seemed just as concerned that my nail polish didn't match my dress as they were about the queen's fainting.

"Those little hands have brought you so much goodwill with the public, Gemma. I promise you, when the proverbial crowns hit the fan when you become the American intruder in the nobility, you will be glad to have that little PR nugget in your publicity handbag." Elliot nodded, wagging his finger at me.

"Won't the public understand that Gemma is assuming a title that should have been bestowed on her British-turned-American forefather after a lie cheated him of his position?" Mama asked, her voice crackled with frustration. She was a loyal advocate for those she loved, especially when it came to any rumble of negative publicity.

"Those are all very good points, Jillian, and we will use that story multiple times to battle any public outrage. You're going to have to realize we're talking about a multi-year campaign here. This isn't a short-term set of issues, but something that will need to be managed over years, truth be told. The slightest, little infraction could set tongues wagging. A political rift between the U.S. and the UK could re-start a Revolutionary War of sorts against Gemma. We don't know what we don't know. I can tell you this, we will have an arsenal of goodwill stories, dossiers on the history of her assuming the title and peerage, and will exploit the connections we have, including being supported by the royals."

Mama and I took a deep breath. This was more than overwhelming. I still couldn't believe my becoming marchioness was that big of a deal to the public, but I trusted Elliot's judgment completely and knew the whims of the public could change in an instant.

"Have you received any word from the palace as to when they'll be announcing my ceremony, Elliot?" I had contacted the queen's office when we returned to let them know that Elliot's firm was handling my public relations and that all inquiries should be henceforth referred to Magnum PR. Elliot was listed as the main point of contact for now, until he felt comfortable turning over my portfolio management to one of his associates.

"The announcement will be made public on Sunday, Gemma. Your days of relative anonymity will be over in less than forty-eight hours. Are you ready, darling? Life is about to become a great deal more hectic for you." Elliot looked at me and Mama and smiled. He put his hand on Mama's shoulder and gave her a squeeze. Her little girl was about to hit the big time from a public relation's perspective.

We spent the next hour going over the documents Elliot was going to send Rosehill Productions, which included changes to my existing contract that limited access to me and increased Kyle's and my salaries, including the compensation that went to the Cherrywood Hall estate for the *Castlewood Manor* series. The salary increases were substantial, given the publicity Rosehill Productions would receive with my becoming Marchioness of Kentshire. The contract for the estate compensation was also increased and included new clauses that would compensate for the feature film(s) if and when they were initiated. Mama had helped with these clauses. Her actress negotiating skills came in quite handy.

Kyle joined us in my bedroom just as we were finishing up. He bent over to kiss my cheek.

"How's the security upgrades going, darling? Everything in place?" Mama asked.

"Steph and her team have the upgrades installed. The Royal Protection Services are on the grounds now too. They're sweeping the property to make sure everything is secure for the queen and Prince Thaddeus' arrival tomorrow. I've hired extra security at the front and back gates now too. They will be manned full-time, 24/7. Starting tomorrow morning, access to Cherrywood Hall will be quite different."

"I'm sure it will, Sir Kyle. You've done the right thing. Why don't Jillian and I leave you two to rest up for this evening. Gemma can fill you in on what we discussed. If you have any questions just let me know. We'll see you downstairs for cocktails. I'll be serving as bartender this evening." Mama and Elliot gave us a finger wave and left. I had a feeling they were going to be doing a little cocktail taste testing beforehand.

Kyle pulled off his boots and fell onto the sofa. I could tell he was tired. He and Steph had been working non-stop getting the security systems upgraded and onboarding the new personnel. I ran my fingers through his hair and massaged his head. He closed his eyes in grateful appreciation.

"Darling, I cannot tell you how good that feels. You're hired for life," he said, smiling as I continued massaging. "So, tell me, what all has Elliot cooked up?"

I went through the different changes, including our new salary increases and compensation to the estate. Kyle was very glad to hear about that given he had just spent a huge sum in updating the technologies and hiring additional staff, including Olivia.

"The queen's announcement of my ceremony will be made on Sunday. Our lives change then, Kyle. Are you positive you still want me?" Kyle rose from his slouched position and pulled me onto his lap.

"Hey, I don't ever want to hear those words from your lips again, Gemma. I'm in this with you, through thick and thin, for better and for worse. There's no going back, darling. You will be my wife and I your husband. I promise I will always be by your side." He kissed me softly, parting my lips with his tongue.

Our passion heated up as we melted closer. Kyle picked me up and carried me to our bed, laying me down. He pulled off his shirt and lay next to me. The next hours were filled in a loving frenzy, any lingering thoughts of Kyle's willingness were obliterated from my mind. My man loved me.

When it was time to dress for cocktails, I asked him to use his room to change. I coyly told him I had a surprise outfit for tonight that I didn't want him to see. He was to wait downstairs in the study with the others for my arrival, no peeking, or else! I showered and did my make-up. I heard a soft knock on my door—it was Mrs. Smythe, accompanied by Olivia. She was going to help us do our hair in the same style and assist in dressing us for our little bluff.

I had Penny pull together two identical outfits for us to wear tonight. We both would dazzle our audience in blue and green, tartan, maxi skirts, with a matching emerald-green, cashmere turtlenecks Sitting at the vanity in my bath, Mrs. Smythe pulled our hair back in matching chignons. I applied Olivia's make-up, matching her eyelids, cheeks and lip color to mine. Penny had sent over matching gold necklaces and earrings to make our deception complete. When we finished, we walked into my bedroom where Mrs. Smythe waited for us. She would be our first test case.

"Oh, my goodness, Miss Gemma and Olivia, you do look like twins. I've never seen anything like it." Mrs. Smythe held her hand to her mouth, shaking her head as she walked around us.

"I can't thank you enough, Mrs. Smythe, for helping us. We have a big crowd downstairs to surprise. Olivia doesn't start as my bodyguard until tomorrow. Tonight, is her social debut here at the hall."

"Your guests are going to be amazed. You ladies have a magnificent time. I think Bridges and I will sneak peeks at you from around the corner. I can't wait to see everyone's surprise, especially his!" she said, giggling.

Mrs. Smythe left my room, giving us a little wave as she shut the door behind her. We were going to wait in my room for a few more minutes to ensure everyone would be in the study when we made our entrance.

"Tell me again, Gemma, who all the guests are that will be here tonight. I know I will get to know them over time, but I just want to be prepared," Olivia said, taking out her phone to jot down notes.

"Okay, you know Kyle of course, and met Steph Rutherford. Her fiancé is Penny Atkins, the wardrobe director for *Castlewood Manor*, and the provider of our costumes tonight. You've met my assistant, Amy Princeton. Her aunt is Sally Prim, the editor and photographer at the Maidenford Banner. Sally's a great friend and will be present at many of our functions, heading up the press pools."

"Right, I've got that. Are there any more people from Rosehill Productions that are here tonight?"

"Yes. Prudence Nell and Reggie Gerard have done all the decorations for the holiday events, with Amy assisting. Lucy Rutherford, the executive vice-president of Rosehill Productions is here, as is Timothy Jones, the director of the upcoming *Castlewood Manor* feature film. They'll be meeting the queen tomorrow. By the way, Timothy and Prudence are an item."

Olivia tapped her phone furiously. "This is a crowd, but it's great for me to meet these folks since they'll be around Cherrywood Hall the next few weeks."

"And that just leaves my mama, Jillian Phillips; my Aunt Margaret—Lady Margaret, mother of my Cousin Evan and the dowager Marchioness of Kentshire; Elliot Pierce, my PR manager and his partner, Max Wellington. Elliot and Max are close friends as well as frequent visitors here at the hall."

"I'm a huge fan of your mother. She's brilliant in her role. I've read about Lady Margaret and the tragedy with your cousin. It's so sad. I understand she's great friends with the queen?"

"Yes, they've been close friends for years and years. The queen is very fond of Aunt Margaret, and she of her."

"Uncle Marky has mentioned that. He also has told me that Elliot and Max are quite the kidders. I understand they enjoy their champers quite a bit," Olivia said, chuckling.

"You would be amazed at the amount of champagne that is consumed here at the hall. Mon Cheri Ltd. does quite a bit of business with us these days. Speaking of which, I think it's showtime. Are you ready?"

"Ready, let's do this," Olivia said, giving me an excited nod.

We walked down the hall to the grand staircase. We could hear the laughter as we went down the stairs, arm in arm. The tree and garland in the grand hallway were glowing, with Christmas carols playing softly in the background. We took a big inhale and smiled just before we entered the study. I gave a loud "harrumph" to get everyone's attention. As all eyes went on us, jaws dropped, and the room went silent.

Olivia and I stood tall, holding our heads high and not saying a word. Kyle broke his stare and walked in front of us, looking us up and down. I laughed when he pretended to kiss Olivia, switching quickly to me at the last second to give me a peck on my lips. The room erupted in laughter.

"Ladies and Gentlemen, may I introduce my new bodyguard, Ms. Olivia Fisher. She begins her role tomorrow morning. Tonight, she is here as our guest." I turned and gestured my hand toward her.

Everyone clapped and made their way over to us to meet her and check us out. I could see Mrs. Smythe and Bridges standing by the dining room entry. She was giggling at the crowd's reactions. Bridges stood with his mouth open. I believe he was gobsmacked.

Mama and Aunt Margaret came up first, shaking their heads and giggling.

"I can't believe it! For a minute I wondered if I had given birth to twins," Mama said, laughing, rolling her eyes over at Max and Elliot.

"You do look like a Lancaster, dear. Very beautiful, just like my niece." Aunt Margaret winked, gently holding our hands.

Amy and Sally came up next to greet us. Sally snapped a picture. To my surprise, Olivia raised her hand in a stop gesture.

"Sorry ma'am, I'm going to have to ask you to delete that photo now please. This is a private event and I wouldn't want Dr. Gemma and my similarities being seen by any perps."

Sally smiled nervously and deleted the photo, showing her phone to Olivia. I was impressed at how quickly Olivia transformed into a figure of authority. I would have deleted the photo if it had been me hearing that tone of voice.

Kyle brought over Steph and Penny next.

"You ladies look marvelous," Penny gushed. "I can't believe the similarities. Just let me know, Olivia if you ever need a similar outfit to Gemma's. We have quite the collection. I'm sure we could find a match." Steph smiled over at her partner.

"I'll walk you through the estate monitoring systems when you get settled too, Olivia. I'm happy to help you."

"Thank you both so much, I'm very grateful. I'll know where to find you," Olivia teased, wagging her finger at them.

Lucy, Prudence, Timothy, and Reggie walked up and shook Olivia's hand. Patch barked, his tail wagging.

"Olivia, please meet Patch, the cutest dog ever." I laughed.

"Ruff!" Patch extended his paw.

"Whoa, I'm going to sign him to be in the film. He'd be smashing," Timothy said, laughing and petting Patch.

"I'm afraid you wouldn't be able to afford him," Reggie said, his nose held up, slightly in the air. "He detests cast food lines. It would never work." Our laughter died out. None of us quite knew how to respond to Reggie's tone or demeanor. "I'm just kidding people! Of course, Patch would star in the movie, if the price is right…" Reggie looked at each of us in shocked surprise.

We giggled at his little joke. I still wasn't quite sure about him though.

Last but not least, Max and Elliot greeted us.

Max's eyes were wide as saucers. "Goodness, I cannot believe my eyes. You darlings are adorable and could be twinsies."

"Better watch it, darling. One of these twinsies could probably kick your sweet little—"

"Dinner is served," Bridges announced.

We laughed at the interruption so perfectly timed by Bridges. I could see a twinkle in Olivia's eye. She had fallen under the enchanted spell of Elliot and Max.

Our group made its way into the dining room. Kyle pulled me back to kiss me as the others went in.

"Gemma, my darling. You never cease to amaze me. I could not believe my eyes when you two walked in. Remind me never to be drunk around Olivia, I might inadvertently slip her into my arms."

I punched Kyle's arm, hard. "Darling, if you do that you had better run. Because after she punches you in the nose, I will, and I won't be as gentle." I bopped him lightly on his nose with my fist.

Kyle swept me in his arms, kissing me so passionately I was going weak at the knees. He stopped and pulled back, still holding me close. I was breathing heavily.

"I know you too well, darling. You have enchanted me with your spell."

I was going in for another kissing session when Mama tapped both of us on our shoulders.

"Come on darlings, your guests are waiting."

Mama took us by the arms and led us into the dining room where our guests stood and clapped at our delayed entrance. Both our cheeks turned red. We had been royally busted. I walked over to the table to take my usual seat at the end when I heard Bridges cough lightly to get my attention. I looked back at him and was somewhat surprised. He was at the head of the table and had pulled out the dining chair. It was for me, my seat as the soon-to-be marchioness.

I took the seat he held for me, dabbing my eyes with my napkin. Kyle was seated next to me as my future husband. I stood and raised my glass of wine for a toast.

"Thank you all for being such incredible friends. Kyle and I appreciate your unwavering support. May God bless you and keep you this holiday season. And please bless our beloved Evan."

The group stood and said, "Hear, hear." We took our seats, the conversations growing boisterous as the food and wine were served. I looked down at the other end of the table where Aunt Margaret was seated. I raised my glass to her, as she did to me. I loved her with all my heart that night.

After dinner we went into the grand hallway for after-dinner drinks and dancing in front of the stately Christmas tree. Jokes were made about the tree falling, causing endless views in the back of the tree to make sure the tethers were holding. Reggie was seated by himself, holding Patch and sipping his brandy. I went over to him and sat down, petting Patch's head.

"The rooms look stunning, Reggie. You, Prudence and Amy have done a smashing job."

"We all want the queen to be impressed tomorrow. I'm glad things worked out after the disaster." Reggie glanced up at the tree, a veil of sadness covering his face.

"Reggie, are you okay? I know things have been hectic, but you've been acting a bit differently. Do you want to talk about it?" I put my hand on his knee as a show of support.

He looked as if an internal struggle was pulling him in all directions. I could sense it. He was just about to answer when I heard—

"David, what are you doing here? I mean, we weren't expecting you for a few more days," Mama said in a rather loud voice, turning back to look at me, motioning for me to come be with her.

I peeked over, seeing my father and his new wife in the entry way. I patted Reggie's knee, giving him an apologetic shrug as I stood and walked over to Mama's side. Kyle joined us. There was an awkwardness in the air as I stared at my father and Elizabeth. She was an attractive woman, brown haired, extremely slight of figure, and tall. Her hair was cut in a sharp wedge that accentuated her cheekbones. Her lips were shaded in bright red. She was stylishly dressed in a black and white striped pantsuit, making my father's tweed suit appear a bit drab next to her. I shook off my awkwardness.

"Daddy, so nice to see you. I'm sorry, I didn't know you'd be here tonight," I said, kissing his cheeks.

He held my hand tightly, his shaking a bit. Was he nervous? "Hello Gemma, Kyle, so good of you to have us. I'm sorry we didn't call—this was a last-minute decision. Elizabeth was very anxious to meet you and to see Cherrywood Hall. I hope you don't mind."

"No, of course not, Daddy." I turned to Elizabeth and shook her hand. "So nice to meet you, finally. Welcome to Cherrywood Hall."

She smiled and looked around the room, her eyes panning the decorations. "You have quite an impressive home, Gemma. I told David you wouldn't mind us coming a few days early. There was no way I wasn't going to seize a chance to meet the queen. I read about her trip here in the tabloids this morning." Elizabeth laughed.

Kyle and I gave each other a quick side-eye. Daddy looked down at his shoes, embarrassed. Mama stared at her with a mouth-half-open look.

"She wanted to meet you, too, of course," Daddy stammered.

"Of course, she did," I said, a forced smile on my lips.

I took Elizabeth's arm and guided her over to our guests to introduce her and my father to them. Daddy and Kyle walked behind us. Mama just stood in place, staring. Elliot walked over to her, handing her a glass of champagne that she rapidly emptied. I clapped my hands in quick succession to get everyone's attention.

"Hello everyone, we have some surprise guests that I'd like to introduce. This is my father, David Phillips and his new wife, Elizabeth. They rearranged their schedules to be with us earlier---please give them a welcome and come say hello."

Our guests clapped and started the introduction line to meet Daddy and Elizabeth. Everyone was very gracious, I could see my father start to relax a bit, especially after Kyle handed him a whiskey. I watched Elizabeth with great interest. She seemed to be making herself the lady of Cherrywood. I glimpsed at Pippa's portrait over the grand hallway fireplace. She appeared to be watching our new family member too, and I didn't think she was glad to see her.

CHAPTER 11
Fit for a Queen

The alarm buzzed, waking Kyle and me from a deep slumber. It felt like we had just gone to bed and here we were, being summoned back to the living by a screeching phone. Kyle turned off the intruder to our sleep and reached over to give me a hug.

"Come-on sleepy head. No rest for the weary today. It's royal show-time." He kissed me on my cheek, pulling the warm covers off me to expose me to the morning air. He was determined to wake me up, and the chill in the room was working.

Kyle left our bed nest to stoke the fire. Grudgingly, I stood up and stretched, walking over to the French doors to look outside. The skies were dark, and snow was beginning to fall. The waves of the sea looked like white-capped-mountains rolling into the cliffs. We were in for some winter chills today.

"I don't like the look of these skies and the snow. I hope it doesn't cause any problems for the queen traveling today. The county roads get awfully slick."

"We weren't supposed to have any snowfall; the weather must have shifted plans overnight. I'll have the crews salt the estate drive and keep it clear. You go get ready to dazzle, my darling. I'll go to my room to get dressed---see you downstairs." Kyle kissed me and held me close. He pulled on a robe and left, blowing me a kiss as he went out the door.

I showered and styled my hair and make-up. I was wearing a festive outfit for the queen's visit today; red, plaid leggings, red turtleneck and a velvet shirtdress overlay in a luscious leopard print, belted at the waist. I wanted to dress in layers, given the chilly temperatures. No matter how high the flames roared in the fireplaces or heat blew through the vents, Cherrywood could become a very cool place. I wore my hair cascading down my back, a thin, red headband keeping the tendrils out of my face. I pulled on my black boots, covered in short fringe. It was an edgy holiday look, I had to admit, but warmth and comfort were a very high priority for me today.

As I turned from the hall to go down the staircase, I saw Daddy and Elizabeth walking ahead, a few steps in front of me. I was going to say good morning, but Elizabeth stopped mid-stair, her seething temper reaching boiling point at my father.

"I don't care what you say. You will talk to her and demand that money back. I'm your wife now and I have a style I want to become accustomed to. She has everything, look at this place." She jerked her hand in front of her, waving it wildly back and forth along the length of the hallway.

My father recoiled, as if afraid of being struck. He looked to be very distressed.

"Good morning you two. I trust you slept well?"

My father looked at me with a shocked expression. I'm sure he wondered what I had overheard.

Elizabeth rolled her eyes and gave me a snarky smile. I could tell she was not thrilled at my intrusion. "Well, good morning to you. Do you always sneak up on your guests? You could have given your poor daddy a heart attack at his age. We do want to take care of him now, don't we Gemma?"

"I'm sorry, I didn't mean to startle anyone. I just turned the corner. I wasn't expecting to see you all this early. Do you need anything, Daddy? I'll be more than glad to see you get whatever you need for your stay."

My father looked at me wistfully and shook his head. "No daughter, I'm fine. Let's go get some breakfast, shall we? I'm looking forward to Karl's creations. I really enjoyed that breakfast he prepared for us before the *Tellys* in Vail. He's an excellent chef."

We continued down the staircase and went across the hallway to the dining room. Kyle was there with Aunt Margaret, Lucy, Prudence, Amy, and Reggie tucking into some yummy looking pumpkin spice waffles. I helped myself to waffles and sausages, taking a seat next to Kyle. Daddy and Elizabeth sat across from me, and next to Aunt Margaret. She was looking very festive today herself in emerald-green slacks and plaid sweater. A diamond and emerald brooch made her sweater dazzle in the light.

"David, so glad to see you here at Cherrywood. We missed you leaving Vail. I understand that you've resigned your position at Columbia. Didn't you like university life?" Aunt Margaret was diving straight into Daddy's latest life change. I was impressed by her inquiring mind.

"He liked it, but we both decided we wanted to live here in the UK. At David's age, we want to take advantage of traveling and living in a new land while we can. I'm so excited to be looking for properties here. Perhaps we can be neighbors," Elizabeth said, jumping in to put the focus on her.

"I never knew you wanted to live here, Daddy. I thought you liked New York City. The gentlemen's club and city vibe seemed to invigorate you."

Elizabeth gave me a sullen look, choosing to butt in once again. "New York is so blasé, Gemma. We decided to move to the UK, the land of our forefathers and settle down with proper folks. I think your daddy will make a fabulous country gentleman, don't you?"

Daddy's face was growing quite red with embarrassment.

"Elizabeth, what about your studies? I thought you were working on a doctorate yourself?"

Daddy gave me a slight cutting wave of hand, trying to warn me to not ask about this. It was too late.

"Hah, I quit the university. They had the audacity to accuse me of cheating on my dissertation. It's a conspiracy to keep talented women out of the academic field. You were so right, Gemma, to leave the academia world behind. It's positively horrid. It will be quite nice to live the lives of ladies in luxury, don't you think?" Elizabeth gave Daddy a pat on his hand, a smug smile on her face.

I was shocked by this conversational exchange. Elizabeth seemed to have morphed into a controlling housewife from Hades. Daddy hadn't even been allowed to speak. The change in his demeanor was shocking and painful for me, seeing him in this state being bullied by his young wife. I wasn't buying any of her story. Something was very wrong here. I was going to have to get Daddy by himself to find out what was going on.

Reggie, Prudence, Amy, and Aunt Margaret left the breakfast table to go do a last round of inspections before the queen's arrival. Lucy asked to speak with me and Kyle in the library. We left Daddy and Elizabeth to finish up their breakfast in silence.

"That was more than strange," Kyle whispered to me, as we walked across to the library. "Elizabeth dominated the entire conversation. I've never seen such a negative transformation as I have with your father. He looks miserable, Gemma."

"I know. I'll have to get him alone. I heard her yelling at him on the stairs this morning, saying something about getting money back. Do you think she's pressuring him to take back his lottery winnings he put in my trust fund?"

"I don't know, darling. Don't let her ramblings upset you. The main thing is seeing what is up with your father. Let's see what Lucy has to say and then I need to make some last-minute checks outside before the royals arrive. Will you be okay?"

I nodded and playfully gave Kyle a quick pat on his bottom.

In the library, we took seats on the leather couch, with Lucy sitting across from us in a wingback chair. I glanced out the bay window and noticed the snowfall intensity had drastically increased. I took a deep breath and hoped all would be well today with the queen's visit.

"Gemma, Kyle, thank you for taking a few minutes with me. Elliot presented the new documents for our legal staff to review. I hope to have everything completed very soon with our contracts team. You both have been so wonderful to work with this past year. I know the coming changes with your position will limit your availability to consult and participate in events with us."

"We're both very committed to the *Castlewood Manor* team, Lucy. It's true our schedules and commitments are about to change in a major way, but we look forward to working with you for a long time. The entire community is too." I smiled.

"We're behind you and Kyle too, Gemma. I've had some discussion with the Rosehill executives. We'd like to do a film feature on your and Kyle's wedding nuptials. It will be a full-blown documentary—how you met, your work on the show, your peerage ceremony with the queen, ending of course with your wedding ceremony. We can make it a huge hit, I'm sure. I mentioned it to Elliot and Jillian last evening. They said I must talk with you first, of course, which I was going to do, I promise. It could be useful to address any naysayers you may have, what do you think?" Lucy was excited about this latest project, no doubt. Her eyes sparkled, and I could see her executive wheels turning in her head. This would be great publicity for *Castlewood Manor*, but was it what Kyle and I wanted?

Kyle and I looked at each other and shrugged, not sure how to take this latest offer.

"Lucy, let Gemma and I mull this over a bit, we're very appreciative, but right now we need to focus on the queen's visit. We'll discuss it, I promise. Now, if you ladies will excuse me, I must check outside to make sure everything's set. As you can see, it looks as if the clouds have opened up with snow."

Kyle gave me a quick kiss and shook Lucy's hand before heading out. Lucy and I stood by the window to look out at the snowfall. You could barely see the drive now; the snow was so thick. I left Lucy to go find Aunt Margaret to see if she had any updates from the queen. I gave a quick wave to Reggie, Amy, and Prudence as I passed them standing next to the Christmas tree, going over the queen's tour one last time. I went down the hall, pausing at the door to his room. Aunt Margaret was looking out the back window at the gardens. I tiptoed in and went to Evan's side. He looked the same, no change. I wondered if we would ever get to talk with him again.

"Hey there, it's really coming down now, isn't it?" I asked, walking over to Aunt Margaret's side.

"Yes, it is. It looks lovely. I was just thinking about the sleigh ride we took into Maidenford for the church service last Christmas Eve. It was such a lovely night. Did you see the Christmas tree over here?" She pointed to a four-foot-tall tree, sitting on a round cherry table, decorated with glimmering, blue mercury glass globes. The lights sparkled against them, making for a beautiful Christmas scene, set against the fireplace on the back wall.

"This is so beautiful, Aunt Margaret. These are Pippa's globes you were talking about. They're so pretty." I touched them gently. They were heavy, the mark of the Irish glass maker on their hook cap.

"I'm glad you like them. I made you up a box of them to use for a tree in your room. Charles gifted these to Pippa on their first Christmas here at Cherrywood. There were plenty, you can have a beautiful tree too."

I pecked her cheek and thanked her for the wonderful gift.

We made our way back to the grand hallway to prepare for the queen's arrival. Sally and a few of her press colleagues had arrived, setting up their equipment in the library. Amy, Prudence and Reggie were making miniscule adjustments fluffing pillows and straightening ornaments. Lucy and Timothy stood by the tree, mentally rehearsing their remarks. Nerves and tensions were running high in the quest to have everything royally perfect.

We had a lovely tea prepared to serve after the queen's tour. Bridges was going over the seating arrangements in the dining room one last time with his staff. Aunt Margaret was very pleased with the table setting and layout, giving him her stamp of approval.

I smiled when I saw Kyle come down the stairs and over to me, having changed into black trousers and matching turtleneck topped with a red sweater, fitting for the holidays. His hair was still damp from his shower. I kissed his cheek, smelling a spicy hint of aftershave.

"I hope the queen's vehicle has snow tires or is four-wheel drive. The weather is brutal outside. The Royal Protection Service members are out front, speaking with Chief Inspector Marquot. Olivia's out there too. He wanted to introduce them to her."

"Where's Mama? I haven't seen her, Elliot or Max yet this morning. Has anyone seen them?'

"They're downstairs, Gemma, in the kitchen. Chef Karl is making what he called a *hangover brekkie*. I think they may have had a little too much bubbly last evening." Lucy teased, her hands tipping a pretend glass.

I didn't doubt it. Mama was very upset by Daddy and Elizabeth's early appearance last evening. Elizabeth didn't do anything to endear herself to us. I was glad she was not at the dining room table for breakfast this morning. I was sure the conversation monopoly and treatment of Daddy would have added to her angst.

"Gemma, is what I'm wearing all right? I've never met a queen before."

I turned to the stairway where Elizabeth posed, dressed in a black slip gown that clung to her slim frame. The material was very sheer. I blinked a few times as I watched her carefully navigate her way down the stairs, holding tightly to Daddy's arm. She was wearing stiletto heels, making her balance very precarious. Daddy was dressed in a black suit and tie, a bit overdressed, but definitely a better choice than Elizabeth's slip dress.

"Um, it's a lovely dress, Elizabeth. Aren't you cold though?" I could see the hairs on her arm standing up.

"I'm fine. David will go get my fur stole if it's too chilly. I'm surprised you're not more dressed for the occasion, Gemma. Don't you want to look good for the queen?"

Kyle grabbed my arm, sensing I was getting ready to leap at her. We were saved by Chief Inspector Marquot and Olivia coming in through the front entry. Bridges took their hats and coats as they brushed the snow off. Kyle and I went up to greet them. We had last been in the company of the Chief Inspector a few months ago, when we were in Malibu. He had last accompanied us as a special envoy on our *Castlewood Manor* tour a few months ago, at the request of the Rosehill Productions.

"Dr. Gemma, Sir Kyle, so very nice to see you again. I was just introducing Livvy, I mean Olivia, to some of my RPS contacts outside. I am very pleased to be here with her on her first day. Even more impressive that she has a visit with the queen as one of her first assignments."

Olivia blushed. I could tell her uncle's opinion meant a great deal to her. She was dressed very professionally today in a tailored black suit, white turtleneck and black leather ankle boots. Fashion meets function. I was impressed.

"Did the RPS give you an ETA for the queen, Chief Inspector? I'm sure no one was prepared for this amount of snowfall."

"The last communication informed us they were about twenty minutes out. The two-lane roads are getting hazardous. They are driving slowly, as one would expect."

Mama, Elliot and Max joined us and greeted the Chief Inspector. The hangover brekkie Chef Karl had prepared for them seemed to have worked its magic. They all seemed very clear eyed and excited for the queen's visit.

"Look Gemma, I'm wearing the cufflinks I bought on our little shopping excursion the other day. Aren't they gorgeous?"

Max's yellow-gold crown links shined bright against his red dress shirt. He wore a tartan vest to give him a festive flare. Elliot's white-gold crown links looked good too against his black, button-down shirt, topped with a navy, watch plaid vest. I looked over at the sitting area by the tree. My father and Elizabeth sat alone, choosing not to interact with anyone. Daddy stared vacantly at the Christmas tree, lost in thought. I knew something was consuming him. I was determined to carve out time with him, if I could just figure out what to do with Elizabeth.

We heard the crackle of the RPS's communication device outside the doorway. The queen's entourage was pulling up the estate drive. Sally and her press photographers were standing close by to catch the queen's entrance. Aunt Margaret came and stood by me and Kyle. We would be first to greet her and Prince Thaddeus.

Mama, Karl, Amy, and Daddy and Elizabeth were standing to our right, near the wall with the fireplace, Elizabeth visibly shivering. Max, Elliot and Reggie stood next to them, followed by Lucy, Prudence and Timothy. Patch was very dapper in a bright-red doggie vest, complete with a bow tie. Chief Inspector Marquot and Olivia took positions near the Christmas tree down the hallway, giving them a clear view of us all.

The snow crunched underneath the royal tires as the queen's vehicle pulled up to the entry. The RPS agents made their way swiftly to the vehicle to assist the queen and husband out to the entry stairs. Bridges opened the door, bowing as Queen Annelyce and Prince Thaddeus walked in. He took their coats, helping them to dislodge any trace of snow. The royals were both attired in bright-colored cashmere sweaters and tweeds; a skirt for the queen and trousers for the prince consort. We walked over to them, Kyle bowing and Aunt Margaret and I curtseying.

"Welcome to Cherrywood Hall, Your Majesty, Your Royal Highness. We're so happy you were able to make it here with all the snow."

I could hear Sally's camera clicking in the background. Aunt Margaret and the royals kissed, with the queen telling her how they were looking forward to seeing Evan. Aunt Margaret's eyes brimmed with happiness at seeing her royal friend.

"Damn frightful at times," Prince Thaddeus exclaimed, his wife giving him a queenly stare. "Hope you have some good spirits, son." Prince Thaddeus gave Kyle a wink.

"Yes Sir, we do. We'll have a seat over by the tree before we begin our tour. Reggie, Amy, and Prudence will give you a run-down on their decorating activities." Kyle motioned to Bridges to get some whiskey offerings prepared pronto.

The queen and prince went down the line, greeting everyone. She stopped when she met Elizabeth and stared a bit as she saw her shiver. She moved on quickly. I'm sure she wondered if the poor girl had forgotten to put a dress on over her slip. We took seats around the tree as Bridges and his staff served tumblers of whiskey.

"Now, this is more like it," the Prince said, taking a large swig of the amber colored liquor. Sally's camera clicked in the background.

Reggie, Prudence, and Amy gave the overview of the upcoming holiday events that Rosehill Productions would be broadcasting. Amy was smiling brightly. This was her second time meeting the queen and she was thrilled. Lucy and Timothy presented the queen with a crystal globe ornament with the silhouette of Cherrywood Hall etched into the glass. It was a beautiful memento. I hoped Lucy had brought more for us.

We stood to start the tour. Kyle, Aunt Margaret, the Rosehill staff, Amy, the press team, and I would be accompanying the queen and the prince. Elizabeth stood too, thinking she could just tag along, but was stopped by a member of the queen's RPS staff.

Elizabeth huffed and was getting ready to make a fuss when she slipped, falling flat on her behind. Her stiletto heel had broken off on her right pump. Her slip dress tore, exposing her undies. Daddy quickly put his jacket around her as they hobbled up the stairs to their room. I was sure he was going to get an ear full.

The queen wasn't fazed at all by Elizabeth's tumble. Truth be told, I think she was relieved to have her gone. I know I was. Our first stop was the conservatory, the showroom for the New Year's Eve broadcast. It had been a few days since I had been in here and I was pleasantly surprised.

Red poinsettias had been brought in, spread around in the plant beds to bring a brilliant pop of red to the black and white space. The red, with the little glass mirrors and fairy lights, made for an elegant backdrop. It would be perfect for the star-studded cast announcement.

"These mirrors are delightful. They lighten up the room and enhance the beauty of the plants. I must have them at the conservatory at the palace. Reggie, you'll call me when I return after the holidays?"

"Of course, Ma'am."

"Ruff!" Patch wagged his tale. He knew a queen's command when he heard one.

We broke into giggles over our little friend's enthusiasm.

We made our way into the dining room where tea had been set up. Before taking her seat, the queen walked around the perimeter of the room, stopping to examine all the ornamental decorations that had been brought out of storage. She was particularly enchanted with a scene of Father Christmas's workshop.

"I think we have one much like this. My mother had it when we were girls."

"It could very well be, Ma'am. This was Pippa's. She and your mama were very good friends as you well know. They could have had duplicates," Aunt Margaret said, nodding her head.

"I believe you're right, Margaret. I must have a look for them in Mama's storage room at the palace. I'd love to have it displayed next year."

The queen's service member jotted down notes.

We sat down to tea. The others joined us, including Elizabeth, who was now dressed in a far more suitable outfit of slacks and a sweater. Daddy took her to the end of the table, farthest away from the queen. He could sense the queen's lack of fondness for his wife.

The food was rolled out and served, including warm mugs of consommé, mushroom and steak tarts, and a variety of sandwiches with savory spreads. For sweets, we were treated to several pumpkin spice offerings, including breads, cupcakes and cookies. The queen was especially fond of the cranberry and cherry turnovers, finding them just the right combination of sweet and tart.

Tea, champagne and cocktails were flowing, and the conversations were getting more and more spirited. Prince Thaddeus was enjoying the whiskey selection from Evan's private reserves very much, helping himself to another serving. Luckily, his staff would be doing the driving to Sandringham.

Inspector Marquot appeared by the dining room entrance from the study, Olivia by his side. He motioned for Kyle and me to join them. We excused ourselves and went into the study.

"I'm sorry to interrupt your festivities. There has been an accident near Maidenford. It's Lady Adela, her car slid off the road. She received a slight cut on her forehead. She is insisting she be brought here to Cherrywood to stay. I must tell you the roads are just about impassable now. We can get Lady Adela here, but I'm afraid there will be no one leaving Cherrywood Hall tonight."

"Are you telling me that the queen and Prince Thaddeus will be spending the night at Cherrywood hall, Chief Inspector? With Lady Adela here too?" I started to panic.

Kyle put his arm around me and gave me a gentle squeeze. "It will be fine darling. We have plenty of rooms. Since your mama moved into the actor's suite, the Royal bedroom next to Lady Margaret's is vacant. The queen and Prince Thaddeus will love that room. Lady Adela can stay in the hall next to my suite. It's very quiet down there. She'll be able to rest quite comfortably."

A member of the RPS came into the room and pulled the Chief Inspector off to one side. The agent gave him the latest info, shaking his head. He nodded and walked over to us.

"That's it, I'm afraid you're going to have several of us as guests this evening. Lady Adela is on her way now. The roads are officially closed. I trust there will be accommodations for us all?"

"Of course, Chief Inspector. There's plenty of room. I think I had better tell our guests the situation and get Bridges and the staff busy setting up rooms. Thank goodness Chef Karl has his sous chef and cooks here. We're going to need food, and a lot of it," I said giggling.

Kyle rolled his eyes at me as we walked back to our guests to break the blizzard news to them.

"Excuse me, Your Majesty, Sir, ladies and gentlemen. It seems mother nature has released more of her fury than expected. We have one more guest that will be joining us shortly, but after her arrival, the roads are closed for the remainder of the day and evening. It seems we are going to have a royal sleepover, Ma'am. Your accommodations are being prepared now. I'm sorry for your delay to Sandringham. I hope the roads can be cleared by tomorrow."

"Well, jolly good," Prince Thaddeus said, winking at the queen. "Sir Kyle, I believe I'll have another whiskey."

Aunt Margaret and Mama came up to me after my announcement. I explained the road conditions.

"Who's coming here, Gemma? We weren't expecting anyone else tonight."

"It's Lady Adela, Aunt Margaret. Her car apparently ran off the road near Maidenford. She received a slight cut on her forehead and apparently insisted on being brought to Cherrywood. She will be our final royal guest tonight."

CHAPTER 12
Regal Intentions

Preparations were in full throttle for our royal sleepover. Everyone was buzzing about being stranded in a snowstorm with the queen. Max was beside himself, taking secret selfies with the queen and Prince Thaddeus in the background every chance he had. Sally and her two colleagues from the press were over the moon. It wasn't often one was an overnight guest with the queen. Sugarplum dreams of a once in a million photo of the queen in her nightgown danced in their heads. Now, if they could just sneak past the RPS agents who guarded her…

Lady Adela arrived, the two-mile trip from Maidenford taking a snail-paced forty minutes. The only reason she was here was because of her ties to the queen. We hovered around her as she sat on the sofa nearest the Christmas tree while her room was prepared. Reggie and Max were her attentive caregivers, fetching pillows, comforters, tea, and of course a smidge of brandy for their injured, royal patient.

Kyle, Elliot and Amy were setting up some fun in the conservatory for later tonight. A screen was being mounted to watch Christmas movie favorites for film fans on the back wall. Bridge tables were lined up across from the waterfall. It was the queen's favorite card game and she was notorious for playing a take-no-prisoners hand. Next to the improvised bar area, Mama and Prince Thaddeus were teaming up to plan out the pantomime themes to be used for charades, a favorite of them both.

The snack bar was being stocked, complete with cocktails, eggnog, popcorn, and holiday mini-bites to keep the players and film watching tummies filled. The queen had insisted that everyone who was stranded tonight at Cherrywood take part in the festivities by royal decree. I was sure, it was going to be an amazing night that members of many families would be talking about for generations to come.

The queen, Aunt Margaret and I went to visit Evan in his room. Olivia and the RPS member followed close behind, keeping watch. It was unlikely anything would happen in our snowed-in state, but one never knew.

Aunt Margaret led the queen over to Evan's bedside. I remained behind them, to give the two friends a chance to talk. I wandered over to the Christmas tree, still shining bright by the fireplace. I looked at Pippa's ornaments again, anxious to get a tree set up in my bedroom and decorate it with Kyle.

I started when I heard a loud moan, turning quickly to go to Evan's bedside. Aunt Margaret had her hand to her mouth--the queen holding on to her arm. Evan was moaning, a deep guttural growl, but the first sounds we had heard from him in months. His caregivers rushed over, checking his vitals to make sure everything was okay.

Nurse Ellie smiled as she backed away. "He's gone back under it would appear. That growl was an encouraging sign, Lady Margaret."

Aunt Margaret's eyes teared up, as did mine and the queen's. Could it be possible that our Christmas wishes might come true?

We decided to sit by the fire for a while, just in case there were any more sounds out of Evan. The queen and Aunt Margaret spoke of bygone days, raising their children. It was good to hear them laugh and reminisce, although Evan remained quiet.

When we left to join in the night of games and Christmas fun, I stopped at Evan's bedside, bending down to air kiss his forehead. "Wish you were here tonight, Cousin. I would so beat you at bridge," I whispered, giggling and giving him just the lightest of punches to his arm, my teasing gesture that was often shared with Evan and Kyle. "Come back to us. We miss you."

I scurried to catch up with Aunt Margaret and the queen. Lady Adela was with them in the hall, leaning on a gilded cane topped with a heavy, crystal knob. She smiled when she saw me coming.

"Gemma, darling. What a magnificent hostess you are, taking in stragglers from all walks of life. I'm sorry to say it, but your father's young wife is ghastly, absolutely no taste whatsoever. We can't have her attend your peerage ceremony. I'm afraid she just isn't the right type. Do you really think it's a good idea for the press and service agents to be joining us this evening as fellow guests? You will be marchioness soon, dear. Your Aunt Pippa must be rolling in her grave."

I didn't quite know how to take Lady Adela's comment, and I could see Aunt Margaret was bristling at her high-horse tone of voice. I had big concerns about Elizabeth myself, but not because of her 'type'. As for the press corps and services members which included Sally and Olivia, I couldn't think of any finer people. Was she insinuating the intermingling of royalty and so-called commoners was a bad thing?

"I think Aunt Pippa would love to be here, Lady Adela. Remember, she was like me, an American and a commoner. It is rather exciting when you think about it. People from all walks of life stranded in a holiday blizzard in a castle by the sea. Sounds perfect for all kinds of Christmas fun and mischief." I laughed. I purposely didn't address her comments on Elizabeth. I would handle that topic privately with my family.

"I quite agree, Gemma. The prince and I were looking forward to being at Sandringham tonight, but given the circumstances this is very exciting. I feel a little like a schoolgirl on an overnight stay," the queen said, chuckling, trying to make up for her niece's snooty comments. Her gaze at Lady Adela was clear. The queen was not amused.

Lady Adela smiled in deferment to her aunt, although I could tell she was a little put off. Did she really feel being surrounded by people not of royal descent beneath her? I tried to shrug it off, thinking her head injury was putting her on edge. The tone of her voice seemed a bit cruel to me and I had a nagging feeling I had heard that tone before. I shrugged it off, I wasn't going to let her attitude spoil the evening.

We walked into the conservatory to check on how things were going in our party room. Kyle was in the back, helping to set up the bar supplies with Elliot. I walked up to him to give him a kiss and share the news of Evan's encouraging sounds.

"Are you sure you didn't imagine it, darling? Everyone makes sounds now and then, even a comatose person."

"I didn't imagine it, Kyle—the queen and Aunt Margaret heard it too. Nurse Ellie thought it might be a positive sign."

Kyle looked at me with loving eyes. He knew how much I wanted my cousin to wake up.

"The conservatory looks magnificent. You've all transformed it into a palatial game room. Movies, cards, charades—it's going to be so much fun."

"And don't forget the cocktails, darling. I'm amazed at Prince Thaddeus' constitution. He could give us all a run if we had a drinking contest. Kyle had to bring out more of the whiskey reserves," Elliot said, his eyes wide with admiration. "I can't wait 'til a little later tonight. We may just see the old boy go skinny-dipping."

We roared with laughter. This princely image not soon forgotten.

Dinner was served at seven, a little earlier than normal, but given the circumstances and the evening of games planned for later, no one was complaining. We changed into more formal attire for our evening of gaiety. I was wearing a leopard print, maxi skirt and black turtleneck with the gold, infinity chain necklace Kyle had given me last Christmas that his mother Honey had made. He looked dapper in a navy turtleneck and tartan sports coat. The men were given a night off from tuxedos to better relax, mingle, and enjoy the games.

Mama wore a bright-yellow maxi sweater dress that hugged her beautiful curves—catching the eye of the teasing prince more than once. Amy looked very mod in a violet jumpsuit with bell sleeves. The queen and Aunt Margaret took a more traditional approach wearing tartan, full-length skirts, vests and silk blouses. Elizabeth's attire sent some tongues wagging when she walked in with a lime-green and orange maxi dress that was more suited for a tropical cruise than a December blizzard party, but at least she was covered up more with this outfit. Lady Adela was magnificent in a royal blue, cashmere sweater and matching maxi skirt, her dark hair pulled back in a low chignon. Her mood seemed to have improved as she laughed and mingled with the commoner crowd.

Chef Karl did us proud with selections that included starters of creamy potato soup sprinkled with chives, spring rolls served with a sweet/sour dipping sauce, and halved roasted red potatoes filled with caviar and crème fraiche For our entre, rotisserie-grilled chickens, pork roasts with cranberry-apple chutney, mince pies, root veggies, and my personal favorite, fingerling potatoes roasted in duck fat, crispy and delicious.

Tonight, dinner was being served in the grand hallway to accommodate our blizzard crowd. Round tables had been set up in the middle of the aisle in front of the stately Christmas tree. We took our seats for dinner, excited by this royally unexpected twist to our plans. Everyone hushed as Queen Annelyce stood, holding her wine glass up for a toast.

"Ladies and gentlemen, it is a rare privilege for the Prince and me to be snowed in with such wonderful guests. It's magical to be here at the beautiful Cherrywood Hall. I wish you a wonderful holiday season, and here's to a very festive night."

"Hear, hear," we replied in unison, tapping our spoons gently on our glasses as the queen took her seat.

The conversations started as the food was served, everyone seemed to be in a very festive mood. Christmas carols played in the background. Our table with the queen was placed near the hallway fireplace. I looked up at Aunt Pippa's portrait hanging above the mantel—she seemed to be smiling down at all the guests. I knew in my heart if she were here, she would have loved this impromptu gathering. I raised my wine glass to her in a ghostly tribute.

I could hear Elizabeth getting louder down at her table. She was seated with Daddy, Mama, Karl, Sally, and Amy, complaining about her food, her wine, and why she was not seated at the queen's table. I could see the other guests' eyes darting over to her.

I excused myself and went to see if I could help her calm down. "Elizabeth, is everything all right? We can hear you down at the other end. We can get you whatever you'd like, but I will ask you to keep your voice down please. You're disrupting everyone's dinner."

Mama and Daddy looked at one another, clearly upset by Elizabeth's whining. Amy and Sally winced at her uncouth tirade.

"I tell you what would make me feel better, Gemma. Much better, in fact…" Elizabeth stood to face me. She snarled. "You can return all the lottery money your daddy gave to you. It should be ours. I want it and you're going to give it to me or else I'm going to go to the press every single day. How about them apples, Gemma?" Elizabeth grabbed her wine glass and took a big swig, proud of herself.

Daddy took her by the arm to lead her out of the hallway and back to her room. Mama was livid at the way she talked to me, both in tone and subject matter. Everyone was watching this unfold as the room went silent. Kyle came by my side, ready to assist if needed. To my surprise, Olivia came and stood next to Daddy, taking Elizabeth's arm in his stead.

She walked the grumbling Elizabeth up the staircase. Elizabeth was stumbling and belligerent, but her attempts to pry away from Olivia's firm grip failed. Mrs. Smythe and one of her maids followed close behind. They would get Elizabeth undressed and stay with her 'til she fell asleep or passed out, much to Daddy's relief.

"Daddy we must talk. Please sit down and enjoy your dinner with everyone. We have a fun evening planned. You deserve it. Mrs. Smythe and Olivia will see that Elizabeth is cared for. She won't be causing any more trouble tonight. I'll join you after dinner." I gently rubbed his shoulder and motioned for him to take his seat. He sat down with Mama and the rest of his table, nervous and a bit embarrassed, but glad this latest outburst was over.

Kyle walked me back to our table.

Queen Annelyce patted my hand. "Well done, Gemma."

Aunt Margaret nodded her approval at me too, making me smile. Lady Adela stared at the staircase, her mind a million miles away. I could tell she was not pleased, her fingers drumming softly on the table.

After dinner, we went into the conservatory—let the games begin! I searched for Daddy, hoping to sequester him. My heart melted when I saw him with Mama and Prince Thaddeus playing charades. He was smiling and laughing. I remembered how much he and Mama used to like playing the different roles when we went on vacations together. Mama was keeping a close eye on him—she still cared for him very much as a friend. He looked like his former self, which was very heartening for me. I decided to let him have fun. We would have our talk later.

Olivia came over to me and pulled me aside. "I just wanted to let you know Elizabeth should be out for the evening. Mrs. Smyth and her staff are keeping watch. There are pill bottles all over her room, Gemma. I'm afraid she might have a drug problem. When you speak to your father, let me know. There are some great treatment facilities here in the area."

She left to go over to her uncle and several RPS members who were keeping a watchful eye on everyone, preferring to stay in the background of the festivities. I secretly thought they were placing wagers on who would pass out first. Amy, Sally and Max were watching Christmas movies, laughing and having fun. At the bridge tables, the queen was ruling, winning hand after hand. Elliot, Timothy and one of Sally's press colleagues were playing with her, amazed at her skills at calling hands. Aunt Margaret watched and observed with a smile. She left the games early to go sit with Evan in his room.

I went back over to watch the charades antics, by far the most boisterous group in the room. Lady Adela was there, watching the pantomimes of Prudence, Reggie and Mama with the Prince. Reggie gave her several tense glances. I wondered if she had criticized any of the decorations as being too common. There seemed to be a chilled silence between them that I couldn't figure out.

The festivities went well into the early morning hours until the effects of the champagne and cocktails started to be felt. We watched as the queen and Prince Thaddeus went up the stairs to their room—calling it a night, followed by their RPS agent. Queen Annelyce turned and waved at us, a big grin on her face. She had every reason to be pleased, Elliot told us she had cleaned house and won fifty pounds.

Daddy came over to me to kiss me goodnight. He was still grinning which made me very happy. "Thank you, daughter, for a lovely evening. I've let this situation with Elizabeth get way too much out of hand. She has problems…"

"I do want to discuss it with you, Daddy. I've heard about some of the issues. Go to bed and rest with that sweet smile on your face. We'll deal with the issues together, as a family." I kissed his cheek and watched him go up the stairs. He had a spring to his step, which was very good to see.

Kyle, Elliot, Max, and I plopped down on the sofa by the tree, the grand hallway still shimmering with the Christmas lights. Elliot was making us laugh as he went over hand after bridge hand. Queen Annelyce was quite the card shark and tolerated no shenanigans. Playing cards with her was serious royal business.

"Amy and Sally are fantastic, Gemma, truly. Sally was telling us all her press inside information. You wouldn't believe it, darlings. We have some very naughty stars and royals in our midst. Sally and I traded phones numbers so we can text." Max was rubbing his hands together in gossip nirvana as Elliot rolled his eyes.

"So darling, do we have any whiskey left in the coffers?" I teased. I had seen Kyle run downstairs to the cellar several times to bring up additional bottles.

"I certainly got my steps in this evening. The prince thoroughly enjoys his whiskey, especially the hundred-year-old variety. No disrespect, but it's a good thing Evan is in a coma this evening, he probably would have fainted seeing his vintage inventory disappearing." Kyle grimaced dramatically, leaving us to roll on the sofa in bittersweet laughs and tears, thinking of his reaction.

It felt good to make merry. The stress of the visit, with everything else, had kept us extremely busy with little time to relax and enjoy the beauty that was here. We decided to have one more brandy before turning in—probably a mistake, but at that point in time none of us really cared.

We sat quietly by the tree, our sides aching. Waves of sleepiness started to hit us. Max had laid his head on Elliot's shoulder and was now starting to snore lightly. I reached over and took his brandy glass from him, setting it down so it wouldn't spill. Elliot gave me a wink and brushed a lock of hair from his partner's forehead, looking at him with loving eyes.

Kyle and I were just about ready to turn in when Patch came running through the grand hallway, barking madly. Kyle and I tried to beckon him over to sit on our laps to calm him, but he stayed away, obviously panicked. I looked around and could see no sign of Reggie, which was strange. He never was far away from his little pooch. Max woke up and tried to get the little dog to come to him, but to no avail.

"Gemma, Gemma!" It was Daddy, dressed in his pajamas, running down the staircase and over to us, quite out of breath. "Elizabeth, she's gone. I was in the bath, changing. I saw what I thought was her lying on the other side of the bed. When I crawled in, I reached for her, but she was gone, it was just a pile of blankets fluffed up. I've searched everywhere in the room, along the hallway. She's vanished."

"Calm down, David. We'll find her. She probably is lost somewhere in the hall; we have over one-hundred-fifty rooms here." Kyle poured Daddy a brandy and handed it to him, making him take a drink.

Patch was still barking, as if trying to get us to follow him. Olivia came down the stairs, still dressed in her black suit. She had been watching us from a sitting niche in the hall upstairs, discreetly observing the unfolding scene.

"I don't understand it. Elizabeth was out cold. I didn't think she'd be up until late in the morning with the drugs she had taken."

"I think we better follow, Patch," Kyle said, a look of worry swept over his face.

Patch led us through the dining room and into the conservatory. We fanned out and looked along the marble pathways but could see no trace of Elizabeth. Patch was barking at the faux rock door that led to the indoor swimming pool. No one had been in there this evening. Elizabeth had not known of the hidden door. We couldn't ignore the pooch's barking—he was adamantly trying to get in the pool room.

Kyle and Olivia led the way to the rock door. She reached behind her back, underneath her blazer, unbuckling her handgun holster snap, her hand placed on the grip. She motioned for me to stay back as she and Kyle entered the pool room. Elliot, Max, Daddy, and I followed her direction, straining our necks to catch a glimpse. We waited, holding our breath so we could hear what was happening by the pool. We heard Olivia yell—

"Stop, put it down and step away from the pool! Hands in the air! I mean it, sir."

Kyle came running out, dialing a number on his phone. "Yes, it's Kyle. Please come down to the indoor pool room. You'd better bring some back-up." He hung up and came over to me, pulling me close.

"Kyle, what's happened? Who is it?" I asked, fear gripping me.

Kyle looked at Daddy, his eyes filled with sorrow. "David, I'm sorry. It's Elizabeth—she's... she's dead, David."

We all gasped in disbelief. Daddy tried to go in, but Kyle stopped him.

"Let me see her," Daddy cried, tears running down his face.

"You can't, not yet, David. Olivia has a suspect in there. I've called Chief Inspector Marquot to come down and bring some RPS members with him. It would be best if you leave things to them for now."

At that moment, Chief Inspector Marquot and three RPS agents ran past us into the pool room.

"Get down on the ground, now. Down!"

We heard the person drop as the agents secured him. Patch had quit barking, it finally dawned on me why. The person being held was his master, Reggie Gerard. I looked at Kyle and shook my head.

"Reggie?" I asked, my eyes wide in disbelief.

Kyle nodded.

"Oh no, he would never..." Max held his hand to his mouth. He couldn't believe his old college friend could do anything as foul as murder.

We went over to one of the bridge tables and sat down. I had my arms around Daddy. He was sobbing inconsolably.

"I was going to get her help. I didn't know she had become so dependent on the drugs. It got worse and worse, Gemma, after we left Vail. They made her personality erratic and volatile. We had been so in love. Everything crashed. She lost her doctoral eligibility. She was caught cheating and plagiarizing on her dissertation. After that loss, she refused to stay in New York. She insisted on relocating over here."

"Why did she keep bringing up the lottery money, Daddy? I'll give the money back. You just have to ask"

"No, no, it's yours, Gemma. I thank God I did give it to you. Elizabeth has spent the lion's share of my winnings. She's been gambling like there's no tomorrow, huge amounts, secretly. I found out about it last month. I have just ten million left. She's lost everything else, gambled away."

"Daddy, are you saying she gambled away ninety-million dollars? It's only been a few months. How could anyone do that?" I was shocked. I had never heard of such a thing. I knew people lost fortunes all the time, but not this much in a matter of months.

Elliot, Max and Kyle were just as shocked as I was at hearing this. Their mouths dropping open.

"I was so embarrassed. I couldn't say anything to you or Jillian. You would have thought me a doddering, old fool. I've always heard there was a curse on lottery winnings. I believe it now."

"Oh, Daddy. We would never think that. You're not old and you're certainly not a fool. You fell in love with a disturbed woman who had many issues. Please be honest with me, Daddy, I'm your daughter, but also your friend. Kyle and I will do anything to help you."

Daddy looked at me and ran his fingers through my hair, gently patting my head. "You're quite the woman, Gemma. My little girl is all grown up. Kyle, I hope—I hope you know what a wonderful woman you have here." Daddy broke down again in uncontrollable sobs.

Chief Inspector Marquot walked over to our table. "Dr. Phillips, the coroner cannot make it here for another few hours. The snow has stopped, and they are making progress clearing the roads, especially since the queen is in residence. My colleagues and I feel that nothing should be touched until his arrival. We are going to leave your wife's body in the pool for now. We will work as quickly as we can and let you see her once we have processed the scene."

"I don't know how she got down here without someone seeing her. In her drugged state she must have been pushed into the pool and drowned. She wouldn't have been able to defend herself."

"No, Dr. Phillips. She did not drown. She was hit on the head with this." The Chief Inspector held up a gilded cane with a crystal knob, bloodied at the end.

"That's Lady Adela's cane, how did Reggie—"

"That's what we will find out, Dr. Gemma." Chief Inspector Marquot shook his head in disgust.

CHAPTER 13
Tinsel Trauma

We took Daddy upstairs to Evan's marquess bedroom suite next to mine to try and get him to rest. We left the secret panel door between the rooms open so I could keep watch over him if he stirred. I was very concerned. He seemed so heartbroken and filled with despair over not being able to help his troubled wife.

Kyle had his crew start the snow removal on the estate roads to have them cleared for when the coroner and his team arrived. We changed into our pajamas and climbed into bed, exhausted, but still reeling from Elizabeth's tragic death. I could hear Daddy snoring softly in the next room.

"Oh, Kyle, I can't believe this. Why would Reggie kill Elizabeth? He just met her. What were they doing in the pool room at that time of night? How on earth did he end up with Lady Adela's cane and use it as a weapon?" My mind was racing with unanswered questions.

"I have no idea, darling. He's been acting strange the past few days, Gemma. Perhaps the strain of the queen's visit and the upcoming broadcasts were too much for him. He could have been up taking a late-night walk when Elizabeth ran into him. You know how caustic she could be. Everyone does have their limits, perhaps he snapped."

"I just don't see him as a murderer though, Kyle. It was a stretch thinking of him sabotaging the Christmas tree and taking the heirloom ornaments."

"We'll know about that soon, Chief Inspector Marquot and Olivia were going to search his room. If the ornaments are there, it will not be good for him."

"Where is Reggie now, Kyle? I assume when the coroner and his team arrive, they'll take him to Maidenford for processing?"

"They're holding him in a small, resting area near the storage rooms. It's used by the staff to catch a quick forty winks if needed. He'll be taken away as soon as the roads are cleared."

"What about Patch?"

Kyle looked at me and smiled. "I suppose we'll have a little dog here for the holidays. He likes Chef Karl's kitchen and seems to have made many friends there. I'm sure they won't mind him staying here."

"The poor little pooch. He's going to be lost without his master."

With thoughts of Patch, I laid my head down on Kyle's chest and finally drifted off to sleep. The winds were calm now, waiting and watching for the light of morn.

After a few hours of sleep, I woke up and slipped out of Kyle's arms, careful not to wake him. I dressed and made my way downstairs. The dining room and conservatory were cut off from entry by crime scene tape so that the coroner and his team could document the details in the pool room. Olivia greeted me in the hallway, handing me a cup of coffee.

"Good morning, Gemma. You should have slept in a bit longer. There won't be much going on this morning with the investigative work."

"Thanks for the coffee, I need it. I came down to see Bridges actually and figure out how we would serve breakfast—"

"No need for that, we, the RPS members I should say, have taken care of that. The queen and Prince Thaddeus have been informed of what has happened. They were served breakfast in their room a half hour ago. They'll be leaving soon. You know how the RPS likes to usher them out when there's been a… when trouble is around. All your guests have been slipped notes under their doors, requesting that they stay put due to unforeseen circumstances. Breakfast will be brought up to them when they wake up."

"I'm impressed, Olivia. You all seem to have thought of everything. I bet the guests will be wondering what's happened though."

"I'm sure they will. We will have a debrief on this later today, once the coroner team leaves and we can open the rooms again. We want to keep things undisturbed for as long as we can. We know you have many events planned the next few days for the holidays. The forensics team should have Elizabeth's body out of the pool in just a bit. You can go wake your father up to get ready if you'd like."

I turned to go upstairs to get Daddy but stopped in my tracks at the bottom stair. The queen, Prince Thaddeus and Aunt Margaret were walking down. They were leaving for Sandringham to avoid being caught up in the crime scene.

"Gemma, dear, such a tragedy. I'm so sorry your evening ended in disaster. Please give our sympathies to your father. It's such a shock about Reggie. I hope they'll get things straightened out soon. Try and have a wonderful holiday, my dear. I know it's upsetting now, but you have some wonderful events coming up—focus on them."

Aunt Margaret and I walked the royals to the door where their RPS service members waited to escort them to their vehicle. We kissed their cheeks and waved goodbye.

Queen Annelyce turned to me, just before going outside. "By the way dear, look at the papers in the society section. Your peerage ceremony hit all the news outlets today. Have a peek under the tree too, I believe Father Christmas has left you an early Christmas present."

Prince Thaddeus slipped his arm around his wife and helped her down the stairs. They waved as they drove off.

Aunt Margaret and I looked at each other and raced over to the Christmas tree. Sure enough, there was a lovely package underneath wrapped in navy blue paper with gold glitter spirals. I opened the paper carefully; I didn't want to tear any of the royal wrapping paper—I wanted everything carefully preserved. Beneath the paper was a blue, velvet box. I opened it. The intense glimmer from within the box took my breath away. It was a diamond star medallion with the Lancaster family crest in the middle, a bespoke creation, with about thirty carats of diamonds beaming their brilliance at me.

"Look at this, Aunt Margaret, have you ever—"

"No, Gemma, I haven't. It's one of the most beautiful pieces I've ever seen, and so thoughtful coming from the queen. You've made quite an impression, niece." She held the medallion and turned it side to side to catch its sparkling dazzle.

I ran up the stairs to go to Mama's room to have her come accompany us when Daddy went to view Elizabeth's body. My mind was a jumble of emotions—I was tense and troubled with the death of Elizabeth, although I didn't really know her at all. I felt sad for my father and wanted to help him deal with his loss. At the same time, I was thrilled at the thought of my peerage ceremony announcement in the papers today and the brilliant gift from the queen. I shook myself to calm down before I knocked on Mama's door, quietly tiptoeing in.

"Good morning, Gemma. Come give Mama a kiss," she said, putting down her morning paper, patting the bed beside her. I climbed in next to her, suddenly having the urge to cuddle in and sleep as a wave of weariness hit. "What is going on? Why can't we leave our rooms? I'm not in a great hurry to get out of bed after the party last night, but it is a bit strange."

"Mama, it's Elizabeth. She was found dead in the pool last night. She didn't drown. She apparently received a fatal blow to the head with Lady Adela's walking stick."

Mama opened her mouth in shock.

"Gemma, I don't believe it. Did Lady Adela kill her? When did this happen?"

"I don't think it was Lady Adela. Reggie Gerard was found holding the bloodied stick, standing by the pool edge looking down at Elizabeth. He's being taken to the police station in Maidenford. The coroner team is finishing up now. I need you to get dressed, Mama. We have to take Daddy down to see the body."

"Does David know? He must be in so much pain. I must go to him." Mama started to get out of bed but sat back down when I pulled her arm.

"He's resting. He came running down the stairs early this morning after everyone had gone up to bed. Kyle, Elliot, Max, and I were still down by the Christmas tree, having one last nightcap. It was awful, Mama. Daddy is so overwrought. Elizabeth was a drug addict, and a gambler. She's gambled away most of his lottery winnings. He has just ten million dollars left. She blew through ninety-million dollars. He's sleeping in Evan's marquess bedroom. I wanted him close to watch over."

Mama reached in the side drawer by her bed and pulled out a flask. We both took a swig of her secret stash.

"I can't believe this. Does everyone know about this? The queen—"

"The queen and Prince Thaddeus just left. The RPS whisked them away as soon as it was safe. Mama, can you turn to the society page for just a sec before we go to get Daddy? My peerage ceremony announcement is supposed to be released today."

Mama went through the paper to find the society section. Sure enough, front and center was an article on me detailing her majesty's announcement. We read through the article twice, relishing every word. Mama hugged me so tight it hurt.

"Look what the queen gave me, Mama." I pulled the velvet box from behind me where I had placed it on the bed when I sat down, opening it to show her the sparkling medallion.

"Oh, Gemma this is stunning, darling. Look at all those diamonds. It almost blinds you."

"That's the Lancaster family crest in the center. Isn't it beautiful?"

"I've never seen anything like this. You'll have to get it to the vault. It must be worth a fortune."

We kissed one another again before I left her to get dressed. I went into my bedroom, putting the queen's brooch gift into my jewelry box. I would show it to Kyle later and have it placed in the jewelry vault downstairs for safe keeping. Kyle was still sleeping. I peeked into Evan's room to check on Daddy. He was just starting to stir. I went over and sat next to him on the bed, giving him a gentle shake on his arm. His face was tensing up as he woke. I knew today would be very hard for him.

"Hey, Daddy. I just wanted to let you know the coroner is just about finished downstairs. You can see Elizabeth now. Kyle and I will go with you, Mama too."

At that moment, Mama barged into the room, walking directly to Daddy's bedside, "Oh, David, I'm so sorry, darling." She bent down to kiss him.

"Thank you, Jillian. It means so much to me for you to be here. I best get ready. I brought some clothes here last night. They were taping up the room that Elizabeth and I stayed in."

"Of course, Daddy. Get changed, I want to freshen up and get Kyle going. We'll meet you in a few minutes."

Mama stayed in the room with Daddy, taking a seat by the window to read her paper while he dressed.

I went back into my room. I was pleasantly surprised to see that Kyle was up, standing by the window looking out at the sea. Today was overcast, but the snow had stopped. The temperatures were dropping—an arctic freeze was expected the next few days. I went over to him, wrapping my arms around his waist.

"Hey there, you've been up for a while I see."

"I'm glad I did. I was able to say goodbye to the queen and Prince Thaddeus before the RPS whisked them away. I saw Olivia downstairs. The coroner is finishing. We can take Daddy down to see Elizabeth."

"Where are the other guests? Do they know?"

"Everyone is still in their rooms. Breakfast will be delivered when they wake up. The RPS and Olivia put notes under the doors of all the guests. They will be giving a debrief to everyone later. The dining room and conservatory are taped off for now. We should have access this evening if not earlier. They're trying to get everything processed quickly for us."

"I'll have the pool drained and cleaned once the police leave. I don't want any tragic reminders of this incident to make your father uncomfortable."

"I have something to show you. The queen gave it to me this morning. The press announcements are out for my peerage ceremony by the way." I walked over to my jewelry case and pulled out the velvet box.

Kyle whistled when he saw the brooch. "Darling, that's an amazing gift. All those diamonds. It will look stunning on you for your ceremony."

"I can't believe she gave this to me. I've never had anything so extravagant. Except for your mother's engagement ring, which I love!"

"They're in different categories, I think. We'd better put that in the vault. I'll do it after we take your father downstairs."

Kyle showered and dressed as I put on my make-up and a fresh change of clothes. I chose a black, turtleneck sweater dress with leggings and popped it with a bit of color with my red and black plaid boots. Kyle stepped out of the bath wearing a black turtleneck and mahogany wool pants. Today was going to be a long, somber day to face. I was sure we'd be inundated with questions from the guests.

When Daddy was ready, we walked him down to the conservatory. Mama had his arm in a tight grip. I think she was afraid of him collapsing. Chief Inspector Marquot and Olivia waited for us by the dining room. The tape had been removed. We walked through the conservatory and into the pool room. The coroner had Elizabeth's body on a stretcher, ready for Daddy to view.

As we walked over, the coroner removed the body bag cover for us to see her face. Daddy gasped when he saw her. Her skin was very pale from being in the water, but she looked as if she were in a peaceful sleep. We did see the gash on her head from where she had been hit with the walking stick.

"I'm sorry for your loss, Dr. Phillips."

"She was heavily sedated, doctor. She had a consuming drug addiction."

The coroner looked over to Chief Inspector Marquot, who nodded. "We will be doing blood analysis at the morgue. The police have gathered all the pill bottles from your room. The body should be ready for release in the next week, so that you can make any final arrangements. Are you staying here at the hall for long?"

"Yes, he is," I said, jumping in. "Daddy and Elizabeth were planning to stay here through the New Year. You will be able to reach him here if you need any information. Thank you, doctor. We appreciate all you've done."

We led Daddy into the grand hallway to sit by the Christmas tree and have some coffee and rolls Chef Karl had sent up. We watched over our shoulders as Elizabeth's body was wheeled out the front entry. Chief Inspector Marquot and Olivia took a seat and joined us.

"Can we let our guests out of their rooms, Chief Inspector? I know the local Maidenford folks would like to go home now that the roads have been cleared."

"We've had calls made to all the rooms. Your guests will be down here momentarily. I'll do the debrief and then anyone who wants to leave may do so."

Sure enough, our stranded party members appeared and walked down the staircase, looking very confused. Sally, Amy and her press team members came down first, followed by Lucy, Prudence and Timothy. Lady Adela was accompanied by Max and Elliot. Aunt Margaret joined us from Evan's recovery room. As they took their seats around the tree, Chief Inspector Marquot stood and began his debriefing.

"I'm very sorry for any inconvenience you experienced this morning. We had an unfortunate incident in the early hours, right after you retired from your festivities. Dr. Phillip's wife Elizabeth has been killed. She was found in the indoor pool room. Mr. Reginal Gerard was found over her body with a walking stick that had been used to strike her on the head. It was your walking stick, Lady Adela."

The group was flabbergasted by the news. Lucy and Prudence turned ashen, thinking about the holiday broadcasts in the next few days. I'm sure they were thinking of how to spin Reggie's arrest. Lady Adela remained calm, her face showing no emotion

"I assume you've charged Reggie with murder then, Chief Inspector? Will I be able to have my walking stick returned to me? It is a family heirloom."

The chief inspector flinched, somewhat taken aback. I was shocked too at her lack of emotion… and there was that tone of voice again that nagged me.

"Yes of course, Lady Adela, eventually. It will be returned to you as soon as we finish processing the case."

"I understand, Chief Inspector. I don't know how Reggie ended up with my stick. I had it by my side last evening, although I was walking around at times without it. I'm afraid I lost track of it watching the charade performers. My uncle was pouring rather large portions of whiskey for us. I don't usually indulge, but this was quite nice."

"Chief Inspector, are all the rooms released from processing? We do have the broadcasts coming up in the next few days…" Lucy looked very worried. There was no way she could reschedule at this late date.

"The forensic team has completed their work, Ms. Lucy. There should be no problem having your broadcasts here, unless of course Dr. Gemma and Lady Margaret feel differently."

All eyes looked at us.

"No, we'll go on with the broadcasts," I answered.

Aunt Margaret nodded her head in agreement.

The Chief Inspector adjourned our session, after answering a few more questions. Sally's press colleagues left first, wanting to get home. Having asked permission, she went into the pool room to take pictures for the afternoon edition of the *Maidenford Banner* before she left. Lucy and Prudence were standing by the tree clearly in a state of panic. I went up to them to see what the issue was.

"I don't know what we're going to do now that Reggie has been arrested. He and Prudence had their scripts memorized for the broadcast. I don't know who we'll get as a replacement," Lucy said, running her fingers through her black hair.

"I'll do it." We looked over at Amy, who was standing behind us. She had overheard Lucy's statement. "I've been working with Prudence and Reggie these past weeks. I know the story behind the decorating decisions. If you get me the script, I'll learn Reggie's lines, although I'm sure you'll have to make some changes now that he's been arrested." Amy looked at us with eager eyes. She was a young woman seizing her chance. I was very proud of her, although it likely meant I was going to be looking for another assistant soon.

Prudence and Lucy went across the room to confer. It was a risk having a newcomer being brought in so late, but they knew Amy's credentials very well. The fact that she had been involved with Penny and Reggie the past few weeks was invaluable. They walked back over to us.

"Amy, you have the job. We have a lot of work to do in the next few days to get you prepared. We'll have to bring in the stylists and make-up artists too as well as the broadcast coach." Lucy shook her new broadcaster's hand.

Amy looked as if she would explode with joy. "I won't let you down, Lucy, I promise. Gemma, it is okay with you, isn't it?"

"Of course, Amy. You deserve it, you've worked so hard with them the past few weeks. Anything you need, just let me know."

"Gemma, do you mind if we use the crew quarters as a home-base to set up for the broadcast? I can have the crew and Amy's instructors do the training there. Penny's team will want to use the mega closet for make-up and costumes."

"That shouldn't be a problem, Lucy. Steph and Penny were coming here this evening. We can speak to Steph. She'll get the crew quarters ready for you. We are celebrating a little tonight, despite the calamity. My peerage ceremony is in the papers. It's official now."

Prudence, Lucy and Amy clapped for me, causing the others to ask what was going on. I noticed Mama and Daddy had gone back upstairs.

"We have two wonderful announcements, which we'll gladly take given the tragedy that has occurred. Today, Amy has agreed to co-host the broadcast announcements with Prudence on Christmas Day and New Year's Eve to show the decorations here at 'Castlewood Manor' for the holidays. I'm also very pleased to announce that Gemma's peerage ceremony has been released to the papers. It won't be long now, 'Lady Gemma'." Lucy beamed at me as our guests applauded, making me feel very loved.

Kyle and I walked Sally to the door. Amy was going to stay here at Cherrywood, now that she would be doing the broadcast with Prudence.

"I'll do a respectful article on your father and his wife, Gemma. We will be reporting on the murder, of course, but hopefully they'll get things done quietly now that Reggie has been taken in for processing. It's so hard to believe he did it. We'll know soon, I'm sure. Thank you so much for having us here with the queen. Don't tell her, but I snuck in a few pictures for my private use. She's so nice, and well, normal. Thank you too for helping our Amy. She's going to do great. I hope Rosehill treats her right."

"I'll have Elliot draw up a little contract for her to give to Lucy. We'll get it right, I promise."

"All right, I will see you on Christmas Eve for the Maidenford village activities and Penny and Steph's wedding. This is going to be a Christmas like no other." Sally gave us a thumbs up gesture as she left.

Kyle and I walked back and sat next to Lady Adela and Aunt Margaret. There was tension in the air between them.

"Lady Adela, will you be leaving to go to Sandringham?"

"I'd prefer to stay, if it's all right with you and Lady Margaret. It's apparent that a little royal protocol is needed here, especially with all the television people. They need to understand that they are in the home of the soon-to-be marchioness. The activities of the past few days have been rather—"

"Common?" I asked, finishing her statement. "Lady Adela, we had a blizzard. We acted as hosts to people that literally had no place else to go. The roads were closed. You yourself were the last person allowed to travel between Maidenford and here. The murder of Elizabeth was tragic too of course, but we can't change what happened. It will be Christmas in a few days. I want them to be filled with joy, with whoever is in attendance here at Cherrywood."

Lady Adela looked at me, assessing what I had said. She did not look pleased, but knew it would not be prudent of her to discuss this topic any further. Kyle took my hand in his as a show of support.

"Of course. I'm sorry if I upset any of you. I guess the horror of my car accident and the death of that young woman has gotten to me."

Lady Adela excused herself and walked away from us, going over to join Elliot and Max. Aunt Margaret frowned and gave a little shake of her head.

Bridges came up to us. "Luncheon will be served in the dining room in thirty minutes. Should I have a tray prepared for your father and mother, Dr. Gemma? They are in Lord Evan's former bedroom I believe."

"I think that would be best, Bridges. I'll go check on them now, just to see how they're doing. Kyle, will you let the others know?"

"Of course, give them my regards."

I raced up the staircase and headed over to Evan's suite. I was still struggling to handle my dual emotions. I knocked on the suite door and went inside. Daddy and Mama were sitting on the sofa overlooking the sea. Mama's arms were wrapped around him, holding him as he wept. Today was testing us all.

CHAPTER 14
Carols and Crisis

"Come on darling, the guests are waiting. Elliot is serving champagne…" Kyle teased, trying to make me hurry up. He was dressed, handsome as always in his black-tie tuxedo, waiting on the sofa in my bedroom.

I took one last check in the mirror before coming out of the en suite to show him my gown. I was wearing a cherry-red lace creation, mock turtleneck, long sleeves, and fitted to every curve, with a slight flare at the knees. My hair was twisted in a high chignon, with twirled tendrils framing my face. It was holiday elegance with a romantic twist—I was going to make sure Kyle noticed me tonight.

"Okay, close your eyes, here I come." I walked over and stood in front of him, tapping him on the shoulder. He looked at me just as I hoped he would, giving me a smile that I knew meant he would be loving me tonight.

He stood and took my hands, gazing into my eyes. "Do you realize how beautiful you are, Gemma? I'm so proud of you, darling. You always make things cheery for everyone. Let's go enjoy our dinner. Later, my dear, you are all mine," Kyle whispered. He took me in a loving embrace, kissing me deep and sweetly. I loved being held in his arms.

"Knock, knock." It was Mama, looking resplendent in a silver, sequin jumpsuit that sparkled at every turn. "Oh, sorry, darlings. I didn't know if you had gone downstairs yet. Gemma, you look beautiful. Don't wear this on New Year's Eve, daughter, we'll clash. You should see the sparkles on my dress."

Kyle and I shrugged, busted once again by my meddling mama. We each took her hand and started walking down the hall to the staircase.

"Mama, are there any sequins left in Maidenford or London? This jumpsuit is as bright as the New Year's ball dropped at Times Square. No one is going to miss you."

"That's the whole purpose, darling. Being an actress, you have to stand out. Our costumes always have that little extra something to make it remembered. Thigh-high slits to reveal your legs, see through fabrics to show your—well, I don't know why people do that." Mama grimaced and shook her head.

Kyle and I laughed. One could always count on Mama's truisms to entertain.

"How's Daddy?" I asked, as we walked down the staircase.

"He's doing much better. He may join us after dinner. He wanted some alone time this evening. He's grieving, but honestly, I can already see an improvement in his demeanor. Elizabeth was so ill and so abusive. It took a big toll on him."

"I could see it, we all could. I do hope he stays with us for a while. It would be good for him to be at Cherrywood Hall and become involved here locally. Maidenford College would be a wonderful place for him to teach. Aunt Margaret knows the chancellor quite well, I believe."

"She does and so do I. The chancellor is Dr. Evelyn Moore. She's Steph's aunt. She'll be at their wedding ceremony on Christmas Eve."

"That sounds perfect. I'll make sure they're introduced. I don't want him moping around." Mama smiled and waltzed into the study dramatically so that everyone could see the sparkle of her jumpsuit, relishing the claps and whistles that followed.

Kyle and Elliot served up the champagne. Lucy, Prudence, Timothy, and Amy sat in a corner talking all things holiday broadcast. Max and Elliot had Aunt Margaret and Lady Adela in stitches. Mama, Penny and Steph were talking fashion.

Kyle tapped his champagne flute with a cocktail spoon to get everyone's attention. "Ladies and gentlemen, I give you Gemma Lancaster Phillips, the future Marchioness of Kentshire, and the future Lady Williams."

"Hear, hear," our guests chimed in, clapping for me.

"Ruff!" Patch announced, as he ran into the study from the kitchen and jumped on Kyle's knee.

"Patch, there's a good boy," I said, reaching down to pet him. "I think you have a new friend, darling."

"He is rather cute. I'm sure he prefers being in the kitchen though. He has quite the support system down there and all the treats he can eat."

"Ruff!"

"Dinner is served," Bridges announced, scooping up Patch to take him back down to his food haven oasis.

We took our seats at the table. I noticed out of the corner of my eye Olivia sitting in the conservatory, watching us discreetly.

Tonight, Chef Karl had gone all out in my honor, offering starters, including lobster-avocado toasts, caprese salad bites, and stuffed mushrooms. For our entre we were served a standing rib roast, Yorkshire pudding, roasted root veggies and a spinach souffle. The table was quieter than usual tonight. I suspected the stress of the last twenty-four hours had boosted everyone's appetite.

"Is there any word on Reggie?" Max asked. He was fretting for his college friend and still could not believe he had been found with the murder weapon.

"Aunt Sally said he was arraigned this morning and is still being held in Maidenford. There's no word as to when he'll be transferred. The court may wait until after the holidays."

"If the murder was committed here, why would he be transferred?"

"She said that they are looking into other crimes actually. There were some materials found in his room." I could tell Amy was hesitating.

"What kind of materials, darling, do tell." Elliot leaned in over the table in an exaggerated manner.

Max swatted his arm and motioned for him to sit back.

"I'm afraid they found schematics of the palace. With the robbery of the queen's vault, it looks pretty incriminating for him."

Our guests looked up, stunned by this news.

"But how could that happen? Reggie has been here at Cherrywood almost full time the past few weeks," Lucy said, holding her hands out in surprise.

"Reggie had been working on a surprise party the queen was planning for Prince Thaddeus' birthday. She wanted to have his closest friends celebrate with them when they returned from Sandringham. He knew the layout at the palace quite well. He's been arranging the queen's events for some time now," Lady Adela explained, shaking her head. "It's a lesson for us all, not to let strangers roam around in one's home, no matter how much you think you can trust them." She looked at me as she cut into her slice of roast.

"Lady Adela, it's a bit late for us here at Cherrywood Hall now, with the *Castlewood Manor* production. Why, thanks to the show we've been able to start major ventures here at the estate. The local economy is blossoming, especially after the *Telly Tiaras* sweep. Evan, Kyle and I are thrilled for them to be here."

"You're going to be a marchioness, Gemma, as I've told you many times. You have a position now to assume. I apologize, if I'm hurting anyone's feelings," she looked at the Rosehill Production guests, Mama, and Aunt Margaret. "I think enough just may be enough. You and Kyle need your space for the estate work and for your future children. I'm just thinking of you."

Mama was breathing rapidly. I could tell she was just about to go off. Steph was holding her arm, just in case she decided to bop lady Adela with the gravy ladle.

"I think we should discuss this privately, Lady Adela. At this time, we're very happy with the way things are going, especially with the plans of the feature film and whatever follow-on efforts there are. I've upped security here at the hall, everyone will be safe."

"I suppose you shouldn't mention that to Gemma's father, darling." Lady Adela looked Kyle in the eye and took a bite of roast, chewing very deliberately.

Max and Elliot's eyes grew wide, enjoying this war of words.

"Gemma, why don't we retire to the grand hallway for our dessert this evening. I think we need some glitzy fun. Can you fetch the medallion the queen gifted you? I'm sure our guests would love to see it," Aunt Margaret said, standing as a sign dinner, and this discussion, were over. She stared at Lady Adela with steely eyes. She didn't appreciate the comments and the fact that she was being left out of the discussion. With Evan in a coma, she was the Dowager Marchioness of Kentshire and had the authority here.

Our guests went into the grand hallway for some after dinner fun, trying to shrug off the veil of disdain Lady Adela had thrown on our dinner party. I went upstairs to get my gift from the queen and check in on Daddy to see how he was doing. I had to admit Lady Adela's snobby attitude and her swipes at the *Castlewood Manor* cast and crew were starting to get to me. She seemed so concerned that I wasn't acting in a marchioness manner, whatever that was. I had always tried to conduct myself with manners and respect for others—to me that was the trademark of a real lady or gentleman. I brushed it off as I knocked on the bedroom door, stepping inside.

"Hey Daddy, I just wanted to see how you were doing. I can have a dinner tray brought up for you. Karl made a delicious rib roast."

"Thank you, Gemma, I'm fine. I had quite a few sandwiches and tarts at teatime. Your mama forced them on me." He smiled.

"She just cares for you, Daddy, like we all do. Would you like to come downstairs? I'm getting ready to show everyone the medallion the queen gifted me. There's some cake, and more of Evan's whiskey," I teased.

"I don't have my tuxedo on…"

"Just grab a jacket, Daddy, you'll be fine. People will love it if you join us."

Daddy picked up his navy wool blazer and followed me into my bedroom. I retrieved the velvet box from my jewelry case, which was unlocked. "Hmm, I thought I locked it, guess not," I shrugged, leaving the room with Daddy arm-in-arm to join the others downstairs.

"Ta-dah, look everyone, Daddy's come to join us," I said, as we walked down the staircase.

"Get the man a drink, Elliot, please," Kyle said, walking over to shake Daddy's hand.

"I'm glad you joined us, David. We've missed you."

Daddy nodded at Kyle and smiled, thankful for the kind words.

"Drum roll everyone," Aunt Margaret said, tapping the table repeatedly, capturing everyone's attention. "Gemma dear, unveil your gift from the queen."

Proudly, I stood in front of the Christmas tree and opened my box, expecting to hear cries of amazement at the beautiful, diamond brooch. Instead, everyone was looking at me questioningly. I laughed, thinking this was some kind of pre-planned prank they had decided upon in my absence.

"What is it?" I looked first at my guests, and then at the blue box, turning it around to look inside. It was empty. "Where is it?!" I screamed, a full-blown panic attack gripping me.

Kyle ran over to me as I started to weave back and forth. He looked around where I had been standing to see if I had dropped it, and then led me over to a chair to sit down. "Are you sure you didn't place it somewhere else, darling? In the en suite, in another drawer?"

"No. It was in this box in my jewelry case. I haven't had it anywhere." I was starting to shake. "This was my gift from the queen. Do you know how valuable it was? Oh, Kyle, what am I going to do?" I put my face down in my arm on the chair and started to sob in total despair.

"It has to be here, no one has been at the estate except us. Everyone, please, help us look for it." Kyle led Max, Elliot, Daddy, Lucy, and Amy upstairs to scour the floors. Prudence and Timothy looked around the downstairs floors in the unlikely event it was down here. Aunt Margaret and Mama stayed by my side, trying to calm me down. Lady Adela stayed seated across from me sipping her brandy.

"It will be found, daughter. Please, Gemma, don't cry."

"I should have put it in the jewelry vault this afternoon. Kyle wanted to but I didn't let him. I kept wanting to sneak peeks at it. He was going to take it to the vault this evening." I sank my head back down into my arm. Olivia came up from behind me and put her hand on my back. She had been behind the Christmas tree, watching this drama unfold.

"We'll find it, Gemma. Something very odd is happening here. I've phoned my uncle. He will be back tomorrow to finalize things with the Maidenford police. I've given him a heads-up on the missing brooch. If anyone tries to sell it on the black-market, it has now been marked as a possible stolen good. No one will touch it."

Aunt Margaret mouthed, "Thank you."

"Don't most jewel thief's take items like that and dismantle them, selling off the individual stones? I've heard that is done quite frequently with so called hot items," Lady Adela asked.

"In some cases that is done, Lady Adela, if the provenance is well known. In this case, it would be a very stupid thing to do."

I raised my head off my arm, listening to Olivia. I wiped my face and nose with a hanky Mama had given me. "Why would it be stupid, Olivia? It sounds as if it would be a way to get rid of a high-profile item," I said, gulping from my anxious state.

"The queen's gems are all engraved, Gemma. Every single piece of jewelry she has at the palace is marked, including those in the recent theft. If the schematics found in Reggie's room indicate he did in fact steal those jewels, he was very ill informed."

"Couldn't the criminals file off the engraving?" Mama asked.

"Not with the hi-tech laser engraving and scribing methods used today, Ms. Jillian. The marks can only be seen at ten times magnification. Anyone trying to remove the mark would risk destroying the gem."

"See there, darling. They'll find it if someone tries to sell it. But don't give up hope, yet, it's probably here at Cherrywood Hall." Mama brushed my hair from my face and gave me a smile.

Lady Adela stood, her face a bit ashen. "I'm sure it will be found too, Gemma. Did anyone think to look under the Christmas tree? You were holding the velvet box behind you. It may have slipped out." She went over and began moving the branches, looking to see if she could spot anything.

"It couldn't have fallen out, Lady Adela. I had the box firmly gripped in my hand the whole time. Someone took it from the jewel case." I bit my lip, trying not to cry.

Kyle and his search group came down the stairs, with Prudence and Timothy joining them in the hallway, their downstairs search completed with no results. Kyle puffed and shrugged, there was no trace of the medallion from his group either. Elliot poured drinks for everyone from the bar in the study.

"Sorry, darling, no luck. I'll call Chief Inspector Marquot and let him know what's happened. Scotland Yard will want to know, since it involves jewels from the queen."

"He already knows. Olivia has called him. They've released an all-points bulletin."

Kyle cocked his head to the side, surprised. "Well done, Olivia. Good work."

Olivia smiled and gave a quick nod.

"Ooh--ooh, I found something..." Lady Adela said, in a singsong tone. She pulled back a branch and grasped something with her hand. She came over to me, a grin on her face. "Is this what you're looking for, Gemma?"

She opened her hand, the diamond medallion shining brilliantly. Gasps came from everyone. I grabbed the medallion and looked at it, overwhelmed with relief.

"I can't believe it. Oh my gosh." I stood and gave Lady Adela an enthusiastic hug.

I started dancing a jig in the hallway, thrilled my royal treasure had been found. Kyle, grabbed me and swung me around, overjoyed to see me smiling again. Our guests swarmed around me to see the treasured piece, oohing and aahing as I tilted it in different directions for them to see its brilliance.

"Sorry, but I am not letting this out of my hands until we take it to the vault and put it in a case." I held the medallion close to my heart.

After everyone had seen the queen's gift, Kyle and I walked down to the vault to put the royal jewels safely away. Kyle's handprint was scanned and the door electronically unlocked. As we walked in, the vault lights went on with the door closing behind us after we entered. We placed the medallion in the brooch case with the other Lancaster heirlooms. I grabbed Kyle around the neck and held him close, the anxiety of the last hour melting away. Kyle held me gently and rocked me back and forth.

"I felt so awful. If it had been lost—"

"Hey, it's jewelry, darling. The important thing is that it's been found, and no one was hurt. It does seem a bit strange that Lady Adela spotted it near the tree. I looked there when I came up to you. I didn't see it. I must have overlooked it in the excitement."

"Thank goodness it was found, that's all I have to say. Let's go upstairs. I think it's time you made me a very large gin and St. Germain martini, Sir Kyle."

Kyle bowed as he led me out of the vault, making sure the door closed securely behind him. "At your service, soon to be Lady Gemma." He laughed.

We walked up the stairs and into the grand hallway. A celebration party had commenced, with everyone laughing and dancing. Lady Adela was the heroine of the evening as people went up to her to congratulate her for finding the lost medallion. Olivia had resumed her observation position from a seat in the back of the Christmas tree. I noticed that she was texting furiously. I assumed she was letting her uncle know the medallion had been found.

Kyle left me to dance with Daddy and Max so that he could mix my favorite martini. My tears had dried and I was enjoying the revelry immensely. The stress of the past forty-eight hours was just about all I could handle with everything that had happened. I heard the front entry bell ring and saw Bridges go to the door. Aunt Margaret came up to my side, curious to see who was calling at this hour.

We shrieked when we saw who it was and ran to the door. It was Simone, Evan's girlfriend. She smiled when she saw us and gave us hugs. Her arrival was such a surprise, but perfect for Christmas.

"Mummy?" We started when we heard a small boy's voice. He had been standing behind Simone, shyly hiding in the folds of her coat.

I was shocked. Simone didn't have any children. In fact, it wasn't clear she wanted any. She was ten years older than Evan and had expressed concerns over having children many times, much to Aunt Margaret's angst.

Simone squatted down so that her face could be at eye level with the boy and spoke softly to him.

"These are your new family, Ajani. Come, let's shake their hand and make Papa proud."

Aunt Margaret and I stood in silence, not knowing what to say or do. Kyle and Mama came and stood by our side. Simone held the boy up in her arms. He was only three or four years old at most, but looked at us with a sweet smile, hiding his face back and forth on Simone's shoulder.

"This is Ajani, son of the gamekeeper who was killed on Evan's ranch. I should have told you sooner, Lady Margaret. After the attack, Evan and I secretly married—we never wanted to be apart again. We learned of the gamekeeper's orphaned son and adopted him. When Evan was kidnapped, I kept everything private because I didn't want anyone to know our news and make it worse for him." Tears welled in Simone's eyes. Her lips trembled.

"All this time, you never said anything to me in London when you visited Evan." Aunt Margaret's eyes searched Simone's face looking for answers.

"I'm so sorry, Lady Margaret. With Evan's condition looking so bleak, I just didn't know how to break the news, or if I even should if he turned for the worse. Please forgive me."

Aunt Margaret stood straight, breathing deep and swallowing hard, her eyes filling with tears. "I think we should introduce ourselves. Hello, Ajani," Aunt Margaret whispered, taking the little boy's hand in her own. "I'm your Papa's mummy, your Grandmama." She hugged them both, sobbing lightly.

Our hearts were bursting, looking at them. Mama, Kyle and I held each other in a tight embrace, our guests behind us watching the scene in awe.

"Grandmama, you're crushing me," Ajani said, laughing with a big smile.

"So I am, I'm so sorry. Come meet your Cousin Gemma and Aunt Jillian."

Simone brought him over first to Mama, where he politely shook her hand. I smiled at him when it was my turn.

"Papa says you like to eat. A lot," he said in an exaggerated little boy's voice, spreading his arms wide.

The room broke into giggles, my secret was out. I laughed myself. I could just hear Evan's voice telling him stories about me. My heart was soaring and breaking all at the same time.

Kyle stood next to me and took Ajani's hand. "Hello there, old man. I'm your Papa's friend, Kyle."

"I'm not old."

"You're right. Hello, young man."

"You saved Papa's life."

Kyle smiled, his chin wavering with emotion. "We had a lot of help. Your Mummy is quite a warrior too." Kyle winked at Simone.

"Papa said you are a knight. Do you have armor and a horse?"

"I do have a horse, and so does your Papa. Tell you what, I'll take you to the barn when it's daylight and show him to you. We can take a ride if you'd like."

Ajani grinned and nodded his head yes.

We walked back through the hallway so that Simone could greet our guests and introduce her and Evan's son to them. For a young boy, he was so polite, taking everyone's hand and shaking it.

Olivia seemed particularly excited to meet Simone and Ajani. "Ms. Alexander, I'm such a fan of yours. You are a ground breaker for women in martial arts," she gushed. Olivia took Ajani's hand. "You, young man, remind me of my little niece, Annie. Sometime, when I'm not working, I'll bring her over to play with you, if you'd like." Ajani smiled and nodded his head, won over by Olivia's kind words.

Once the guests were introduced, we led him and Simone over to the Christmas tree to see the lights.

"That's a big tree," Ajani said, with all the wonder of a child at Christmas.

"Yes, it is," Aunt Margaret said, bending down to talk to him in a sweet Grandmama voice. "In a few days, Father Christmas will be here. We're having all kinds of parties too. There will be children from the village here to play with. It's always so much fun."

Ajani smiled, and touched Aunt Margaret's cheek. "You're pretty. Papa told me how pretty you are. You're nice too. Except when he does something you don't like. He said you say to him, 'Evan'…" the little boy tilted his voice, enchanting us.

We all could imagine Evan talking with him. It was as if he were here. Aunt Margaret closed her eyes, and smiled, hearing the words of her son warmed her heart.

"How about we go see Papa," Simone whispered, tears trickling down her face.

"I think that's a splendid idea, dear. Ajani, will you take Grandmama's hand? I think it will do your Papa a world of good to hear your voice."

We watched as Simone and Aunt Margaret walked back to Evan's room, Ajani between them, holding each woman's hand. It was one of the most heartwarming scenes I had ever experienced. The news of Evan and Simone's secret nuptials, the adoption of the orphaned boy, all pulled at the strings of our hearts. There was not a dry eye in the house.

We turned and hugged each other after they went into Evan's room. Daddy, Mama, Prudence, Lucy, Timothy, Amy---all of us touched by the spirit of the season. Elliot brought Max over to us. He was crying like a baby. He was so overcome. We hugged him close, loving our sweet friend even more.

"Darlings, I think it's time for some champagne," Elliot announced, sending a cork flying into the air.

We laughed, standing in front of him as he poured the bubbling liquid, Christmas carols ringing through the hallway. I didn't notice Lady Adela leaving us, slinking up the staircase to her room. If I had, I would have seen a dark scowl covering her face.

CHAPTER 15

Christmas Eve I Dos and Don'ts

"Come on, Ajani, let's go down to the barn to make sure the sleigh is all ready for our guests. Everyone wants to ride in Father Christmas' sleigh," Kyle said, grinning. He stood by the front entry as Ajani ran to him, bundled up to keep warm in the arctic air that had gripped the region.

"Coming, Cousin Kyle," Ajani yelled. "Mummy has me wrapped up like a Christmas present."

"Ruff!" Patch ran up behind his new-found friend. He was wearing a doggie, puffer jacket and booties to protect the tiny pup from the cold. Ajani and Patch had taken to each other immediately upon meeting and had become inseparable.

Kyle swept the little boy and dog into his arms to head off to the barn. He had a four-wheel drive Gator waiting outside for their trip, complete with blankets to put over their laps for the drive and thermoses of hot chocolate to drink. Kyle hooked Ajani's seatbelt and placed Patch on his lap. The engine sputtered in the cold as they drove off for the last-minute inspection at the barn.

"Okay, quick, let's do the last of the wrapping," I squealed, as Simone and I ran upstairs to my office to get our Christmas gifts ready for the evening's festivities.

The grand hallway was bustling as the staff added extra seats and tables for the Maidenford villagers that were coming today for the traditional lunch and Father Christmas gifting, ending with sleigh rides and sledding. The majority of people attending were villagers who worked on the estate, but also included the staff and their families that were tied to the *Castlewood Manor* production.

Tonight, was also the nuptial event for Penny and Steph. Prudence and Amy were making sure the conservatory was adorned with extra flowers and candles for the ceremony. Chef Karl and his staff were in full throttle preparing the Christmas Eve feast for us to enjoy.

I opened my locked office door. We didn't want any prying eyes sneaking a peek. We closed the door behind us and went to work. Aunt Margaret, Mama and I had gone to Maidenford yesterday to pick up Christmas gifts for Ajani to open tonight. Simone had given us a list of items she wanted, and we had supplemented the list with picks of our own. We had a ton of fun looking at the toys and picking gifts out for our new grandson, cousin, nephew in the family. The little boy had charmed our hearts and Aunt Margaret beamed as a new grandmama, showing pictures of him to anyone who asked.

Our shopping bounty was stacked on my conference table, waiting to be adorned with fancy Christmas finery. We started with the toys first, adding colorful streamers and balloons to the gift bags and wrappings. Father Christmas was bringing a push riding horse, puzzles, story books and a football to our little boy. I couldn't wait to see his eyes open wide in delight.

"Simone, I'm so glad you and Ajani are with us for Christmas. It means so much for you to be here. Aunt Margaret has simply blossomed since your arrival. I haven't seen her this happy in so long. She adores her new grandson, and her new daughter." I placed my hand on hers. Her presence gave us all renewed hope for Evan.

"I'm sorry I didn't tell you all sooner that we would be coming. I was rushing around in South Africa to get everything ready for our departure. I know Evan would want Ajani and me here with him at Christmas. I pray that my man can come back to us. I don't know what I'd do without him, Gemma."

"Simone, do you think Evan would have any problem with my becoming the Marchioness of Kentshire? I feel so bad that he never knew about the history and what the research revealed for my American ancestor, John."

Simone came to my side and hugged me. "Look at me. This would be what Evan would want with all his heart. You know how much he struggled with the weight of serving his peerage and title yet wanting to be with me on the ranch in South Africa. He would support you one hundred percent. This is your destiny, Gemma."

"It means a great deal to hear you say that, Simone. Hurting Evan's feelings has been my biggest fear. I love him and Aunt Margaret so much. I would never let anything cause a rift in our family."

"Lady Margaret wants her son to be happy, first and foremost. She knew how torn he was. My only regret is that he's not able to celebrate it with you. He looks as if he's just taking a nap. I expect to see him wake up at any minute."

"I know, I think the same thing every time I go down to his room. I miss him so much."

We finished wrapping the gifts, humming Christmas tunes to lift our spirits. I had all my personal gifts wrapped and hidden in my bedroom, including the Lancaster signet ring I was presenting to Kyle tonight. The jeweler in Maidenford had it cleaned and gleaming. It was his opinion that it was indeed from the late seventeen-hundreds, making it very likely it once belonged to my British-turned-American forefather, John Lancaster. It was my wish that Kyle would use this as his wedding ring someday soon.

We went downstairs to the grand hallway to wait for Kyle and Ajani to return. It would soon be time to get dressed for the Maidenford luncheon and gift exchange. Rosehill Productions had one of their contract actors here in full, Father Christmas regalia to hand out presents and mingle with the children. The gilded chair with red velvet tufting was placed next to the Christmas tree, waiting for the special arrival of the beloved man of the day.

The studio also was catering the luncheon today to give Chef Karl and his team plenty of time to prepare our Christmas Eve dinner. The caterers had several, large round tables put in the dining room to accommodate everyone and were setting up the buffet line with culinary precision. No one would be leaving hungry today.

We found Lady Adela and Aunt Margaret sitting by the tree, having a glass of sherry before the festivities began.

"Did you get all the gifts wrapped for our little angel?" Aunt Margaret asked, her eyes shining.

"Yes, we did. Everything's ready for the gift exchange tonight. Santa, I mean Father Christmas, will have loads of gifts to hand out." I cringed. I was still getting used to British terms.

Lady Adela looked at me, her eyebrows arched. "Whatever happened to a good old 'family only' Christmas Eve? Today we have a village fete, a wedding… it's really a lot to take on, Gemma."

"Lady Adela, many of these people attending today have become almost like family members to us. I'm sorry if it's overwhelming for you, but we're celebrating with our friends and family in a beautiful setting. Please, go upstairs if you feel you cannot handle the festivities. Don't ruin it for the others." I had had enough of her cruel-toned admonishments.

Lady Adela stared at me in silence. I could tell she was furious, but she knew I was too. The tension eased when Kyle and Ajani came in through the front entry, cold but with huge smiles on their faces. Patch followed close behind, wagging his tail.

"Mummy, I saw Father Christmas' sleigh. We're going to take a ride later. Will you and Grandmama come with me?"

Simone and Aunt Margaret bobbed their heads yes. "Of course, we will, Ajani. Come give Grandmama a kiss. We need to all get upstairs to change for the luncheon and be ready for you know who…"

We took our cue from Aunt Margaret and disbanded. Lady Adela waved us off and poured herself another sherry. I hadn't seen Mama, Daddy, Elliot, or Max yet this morning. As Kyle and I walked to my bedroom we heard howling laughter coming from Evan's former bedroom— they were all in there with an open bottle of champagne, of course.

"Gemma, Kyle, come join us, darlings," Mama said, raising her flute to us.

"Mama, it's time to get dressed for the luncheon. The guests will be here soon. You need to be on your best behavior now. Father Christmas is coming."

"Gemma, don't be such a marchioness, darling. Come have one drink." Mama pouted.

Kyle and I rolled our eyes and went into the room for a glass of bubbly. I knew it would be the only way to satisfy Mama. Elliot topped off our flutes and handed them to us.

"Here's to a great day, great friends, and a wonderful family," I toasted, holding my glass up.

"Hear, hear."

We drank up quickly to entice the others to do so too. Daddy saw me beginning to panic and rallied the others.

"Come on now, Gemma's right. We must get ready for the day's festivities."

I gave Daddy a grateful look and mouthed "Thank you" as the others departed to go change.

Today, I was wearing a lovely, turquoise, velvet jacket belted at the waist over a hot-pink and aqua, plaid, maxi skirt. It was a change from the traditional colors of Christmas, but I was excited to wear the bright hues. They reflected my happiness this day and I couldn't wait to celebrate. Kyle was wearing dapper, green and blue, tartan pants and jacket with a navy turtleneck, looking very festive.

We walked down to the grand hallway to be ready to greet the guests as they arrived. Father Christmas was hiding in the conservatory, waiting for his cue to come out and surprise the children. Aunt Margaret, Simone and Ajani were wearing matching red jumpers and red and white tartan skirts, with matching knickers for Ajani. She had insisted on buying them when we were shopping in Maidenford. She wanted everyone to know her new family members.

Cars started pulling up the drive signaling it was time to start the holiday celebrations. Kyle, Aunt Margaret, Simone, Ajani, and I made up the receiving line, giving Christmas hugs and handshakes to our guests as they walked into the hallway gleaming with Christmas lights. Songs of the season played in the background and were soon drowned out a bit as laughter and conversation filled the air. Waiters were serving Christmas wassail, eggnog, and spirits for those who were so inclined.

Mama, Daddy, Elliot, and Max were mingling with the villagers. Vicar Hawthorne never left Mama's side. He was her most devoted fan. Amy, Prudence, Timothy, and Lucy were taking questions about the rumored feature film, dodging direct answers, but dangling teasers, telling the fans to be sure and watch the broadcast tomorrow evening.

The time came for the big moment, Father Christmas' arrival. The children waited around the tree laughing and clapping their hands together.

"Ho, ho, ho," Father Christmas said, walking into the hallway with a huge bag of presents thrown over his shoulder. The children roared as he came into the hallway, rushing over to greet him.

Kyle hugged me tight and whispered, "Our children will be there one day, darling. I can't wait."

I kissed Kyle's cheek and smiled. "I think little Ajani has captivated you, I know he has me. It was so much fun shopping in the toy store the other day. I do hope we have girls—there's so many pretty things."

Kyle laughed. "Lord help me if I have a household of Lancaster women, I'll be doomed."

"You would love it and you know it," I said, punching his arm.

Kyle hugged me closer to him.

Father Christmas made his way over to the gilded throne to hand out the presents. The children sat down by the tree, anxious for their names to be called. Ajani was beaming, smiling and clapping with the other children.

Father Christmas sat down on his chair and reached into the present bag. "CRACK, THUD, OOF". The sound of the chair leg breaking and Father Christmas hitting the floor like a ton of rocks jolted us out of our holiday daze as the adults ran over to help the beloved idol back up to his feet.

"Ho, ho, ho—Father Christmas needs to lay off the Christmas cookies," the acting Father Christmas said, trying to brush himself off.

The entire room roared, relieved to see that he was not seriously harmed. Kyle brought over a replacement chair, sitting in it first to show the red-suited man he would be safe in this one.

"Nice save, Sir Kyle. What in the world could have happened? That chair is solid. There is no way he could have caused it to collapse," I said, as Kyle rejoined me.

"He didn't cause it to break. The chair leg was sawed through. This was deliberate, Gemma." Kyle's eyes scanned the room looking for anyone who might be guilty of a prank gone wrong.

"Sawed through?" I whispered, stunned. Kyle nodded.

"We'll look at it after the guests leave for the barn and sleigh rides. Someone deserves some very, large, lumps of coal in their stocking."

I couldn't believe anyone would do such an unbelievably, cruel act. Suppose there had been a child sitting on his lap—I was growing furious about the Christmas sabotage we had experienced. First the Christmas tree tethers and now this. We had to find this elf gone wrong before someone gets killed.

The children were elated with their gifts. Rosehill Productions had gone all out splurging on the hottest selling toys their marketing group had identified, shopping early so that the kiddies would not be disappointed. The adults were smiling too, everyone had received a crystal globe ornament with *Castlewood Manor* aka Cherrywood Hall engraved on it— much like the one given to the queen, although the *commoner* version was a bit smaller. Pictures of the Cherrywood Hall heirloom ornaments were featured in a tiny booklet handed out with the crystal globes. I had to admit, Reggie had done a marvelous job putting the booklet together.

After lunch, coats were donned, and everyone headed down to the barn for sleigh rides and sledding. There were two, horse-drawn sleighs, and a hill next to the barn had been groomed for icy rides on sleds and snow saucers, complete with a tow rope to pull up the brave riders from the bottom of the hill. Aunt Margaret and Simone took Ajani down to experience his first sleigh ride, the little tyke squealing with delight.

Mama, Daddy, Max and Elliot sat down on the sofa next to the Christmas tree to enjoy an after-lunch cocktail. Kyle and I made our way to the gilded chair, now laying dethroned on its side.

"What in the world happened with the chair, Kyle? I thought I'd die when Father Christmas crashed on the floor," Mama said, shaking her head.

"I was afraid Father Christmas may have drunk a bit too much nog." Elliot grimaced.

Kyle and I bent down to examine the damaged chair. Sure enough, you could see the clean cut of a saw on the leg and a little of the shavings on the floor. We shook our heads in disgust, not only for the prank that could have hurt someone, but also for the damage to a lovely heirloom.

"The chair leg has been sawed through, deliberately."

"Who would want to sabotage Father Christmas giving gifts to the children?" Daddy asked. "There is someone seriously ill doing this. First the Christmas tree crashes down on Margaret and now this."

We shut down the discussion as our village guests trooped back in, anxious for cups of hot cocoa and tea after being out in the cold. The caterers put out trays of cookies and tarts for the guests to enjoy with their drinks. Gift bags were set out for everyone, complete with bottles of our Cherrywood wine and sherry, and tins of cookies and cakes. By three o'clock the last of our visitors had waved goodbye, leaving us to prepare for the next event, Penny and Steph's wedding.

I went upstairs to my room to rest and before changing into my evening dress. I was going to be Penny's attendant for the ceremony. She had created a special design for me to wear tonight; a taffeta maxi skirt in red and ivory, gingham-pattern topped with a velvet, long-sleeved shirt trimmed in white, faux fur. It was very holiday chic and would go perfectly with her red wedding dress that her wardrobe staff had made for her. The brides had requested that everyone wear something red tonight in honor of their wedding. Kyle had selected a red bow tie and cummerbund to wear with his tuxedo to complement my outfit and make the brides happy.

I placed a washcloth on my head that had been soaked in cool water. My head hurt, spinning from the thought of someone intentionally destroying the gilded chair, as I lay down on the sofa in front of the fireplace. I pulled a comforter over me as I stared at the flames, trying to relax.

Out of the corner of my eye, I saw some wood scrapings on the floor from my jewelry case next to the fireplace. I sat up and went over to the case. It had been jarred open. I hadn't noticed the scrapes yesterday. I was so relieved that the medallion had been found, I thought nothing about checking the jewelry case last night. I sometimes locked it and sometimes not. I trusted everyone at Cherrywood and had never experienced any thefts.

I thought back to when I retrieved the velvet box from the case. The door had been unlocked. That should have been a red flag for me. I had specifically locked the case when I put the queen's medallion in there. Someone had been in my room and taken the medallion. But why would the thief drop it under the Christmas tree after taking such drastic measures to steal it from my case? Even more bothersome, who was this thief? It was hard to imagine another of our guests had evil intentions.

I laid back down on the couch, my head reeling from this latest find and the many questions. The door to my room opened slowly, it was Kyle, tiptoeing in to be quiet.

"It's okay, I'm not asleep."

He came over and sat down next to me, putting my legs on his lap.

"What's wrong, darling? Don't let the chair bother you. Prudence has a craftsman in Maidenford that does outstanding restoration work. She's already put in a call to him. He's picking up the chair after the holidays to fix it."

"I think we'll need him to fix my jewelry case too. Take a look."

I pointed over to the shavings on the rug. Kyle lifted my legs and bent over the chest to inspect the damage.

"It's been broken into, no doubt. Didn't you notice the door being unlocked when you retrieved the box?"

"No, I sometimes lock it, but most of the time don't. I guess in my rush to get it last night I just let it go. I was excited Daddy was coming down to join us."

Kyle knelt down by the couch and put his hand under my chin. "Darling, we'll catch whoever is doing this. Obviously, someone is carrying a big grudge. A mentally unstable one at that."

"Kyle, you don't think Lady Kimberly is on the loose, do you? She was being transferred to another care facility." Lady Kimberly was the jilted, royal bride that had tried to kill me when we were in Malibu a few months ago. She had a deep hatred for me and the Lancaster family, unfairly blaming us for her family's decline.

"I'll have Olivia run a check. Surely, she hasn't escaped, it would have been in the papers."

"Maybe the queen has banned coverage. She was engaged to her grandson."

"We can ask Sally tonight at the wedding. She'll know if any royal bans have been placed. Now, come on, I think a nice bubble bath is just what you need. I'll rub your back…" Kyle led me into the en suite, where we remained the rest of the afternoon.

Kyle and I made our way down to the conservatory at five o'clock, just in time to see the brides arrive, both looking resplendent in red. Penny's bespoke creation was a fitted, mermaid-style dress in stunning, red satin. She topped off her look with a red, feather fascinator that looked gorgeous against her black bob. Steph was also wearing a custom, red tuxedo, fitted to her curves, with bright, red stilettos. They made a beautiful couple, laughing and giggling as they greeted their guests who had gathered in the conservatory

Vicar Hawthorne motioned for everyone to take their seats promptly at six o'clock. A harpist played the bridal song as I walked down the aisle first, with Penny following close behind. Kyle was Steph's best man. They had been close friends since university. I smiled when I saw him, thinking of our own ceremony to be held one day soon.

The conservatory looked magical with red and white twinkling lights and the candles and flowers Amy and Prudence had brought in for the special occasion. The brides joined hands and Vicar Hawthorne began the ceremony. I looked over at our guests, many had tears in their eyes as they watched. Mama blew me a kiss. Daddy was seated next to Steph's aunt, Dr. Evelyn Moore, the two exchanging quick glances at one another throughout the ceremony. Aunt Margaret and Simone smiled, with a drowsy Ajani held in her lap.

Lady Adela sat in the back alone. Staring at the wedding with a vacant look on her face. This was the first I'd seen of her after our encounter this morning. She had not come down to meet the villagers for our luncheon gala. I was glad actually; her ill humor would have put a damper on the afternoon. I couldn't figure out why her normally nice demeanor had changed so drastically—or was the real Lady Adela emerging? I'd had just about as much as I could take of her in this mode, that I knew.

The ceremony was brief but filled with love and joy. As the service ended, the brides kissed as the guests stood and clapped for the happy couple. We went into the dining room where champagne and hor d'oeuvres were served, followed by a scrumptious Christmas Eve feast of leg of lamb, salmon mousse, sourdough stuffing, and a variety of vegetables and gravy sauces to please every appetite. Dessert was a five-tier wedding cake, each tier a different flavor, sliced by the brides and handed to the guests.

After the cake was consumed, the brides made their exit, off to a beautiful honeymoon in the Bahamas for the next week—they were escaping the cold and wanted nothing to do, but walk the pink sands of the beach. We waved them goodbye with happy hearts.

"Okay everyone, time to gather in the grand hallway by the tree to exchange gifts," I called, pointing for everyone to go into the next room. The group was in high spirits now, having eaten their fill of savory and sweet, topped off with more champagne.

There were lots of oohs and aahs as the guests entered. I had Bridges and the staff light candles around the room, their flickering flames giving the room a holiday magic glow for our gift exchange. I had bought sterling wine glasses for Elliot and Max to add to their collection. Amy adored her ruby, sapphire and emerald earrings. Mama and Aunt Margaret loved the sapphire and diamond brooches I bought in the London shop. I was surprised to see Lady Adela's mouth drop when she saw their gifts. Surely, she could not fault diamonds and sapphires.

Ajani kept us all entertained riding his push horse up and down the grand hallway, delighted with his gift from Father Christmas. As the others opened their gifts, Kyle and I waited 'til the end to do our exchange, laughing at the gag gifts that included whoopee cushions and whiskey of dubious origins, making Lady Adela roll her eyes. The guests all watched when it was time for Kyle and me to exchange our gifts.

I opened mine first and gasped. It was a diamond and sapphire tiara set in platinum, the gems sparkling bright in the candle-lit room.

"I thought you could wear this for your peerage ceremony at Hampton Court with the queen. It's befitting for the next Marchioness of Kentshire." Kyle bent and kissed my lips.

"Thank you, darling. It's so beautiful. I love it."

I handed my gift to Kyle. His hand shook as he opened the ring box. He stared at it for some time, slipping the ring onto his left pinky finger.

"This ring is believed to have belonged to John Lancaster, Kyle, my American forefather. Through a fluke it has found its way back to the family after all these centuries. I would be honored if you would wear it as your wedding ring."

"Of course, I will. I love you, Gemma."

We kissed as our guests clapped, moved by the love they saw between us. A log dropped in the main fireplace, causing a few of us to jump. I looked over as the sparks flew up the chimney, Pippa's portrait highlighted with their shimmer. I swore I saw a twinkle in her eyes looking down at us. I realized then it was no fluke that this ring had made its way back into the family. I knew it had a spiritual helping hand.

CHAPTER 16
Yuletide Showtime

Christmas Day rushed in on a giant wave of arctic air that threatened to shut down the region. The winds raged outside, their howls whirling through the many chimneys of Cherrywood. It was made for a jumpy morning, the wailing sounded like ghosts of Christmas past roaming and screeching in the halls.

"I can't believe these winds," Kyle said, pulling a green sweater over his shirt as he stared out the French doors overlooking the sea. Whitecap after whitecap rolled into the shore with a vengeance.

"I woke up several times last night convinced we lived in a haunted mansion. Some of the groans these chimneys produce are spine tingling," I said, gritting my teeth.

"Let's hope your Aunt Pippa keeps the Cherrywood spirits in line for the broadcast today. With these winds a power outage is very likely. We have our generators ready for backup if needed. I hope Rosehill has alternatives in place for the broadcast, just in case."

"I peeked downstairs earlier. Lucy and Timothy were up before dawn, letting in the crews to set up. The feature film announcement is a big one for them. I'm sure they have backups to their backups. Lucy will not be having any mistakes, not tonight."

I finished pinning up my hair in a chignon and took a final look at myself in the mirror. I was wearing wool, ivory slacks today with a matching cashmere turtleneck. I threw my faux fur stole over my shoulders for added warmth. When I came out, Kyle was standing by the French doors, next to a Christmas tree adorned with the same blue ornaments that were on Evan's tree downstairs. I gasped in delight seeing the sparkle of the blue mercury glass ornaments, skipping over to give him a big hug and kiss.

"I have one other little gift for you, Gemma." He pulled out a ring box from his pocket and handed it to me.

"Kyle, you didn't have to get me anything else, darling. The tiara was—" I stopped mid-sentence as I opened the box. Inside was a gleaming, baguette, diamond band.

"This was my mother's wedding band. It was made to fit with your engagement ring. I thought since you gave me the signet ring you want me to wear when we're married, I would give you yours. She would have loved knowing you would wear it someday."

I threw my arms around Kyle's neck and kissed him, loving him more this morning than I ever had. He placed the ring on my right-hand finger, to wear until our big day. It sparkled and shined in the morning light, made even more beautiful by knowing his mother Honey had worn it.

We walked hand in hand down the staircase, beaming with the promise of a fun-filled day to come. I couldn't wait to get down for breakfast, Chef Karl had prepared croissant bread pudding with custard and eggs benedict for our Yuletide feast this morning. My tummy was growling in anticipation, giving the chimneys a run for their money.

The grand hallway was filled with cameras and stands as the crew placed high intensity lighting and mics around the area. We waved at Lucy and Timothy as we went across to the dining room. To our surprise and delight, Penny, Steph and her aunt Evelyn were at the table, sitting next to Daddy, Mama, Max and Elliot.

"What are you all doing here? You should be running through pink sand about now." I laughed. Steph and Penny rolled their eyes. "Happy Christmas!"

"Happy Christmas, Gemma. All flights are cancelled today. Evelyn was a dear this morning, coming over to drive us to London. The airline called right as we were getting ready to leave, all flights cancelled for the next forty-eight hours." Penny shrugged.

"It was horrid driving here this morning. I thought my Rover would tip over several times just coming to the estate from Maidenford," Evelyn said.

Daddy looked at her and smiled. I think he had found a new friend.

"We'll go after New Year's. Penny has a few days left before season two filming starts. Hopefully by then the weather will have cleared." Steph kissed her bride on her cheek.

The chandelier lights flickered on and off as the growl of the wind was heard coming from the dining room fireplace. We looked at each other in surprise, hoping this was not a sign of things to come.

"I'm going to check the generators to make sure everything's in working order. I don't want to take any chances."

"I'll come with you, Kyle," Steph chimed in. "I might as well make myself useful too."

"Both of you need to wrap up when you make the generator rounds. I want no frozen casualties this Christmas day, thank you. Has anyone seen Aunt Margaret and Simone this morning?"

Ajani came running into the room with Patch by his side, followed by my aunt and Simone.

"Happy Christmas, everyone!" the little tyke shouted.

"Happy Christmas, Ajani!"

The toddler grinned ear to ear at our greeting. Aunt Margaret and Simone took a seat with him in between. Simone went to the buffet to fix plates for them.

"We were just sitting with Evan. The winds are gusting so hard I closed the shutters in his room. This wind is unprecedented, as are the howls in the chimneys. We must ask Auntie Pippa to quiet down her ghosts." Aunt Margaret smiled, giving Ajani a wink.

"Are there ghosts here, Grandmama?" Ajani asked, his eyes open wide.

"Just family ones, Ajani. Auntie Pippa keeps them all in line. She'll watch over us, I promise." I scrunched up my nose to make him laugh. "Have you seen Lady Adela this morning, Aunt Margaret?"

"She's left."

"Left? On Christmas day? I thought she wanted to be here for the broadcasts?" I was stunned. She had made it clear to me that she was here to make sure my marchioness reputation didn't get spoiled by the commoners.

Aunt Margaret pulled a note from her pocket and handed it to me. Kyle scooted his chair up close so that we could read it together. It was addressed to both of us and read:

Dearest Gemma and Kyle,

My apologies for leaving, but I thought it best. I can tell my presence and observations have been upsetting for you. I think it wise to give us a little space—I'm going to drive up to Sandringham for the remainder of the holidays. I'll touch base after the New Year to help you prepare for the peerage ceremony in any capacity that will be useful. I wish you all success with your broadcast events.

Happy Christmas,

Adela

I folded up the note and passed it over to Mama to read. I was sad that she had left, but also relieved. She didn't seem to approve of our activities here at Cherrywood. With everything we had going on there wasn't time to deal with someone who was just here to criticize.

"Her car is still in Maidenford. I don't know if they've completed the repairs after her accident. How did she get into town?" Kyle asked.

I could tell he was worried about her.

"I saw a taxi leaving the estate as I pulled in to pick up Steph and Penny. It may have been her, although it was only five o'clock," Evelyn volunteered.

"The queen will get her back on track. She did seem very odd these past few days," Aunt Margaret said, taking a bite of the croissant-laden custard.

"Mama, are you or any of the stars going to be on tonight's broadcast, or just Amy, Prudence, Timothy, and Lucy?"

"Just them. They'll be focusing on the grand hallway décor and end with the big announcement of the feature film. They only have a half hour of airtime with the British television network. Christmas day is so busy with the queen's speech and re-runs of all the holiday classic shows and movies. They don't want any of the stars stealing the spotlight tonight. We're just going to see the beauty of *Castlewood Manor*, aka Cherrywood Hall and end with the big announcement. The stars will come out on New Year's Eve." Mama's eyes glistened with anticipation.

"You will steal the show, darling," Max said, his puppy-dog eyes looking lovingly at Mama.

"Dame Agnes will be here. She texted me yesterday," Elliot said, a big, cat-eating-the-canary grin on his face.

Dame Agnes Knight was Mama's co-star on the Castlewood Manor series. There had been rumors that she may not be in the feature film due to salary negotiation standoffs. Elliot had been in on her talks with the studio via conference calls, which had just ended yesterday.

"Oh, I am so relieved. She was a holdout to the very end. You little rat, why didn't you tell me sooner?" Mama asked, playfully swatting Elliot's arm.

"Happy Christmas, darling. I know you were worried about her not being included. The film would not have been the same without her, as brilliant as you are, of course."

"Well, that just leaves Freddie then," Mama blurted, before realizing that saying his name might make Aunt Margaret upset.

Aunt Margaret gave her a little hand-wave signaling it was all right. She and Freddie Alton-Jones, the lead male actor on the series had dated during the summer. She walked down the red carpet with him in Vail for the *Telly Tiaras*. After Evan's kidnapping, she had broken off their relationship suddenly citing the need to care for her son. Freddie had been trying to reach her, but she kept him at arm's length.

"So, what does everyone have planned for today now that we're housebound?" I asked, trying to change the subject.

"I was going to take Ajani swimming. This little boy just started lessons before we left Johannesburg. And Olivia and I are going to practice a little martial art sparring later. I think she can give me a run for my money." Simone laughed.

"The pool's ready for some swimming fun," Kyle said, giving a glance over to Daddy. He had the pool drained and cleaned after Elizabeth's body was removed.

"Yay!" Ajani cried, clapping his hands.

"Evelyn and I were going to explore the library. There are some wonderful texts there. The Lancaster's have accumulated quite the inventory," Daddy said, smiling at Evelyn.

I was relieved that he was coming out of his broken shell that Elizabeth had him in these past few months. He deserved better—hopefully, Evelyn could help pull him back to his beloved academia world.

"Max and I will be playing billiards if anyone would like to join us. It doesn't look as if anyone has played there in ages. If it's okay with you Lady Margaret, we'd like to imbibe in some of Evan's finest whiskey and maybe even enjoy a cigar, it being Christmas and all."

Daddy and Kyle looked up and smiled, they enjoyed a good cigar themselves.

"Yes, yes of course, although I really don't understand the attraction of the cigars. Evan and Kyle…." Aunt Margaret choked up for a moment, thinking of her son. "Evan and Kyle used to go in there all the time to play away and smoke cigars, thinking I didn't know." She laughed. "Just please, keep the doors shut. We don't want the grand hallway smelling of cigar smoke."

Elliot gave her a salute and embellished bow.

Our group broke up to enjoy their Christmas playtime. Mama and Aunt Margaret were going to join Ajani and Simone in the pool. Max and Elliot went downstairs to raid Evan's whiskey coffers. Kyle and Steph went to suit up to check on the generators outside. Penny joined the Rosehill team to offer her help. Daddy and Evelyn went into the library to look for literary treasures.

I decided to go upstairs. I wanted to examine the room where Lady Adela had stayed. I still had a nagging suspicion about her, something felt very off kilter with her mood and actions the past few days. I opened the suite door and to my surprise, saw Olivia in there, kneeling down to look under the bed. Kyle had told her about the gilded chair yesterday. She was going to follow up on it with her uncle, Chief Inspector Marquot later this week.

"Hey you, Happy Christmas. You're not supposed to be working today, you know."

Olivia looked at me and smiled. "I hadn't planned on it, but with the weather being so wicked outside I decided to come up to the hall from my apartment to, ahem, explore a bit. Simone is going to show me a few more martial arts moves later too, that I am so looking forward to. I saw a taxi enter the estate this morning on the camera link Kyle provided me. I saw Lady Adela leaving with two large suitcases and two boxes. I don't remember her having that many items when she arrived here after her accident."

"Boxes? She arrived with two large suitcases and a makeup case. Her Christmas gifts were all small items—a pair of leather gloves from Aunt Margaret, a fringe belt similar to the one I wore last spring at the fashion show at Buckingham Palace that she had admired, silk scarves from Mama, and a vintage, lace shawl from Elliot and Max. All the gifts combined would not take up a box, much less two."

"It doesn't make sense, just like her finding the medallion by the Christmas tree. I had searched there first thing when you cried out."

"Kyle said the same thing. I found some wood shavings by my jewel case last evening before the wedding. I hadn't noticed it the night before when I grabbed the medallion box from the case, and I didn't remember 'til later that I had, in fact, locked the case. Someone jimmied it open. Do you really think she would have done that though? She has been on a rampage wanting me to drop all things not nobility or royal related. Why would she steal a gift that her own aunt had given me?"

"To create a distraction, maybe, prove to people her statements were correct when chaos reared its devious little head. She seemed very determined to put a halt to your public functions. Or perhaps she likes very expensive jewelry… of the royal kind."

"I don't know what's going on in her head. I was feeling more than a bit stifled and I did not appreciate her comments on the so-called social status of my friends. I'm a commoner myself, for Pete's sake."

"Not really, Gemma. Your Lancaster lineage has you of noble birth. It may have been sidetracked for a few centuries, but here you are now, about to become Marchioness of Kentshire. It's a big deal to us."

"Yes, I know. You just have to appreciate being raised as an American the whole topic of royal versus commoner isn't really emphasized there. We're all equal, or at least are supposed to be."

Olivia smiled and took my arm. "Come on, let's call it an afternoon. I didn't find anything here of significance."

As we walked from the room, I stepped on something causing a crackle in the carpet. I stooped and picked up a silver piece that was now crunched by my size-ten shoe. I looked at it to see what it was.

"It looks like an ornament hook. See, here's the cap. It's engraved and pretty heavy," I said, flipping the piece in my hand.

"Ornaments? Why would there be ornaments in her room? There's no tree in here."

A bulb switched on in my head. This could be from an heirloom ornament. I raced down to my bedroom with Olivia following close behind. I wanted to see if the ornament cap matched the ones on my tree Kyle had given me this morning. We ran over to the tree as I removed an ornament and put the smashed piece next to it to look for any trace of similarity. The sterling caps were identical in weight and style. There was no doubt this was from one of the heirloom ornaments.

"They're a match, I think. You can see here on one of the engraving swirls. You don't think she and Reggie were in on the Christmas ornament switch, do you?" My head was spinning. We hadn't found any of the heirloom ornaments yet even though we had suspected Reggie. His room had been searched when he was arrested. We found no traces of the missing heirlooms.

"I don't know what to believe right now. I will call my uncle first thing in the morning. I was focused on the brooch myself. I just don't understand why she would be involved in stealing these items. It seems such a cruel thing to do, especially to someone she professes to care so much about."

"The death of her daughter could have driven her over the edge. She seemed fixated on me lately. I thought at first it was just because she needed someone to be close to, and she was a friend of Kyle's mother, Honey, so I accepted it. Her daughter, Evangeline, was somewhat of a rebel. Maybe too much of a mother's love is a bad thing."

We decided to put our speculations aside to go downstairs and enjoy the Christmas day. Olivia was invited into the billiards room to enjoy a game and a glass of Evan's finest before meeting up with Simone. I went to the indoor pool and was overjoyed to see Ajani and Simone swimming around enjoying the warm waters. Mama and Aunt Margaret were seated in chairs by the pool, sipping a glass of wine.

"Come sit with us, darling. Do you fancy a glass of wine?" Mama asked.

"That sounds lovely, thank you, Mama." She handed me a glass of the sparkling wine, clinking her glass to mine.

"Gemma, is that a new ring I see on your finger?" Mama grabbed my right hand for a closer look at the ring that had dazzled her eyes.

"It's Kyle's mother's ring, Mama. It was made to fit with my engagement ring. Since I gave the signet ring to him to wear as his eventual wedding ring, he gave this to me this morning. He is so sweet. He also presented me with a tree that had Pippa's ornaments on it. You should see it. I love the way those ornaments sparkle."

"He's a good man, Gemma. He'll make a fine husband and he's already done so much for the estate."

"Thank you, Lady Margaret," Kyle said, walking up behind us.

He was rubbing his hands to get them warm after being outside. He bent down to give us kisses and pulled up a seat. Mama poured him a glass of wine. Simone and Ajani squealed in laughter in the pool.

"Save me some of that wine, please. My fingers are getting shriveled. I need to get warmed up before taking on Olivia."

"Mummy and Olivia are playing superheroes." Ajani laughed, clearly adoring his mummy and her new friend's sparring.

We were tickled by his comments and held up our glasses to Simone to assure her there would be plenty of wine.

"Are the generators working okay? The winds look like they've actually picked up."

"They have, Gemma. Steph and I put some canvas toppers on them to protect them from the blowing snow and ice. I don't want any of the device controls damaged before we turn them on. Karl said the lights in the kitchen have been going on and off. He's roasting pork and beef roasts on the spit by the fireplace. It smells divine down there."

My mouth started to water thinking about the grilled meats. "We'll have a feast after the Christmas broadcast. We may have to expand into the grand hallway for dinner. If the weather keeps up, the broadcast crew may be spending the night here at Cherrywood Hall."

"That will be just fine. The more the merrier," Aunt Margaret said.

"Without Lady Adela here, we'll have a good time. I'm sorry Margaret, but I was getting a little tired of all her royal blabbers."

"As I said this morning, Jillian, the queen will have words with her at Sandringham. I don't think she appreciated Adela's comments."

Our poolside party ended when Simone and Ajani got out of the water to go upstairs to rest and get changed. It was getting close to broadcast time, which would be right after the queen's annual Christmas day speech. We left the pool area and gathered in the library to watch the queen's speech while the Rosehill crew made their final preparations. We saw Penny making last-minute adjustments to Amy and Prudence's garments. They waved nervously as we went into the library. Lucy was by the Christmas tree with Timothy rehearsing their comments on the feature film.

We watched as Queen Annelyce made her annual speech to the nation, wishing her subjects hope, health and happiness for the holidays and New Year. It felt surreal for me to watch her on the television this year. I had the opportunity to have quite a few meetings with her and had come to respect her and her position very much. She was an honorable leader, filled with integrity to do the right thing. We sat together and smiled at the woman who had become our friend.

As her speech ended, we had a quick moment to stand and stretch and refill our cocktails. The studio production assistant signaled us to get back in our seats and remain quiet as he counted down 3-2-1, the *Castlewood Manor* theme song playing in the background:

"*Happy Christmas from the lovely halls of Castlewood Manor, or for some, Cherrywood Hall,*" Prudence announced, starting the broadcast.

"*Tonight, we are very pleased to show you the beautiful holiday decorations at the beloved estate we've all come to love. We have a special announcement at the end, that we think will fill you with even more Christmas cheer, so stay tuned,"* Lucy teased, with a sly smile on her face.

We watched as Amy and Prudence went through the history of the grand hallway, featuring the fine portraits lining the corridor, ending with Aunt Pippa's over the fireplace.

"Lady Pippa Lancaster was the American heiress who came to Cherrywood Hall to marry her distant British cousin. In an extraordinary change of circumstance, her great, great niece, Dr. Gemma Lancaster Phillips, will be assuming the title and peerage as the Marchioness of Kentshire on January fifteenth, as announced by the queen this past weekend."

Everyone raised their glass to me when this announcement was made. Mama clapped her hands silently, blowing me a kiss. The broadcast came to an end, with the highly anticipated announcement. Lucy and Timothy stood in front of the shimmering Christmas tree.

"We at Rosehill productions are very pleased to announce that there will be a feature film for all of you lovely, Castlewood Manor fans. Shooting will begin next spring, just after season two filming completes. The premier will be just in time for next Christmas! Stay tuned for our next big announcement on New Year's Eve where we'll announce the cast for the new film."

The Castlewood Manor theme song ended the broadcast with Amy, Prudence, Lucy, and Timothy waving goodbye. In 3-2-1, the production assistant took off his earphones and called it a wrap. We were free to talk and clap. Mama stood, elated at the announcement, giving everyone hugs as she flitted around the room.

We walked into the grand hallway, clapping for the Rosehill crew who had done such a splendid job. Amy was beside herself, laughing and giggling at her first television appearance. She was on her way, I thought with just a tinge of sadness. Champagne corks were popping as we readied ourselves for a big celebration. Personally, I was looking forward to the spit-fired roasts that were being cooked over the fire. We stood by the Christmas tree, clinking our glasses in honor of this festive night.

We held our collective breaths as the lights flickered on the first floor, the wind howling a menacing growl through the chimneys. To our dismay, we heard a loud "C-R-A-C-K' as the power shut off. The hallway glimmered with just the light of the fireplace. Kyle and Steph went running downstairs to go outdoors to make sure there were no issues with the generators. We huddled by the fireplace, standing under Pippa's portrait. The hairs on our arms stood up as we heard a scraping sound on the floor from across the hallway. We strained to see in the dark but couldn't detect anything visually. By the sound, it was getting closer. I drew a deep breath as I finally saw a blue-gowned figure, slowly coming toward us. We stared at the apparition in disbelief. Were the ghosts of Cherrywood Christmas past coming to join us?

"Oh, my Lord," Aunt Margaret gasped, dropping her champagne flute, the stemware shattering on the floor.

She ran toward the figure. I followed her, concerned and a bit frightened. I stopped dead in my tracks as we stepped in front of our Christmas apparition, and sank down to my knees.

"Hello, Cousin."

It was Evan. Our Christmas wishes had just come true.

CHAPTER 17
Mistletoe Miracle

Aunt Margaret threw her arms around her son, sobbing with joy. Simone, holding Ajani, made her way up to her husband, tears streaming down her face. They embraced, holding their young son between them, crying, laughing, kissing—a muddled mass of love that now radiated from the darkness of the past months.

I stood up and slowly made my way to him as Simone beckoned me to come over. She stepped back as Evan and I embraced, holding each other close, relishing the moment. I tilted my head back and punched him lightly on his arm, teasing him like I had done so many times the past year.

"Ow," Evan said, pretending to be hurt, giving me a wink. "See son, just like I told you. Your Cousin Gemma packs a mean punch."

"She does like to eat too, Papa."

Our guests started laughing, and ran over to join us, thrilled to see Evan awake.

"Hurry, let's get him in a comfy chair," I said, slowly leading him over to a seat by the tree, careful to keep the path for his IV pole clear. I could see Evan was growing weaker and less stable after his miraculous journey across the hallway.

As soon as he sat down, the lights flickered and came on once again, the generators working their electrical magic perfectly. I stepped back to let the others greet him, watching the miracle of his return unfold. Kyle and Steph stepped into the hallway from downstairs, still shivering from the cold outside.

"There, we have power. No more darkness—" Kyle stopped talking and stared, not believing his eyes. He turned to me as if to ask if what he was seeing was real.

I nodded my head and whispered, "Yes."

Elliot and Max, who were bent over Evan, stood up and moved away when they saw Kyle. He rushed over and fell to his knees, hugging his dear friend close. They both cried tears of man-joy at seeing one another again after the ghastly experience of the past few months.

Evan gently placed his hands against Kyle's cheeks and raised his head. "Thank you, old man. I believe you are the one who rescued me."

"You would have done the same for me, Evan. I can't tell you how happy I am to have you back. You gave us a scare, my friend."

"Lady Margaret, Lady Margaret!" Nurse Ellie yelled, running over to us. "Lord Evan he's—"

"He's here, Nurse Ellie," I answered, laughing.

Nurse Ellie came to an abrupt halt, her hand on her mouth. "Why you little dickens, giving me a start like that. I had just gone in the back for a cup of Christmas tea with the staff. Chef Karl sent us up a lovely tray of goodies." She went over to Evan to feel his pulse and check his bags which were still attached to his abdomen.

"Is he all right, Nurse Ellie?" Aunt Margaret asked, a look of concern hitting her face.

"He's fine, Lady Margaret, but very drained," she replied. "I'm going to get a wheelchair and take you back to your room, Lord Evan, to do a more thorough exam. We need to get you some warmer clothes too. You'll catch your death."

"By all means, then, Nurse Ellie. I'll be your willing patient. I didn't come this far to die by a cold."

Nurse Ellie grinned and went to fetch the wheelchair.

Kyle stood, giving Evan a playful rub on his head. Aunt Margaret just stared at her son, tears streaming down her face. Simone and Ajani went to kneel by Evan.

"Are you back alive now, Papa?"

"Yes, son. I believe I am." Evan kissed Simone's hand and hugged his son close.

Nurse Ellie brought the chair. Kyle and Simone helped him stand and sit down in the wheelchair, positioning his IV pole between his knees. Aunt Margaret, Simone, and Ajani followed him back to his care room, not wanting to let him out of their sight.

We took seats next to the tree, still flabbergasted by Evan's return. Elliot and Max served tumblers of whiskey to everyone. We needed it.

"I cannot believe what just happened. Here I thought we were about to see a ghost with rattling chains, and it was Evan, dragging his IV pole. My word, I need to remember these feelings," Mama gushed, fanning her face.

"I couldn't believe it; I was half hiding behind Elliot's back. I didn't know what was happening," Max said, taking a long sip of whiskey.

"I was getting ready to stand behind Jillian. I figured we could use her stilettos as a weapon if push came to shove," Elliot deadpanned, sending us all into giggles.

"I was not expecting this; I can tell you. I thought I was hallucinating when I first saw him. Evan has always been a fighter, ever since we were small boys," Kyle reminisced, a smile of relief and gratitude swept across his face.

"I just ran after Aunt Margaret; I didn't know what was coming. When she started hugging him and sobbing, I knew. I just sank to my knees. My Christmas wish, many of our Christmas wishes, had just come true. Aunt Margaret was right all along, knowing that Evan needed to get back to Cherrywood Hall. I'm so, so happy." I wiped tears of joy from my face, the emotions from the past month flooded out.

Bridges came over to our group, his eyes reddened by tears of joy. All the staff had gathered to watch with us as their dear lord walked the halls of the estate again. News of his revival spread fast here in the halls of Cherrywood.

"Miss Gemma, would you like to have dinner served now?" He gulped, trying to control his emotions. My hunger pangs kicked in at the mention of food.

"I think that would be a fantastic idea, Bridges. Come on everyone, to the dining room."

We trooped in, smiling happily and grateful for the wonder of the day. As we took our seats, I glanced at a small portrait of Pippa hanging in the dining room and tipped my wine glass to her. I was sure she had some part in Evan's miraculous return.

Chef Karl once again graced our dinner plates with a variety of spit-roasted meats, mashed potatoes, roasted veggies and a delightful cranberry chutney. Our conversation was spirited this evening after the successful, feature-film announcement and Evan's awakening. We drank and partied through the evening. Aunt Margaret finally joined us to give us an update on Evan.

"He's doing fine, still very spent and a little muddled at times, but he's eating on his own. He's going to have to take it slow for the next few weeks, but it's Nurse Ellie's and the other caregivers' opinion that he's doing well. I'll have the doctor come in tomorrow for another exam, but for now it looks good."

"Do you want anything to eat, Aunt Margaret? What about Simone and Ajani?"

"The caregivers brought us some trays. We had Christmas dinner in Evan's room. He wanted a sip of wine, but Nurse Ellie was not going to allow that." She laughed.

"Does he remember anything from the rescue?" Kyle asked.

"Not too much. His thoughts are still a bit jumbled. Nurse Ellie said that was typical, that it would take some time for the brain to acclimate to being back in service, so to speak. He does say that he remembers hearing conversations around him, which is just unbelievable to me. He said he knew the night the queen visited him. Gemma punched his arm that night," Aunt Margaret teased, giving me a wink.

I couldn't believe it. "I did, seriously. How could he know that?"

Aunt Margaret shrugged.

"Does he know anything of the change in peerage?" Kyle asked, worried that the news may upset him.

"He knows a bit. Simone is going to talk with him tonight to give him more details. The caregivers moved in two beds so that their little family could sleep together this magical night. He does want to talk with you, Gemma, in the morning," she said, looking at me. "Now, if you'll excuse me, it's time for me to retire. I have a lot of thank you prayers to make tonight." A few of us blew kisses at her as she went upstairs. I had a feeling she would be up and down a few times tonight to check on Evan.

"What a brave woman," Elliot said, holding his glass up.

"Hear, hear," we chimed in.

Kyle and I were the next to turn in, a wave of fatigue hitting me, and I wanted to get up early to go talk with my beloved Cousin. The others decided it was time for a Christmas cha-cha-cha dance session, changing the carol music playing in the hall to a sultry rhythm beat.

"I don't think I've ever had such a happy Christmas," I said, as I slipped into Kyle's pajama top.

I threw his bottoms over to him, landing across the bed. He came over to me and unbuttoned the few buttons I had managed to close, opening the shirt wide so he could look at me, taking me in. His stare was intense as he caressed me lightly with his fingers, until I could stand it no more. We melded together in our love; our passion fueled by the joy of this special night.

I woke the next morning, slipping quietly out of Kyle's arms. I looked down at him, still in a deep slumber, a soft smile on his lips. He looked so peaceful. My heart filled with joy just watching him. I changed into a pair of jeans and a turtleneck sweater. It was eerily quiet outside compared to the past few days. I tiptoed over to the French doors to see what the weather was doing today. To my delight, it was snowing again, heavy, and showing no signs of stopping. I pulled on my faux fur boots and crept outside to the hall to go downstairs.

The lights in Evan's room were on. I could hear laughter as I approached. I gave a small knock as I turned to go into the room. Ajani was in his pajamas sitting on his papa's bed. Aunt Margaret and Simone were seated by the fireplace next to Evan's bed, sipping cups of tea.

"Good morning," I said, walking in and bending over to kiss Evan. Ajani jumped into my arms.

"Papa slept well, and the doctor says he's going to be fine," the tyke said, pointing down his chin in affirmation.

"He did? Well, that is good news, isn't it?" I spun Ajani around.

"Dr. Moore just left a while ago, dear. He concurs with Nurse Ellie and the caregivers. Evan looks to be fine. They removed his IV lines and feeding tube. He needs to take things very slow." Aunt Margaret couldn't have looked any happier.

I handed Ajani to Simone. She was going to take him upstairs for a bath and nap—they had been up since early morning. Aunt Margaret stood and kissed her son good-by, leaving us to talk. I pulled a chair over next to Evan's bed, taking his hand in mine.

"Do you have any earthly idea how happy you made people yesterday? Well, once we found out it was you." I clarified, giggling. "At first, we thought it was a ghost of Christmas past coming to haunt us."

"I'm pretty happy myself, Cousin This has all been such a surreal experience. The entire time I was in a coma it was as if I was floating above everyone in the room. At times, I could see you from my mental loft position, and other times I could hear every word. I tried to speak, but my lips wouldn't move."

"You owe your mother a lot of thanks, Evan. The doctors wanted you to stay at the care facility. Your condition was grave, but your mother didn't give up. She wanted you here at Cherrywood Hall this Christmas. She thought all the caroling and decorations would somehow lift your spirits, bringing you back to us."

"It looks as if she was right. I can't tell you how many conversations I've had with Pippa since I've been back. She's come to visit me every day you know." Evan winked.

"Oh, I believe it. I've talked with her many times, asking for her help. I think she cares a great deal for us, especially you."

"Gemma…"

"Evan…"

We laughed, both of us starting to speak at the same time. Evan, ever the gentleman, waved his hand in a twirl to let me speak first.

"Evan, there's been some research that has surfaced. My American forefather, John Lancaster, was found to be the rightful heir to the Lancaster peerage and title. His older brother was illegitimate and not a Lancaster. The queen wants to rectify the wrong done centuries ago…"

"I know, Gemma," Evan whispered. "Simone told me last night. Do you know what this means?" He looked at me, struggling for words, yet with a new look of hope in his eyes. "This means I get to do what I've dreamed of for so long with my wife and our son. The research has set me free, Gemma."

"Really? I didn't want you to be upset with me. I couldn't stand it if our family was split apart again. I would never let that happen, Evan." My eyes brimmed with emotion.

"Darling, don't you think I know that? You've brought such a fresh, new outlook to our family and community that I could never do. I was faithful, sure. But my heart was not in it. I truly believe you were brought here for a reason, Gemma." He held my hand, feeling my fingers, and looked at my engagement ring. "This is new. Are congratulations in order, Cousin?"

I blushed. We were going to have a lot to catch up on. "Kyle took me to Iceland on our way back from Los Angeles. We went snorkeling in the Silfra Fissure, and golly, was it cold. His parents became engaged in the lagoon, so that's where he popped the question to me. This is his mother Honey's ring. I love it."

Evan put my fingers to his mouth and kissed them. "You two are my best friends. I couldn't be happier for you. Kyle belongs here at Cherrywood too. He has a way with the estate that I could never hope to have. I know it will be run in good hands for generations to come."

"Evan, aren't you afraid to go back to South Africa? I know the kidnappers were arrested and convicted, but they have deep roots and connections."

"That's what was strange, Gemma—they did seem hell bent on destroying the ranch and committing horrific deeds. There was something else in play though, that I was never able to get to the bottom of. It was like they knew every move I was going to make. They were well funded too. Someone with deep pockets was fueling their actions."

"Weren't the police able to track down who was enabling them, either through bank accounts or money transfers?"

"No. It was as if the moneys came from a secured account with no trace. There aren't many people in the world with those kinds of resources, not unless you're a billionaire or a royal." Evan sighed, giving a little shrug.

"I can't imagine why anyone would want to fund that kind of operation. It seemed as if a vendetta was taken out on you."

"Simone thinks the same thing. She had her firm's attorneys do some investigating, thinking it was an act of violence toward her, through me. There was no trace though, nothing. None of the local snitches could provide any details either, leading the police to believe it was an operation from abroad."

"I don't understand. I'll talk to Olivia about this, perhaps she can get her uncle to do some checking for us."

"Who's Olivia, darling?"

I covered my hands over my face in embarrassment, remembering that Evan wasn't up to speed with the new personnel.

"My-bad. Olivia Fisher, she's my bodyguard. With me becoming Marchioness of Kentshire, Elliot and Kyle were concerned that I may receive a bit of public backlash as an American assuming a British title. Elliot has put together a whole PR campaign to tell the story and history of why I'm taking on the peerage, and a list of all the projects I've managed with the *Castlewood Manor* series that has brought benefits to the local community. My peerage ceremony will be on January fifteenth. Kyle wants to make sure I'm physically protected. Chief Inspector Marquot just happens to be Olivia's uncle."

"Surely the queen will help with this too. After all, you were the *royal avenger* who saved her from being seen in a rather unroyal position," Evan teased, putting his hands out in my now infamous pose seen round the world.

"She is, and I've come to respect her so much. She gave me a beautiful diamond medallion to wear for my ceremony. It was lost for a bit, but Lady Adela spotted it by the Christmas tree, much to my relief."

"Lost? Gemma, are you not telling me something? I can see it in your eyes dear Cousin."

"We've had some accidents here, Evan. One of which was deadly. The Christmas tree in the grand hallway was felled. Someone had unscrewed the hooks of the tethers holding it up. It crashed down and nearly crushed your mother. She had bandages on her arm and hand."

"What? She said nothing of this to me." Evan frowned, dismayed that his mother had been hurt.

"She probably didn't want to worry you. I probably shouldn't be telling you any of this. My father's new wife, Elizabeth, was found murdered in the indoor pool. Our broadcast decorator, Reggie Gerard, was found by the pool side, holding a walking stick that was used to kill her. It belonged to Lady Adela."

"You're kidding me. How awful for David."

"He took her death very hard. Elizabeth was a very troubled person, Evan, with many, many issues. She did not deserve to be murdered though. It's all very puzzling. Reggie had only met her recently. Why would he kill her?"

"Hey, you two." Kyle smiled at us as he walked into the room. He kissed the top of my head and gave Evan a hug, pulling up a chair to sit next to me.

"Gemma's been filling me in on the latest happenings at Cherrywood Hall. I think I'm glad I was in a coma," Evan deadpanned.

"Not when you see how much your whiskey reserves have been depleted old man." Kyle joked.

Evan's eyes went wide. He waved his hands signaling Kyle not to tell him. "Some things are better not known. So, has this Reggie person been arrested and charged?"

"He's being held in Maidenford. We don't have all the details of his arraignment yet. Olivia was going to call Chief Inspector Marquot to find out the latest and share some other tidbits."

"Father Christmas's throne was sabotaged for our Christmas Eve village event. He sat and came tumbling down in front of everyone. Luckily, no children were hurt. The chair leg had been sawed through," I said, jumping in. "My jewelry case was broken into as well, so it is very likely the medallion given to me by the queen was stolen, not lost."

"You think this was done by someone at Cherrywood? Who?"

"It's not clear, Evan. There are things that point to Reggie. But there are also suggestions that Lady Adela may have been involved too. No proof, not yet. And no motive that we know of for Elizabeth's murder."

"Gemma, are you saying the queen's niece may be involved? Why on earth would she want to do anything that cruel? I thought she always liked you, and she was a great friend of your mother's, Kyle."

"Lady Adela's behavior has been very strange, Evan. She's been rude, speaking to everyone in a cruel tone and manner, belittling those not of royal birth. It doesn't explain the gilded chair, nor the Christmas tree crash, but the heirloom ornaments on the tree were switched with cheaper substitutes. Reggie was a big fan of the ornaments and they would fetch a good price, if he or Lady Adela need cash."

"Olivia and I found a piece of an ornament cap in Lady Adela's room yesterday afternoon." Kyle looked at me. I hadn't had a chance to tell him about our find. "Lady Adela left very early yesterday morning, citing that she felt I didn't appreciate her commentary on the events and people being hosted here at Cherrywood Hall. I agree with Kyle; she was being very demeaning the past few days. Olivia saw her get into the cab when she left. In addition to her two suitcases, she had a couple of boxes. We don't know what she had in them. It could have been the missing ornaments." I knew it was a big conjecture, but I wanted it out so that Kyle, and now Evan could help me think it through.

We heard a clap at the door. "Okay young people, it's time for you to leave, please. I need to get Lord Evan cleaned up and dressed. I will wheel him out in a bit." Nurse Ellie smiled, holding the door open to let us out. We waved goodbye and headed to the dining room for breakfast.

"So, I gather that you and Evan had a chance to talk?"

"Yes, he knows everything, Kyle. I'm so relieved. He supports me and is happy for me, just as you said he would be. I can't tell you what a weight it is lifted from my shoulders. I can go into the peerage ceremony with no guilt now that I know the family will stay united."

"I knew it, darling. Evan was here by duty. You will be taking over from love."

"We spoke about his kidnapping and the poachers. He told me they were well funded and always seemed to know what his plans would be. They were fixated on bringing him down, almost like a vendetta had been placed on him. Neither the police nor Simone's attorneys could find any leads. They told him there were only a few people in the world that could buy that type information protection---billionaires or royals."

"Darling, the queen had your father do the research that unearthed the information that has led you to becoming marchioness. She would not have anything sinister done to Evan, nor anyone for that matter. My money is on one of Simone's competitors, harming Evan to get to her."

"He said they looked into that aspect, but could come up with nothing."

"Let's have Olivia talk with the Chief Inspector later today and get Scotland Yard working on this. I need some food and I know you do," Kyle said, laughing as he picked me up, carrying me into the dining room over his shoulder.

Mama, Daddy, Elliot and Max smiled when they saw us come in so dramatically, me screeching.

"You two look way too energetic this morning," Elliot said, sipping on a hair of the dog Bloody Mary. He had obviously partied too much after we went to bed. Max didn't look much better, giving us a little finger wave, but saying nothing.

Kyle dropped me to my feet. "We just had a visit with Evan. He's slowly, but surely being brought up to speed on what he's missed."

"Did you speak to him about you becoming marchioness, darling?"

"Yes, Mama. Simone had told him some of the details. I filled in the rest. The bottom line is he's very relieved. He wants to have his own life with Simone and Ajani down in South Africa."

Kyle and I loaded our plates with the usual yummies from the buffet and sat down to tuck in. Elliot watched as I took big bites of my favorite mushrooms, tomatoes and baked beans, turning his face away from those of us who were eating, every now and then. He truly looked like he didn't feel well.

"Good morning, everyone," Evan said, smiling as Nurse Ellie wheeled him in.

Mama stood and went over to give him a kiss.

"Jillian, tell me, no one has told me about the *Tellys*. Did you win?"

Mama's eyes lit up as she filled Evan in on all the details of the awards show, bringing up pictures on her phone to show him. It warmed my heart to have him back with us. I loved Evan so much. The laughter and stories made me smile, I was so thankful this piece of our family history ended happily.

I still had a nagging feeling about who would have wanted to go after Evan like that. The comment of the royals stuck in my head. We had to get to the bottom of this, before anyone else was killed or hurt. Sparks popped in the fireplace. Aunt Pippa agreed with me.

CHAPTER 18

Untangling the Tinsel

The next few days were filled with events and news, some of which threw us for a loop. Reggie Gerard was released from the Maidenford jail. He was still under suspicion since he had been found with the murder weapon in his hand, but there was no motive and no other circumstantial evidence that could be found that implicated him at this time. Reggie explained the schematics that were found, saying that he always had those types of details drawn up for the venues that he planned events for. He was cautioned not to leave the country as the investigation was still ongoing.

Mama, Daddy, and I were taken in for questioning by the police, plied with questions about Elizabeth. Daddy had now become the main person of interest it seemed. The police had found out about Elizabeth's drug and gambling addictions. The fact that she had lost ninety percent of his lottery winnings (not including those given to me), was leading to a case against him. Was he driven to kill her out of fear she would lose everything he had? Had her continuous henpecking caused him to strike out against her in rage?

Mama was questioned as the ex-wife and protective mother of me. Was she still in love with her ex-husband, jealous of his intelligent, younger, beautiful wife? Did she strike out of revenge because she feared for her daughter's safety and livelihood after Elizabeth made claims to the lottery winnings that Daddy had transferred to her daughter?

I was questioned briefly by the police. They wanted to know about the lottery statements made to me by Elizabeth. Did her comments inflame me? Yes, only because I could see the torment her outbursts were causing my father. The main advantage I had that quickly dismissed suspicions about me was that my bodyguard Olivia could vouch for just about every second of my time, thus putting me in the clear.

It was disturbing to be in the focus of the investigation, but even more so because there were no substantive facts that could link any of us to a motive to kill her. Couple that with a lack of forensic evidence and we were back to square one.

After my questioning, Kyle, Olivia, Chief Inspector Marquot, and I went to the Howling Pig Pub for lunch—Mama and Daddy had gone back to Cherrywood Hall. Henry, the barkeep and owner, greeted us.

"Hiya, Sir Kyle, Dr. Gemma, will you be staying for lunch or just drinks?"

"Hi, Henry, we'll be having lunch. An area with a little privacy would be appreciated," Kyle said.

The ears at the pub had supersonic hearing abilities when they wanted. Henry walked us to the back room.

"Henry, I'd like to introduce my new bodyguard, Ms. Olivia Fisher, and her uncle, Chief Inspector Marquot from Scotland Yard."

Henry's eyes went wide at the mention of the world-famed crime agency as he shook hands with the chief inspector. His eyes softened when he went to greet Olivia, looking first at her and then at me. He seemed a little confused, but I sensed he was smitten with Olivia.

"You ladies look like you could be twins! I'll have Debra here in a minute to take your orders. In the meantime, the usual?"

Kyle and I nodded our heads yes—an apple cider on draft for me and a lager for him. Chief Inspector Marquot and Olivia ordered tea since they were on duty. Henry left with a wink to Olivia as he went to fetch our drinks.

"This looks like a nice hangout, Gemma. What do you suggest?"

"It's a great place to come and chill with the locals, Olivia. Henry brings in musicians to play at night. They get a good crowd. As for food, I love just about everything. The shepherd's pie is my favorite."

"The lamb burger and thyme fries get my vote," Kyle chimed in.

Our drinks were served by Debra and Henry, who personally poured Olivia's tea for her. Debra took our orders—two shepherd's pie and two lamb burgers.

"Here's to a good year," Chief Inspector toasted, as we clinked our glasses and mugs. "Thank you for meeting with me, and Olivia," he smiled, not wanting to leave his niece out. "I wanted to get your reactions to Mr. Gerard's release, and answer any questions you may have on the interrogations made to your family. I want you to know that Scotland Yard is leading the investigation, not just the local force."

"Chief Inspector, can you divulge any of the details that led to Reggie's release? I can understand there not being a strong motive—he just met Elizabeth, at the same time Mama and I did, actually. Why was he in the indoor pool room at that hour? Most importantly, why did he have Lady Adela's walking stick in his hands if it was the murder weapon?"

"Good questions, Dr. Gemma. He claims he was in the conservatory to allow his little dog to use the, ahem, planting facilities, citing it was too dark and cold to take the pooch outside. He claims the pool door was ajar. He could hear the lapping of the water against the sides of the pool. He went inside to investigate and found Elizabeth floating in the water, a small wisp of blood coming from her head. He saw the walking stick lying on the side of the pool. He claims he picked it up to try and get Elizabeth's body to the edge."

"Were there any other fingerprints on the stick, Chief Inspector?"

"There were three sets of prints, Sir Kyle. Mr. Gerard's, Lady Adela's, and Elizabeth's. It was apparent from the angle of the prints the deceased tried to fend off her attacker."

"May I ask, Chief Inspector, why Lady Adela wasn't questioned?"

The Chief Inspector and Olivia quickly glanced at one another before he answered.

"One needs to be very careful in incidents involving royals, Dr. Gemma. The queen gives her total support to any inquiries, but extreme measures are used to keep any type of investigation involving them very discreet. In the case of Lady Adela, as you heard, we did get a statement from her saying that she must have left it in the conservatory while she was watching the charades games. She claims she forgot about it due to imbibing in the whiskey being poured generously that evening. It was left downstairs, for anyone to take or use, so she said."

Our food was served by Debra, so questions were put aside for a while as we tucked into our lunch. I still could not get the suspicions of Lady Adela out of my head. She had come to Cherrywood Hall in a very unexpected manner after her accident. If the blizzard had not hit the roads she would have been up at Sandringham with the queen and never come to Cherrywood, so she led us to believe.

"Chief Inspector, did Lady Adela tell you why she didn't drive with the queen and Prince Thaddeus up to Sandringham? From what I understand, she goes with them every year. How did it happen that she drove separately and just happened to crash in Maidenford? What was she doing up this way? It's not on the route from London. The queen and Prince

Thaddeus stopped here purposely to see the Christmas decorations and Evan, of course."

Everyone seemed very interested in my observation, especially the chief inspector, who turned to his niece. "See, Olivia. I told you that Dr. Gemma has a keen eye and mind." He smiled.

"She doesn't have a clear rationale for that, Dr. Gemma. She first told us that she hadn't wished to go to Cherrywood. She then stated she wasn't ready to leave when the queen and Prince Thaddeus left London. Finally, she stated she was just confused when asked how she crashed in Maidenford off the main road to Sandringham. She cites her head injury has caused her memory to lapse."

"The royals' diaries are usually known for months at a time. Isn't it strange that for one of the biggest holiday events of the year the queen's favorite niece's memory gets muddled? For someone who was tentative about wanting to come to Cherrywood, she became adamant about staying over for the holidays, leaving her beloved aunt and uncle to go to Sandringham without her." Kyle took a bite of his lamb burger, shaking his head as he chewed.

"She was concerned I was making un-marchioness like decisions with respect to the events I hosted, and the people invited into the hall were---um, common," I piped in.

The chief inspector sat back in his chair and contemplated our statements, trying to match them with the others he knew about that we weren't privy to.

"May I ask… have you had much interaction with Lady Adela since the death of her daughter Evangeline last spring?"

Kyle and I looked at each other, trying to remember.

"You were with us when we caught Sir James at Lady Adela's home behind Kensington Palace, Chief Inspector. That was after Evangeline's murder."

Sir James Dennison was one of the first male leading actors on the *Castlewood Manor* series. He was a first-rate cad, having affairs with not only Lady Adela and her daughter, Evangeline, but also Aunt Margaret during the season one filming of the series. He murdered Evangeline because she threatened to go public. He was set to murder Lady Adela, but Kyle and my arrival at her home thwarted his plans and gave Chief Inspector Marquot and his team time to get to Lady Adela's quarters and capture him.

"She was at my knighting ceremony at Buckingham Palace too. She was a very close friend of my mother. Other than that, we haven't spent much time with her. We were so busy with the royal wedding and then the series premiere and American tour, there just hasn't been much time. She's been visiting us more once she learned that Gemma was to become the Marchioness of Kentshire. She was a bit pushy, trying to force Lady Margaret to endorse Gemma's taking of the title. It was a difficult time, especially with Evan being in a coma."

"It was such a sad situation. I remember following her daughter, Lady Evangeline on social media. I was about the same age as she was. She was 'the' royal it-girl. The darling of the fashion houses and nightclub scenes. I was so shocked to hear of her death. She seemed so close to her mother, too. They went around the world on many adventures; mountain climbing, glacier hiking—both were very athletic and acted more like sisters than mother and daughter," Olivia observed, taking the last bite of her thyme fries.

Chief Inspector looked at his niece in wonder and startled us all by kissing her on the forehead. Olivia looked shocked at this public display in front of her employers, and especially by her reserved uncle.

"I didn't mean to embarrass you, Olivia, but your observations have made me very happy. Very happy indeed. May I ask, does anyone wear a blonde wig at Cherrywood Hall?"

"Not that I know of, Chief Inspector. Mama and Aunt Margaret get a little blond help from their hairdressers, but neither wear wigs. There may be some stored at the crew quarters down the road from the estate. They're used during filming for wardrobe changes. The mega closet upstairs by my office just has clothes and accessories, no wigs."

"No, I think the weather would have been too formidable for someone to go out and retrieve items from the crew quarters. I was thinking if one of the ladies staying in the house was wearing a wig."

Kyle and I looked at each other thinking but shook our heads.

"Amy's hair is dark brown, as is Lucy's. Prudence is more of an ash blond. Sally was there, but she has short blond hair. May I ask why you want to know?"

The chief inspector stared down at his hands for a few minutes before looking up at me to answer. "Elizabeth had strands of what looked like hair wrapped in her fingers. They were long blond strands. They were not human hair. They were synthetic, from fibers used in lower quality wigs. That was one of the main reasons Reginald Gerard was let go. There was nothing in his possession that matched an item such as that, nor did he know of anything."

We finished our lunch, Kyle and I heading back to Cherrywood Hall and Olivia staying behind to talk more with her uncle on the suspicions we had on the Father Christmas chair and jewelry case, and possibly even the ornaments. My mind was reeling trying to put two and two together, but I had nothing.

"I had forgotten about Lady Adela and Evangeline's mountain climbing. They were the talk of the polo set a few years back. It takes a lot of funds to set up those excursions, especially these days. You need crews to manage the supplies, guides to manage the navigation, it's very complex. They climbed mountains all over the world. Lady Adela had no qualms about using her royal connections to get funds and endorsements from the corporate and playboy billionaires. Her lifestyle was lavish and had considerable influence on Evangeline. They appeared to have strong family ties, but I wonder…"

"It seems she gets around through using people. Do you think some of her corporate and playboy cronies have tired of her? That could account for the personality change."

"It could also account for using other measures to get the monies she needs for her lifestyle."

"Do you really think she was behind the vault theft at the palace? It just seems so incredible to me that she would do it. Do you think Chief Inspector Marquot is investigating her, or Reggie? I still don't know what their connection might be."

"The chief inspector was keeping many things from us, I think. He said it best, when it comes to the royals, the utmost of discretion is deployed, no matter how heinous the crime might be."

Kyle drove the Rover in front of the hall. More snow and cold was predicted for the New Year's event tomorrow evening. The Rosehill staff was once again in final prep for the cast announcement broadcasts to be made from the conservatory. The grand hallway was bustling with staff who were getting the equipment and lighting sorted for installation. Elliot and Max were seated by the Christmas tree. They stood when they saw us enter, motioning for us to come join them. Max looked nervous.

"Was it horrid at the police station, darling? I can't imagine. Jillian went up to her room. David's in the library, of course."

"Just some basic questions, I think, not too bad. Daddy's taking the worst of it as the husband of the deceased. We were a bit surprised to hear about Reggie's release."

"Reggie just called me. He wanted to come here to retrieve Patch. I told him I would have to talk with you of course. I know little Ajani has become attached to the doggie. I didn't know what to tell him." Max clenched his hands tightly.

I inhaled deeply. It was going to be tough to separate Ajani and Patch. I looked at Kyle and gave a little shrug.

"You can tell him he may come to pick up the dog. I don't want him going inside the hall. We can have the dog brought to him at the entry. Have him come this evening. We don't want him here on New Year's Eve," Kyle said.

Max nodded his head. He understood that with the current uncertainty of Elizabeth's death, he would not be welcome back to stay or visit at Cherrywood Hall.

I went over to Evan's room to see how he was doing and to talk to Ajani about giving up the pooch he had become so attached to. Simone and Evan were sitting by the fireplace, watching their son play with Patch. I pulled up a chair to join them, whispering to Evan and Simone.

"Reggie wants to come and pick up Patch. I know it's going to be so hard on Ajani."

The little tyke squealed as he threw a ball for Patch to fetch. Evan and Simone understood, nodding their head.

"Ajani, come to Papa, will you?" Evan asked.

He ran over, with Patch following close behind. He pulled Ajani on his lap.

"Do you remember how you felt when you were waiting for me to wake up? You were a little sad, weren't you?"

"Yes, Papa. Mummy and I prayed for you every night."

Evan kissed his son's forehead. "Patch's papa was away too, but he's come back. He wants to come here and take Patch home."

The little boy's eyes teared up. His bottom lip started to tremble. Evan rubbed his son's back to calm him.

"Ajani, we will have many animals at the ranch when we go back home. You can have as many pets as you'd like," Simone cooed, trying to soothe her son.

Ajani climbed down from Evan's lap and bent to pet his little friend. "You need to go to your papa now, Patch. Happy Christmas and New Year's." We all had tears rolling down our face as the little boy petted the dog for a last time and handed him to me. "Bye Patch."

Patch whined, his eyes wide with sorrow as he left his little friend.

Simone and Evan held Ajani close as I left the room carrying the dog to the front entry. Max and Elliot were at the door with two large duffle bags, Patch's belongings I assumed. I wiped my face and handed the dog over to Max. The doorbell rang, and Bridges opened it, letting Reggie into the front entry to get out of the cold. Kyle and I stood behind Max and Elliot as they shook hands with their friend and handed him his dog. Patch wagged his tail, torn between his love of his master and the little boy who had stolen his doggie heart the past few days.

"Gemma, Kyle—I—thank you for taking care of Patch. I can see he's been very happy. Please give my regards to… give my regards to everyone." Reggie choked up and turned taking his little dog.

Max and Elliot carried Patch's luggage to his car. We waited for them to come back in.

It was time for a cocktail in the study, and after this, I definitely needed one. The episode with Patch was heartbreaking. Kyle started mixing my gin and St. Germain martini and poured whiskey tumblers for him, Elliot and Max. They joined us in the study, just in time to say cheers.

"Oh, my goodness, be still my heart," Max said, taking his cocktail and downing it, holding it up for a refill.

"You guys didn't have to go to Evan's room and take Patch from a little boy's arms," I sobbed, taking a generous drink of my martini. "Evan told him Patch's papa had come back, just like he did for Ajani. If you had seen his face—"

Kyle came over and hugged me, wiping tears from his eyes too.

"For such a small dog, Patch sure had a lot of gear. I ended up dropping the bag on the way to the car. Can anyone tell me why a pooch that small needs a rappelling rope? A shoestring would hold that pooch," Elliot said, shaking his head.

"A rappelling rope? Are you sure?" Kyle asked.

"Yes, it had the hooks, or whatever you call them. There was a harness in there too, come to think of it. It was much too big for Patch…"

"We never checked Patch's bags. They were in the kitchen. I need to call Chief Inspector Marquot." Kyle pulled out his phone and dialed, going into the dining room to talk.

"What's he calling the chief inspector for? Surely, he won't be accusing the dog," Elliot teased.

Kyle rejoined us, a big grin on his face.

"What is it, darling? You have my interest."

He pulled me up from the chair and motioned Elliot and Max to follow us. We went over to the Christmas tree down at the end of the grand hallway.

"See the beams near the ceiling? Rappelling ropes could have been swung over them. A skilled climber could have easily scaled the wall to untether the tree. I couldn't figure out how those hooks were loosened, being up so high."

"Does Reggie climb?" I asked.

"He did a bit of climbing in university. He even travelled with Lady Adela years back on one of her mountain excursions. I thought he gave it up. He took a fall that shook him up pretty badly," Max explained.

"I've told the chief inspector to get a warrant. He's sending a forensics crew here now to inspect the beams. They have a hewn surface, there may still be traces of the rope fibers on them."

We didn't have to wait long for the police to arrive with Chief Inspector Marquot in tow. They used a ladder that Kyle's crew had brought to the house to inspect the beams. We stood at the base, watching the forensics expert take samples. He climbed down and nodded his head. He had found strands from a rope.

"Is Lord Evan available? I'd like to have a word with you. I have some information that includes him," Chief Inspector Marquot said, looking at Kyle and me.

Kyle went to Evan's room to get him, pushing him in the wheelchair to the library where the chief inspector and I had taken a seat. Kyle sat down next to me as Chief Inspector Marquot shook Evan's hand.

"We have had several breaks in cases related to the events here in Cherrywood Hall. I cannot disclose all the details to you yet, but I fear all three of you may be in grave danger. It would appear that Lady Adela and Reginald Gerard are the leaders of an international network that has been involved in major crimes of late, including the theft of the queen's jewels from her vault at the palace."

"I can't believe this. They're robbers?"

"More than mere robbers, Dr. Gemma. They have been involved in blackmail, taking pictures and making audio tapes to extort millions of dollars from their unsuspecting victims. They surrounded themselves with the rich and famous, including many royals around the world. Lady Adela used her position as the queen's niece to open many doors for her. Reggie is her accomplice. As he arranged royal weddings and other events, he was an inside mole, discovering where safes were located, taking pictures and drawing schematics of their locations. When the time was right, he and Lady Adela would make their moves."

"How horrible, does the queen know?"

"I informed her yesterday, Lord Evan. Lady Adela has not been seen nor heard from since she left Cherrywood Hall, with the exception of a very angry garage owner who was rudely awakened on Christmas day. The cab drove her into Maidenford, where she picked up her car and drove off without a trace."

"This is so strange. The queen must be heartbroken. How long has this been going on Chief Inspector?"

"For many years, Sir Kyle. Interpol has been watching them for quite some time. They have been guests at several locations when the thefts or blackmail occurred."

"Why do you think we're in grave danger, Chief Inspector? If Lady Adela has disappeared with Reggie following close behind, don't you think they'll be long gone, possibly out of the country?"

"We've put out alerts to all airports, train and ship locations. They wouldn't get far."

"Do you think they're planning to come back to Cherrywood Hall?" I asked.

"You're having a New Year's Eve broadcast and celebration here at Cherrywood Hall tomorrow night with many viewers from around the world watching for the news of the film cast. I think your vault downstairs may be a temptation they won't be able to resist. They both stayed here at Cherrywood with full access. They would have had plenty of time to figure out a way to get access to the vault."

"The access to the vault is digital, Chief Inspector. You have to scan either Evan's hand or mine to open it. Gemma's handprint isn't yet authorized."

"I understand. They don't know about Dr. Gemma not having access. They could hold you at gunpoint to open the vault or kill you and place your dead hand on the reading device."

"Do you really think they would kill us?" I asked.

"I'm convinced they killed Elizabeth—she must have heard or seen something, unwittingly. I think with you, there's another factor in play here. Revenge—revenge for the death of Lady Adela's daughter, Evangeline. Sir James Dennison was found murdered in his cell yesterday, killed by a cellmate who was paid to commit the act. I believe Lady Adela is holding everyone here at Cherrywood to blame as well. You see, we have found out the source of funds used to pay for your kidnapping, Lord Evan. It was Lady Adela, who gave the orders and paid the poachers. You weren't expected to live."

CHAPTER 19
Midnight Madness

The ladies of Cherrywood Hall had gathered in the mega closet to prepare for the *Castlewood Manor* New Year's Eve broadcast. Hair was being fluffed and teased. Eyeliner was applied by the buckets as the stylists worked their makeover magic. We were being transformed into glittering muses for the big cast reveal. Lucy and Timothy wanted to start the broadcast with us dressed in our golden finery, descending the staircase into the grand hallway, complete with shimmering masks to add to the New Year mystery.

There was a dire rationale for the slight change to the broadcast content. After receiving Chief Inspector Marquot's devastating news on Lady Adela and Reggie, our first reaction was to cancel the broadcast. We had brought Lucy and Timothy into the library along with Aunt Margaret, Mama, Olivia, and Elliot to brief them on the news. Aunt Margaret was beside herself upon learning it was her conversations with the queen that fed Lady Adela's devious mind in devising Evan's kidnapping.

"I know you are concerned for everyone's safety, but it seems Lady Adela and Reggie are bent on being in the spotlight to fuel their unhinged egos. If the broadcast is cancelled, it's likely they'll try to attack at the next big event, Gemma's peerage ceremony. The queen will be there and could become a target herself. I'd recommend going ahead with the broadcast and try to capture them. The more time that passes will enable them to gather more resources to support their sinister plot. If we act quickly, there are lots of ways we can stir the pot to draw them out."

"Elliot, I don't want to endanger my family anymore," Aunt Margaret cried. "It's bad enough that my private conversations were used to attack and almost kill my son."

Evan put his arm around his mother to comfort her, as she sobbed. Lucy and Timothy visibly cringed.

"What would you recommend we do, Mr. Elliot, to stir the pot, so to speak?" Chief Inspector Marquot asked, intrigued.

"Suppose we throw a masked ball type event, with the ladies all dressed in similar dresses, the men attired in matching tuxedos, and everyone wearing masks. If their goal is to try and take retribution against Lord Evan, Sir Kyle and/or Gemma, let's make their job harder. With everyone dressed alike, they will be the ones to stand out as they go around the room to try and find their targets. You can have the rooms loaded with police to observe the crowds and brief all the guests on what to be on the lookout for. Twist the element of surprise back at them."

We sat in silence, pondering Elliot's plan. He was right in one respect—the more time they had to plan, the more deadly the outcome could be. I shivered at the thought of them being at my peerage ceremony with the queen. It would be horrible if anything was to happen to her.

"How do you propose getting the matching costumes in time for the event? I can see the tuxedos for the men, but the ladies? Where would we get matching dresses for so many?"

"Chief Inspector, darling, Rosehill Productions is hosting the event. They're one of the largest studios in the country. I do think they can manage to come up with the costumes, don't you think, Lucy?" Elliot winked.

"Of course, I can get Penny's team on it now. We can have all the guests arrive early and get them dressed upstairs in the mega closet. I'll have make-up artists and stylists here in force to get everyone fancied up." Lucy was visibly relieved at the possible lifeline. The cancellation of the broadcast would be a disaster for the new feature film. Rosehill had spent millions promoting the New Year's Eve broadcast.

"It's actually a brilliant idea. With everyone dressed the same, it will make it easier to flush out Lady Adela and Reggie if they decide to make an appearance. The tables will be turned because you'll have all eyes watching for them. I can be styled identically to Gemma to confuse them more. We won't have many opportunities such as this uncle." Olivia observed.

"Lord Evan, Sir Kyle, Dr. Gemma, the decision is yours. I appreciate your safety concerns, but I agree with Olivia and Elliot, we won't have this chance again. I can have the hall completely surrounded by police."

Kyle, Evan and I looked at each other, dreading the encounter with the devious pair, yet wishing their reign of madness to be extinguished. Evan nodded at me to make the final decision. I looked at the anxious faces of the people I cared very much about.

"I vote to go ahead then, if it's our best way to capture these fiends before they can harm anyone else." So, it had been decided, the golden, masked ball would be our chance to catch the thieves.

And so, New Year's Eve prep was now in full swing.

"Are you ready for your honeymoon, Penny?" Mama asked, as she sipped a glass of champagne while getting her make-up applied.

"Yes indeed, Jillian. I will be so glad to get out of this winter wind tunnel and into the pink sands of the Bahamas. I told Steph yesterday if our flights get cancelled again, we're getting a rowboat." Penny laughed.

"It's dreadful outside. We barely made it here from London. There were lorries on their sides with produce and boxes all over the highway. I felt as if we were in a motorized rugby tournament the way our chauffeur weaved back and forth on the roads to stay clear of obstacles. I had my eyes closed most of the drive here." Dame Agnes grimaced.

She and Freddie Alton-Jones would be on the broadcast tonight with Mama as the *Castlewood Manor* feature film cast was introduced.

"Freddie was quite the gentleman. He brought me flowers," Aunt Margaret said, a twinkle in her eye.

He cared for her very much and wanted to rekindle their relationship.

I was glad to see it. The past twenty-four hours had been very hard on her. She and the queen blamed themselves for unknowingly enabling Evan's kidnapping. The queen shortened her Christmas stay at Sandringham to head back to Buckingham Palace. She put out an official decree for her law enforcement services; she wanted Lady Adela and Reggie caught as soon as possible. All traces of her royal niece were being purged from the palace websites. The palace expected there to be public outrage once the news of Lady Adela hit the airwaves. They were taking unprecedented measures to ramp up the capture plans and start the royal messaging. A favorite niece or not, the queen was most definitely not amused.

Olivia was sitting next to me as our stylists set our hair and applied our make-up. I was amazed once again at our resemblance, made even more remarkable once the make-up and hairstyles were completed. We donned our gold gowns and slippers and tied our masks on. I gasped when I saw our reflections in the mirror. It would be very difficult for Lady Adela to tell us apart. Penny paraded us to the center of the mega closet to show off our completed looks.

"I still think you must be a long-lost daughter, Olivia." Mama teased. "I can't get over how much you two look alike."

"I hope our transformation works, Ms. Jillian. If Lady Adela or Reggie try to nab me, they'll have to fight this." Olivia raised her skirt to show a small pistol, strapped to her leg. She was dressed for business tonight.

"I wish Simone was joining us tonight. With her martial arts skills I'm sure she could take out any intruder."

"She's afraid to leave Ajani alone, Jillian, even with a nanny and police officers guarding their doors. I've never seen her so frightened. Evan has tried to reassure her, but she will have none of it," Aunt Margaret said, shaking her head.

3-2-1, at nine o'clock we began our masked procession down the staircase as Mama, Lucy, Dame Agnes, Timothy, and Freddie began the broadcast. Amy and Prudence were stationed in the conservatory to highlight the New Year's Eve décor. Red, gold and black metallic streamers hung from the ceiling, camouflaging a net filled with balloons that would be released at the strike of twelve to ring in the new year.

The cameras zoomed in on the grand hall finery, with a final look at the stately Christmas tree that was still a gleaming centerpiece this last night of the year. Our gentleman escorts waited for us as we descended the stairs, Elliot taking Aunt Margaret's arm, Max taking Penny's, Evan, who was using a walker, escorting Olivia, and Kyle as my partner.

Daddy had decided to go over to Evelyn's tonight. The news of Lady Adela and Reggie's murder of Elizabeth had upset him a great deal, thinking of his wife being murdered as she wandered around in a drug-induced stupor. He was no longer a person of interest in Elizabeth's murder, news that relieved us all. We would be having a small ceremony next week to release Elizabeth's ashes to the sea. I hoped it would bring closure to my father's broken spirit.

Kyle led me to the conservatory as I greeted my guests, waving a fan in front of me in an overly flirtatious manner. Olivia and I had matching ones, fitted with a transponder to monitor our every move. I saw Chief Inspector Marquot in the dining room, watching as the guests trooped in. He was determined to knab Lady Adela and Reggie tonight.

The television cameras in the conservatory zoomed in on Prudence and Amy as they showed off the gorgeous room features and décor, explaining the history and the design of Pippa's thirty-foot waterfall that prominently featured red holographic lights beaming in the splashing waters.

We all were waiting and watching for any sign out of the ordinary as the background music played. Mama, Dame Agnes and Freddie were up next, to make the big casting announcement for the film. In 3-2-1, the cameras were on as the lead stars began their excited banter.

We were startled to hear a loud 'POP' noise come from the dining room just as they were about to make the starring actresses announcement. It sounded like a gun going off, or a very loud New Year's Eve popper that had been triggered early. Evan, Kyle, and I dropped our mouths as we turned to see what had caused the commotion.

To our shock and horror, Simone, carrying Ajani, walked into the conservatory, with Lady Adela following close behind, a gun pointed at her back. She was wearing a vest loaded with what appeared to be explosive devices, threatening anyone who came close to her. Her hair was covered by a long, blonde wig that was styled in the same way her daughter Evangeline had worn her hair, giving her a very creepy resemblance to the deceased. The police tried to move as many guests as they could out to the hallway and through the front doors to take them to safety.

"Everyone stop now, I demand it! No one will be leaving the halls of Cherrywood tonight. I intend to blow up the house that killed my daughter. If anyone tries to leave, I'll set the explosives off now!" the mad woman screeched, turning on a clock device.

We had fifteen minutes to stop her before we all perished in a fiery end. The broadcast cameras zoomed in on the crazed woman and her hostages, playing for all the world to watch as the drama unfolded.

"Lady Adela, let my wife and son go, they've done nothing to you." Evan pleaded.

Kyle grabbed him by the wrist so that he couldn't move forward. Now, wasn't the time to make her angry.

"I will not. You should be dead, Evan Lancaster. My daughter was killed in our stately house, right in the room next door. You have no right to be marquess, you did nothing…" Lady Adela's shouts seemed to vibrate the glass in the frames.

I had never heard such a deranged cry of rage. It sounded almost unhuman. Her cruel tones dawned on me finally—it was Lady Adela's voice in the jewelry store we heard that day. She was the royal ladyship selling the queen's jewels!

"Lady Adela, please stop this. I want you at my peerage ceremony to celebrate with me. You loved Kyle and me, remember?" For just a moment, there was a trace of kindness on Lady Adela's face as she looked at me. Her face morphed between love and madness, the latter winning in her crazed mind.

"I'm sorry, but you're not going to be marchioness, Gemma. You and Kyle let me down. I'm so disappointed in you. You had everything I dreamed for my darling Evangeline. You see, I wanted her to marry Kyle, just as Honey and I used to talk about. It would have been a lovely wedding."

The crowd gasped as she ranted on, unsure of how to react to the lunacy that was being spewed. Simone remained extremely calm as her eyes darted back and forth around the room, looking for an opportunity to escape and save her son. She saw the police snipers on the camera scaffolding, trying to aim at Lady Adela, but she held Simone and Ajani too close. They were afraid to take the shot.

I saw a veil of calmness cross over Simone's face as the clock of the bomb ticked away. She looked at Evan with love in her eyes as she made up her mind to try and save the people she loved most. We screamed as she threw Ajani into the air, floating to safety as Evan made a desperate grab to catch him, cradling him in his arms as he turned away.

Simone kicked out her legs at the madwoman, giving her deadly, swift kicks to her extremities. Lady Adela lost her balance and fell into the pool under the waterfall. Simone dove in to pull the woman as deep into the watery depths as possible. She wrapped her body around the bomb vest to try and absorb as much of the explosive brunt as possible.

The police swarmed the pool trying to get a shot to take the mad woman out. Chief Inspector Marquot and his men pushed us out as we waited for the inevitable explosion.

"Get out, everyone run to the front entry, now!" he shouted.

We had less than five minutes to vacate the house, running outside into the freezing night air. Aunt Margaret, Evan and Ajani hobbled down the drive as quickly as his weakened legs and walker could go to get as far away as possible. Kyle, Mama, and I followed close behind, not knowing what was happening in the final moments at the house. Our guests gathered around as we took refuge behind the massive, stone, retaining wall that protected the final hill to the estate. We watched the manor house that was the favorite of millions draw its final breath.

The explosion was immense, sending a fireball out into the night sky, a brilliant orange glow illuminating the area for miles. Shards of glass and steel blew all around us as we knelt and covered our heads with our hands to protect ourselves.

"Nooooo!" Evan wailed, as he handed Ajani to Aunt Margaret, crying for the wife who had so bravely saved us.

His cries of pain and sorrow chilled us all to the bone. We stood and cried as Kyle held Evan in his arms, trying to comfort a man collapsed with grief who had been through so much.

The fiery ball over the house finally calmed as the night sky reverted to its shining stars overhead. We could see an orange glow emanating from the back of the house. I ran up the hill with Kyle and Evan to learn of Simone's fate and assess the damage to the house. We made our way through the entry, surprised to see the grand hallway virtually untouched. The generators had kicked on, supplying power after the explosion took out the main junction to the house. We went through the study into the dining room, where the explosion had caused a major hole through the wall dividing the room from the conservatory.

We climbed over the wreckage of glass and steel that covered the floor, embers still glowing from the heat. Chief Inspector Marquot was sitting on the rocks where the waterfall had been, cradling his face in his hands. The entire wall behind the falls was gone, blown away by the explosive force. Charred plants and melted balloons littered the marble pathways. We made our way over to the chief inspector as we prepared for the worst news one could hear.

I looked over the chief inspector's shoulder and gasped. The body of a woman in a shimmering, gold gown floated on the brackish water, her long, blond hair spreading out like a golden crown. I realized now why the chief inspector was crying. The body was that of his niece, Olivia. She had dived into the water after Simone to try and protect us as well.

Kyle cradled me as I started to cry for the brave, young woman who had given her life to protect others. Evan fell to his knees as he looked at the devastation around, sobbing uncontrollably. The heart-wrenching cries were almost too hard to hear.

"Evan, I'm here," Simone whispered, bending down to hug her husband.

We turned and stared, not believing our eyes.

Evan grabbed her, hugging her tighter than he ever had, kissing her face and hands. "I thought--we thought you were dead, darling. How in the world did you survive?"

"Olivia dove in after me to help take Lady Adela to the bottom of the pool and stuff that maniac in the drainage tank. We both managed to get her in, but Olivia's dress stuck on the grate; she couldn't pull it loose. I tried to pull her free, but there just wasn't time. She was so brave—she smiled as she pushed me away. I will never forget the love and compassion that she showed to me." Simone held Evan's sobbing frame in her arms, protecting the man she loved with all her heart.

"Your wife is an amazing woman, Lord Evan. She managed to swim up and climb out of the pool, putting herself behind the rock pillars to shield her from the explosion that came. We owe our lives to these brave women. If they had not caged her in that drainage tank, the house would have been damaged much worse with many casualties," the Chief Inspector sobbed, shaking his head in sorrow for his beloved niece. "I don't know how I will explain this loss to my little girl, Annie. She loved her cousin so much…"

We walked out the front entry into the night air, Evan and Simone holding each other close, and the chief inspector walking between Kyle and me. The crowd gasped when they saw Simone—Aunt Margaret carrying Ajani raced toward her, ecstatic at seeing her alive. Mama, Elliot and Max were close behind. They threw their arms around us as Ajani squealed in delight at seeing his mummy and papa. They held him in their arms rejoicing at being together again.

The police gathered our guests and allowed them to go after being debriefed. We went back into the hall to sit by the Christmas tree that acted as our family beacon these past weeks. The doors to the dining room and conservatory were shut as the forensics team began their analysis and collection of evidence.

It was amazing that we were sitting in the room that had been so close to the explosion but had escaped unharmed. Bridges and his staff brought us blankets and drinks to warm us up, handing a bottle of Evan's private reserve whiskey to Elliot to pour us a tumbler. The Chief Inspector spoke with one of his guards on the stairs leading to the kitchen, shaking his head as he took a crumpled piece of paper from his colleague. He joined us by the tree, and even accepted a tumbler of whiskey from Elliot.

"I wanted to let you know that the body of Reginald Gerard has been found at the bottom of the cliff along the sea path. He was stabbed with a Damascus knife through his heart. There are rappelling ropes at the cliffside. That's how Lady Adela made her way to Cherrywood. They brought a dinghy over, landing it on the beach."

"Simone, how did Lady Adela get to you and Ajani? You had guards outside your doors."

Simone looked at me and smiled as she choked back tears holding her now sleeping boy. "I was putting Ajani to bed when I heard the creak of a door opening. I looked at the room door, but it was closed. I turned by the fireplace and looked over my shoulder. Lady Adela was climbing out of a secret panel door in the wall adjoining the fireplace. She had a gun pointed at me. She told me to pick up my son and follow her directions or be shot. She killed the two guards outside my door, and we began our walk to the conservatory. She kept rambling on and on about justice for the dead. The police who saw us backed away as she threatened to kill us. There was nothing else to do. I couldn't bear to think of our baby being killed."

"How did she know about a paneled door? She had only been here for a few days."

"I showed it to her," Aunt Margaret said, tears streaming down her face. "She was with the queen and me when we were visiting Evan. Kyle showed it to me earlier during the renovation. It's what they call a priest hole, used centuries ago to hide persons of the Catholic faith. Once again, my blathering's almost got everyone killed," she sobbed.

"Aunt Margaret, stop. No one knew Lady Adela was so evil." My heart broke for my grieving aunt.

"She entered the house from a window in the adjoining room. She found a way into the house that no one had suspected. She and Reggie were masters at staking out these old manor houses," Chief Inspector Marquot said, sighing.

"Chief Inspector, why did she kill Reggie? I thought he was in this with her."

"This note was found on his body. I think it explains what happened," he said, handing the crumpled note to me to read to the group.

It read:

Final Confession of Reginald Gerard,

If you are reading this, then unfortunately, I must be dead. I have been blackmailed by Lady Adela to help her with her theft rings since she caught me taking a Damascus knife from the queen's collection five years ago. She threatened to expose me and have me jailed if I did not cooperate with her. I must admit it was my own weakness that led me down this path. She introduced me to a whole new way of living in a lavish lifestyle that had seduced my heart.

Lady Adela has been driven over the edge, consumed by rage stemming from the death of her daughter, Evangeline. I wanted no part in Lord Evan's kidnapping, but I was in too deep and didn't know which way to turn. When I came to Cherrywood, I could see how lovely your family was. I knew that Lady Adela's rage was heightened by insanity. She is the one who damaged Lord Evan's tubes, trying to put the blame on my beloved Patch.

Elizabeth walked into the indoor pool room and heard us arguing about her final plan of exploding the hall. Elizabeth tried to run, but, in her drug-induced state she didn't get far. Lady Adela cracked her over the head and dumped her body into the pool. We concocted the story of me being found to cover her participation. We thought we could get away with the deception.

Tonight, I tried to talk her out of this insanity, but she wasn't listening. I made up my mind to kill her myself. Alas, if you've found this note, I was not successful.

I have two final requests. My dog Patch is in a room at the Maidenford Hotel where we were hiding out under the name of Pettiford. I would ask that he be returned to the little boy. My friend Max said the two had become very attached. Please tell Lady Gemma her beloved heirloom ornaments are in the room as well. I could never stand to see beautiful items destroyed.

Thus, endeth the day.

Reginald Gerard, Esq.

CHAPTER 20
American Marchioness

January fourteenth, the day before my peerage ceremony was a joyful day for us all. We were in London, staying at Aunt Margaret's Belgravia home to have a small party before we left for Hampton Court Palace in the morning. Our friends and colleagues from Maidenford and Rosehill Productions had been invited to attend the ceremony, it was my wish that they be included in my special day.

The past few weeks had been a tumultuous time, dealing with the demolition of the structures that had been destroyed or damaged by the explosion at Cherrywood. I was proud of our stately manor and wanted it repaired as quickly as possible.

Kyle and Steph had changed the layout of the conservatory to now combine it with the space from the indoor pool room. Our swimming area would now be part of the waterfall feature, giving more room for entertaining in the space that was converted from the pool to a luscious sunroom and bar area overlooking the sea. There would be more room for dining and dancing. With all that had happened this past year, we felt a new space design was the best option for us.

The queen had made sure that all our Cherrywood Hall expenses were paid for out of Lady Adela's inheritance funds. Her estate funds were being used to pay back all the victims that had been stolen from over the years. She had offered a special fund to Evan and Ajani, but it was turned down. Evan and Simone were billionaires now with their marriage. They did not want any of Lady Adela's monies.

Daddy had Elizabeth's remains cremated, with a short ceremony to scatter them off the cliffs into the ocean. It was a bittersweet moment for us all. We hoped that the young woman's soul was finally at peace. Daddy would be staying with us at Cherrywood for a while as he decided his future.

Season two filming of *Castlewood Manor* was delayed for another few weeks due to the fallout from the explosion shown on the cast announcement broadcast. The executives wanted all their employees to take all-expenses paid vacations to try and relax after the horrible experience. Penny and Steph had joyfully left for their delayed honeymoon, sending cards from the pink sands of the Bahamas.

As disastrous as that evening was, it had been a ratings bonanza as the live feed streamed around the globe. The television cameras captured everything until they were destroyed by the explosion. The infamous film made the *Castlewood Manor* feature film the talk of the industry.

Olivia Fisher's funeral had the highest honors and was attended by the queen. She was awarded a Victoria Cross for bravery in the course of duty, one of the queen's most coveted awards. Her family was also compensated for her loss of life in a fund given personally by the queen.

Our dinner the night before the peerage ceremony, hosted by Aunt Margaret and Freddie Alton-Jones, was to include Daddy and Evelyn, Mama and Karl, Max and Elliot, and Evan, Simone, and Ajani, accompanied by his best canine friend, Patch. We gathered in Aunt Margaret's sunroom for cocktails, ready to enjoy a quiet evening with friends.

"POP" the first cork of champagne was unleashed by Elliot as he filled our flutes with the sparkling bubbly. As the champagne was poured the doorbell rang, answered by Aunt Margaret's butler, James. He came to the sunroom and announced, "Her Majesty, the Queen and His Royal Highness, Prince Thaddeus."

We turned to them and bowed and curtsied as they entered the room, shocked to see them here. Queen Annelyce came over to me and kissed my cheeks.

"Gemma darling, we just wanted to wish you well before your ceremony tomorrow. We were passing by and thought we'd take a chance you were here," she said, with a twinkle in her eye.

I was pretty sure one of her staff had called beforehand to make sure we were in attendance.

She then walked over to Evan and Simone, bending down to Ajani to shake his hand.

"Ruff!" Patch wagged his tail.

"Ruff to you, little Patch. You take care of this young man now. I'm the queen, you must do as I say."

"Ruff!" Patch responded. He knew a queen's mandate when he heard one. It also helped that she just happened to pull a dog treat from her handbag to give the tiny pooch a royal snack.

The queen stood and looked over to Simone and Evan. "I don't know how to thank you for saving so many people that horrid night, Simone. You are an honor to know. Evan, I trust you will include us in your visits when you travel here on holiday from South Africa?"

"Of course, Ma'am. It will be an honor, thank you."

"Good then. Elliot, do you think you could pour your queen and prince a glass of champagne? We would love to participate in a toast."

Elliot scurried to find two more flutes and filled them. Max handed them to the queen and Prince Thaddeus with a smile.

"A toast to Lady Gemma Lancaster Phillips, the soon-to-be Marchioness of Kentshire. Welcome to your new role, Lady Gemma."

"Hear, hear," the group said in unison.

"Ruff!" Patch agreed, as well sending us into waves of laughter.

I walked the queen out to her car when she was ready to leave. Kyle walked behind with Prince Thaddeus.

"Your majesty, I have a special request after my ceremony tomorrow."

"I'll do whatever I can, dear. What is it?"

I bent down to whisper in her ear.

"Uh-hum, yes, I understand. I think that should be no problem, dear. I will see you in the morning."

Kyle and I waved as the royal couple departed, our arms wrapped around one another. "Come on now darling, what were you whispering to the queen? Remember, a husband and wife must have no secrets between them."

"I do agree, Sir Kyle, but alas, we are not married, yet." I teased, tickling him as we walked back inside.

That night we had a feast of roasted prime rib with root vegetables, mushroom tarts, and Mama's favorite, dates wrapped in sausage and bacon. I finally felt a sense of relief and closure as I shared my last night of being Gemma Lancaster Phillips, PhD with my family and friends. After the ceremony tomorrow, I would be known as Lady Gemma Lancaster Phillips, Marchioness of Kentshire.

Evan, Simone, Ajani, and Patch would be leaving for South Africa after the ceremony. Evan was anxious to start his new life with his wife and son, and he still had a long way to go with his recovery. I would miss them so much—we had grown even closer the past few weeks, taking walks around Cherrywood one last time before everything changed. I remembered our final day, Evan and I walked along the sea path before we left for London for one last cousin-to-cousin chat.

"Pippa would be very proud of you, Gemma. You're breaking new ground for all the Lancaster ladies you know."

"I hope to make her and all of you proud of me, Evan. It's scary, but with Kyle by my side, I'm very excited to give it my best. I'll miss you so much."

We hugged on the cliffside, holding each other close. It was a bittersweet moment, but I was proud of my cousin too. He was going to get to live the life of his dreams, and in the end, that's all that mattered.

Our dinner ended with an after-dinner drink. It was to be an early evening for us since we had to be at the palace on time in the morning. Aunt Margaret was a firm ruler of royal etiquette, no exceptions.

As we crawled into bed, Kyle pulled me close and kissed me. "You do know you'll be magnificent tomorrow, don't you?"

"Yes, I think I rather will, Sir Kyle. Wait 'til you see me dressed in Pippa's anniversary gown, bejeweled with the queen's medallion and the lovely tiara you gave me at Christmas. I do look stunning if I don't say so myself."

"There's my American girl, full of self-confidence and grit. I wonder if our noble lords and ladies know what they are in for?" He laughed.

"It's taken me a few hundred years to get here. Hopefully, they'll cut me some slack."

"Elliot was talking of the spread that is going to be placed in the papers after your ceremony. You're going to be quite famous very soon, darling."

"I don't know about famous. There will be interest at first, I'm sure. I think over time it will fade. We'll become part of the 'Turnip Toffs' set, with maybe a few pictures of us at the *Castlewood Manor* events. Everyone will want to see pictures of our babies."

"I want to get married, Gemma, soon." Kyle smiled, kissing my hand.

"I do too, Kyle, more than you know. I promise everything will be done, soon." I kissed Kyle warmly and deeply as our passion grew. There was no way this man would not be in my life. I loved him more than ever—being his wife and having his children would fulfill my dreams.

The next morning, a limo arrived to take Aunt Margaret, Mama and me to Hampton Court Palace. I wanted us to get there earlier than the rest of the guests so that I could prepare and dress in my ceremony finery. Penny's wardrobe team had altered Pippa's anniversary gown so that it fit me to a tee. I requested all my female guests to wear blue to the ceremony today in honor of my American turned British auntie. Mama was wearing a lovely, periwinkle-blue wool dress with a half cape that draped her figure beautifully. Aunt Margaret was wearing an elegant, blue and gold brocade coat dress with faux, blue fur around the collar and cuffs.

As we drove to the palace Mama held my hand, tears brimming in her eyes.

"You look so lovely, daughter. I can't believe this is really happening. I always knew you were special. You're going to be a fine marchioness."

"Thank you, Mama. I had no idea my life would take this direction, but there's no place I'd rather be. All our lives have changed so much in the past year and a half. It's been a journey I never could have anticipated."

"I'm very blessed with the way things have turned out. My son is married to the woman he adores and is about to start his life doing what he loves. I have to tell you though, having Ajani as my grandson has been the best blessing ever—in addition to Evan's recovery of course. That little tyke has melted this grandmama's heart." Aunt Margaret wiped tears from her eyes.

"He's melted all our hearts, Aunt Margaret. I don't think I've laughed as much, seeing him and Patch run around the corridors of Cherrywood Hall. His laughter and the pooch's barking made me smile every time. I think I'm going to have to get a dog for Kyle. He grew close to Patch, too." I laughed.

"Gemma, darling, have you thought anymore about your wedding? I know that dreadful Reggie was going to do the planning, but obviously that will not happen now. I bet Max knows another great wedding planner we can call in. You do want to make a big splash, don't you?"

"Mama, you're incorrigible. I promise you this—the wedding will be sooner rather than later. As for a splash, I think as long as Kyle and I are pleased, then you should be too." I winked.

"Every mama wants her daughter to have a big wedding, darling. It's the one time we get to beam with pride as our daughter takes center stage, dressed in a beautiful gown, surrounded by hundreds of your closest friends and family."

"Mama, we don't have hundreds of closest friends and family—at least Kyle and I don't." I giggled, rolling my eyes. "You're the one with the hundreds of parades of stars and industry friends. I'm going to ask that this one time, for you to trust me. I promise, when we do get married, you will remember it."

"Gemma has a valid point, Jillian. All these years I wanted Evan to have a huge wedding at Cherrywood Hall. Now, though, none of that matters. He's the happiest I've seen him, and that makes my heart very glad."

Our limo pulled to the front of the palace gate. Queen Annelyce had requested the palace be closed today to the public, so that safety and privacy could be assured. Our credentials were checked, and the limo swept. We were waved through the gates and escorted to the private rooms in the back of the palace near the gardens. My heart started to beat rapidly as it finally hit me that this was really going to take place.

We were escorted to the suite where I would wait until it was time for the ceremony. It was a cheery group of rooms in yellow and red chintz that included a sitting area overlooking the main garden and fountains, and a bedroom/changing area complete with en suite bath. Queen Annelyce had provided me with a maid to help me don my dress as Mama and Aunt Margaret waited in the sitting room for me.

I looked at myself in the full-length mirror as the maid fastened the buttons in the back. The ivory satin with gold stitchery glimmered with a soft sheen. We attached the blue, tulle train at the waist. The maid fluffed it out in the back and the sides. The beauty and elegance of the gown took my breath away. We pinned the diamond, medallion brooch in the center of the sweetheart neckline, its regal brilliance dazzling my eyes. I was wearing the pear-shaped, diamond, lever back earrings Daddy and Mama had given me last fall during the American tour. They matched my engagement ring. I wore the matching wedding band on my right hand. My hair was pulled in a low chignon with soft tendrils framing my face.

"You look beautiful, miss," the maid said, as she opened the door for me to walk into the sitting room.

"Thank you." I smiled.

To my surprise, Mama and Aunt Margaret were not alone. Queen Annelyce was with them, dressed in a powder blue skirt and blazer, belted at the waist. The petite woman looked every bit as regal as expected. I curtseyed when I saw her. She walked over to me and kissed my cheeks.

"You look lovely, Gemma."

Mama, Aunt Margaret and the queen circled around me several times—touching the fabric, fluffing the tulle skirt. The gown looked even more elegant in the morning sunshine, giving me a regal glow.

"Gemma, the ceremony today will be a short one. You will kneel and bow your head as I take a sword and touch each side of your shoulders. I will place your chosen tiara on your head, your mama gave it to my service assistant. It will be on a table by my throne. You will rise and turn as I pronounce your name and title, Lady Gemma Lancaster Phillips, the first reigning Marchioness of Kentshire, to the audience. Your guests have arrived and are seated in the grand hall. Are you ready my dear?"

"Yes Ma'am, I am."

"Good. The main thing is to relax. We will have a lovely reception afterwards in the conservatory." She winked.

The queen motioned to Mama and Aunt Margaret to follow her escort to the hall to wait for us.

"I believe you may need this," she smiled, handing me a blue, satin pouch. I looked inside and smiled, pulling on the surprise gift.

"Let's do this." I laughed, as we walked into the hall to join Mama and Aunt Margaret.

I followed them as we made our way to the grand hall where the ceremony was to be held. The queen pointed out paintings and made little jokes about her ancestors. When we reached the entrance to the grand hall she stopped.

"I will be leaving you here. I'm going through the secret panel that goes to my throne. Jillian, Margaret, after they conclude the "God Save The Queen" anthem, you will walk down the aisle first and take your seats in the front row. Margaret, you will sit on the right with Evan and Simone, Jillian, you will sit on the left with Kyle and Gemma's father.

Gemma, you will begin walking down the aisle as the canon arrangement I've had composed for you begins playing.

The queen went through her secret door and we waited by the main entrance. As the queen entered, the orchestra began playing her song. When it concluded, Mama and Aunt Margaret walked down the aisle, side by side. The only sound was the click of their heels on the marble tiles. They took their seats as the queen had directed.

I waited for the first chords of the canon and began my walk down the aisle. I smiled as I saw my friends from Maidenford; Sally snapping pictures, Amy waving, Vicar Hawthorne winking, Prudence and Timothy smiling. The Rosehill Productions cast, and crew were there—Lucy, Dame Agnes, Penny and Steph, and Freddie Alton-Jones. Elliot and Max were seated behind Mama, Kyle and Daddy, blowing me kisses. Daddy bowed his head, Mama smiled, tears streaming down her face. Kyle stood and bowed, mouthing 'I love you.'

I looked over to Aunt Margaret, Evan, Simone, and Ajani—my British family that I loved so much. They were beaming their love to me. I proceeded up the stairs to kneel in front of the throne.

True to her word, the queen stood and took her ancient sword, placing it gently on my right shoulder and then on my left. Her assistant took the sword from her and handed her my diamond and sapphire tiara which Kyle had given me for Christmas. I bowed as she placed it on my head.

"You may stand."

I stood and turned to face my guests, who were smiling and crying at this beautiful moment.

"Ladies and gentlemen, Lords and Ladies, I present Lady Gemma Lancaster Phillips, first to reign as Marchioness of Kentshire."

The room erupted in applause. "Hear, hear," they cried.

The queen motioned for them to be silent and take their seats. I stepped to the left of the kneeling pad, turning sideways so that I could see the queen and the audience.

"I have had an official request to do something I've never done, ladies and gentlemen," the queen said, smiling. "Sir Kyle, will you please join Lady Gemma and me here please." She pointed to the right-hand side of the kneeling pad. Kyle looked at me as he stepped up, not believing what was about to happen.

The audience buzzed, "What was going on? What's this?"

"It has been requested that I officiate the wedding between Lady Gemma and Sir Kyle. If there is anyone who objects, speak now or forever hold your peace."

The guests gasped. Mama's mouth dropped down to her chin. Evan shook his head and smiled, giving me a thumbs up. I heard the click-click-click of Sally's camera, capturing yet another royal first.

"Sir Kyle, will you please take Lady Gemma's hand. Do you have the rings?"

I nodded and gave her the wedding band from my right hand. Kyle took the signet ring from my ancestor, John Lancaster, off his left hand and gave it to her.

"Lady Gemma, do you take Sir Kyle as your lawful husband, to have and to hold from this day forward?"

"I do, Your Majesty."

The queen handed Kyle the diamond wedding band. He placed it on my ring finger.

"Sir Kyle, do you take Lady Gemma as your wife, to have and to hold from this day forward?"

"I do, Your Majesty."

I took the signet ring from the queen's hand and placed it on his pinky finger.

"By the power vested in me as monarch of this kingdom, I now pronounce you husband and wife. May your lives be blessed with happiness and love. You may kiss your bride, Sir Kyle."

Kyle looked at me with adoration and pulled me to him, kissing my lips. We stared at each other and smiled, turning to face our audience.

"Ladies and gentlemen, Lady Gemma and Sir Kyle Williams, husband and wife."

This time our guests gave us a standing ovation with whistles and congratulations. We stopped at the front rows so that I could kiss Mama and Daddy, and then Aunt Margaret, Evan, Simone, and little Ajani. We strolled down the aisle receiving smiles and waves from our friends who had become so dear. When we walked out into the grand hallway, Kyle swept me up in his arms, kissing me deeply.

"I knew you were up to something, you little minx." He laughed. "You could have knocked me over with a feather when the queen asked me to come stand next to you. I have never seen this happen, Gemma. You have certainly made history on this day."

"I wanted our wedding to be as unique as our love for each other, Kyle. This is the most special day of my life, accepting the peerage of my family, but most of all being able to cement everything with my marriage to you. You're my everything and I hope to be yours."

"Oh, Gemma—" Kyle pulled me close and kissed me. Our love had never felt so right.

The hall room door opened as our quests surrounded us with more hugs and kisses. We went into the conservatory—today's reception would fill a dual purpose.

We laughed with our friends, took loads of pictures and had a swinging time on the royal dance floor. The news coverage the next day made us their headline as Sally's pictures were wired around the globe. Mama was beside herself, drinking champagne and telling anyone who'd listen, "That's my girl!" She beamed with love and pride at me. She had received her wish of a big, royal, splash of a wedding like no other couple ever had.

Our celebrations went late into the evening. The queen arranged for Kyle and me to spend our wedding night at the palace. In our room, Kyle slowly unbuttoned my dress. As I slipped it off, he looked at me, running his fingers down my body. They stopped when they reached a garter on my leg.

"Wait a minute, where did you get this?" He laughed.

"The queen gave it to me before my ceremony. It's my something borrowed, every bride needs it."

"Well, here, let me remove it then. We'll have to keep it in the vault."

I groaned as his hands slipped it down my leg and over my foot. I pulled him into a standing position to kiss him. "Do you want to know what the queen told me as I slipped it on my leg?" I teased.

Kyle kissed my neck and whispered, "What did she say?"

I bent my head back, relishing his kisses. "She told me that when you take it off my leg, we should start trying to make those babies."

My knight, not in shining armor at this moment, did as he was commanded by his queen, lifting me in his arms and laying me down on the bed. I'll end the discussion here; some things are better left to the almost-royal imagination.

The Next Four Months...

The Almost Royal Wedding that Changed History

American heiress and now Lady Gemma Lancaster Phillips Williams, Marchioness of Kentshire, made royal history after her peerage ceremony by having the Queen perform a marriage ceremony between her and her longtime love, Sir Kyle Williams. The audience watched in shocked disbelief as this never before seen, almost royal matrimony took place....

Filming Commences on the *Castlewood Manor* Movie Feature

Cast furs are flying according to our secret source on the set. A new leading lady, actress Kay Moyer has joined lead stars Jillian Phillips and Dame Agnes Knight, causing tensions to run high on the set...

Cherrywood Hall Opens New Gin Distillery

Residents of Maidenford and the surrounding community were treated to a night of merriment as the estate opened its latest business venture. Lady Gemma and Sir Kyle led the toasts. Whispers were racing around the hall as it was observed Lady Gemma did not drink her gin libation. Will we be hearing the pitter-patter of little feet at Cherrywood Hall soon? This story is developing...

Crowns and Kisses.

The End

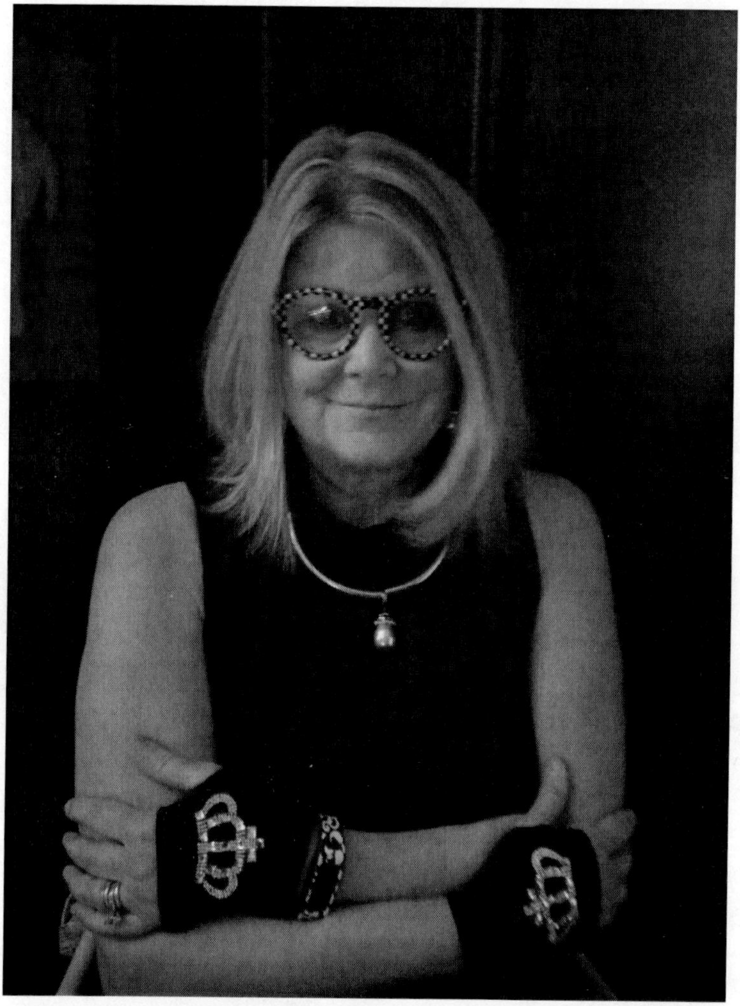

A word from the author…

I wanted to thank you, the readers, for joining me on this latest adventure with Gemma and her family and friends this Yuletide season, it's such a special story for me! I have been supported by so many people throughout my writing journey, I wanted to give a few shout outs to those who have worked with me on this latest read. I am very grateful for the editing services provided by author Theresa Snyder---her support, suggestions and literary guidance is very much appreciated. Proofreading has been provided by the Hyper-Speller at wordrefiner.com. I'm very grateful for the support and encouragement of the #WritingCommunity, # Readers, and #BookBloggers on social media—you're so awesome! Finally, a special thank you to my beta readers: Brenda, Jackie, Gayle, Trisha, Sonia and Bibiana, crowns & kisses!

Award winning author Veronica Cline Barton earned graduate degrees in both engineering and business and has had successful careers in the software and technology industries. Her lifelong love affair with British cozy murder mysteries inspired her to embark on a literary career. The Crown for Castlewood Manor is the first book in the My American Almost Royal Cousin Series, followed by Cast, Crew, & Carnage; the Filming of Castlewood Manor, and Deadly Receptions: the Debut of Castlewood Manor. When not traveling and spinning mystery yarns, she lives in California with her husband, Bruce, and her two cats, Daisy and Ebbie.